An American Mystic

VIKING

ARKANA

An American Mystic

✣

A NOVEL OF

SPIRITUAL ADVENTURE

Michael Gurian

VIKING/ARKANA

VIKING ARKANA
Published by the Penguin Group
Penguin Putnam Inc., 375 Hudson Street,
New York, New York 10014, U.S.A.
Penguin Books Ltd, 27 Wrights Lane, London W8 5TZ, England
Penguin Books Australia Ltd, Ringwood,
Victoria, Australia
Penguin Books Canada Ltd, 10 Alcorn Avenue,
Toronto, Ontario, Canada M4V 3B2
Penguin Books (N.Z.) Ltd, 182–190 Wairau Road,
Auckland 10, New Zealand

Penguin Books Ltd, Registered Offices:
Harmondsworth, Middlesex, England

First published in 2000 by Viking Arkana,
a member of Penguin Putnam Inc.

1 3 5 7 9 10 8 6 4 2

PUBLISHER'S NOTE
This is a work of fiction. Names, characters, places and incidents are either the product of the
author's imagination or are used fictitiously, and any resemblance to actual persons, living or dead,
business establishments, events or locales is entirely coincidental.

Library of Congress Cataloging-in-Publication Data

Gurian, Michael.
An American mystic : a novel of spiritual adventure / Michael Gurian.
p.   cm.
ISBN 0-670-88296-8
I. Title.
PS3557.U8147A8   2000
813'.5—dc21   99-33509

This book is printed on acid-free paper.
∞
Printed in the United States of America
Set in Goudy
Designed by Jaye Zimet

Dedicated by Ben Brickman to
Joseph Kader
and all the millennial mystics

Dedicated by Michael Gurian to
Jim McNeill and in memory of Vicki McNeill,
and Gail, Gabrielle, and Davita

ACKNOWLEDGMENTS

This book could not have been published without the help of some very important people.

My thanks to Janet Goldstein and her colleagues at Viking Arkana. They have been gracious and caring. This book has benefited from their help in ways I cannot begin to describe. My thanks also to David Stanford, who began this book's editorial journey.

My thanks to Susan Schulman and her staff; also to Jeremy Tarcher, Joel Futinos and Mitch Horowitz—without all of them, this book would not have found a home.

Finally, my thanks to the people of Turkey, who taught me what hospitality and friendship truly mean.

CONTENTS

EDITOR'S FOREWORD

Mysticism refers to a pervasive sense of connect-
edness *and* an openness to all experience, ratio-
nal and nonrational. When a person comments
about feeling "at one" with the cosmos, he or she
is making a mystical statement. Similarly, when
someone expresses an openness to mystery or
the unknown, that person is making a mystical
statement.

— REVEREND WILLIAM HARPER HOUFF

Mystical experience is always available—like the
divine grace it is—to any who really want it; and
all human beings are given in the course of their
lives glimpses into the heart of the Real which
they are free to pursue or forget.

— ANDREW HARVEY

*T*he book you are about to read is Benjamin Brickman's diary of his
spiritual adventures and discoveries, which I have edited and
shaped, at his request, into a coherent narrative. It chronicles not only his
experiences, but also the lives of individuals who call themselves "millen-

nial mystics." By word of mouth, mystics around the world quickly learned of Ben Brickman's spiritual awakening, and many have claimed it to be a watershed, prophetic experience for the new millennium.

Over the period of almost three months, in the summer of 1988, across two continents, and through many quiescent as well as harrowing adventures, this young man of thirty, a graduate student in psychology, discovered, in his words, "a blueprint for the ten tasks of enlightenment." When I, a young visiting professor at Ankara University, first met him in the fall of 1988, I did not believe his bold claim. But after I read his journals, my skepticism disappeared. As I got to know him, I saw a person who had been changed by spiritual life, a person who had once lived in a kind of chaos, then found an inner order, a deep holiness. Having now spent more than a dozen years working with his material, as well as with many mystics like him, I am convinced that their passion as well as Ben's discoveries will change the way religious and spiritual people understand humanity's relationship with God.

Ben Brickman was tall with olive skin, dark blond hair, deep brown eyes, and seemingly endless energy. An American, he had grown up in many parts of the world, his family moving a great deal—mainly in Asia and in the western part of the United States. He was of German Jewish extraction on his father's side and Italian Catholic on his mother's.

Our first meeting took place at the Turkish-American Cultural Center in Ankara, Turkey, in the fall of 1988, where he mesmerized a standing-room-only audience with his uncanny abilities. People would stand up at random and hear him relate their life histories. I wanted personal proof, so I stood up myself. Knowing me not at all, he revealed to the audience a recurring dream I'd been having, one I had told no one except my wife about. He also revealed where I had lived as a boy, down to exact details of one of my family's houses. It was as if, for a moment, his and my minds and memories were attached. He told me what my ambitions were, and he revealed aspects of my future, including two books I would write, that have come exactly true.

I had met "psychics" and distrusted many of them, but Ben Brickman was a kind of magician of the mind I had never met. When I went up to him after the lecture, and as I got to know him over the next weeks, I could see that he was a true mystic, a person who makes direct and constant contact with God. He was, in my life experience, a model of some kind of new man. I became very interested in learning more about how he had journeyed from being what he called "an ordinary person" to "a millennial mystic." He obliged my curiosity not only with his conversation and friendship but also by showing me the detailed journal he had kept during his transformation, which he asked me to turn into a book.

Though Ben wrote in the margins and often in unreadable script, the structure of his journal-record divided easily into ten sections, one for each of the "ten tasks of enlightenment." Ben asked me to divide the published book—which I suggested we call An American Mystic—into the same ten sections. Thus, the book you are about to read is divided into ten chapters, revealing the accomplishment of each mystical task in separate episodes. Ben was vehement, also, that his book not be published until after the turn of the millennium. He predicted that the 1990s would include a "millennial frenzy," an inordinate attention to endgames, despair, and Armageddon-type psychologies that would dissipate once the new millennium safely began. "The millennial mysticism I've discovered," he explained, "is rooted in our past but is, in the end, the flower of the new millennium." He also gave me the names and locations of other men, women, and children whose adventures and stories he asked me to pursue for future publication. He predicted I would publish seven stories like his, which would continue to emerge for many years after our own lifetimes, to form a "Millennial Testament."

In his words:

"This Testament will be read by millions of people who seek the direct experience of God—to know divinity in their own way. This Testament will be our era's equivalent of the Old and New Testaments, a third Testament. The Old Testament was a record of the lives of a group of mystics now called the Jews who were led by Moses and others. The New Testament was a record of a new group, led by a young Jewish mystic, Jesus. The Koran was a record of yet another group of mystics, led by Mohammed. The Millennial Testament will record the lives and teachings of mystics of the new millennium. Like its predecessors, it will be a narrative, but, unlike the New Testament, it will not center mainly on the life of one prophet."

"And yet," I challenged him, "you appear as one of the central figures in your own narrative. You are already considered a leader of the millennial mystics. How can it not focus on you?"

"I am just one of many servant leaders," he corrected me. "My spiritual adventure is a template, not an end; my life is an example, but I am not a guru. I have gained a complete trust of the universe, and from that trust come immense gifts, but anyone can experience these gifts if they fulfill the tasks of enlightenment authentically. Anyone can become a full member of God's house, should he or she focus on this mission freely and completely. My experiences are *a* map, not *the* map. There is no single true way to become enlightened, no single true way to accomplish each of the tasks of enlightenment. But there is a map, and finding the map in our era, as I have, can only help seekers."

If you have picked up this book, you are a spiritual searcher, as I am. The millennial mystics would say that you are helping humanity evolve into the next stage of consciousness. Whether you feel you are a mystic or not, you must decide for yourself. If you do decide, after reading this book, that you are one, you will meet the companion who always walks beside you. Your life will be changed, as mine has been. Change is the miracle that awaits us all.

—Michael Gurian
Spokane, Washington
January 2000

PART ONE

The
Mission

After all, if you can be born once, you can be

born twice.

— VOLTAIRE

A human being must be born twice: once from

his mother, and then again from his own body

and existence. The body is like an egg and

the essence of a human being must become a

bird in that egg through the warmth of love,

and then must go beyond the body and fly in

the eternal world of the soul.

— SULTAN VALAD

Editor's note: The epigraphs that introduce each section
of the book were culled from Ben Brickman's journal.

FIRST ✼ DREAM

Ben Brickman called this "The Sad Soldier Dream." It was the first of seven dream visions he experienced during his transformative journey in the summer of 1988. He later felt that in some way he blended with the people in the dreams, as if their separate personalities had been set aside. Each dream was distinct, and each could not have grown from his imagination alone, for each of them not only consisted of an unusual quality of experience but took place in the future, as does this first one, dreamt by Ben in 1988 but taking place early in the new millennium.

A tall American, his hair almost white in its blondness, in his early thirties, steps out of Dojo Ramone in Paris on a balmy evening in May. He carries a gray workout bag with a Nike swoosh; his step and slightly red cheeks are lit up by the physical release of his workout. His body is well muscled, thighs and calves tight in his blue jeans, biceps and pectorals tight in his white button-down shirt. His sleeves are rolled up to his elbows, revealing a sheen of hair on his forearms.

Breathing in the scent of lilacs and the evening breeze, the man turns right, toward the Musée des Beaux-Arts, one of Paris's smaller museums. It is under reconstruction and temporarily closed to the public. Among its buttresses and in its tower, men wander like ants. Responding to the loud construction sounds—taps, cuts, saws, grinding, sanding—the tall American momentarily closes his eyes and moves inward, recalling a teacher's words from long ago: "Every young man should wander in the extremes of youth and without compass through civilizations that have spawned him. One day you will do that." This prediction is finally being fulfilled.

"Monsieur, parlez-vous anglais?"

The American turns to see a skinny, stoop-shouldered Englishman wearing a jacket and a green bow tie. A few yards behind the elderly man waits a black limousine.

"I'm American," he responds calmly, though he speaks French. The hair on the

back of his neck is standing up straight, and a chill ripples through him. He is military trained, and even when he is not on assignment, his professional instincts are never completely relaxed.

In his peripheral vision he sees a man in a long coat hail a taxi. He sees a crowd milling around in front of the closed museum, a woman and two children entering a shop, and the sound of a window opening above. In a split second, for no apparent reason except the presence of this Englishman, his energies snap from reverie to vigilance.

The Englishman claps his hands. "Thank God you understand me, young man. Do you know where the rue des Beaux-Arts is?" He shoves a map at the American's free hand and moves beside him to take a look at it with him. "We've been circling and circling," he frets.

"That is the Beaux-Arts museum." The American points with the map in his left hand, the gym bag clutched in his right. "The street you're looking for runs right past it—there, that way."

As he gestures, he feels a sharp prick in his neck, like a bee sting. His body tightens its muscles against the dart, the worst thing it can do. The poison enters his system rapidly, before he can drop either map or bag and reach a hand up.

"My Lord, he's fainted!" the Englishman calls out to passersby. Drifting away, the young American knows better. Hands are on him, practiced hands. They move him to a car. He becomes the car seat, his skin vinyl, his eyes its buttons, the green bow tie the last bit of color he holds on to before disappearing into darkness.

"He's the right choice, no doubt," the Englishman says to his colleagues. "Right in a multitude of ways. But does this technology truly work? If he learned the truth, where would we be?"

"He's waking up."

"So he is. And how are you, young man?"

"Expect no answer, gentlemen, he can't speak."

One man has a Middle Eastern accent of some kind; another, American. The third is the Englishman. They all seem vaguely familiar.

The young American sits in a hard chair in a room that is damp and clammy and smells like the basement of a factory. He is numb, blindfolded, but not tied or gagged—these are unnecessary. He has been given drugs of some kind; he can't talk, and he can't move.

He can hear and sense in other ways that exceed most people's capabilities. He senses the living energies in the room. There are four besides himself: one at the door, stoic, and three in front of him. He smells the cigarette of one, the cologne of another. He senses in the Englishman, to his left, a clear focus. He feels an overwhelming rage in the man to his right. This voice, heavily accented—perhaps Egyptian or Saudi— had announced his waking up.

It's been years since the experimental training he underwent. He had left that training behind and turned off his gifts, especially avoiding perception-enhancing drugs, whether DH 9, mescaline, or even marijuana. The military had identified him after a tip from a psychology professor and used him because of his sensitivity to extrasensory experience (pretersensation, they called it). "You're going to be a new kind of soldier for new kinds of war," they had told him, and he tried to be just that.

The men in this room must know his history well. They want his paranormal abilities mobilized. He knows they have him here for a reason.

Now he feels the lacy, quiescent wave of DH 9, also some MH 9 and other agents he doesn't recognize, coursing through him. The drugs seem to affect the very nature of his emotional intake, or at least try to, working on his neurotransmission, serotonin levels, and amygdala. He knows that his survival depends on continuing to sense, to process. He senses that the person right in front of him is the most dangerous, a man who is examining him with clarity and purpose but also a laconic indifference to life itself.

"He's holding up just fine at this point," the examiner says. "The quicker we program him, the better." It is an American voice, with a slight southern lilt. There is a sound of metal—surgical equipment on a metal table?

"Agreed." It is the third voice, the Middle Eastern, deep toned. "Program him to kill Nathan within the month. He's more than capable."

"Not agreed in the least." The Englishman. "There's much more to learn from Nathan. I want to learn everything before killing him."

"Nathan is a danger. It is time, now, to remove him!"

"Don't think, Bilkent, that because I'm a wee scholar from England, I'll give in when your neck gets hot. We saw each other through the Cold War. We got through the end of the millennium. It's a new century now, and we don't have to do everything the way we used to. The urgency just isn't there anymore."

"For me the important things are always urgent."

"But I need to know the full theory, everything—all Nathan's new neural technology, this 'spiritual' power these mystics seem to have, these windows into the future they possess. I need to know. That is why I'm bankrolling my share—and why we will not just blindly do whatever you wish."

"Over and over," the examiner says quietly, firmly. "The same argument. You two are like dogs fighting over a bone. You forget, my friend, that once programmed, our friend here can be triggered at will. We will reconnoiter every month as he progresses toward the target, and we will not trigger him until we have all the information we need."

"And everything will work?" The Englishman.

"He'll remember nothing, just as he doesn't remember the lab work or the three of us. He'll receive the phone call, then the trigger. He'll complete. Unfortunately for him, he will not know his own motivation when he's done. That's a cruel thing to do to a trained and brilliant soldier, especially one with his gifts—but it's necessary." There is a strange regret in the voice, a regret the young American feels like a current in the room.

"We stand on the edge of so much!" the Englishman assures the room.

The Middle Eastern voice: "We must continue to meet frequently during the penetration."

The American examiner: "We will. Let me get to work. Lieutenant Krane, show these two gentlemen to the observation room."

"Yes, sir." The door opens. Beyond it is a sound of banging, some kind of hammering. The fourth presence is this lieutenant. Footsteps toward the door. The Englishman's shoes make almost no sound. The other man's are heavier.

A wooden door closes. The doctor sits in silence, his breathing very fine. He is alert, like an animal watching from camouflage. There is an ambivalence in him, but very slight.

The doctor stirs. "All right, son." Clicks a machine on. Not a tape recorder, but something that hisses slightly. A song begins, a song the young American knows well—Led Zeppelin's "Stairway to Heaven." Somehow his captors know this is his favorite song from adolescence. The American understands that the doctor is going to use it as a trigger. What did he mean "he doesn't remember us"?

"There's a sign on the wall . . ."

Jimmy Page's slow, symphonic guitar.

The music is turned down.

"Son," the doctor says softly, "I want you to listen carefully now. Can you do that? Listen as my voice becomes one of the voices in this music." Yes, the doctor will use the song as a hypnotic trigger. "This will sting a little, but it'll help you. There you are. Give it a second." The sting of the bee again, hot, harsh. "Listen to that music, hear my voice in it. The music's not enough. You have to hear my voice too, and a suggestion, my suggestion."

The young American loses himself in the music, washed by the fluids in his blood. The drug erases everything, effaces it into the music, the words, a feeling of comfort, Robert Plant's tenor.

"As we wind on down the road . . ."

The music clicks off. "Right there, son, did you hear it? Did you hear me say it? Hear me say it, son—right after 'gold'—listen carefully, this is what you'll hear me say. And you'll forget everything."

A strange presence has entered the room. It makes it difficult to hear the doctor's words. It is huge, white, beautiful energy. Very loving. Surrounding. Magical. It causes the American to relax. He becomes joyful, begins to move within himself, though his body is still imprisoned in the chair. Immense gentleness, like a quiet ocean. Another presence, caring for him.

Suddenly the doctor yells out.

The three other men are back.

"What's happening?"

"Dammit, what the—"

"A seizure. Get back. Get back!"

I awoke sweating, startled. It took me a second to realize I was Ben Brickman, not the man drugged in the dream. I was not having a seizure, yet I shook and was chilled. The doctor's voice was so sinister. It all seemed so sinister—all except that immensely joyful presence. What a strange dream! And so real—it felt different from any other dream I'd ever had. I'd experienced strange things in my life, but I'd never felt so completely immersed in someone else's being. Earlier in my life, I'd had premonitional dreams, but never one so detailed and lifelike—and set so far in the future.

I trembled as I tried to write everything down exactly as I had experienced it in the dream. Could I meet this "target"? His first name, or last name, was Nathan. Could I find him and warn him? Was it all a work of my imagination? Yet I knew it wasn't. I was sure some new kind of process or technology or ability was being used here, and I was somehow a part of it.

CHAPTER 1

The Invitation

> *The first task of the mystic is to answer the invitation to the journey with the choice of adventure rather than comfort, action rather than stasis. Every mystic is called to the journey of discovery in his own way. Often the call comes unnoticed at the time. Often it is accompanied by uncanny coincidences and small experiences. Strings of energy weave around us constantly, strings we may not notice until the call to the journey of Union and Oneness begins.*
>
> *No matter the quality of the call—no matter its high drama or droll simplicity—the duty of the mystic is to answer the call authentically, fearlessly, decisively. The adventure of Union begins with swords or with sitting in silence, but it always begins when you choose to let it begin. Until that moment of choice, you are a resistor rather than a transmitter. Once you choose, however, it is difficult to turn back.*
>
> *—The Magician*

In Paris in July the weather is moody—gray and humid for a few hours in the morning, then, with just a half hour of breeze, the humidity lifts by midafternoon, the sky clears, lifting a weight off the shoppers, the café chatterers, the office workers, the tourists. When morning is like a first awakening, into moroseness, the city has a second awakening of tenderness, vitality, and the promise of evening adventures.

On this kind of Saturday in July 1988, at around 4:00 P.M., I sat at Café Le Roc, just west of Notre Dame Cathedral, with my old mentor, Professor Mick Laur. I had not slept since awakening from the strange dream the night before, yet I felt more alert than I had in a long time. I didn't know if the dream had made me this way or if Mick's presence was giving me energy. Seeing my friend after six months was a pleasure, and it brought intrigue too—his visit, from across the Atlantic, was not altogether social.

After we embraced and caught up on doings and people back in Berkeley, he handed me a thick manila file. It's opening pages contained the highlights of interviews with a hundred or so people from all over the world, most of whom had gone to the Aegean and Mediterranean coasts of Turkey as tourists, then experienced a complex, extended hallucination. Each person's hallucination contained differences from the others, yet each was remarkably similar.

I woke up naked on a hill on the southeast coast of Turkey, near Kaş. My skin felt translucent like water, my vision was blurry, my mouth dry. Swallowing hard, I tried to get my bearings as bird shadows flew above me, screeching. The air smelled like ocean air, thick and salty. This is a dream, I told myself, it must be. And then I saw him, the Magician—all lit up, like Jesus with a halo, but no hair. Light coursing through his gray eyes. I felt an immense rapture. All pain was over. The bliss was here, a sudden and immense peace.
    —Transcript of psychiatric session with Joshua Millicent, 21, North Carolina State Mental Facility, files of Dr. V. Nesbitt, November 26, 1987

He was silky, tall, completely bald, standing with me at a doorway to an abandoned stone building. I could see the ocean behind the building, placid like the belly of a sleeping giant. His skin pigment was dark like mine and his Urdu perfect; light flowed from within him at the heart center. He told me to rest easier now, for all was well and the world belonged to the spirits again. A beautiful completeness flowed from me to him, from him to me. I became whole.
    —Transcript of interview with Bulaza Tanvier, 39, at the U.S. Embassy in Islamabad, by the Independent Investigative Team, Grant II, December 17, 1987

He sits on a rock, dressed in a white robe, completely bald, brown skin. I
am coming out of the ocean after a swim and see him there. I say, "The
sun, is it not dangerous, sir, on your head?" He smiles at me, speaking per-
fect Berlinese German. "There is no danger," he says. "There is no depri-
vation. Your worries are over. I have been sent to teach you that Love is
everywhere." Like this he speaks to me. I am touched. The light from his
bald head—it is swirling everywhere. I am very touched by the light. My
body aches with the light. It is like pain, pain of a sickness leaving my body.
I am different after that time with him, no more worries. I am, so to speak,
one with God.

    —Transcript of interview with Ingrid Bruener, 69, by the Inde-
        pendent Investigative Team, Grant II, April 20, 1988

At the table next to ours, sunlight glinted off a watch, then a man's
glasses. I put the file down, took off my own glasses and rubbed my eyes.
The Magician file, compiled by my former colleagues at the California Institute of Transpersonal Psychology at Berkeley under a $200,000 grant,
contained many vignettes like these, all describing contact with a presence called the "Magician."

    I looked up at Mick. "All the hallucinations occurred within a few
hundred miles, in coastal areas of Turkey?"

    Mick nodded. "Careers are made with things like this. We've got
people from all walks of life and fourteen countries seeing this bald appa-
ration, this 'Magician.' Tufts and swirls and beams of light shine around
him. His presence heals the individuals who encounter him or makes
them feel 'complete.' This has all happened over the last year or so."

    Follow-up interviews had been undertaken with most of the hundred
individuals. Nearly all of them enjoyed, even a year later, a peace of mind
that was, quite frankly, abnormal.

    I thought of similar "miracles": the sightings of the Virgin at Zeitun,
Egypt, in 1968; the bleeding in Japan, between 1975 and 1981, of the
Akita statue; the healings and unexplainable gyrations of the sun at Med-
jugorje, Yugoslavia; in India, the statues of elephants and cows that drank
milk from people's hands—all bizarre events that would have been unbe-
lievable if not recorded on video cameras, as the recent ones, at least, had

been, confirming the incredible. In all cases, people came away from these miracles "changed." Unfortunately, thus far no one had used a video camera to capture a Magician encounter.

"Are there any similarities in the psychological profiles of the participants?" I asked.

"None except that all subjects have a substantial spiritual discipline in place. Each person meditated or prayed almost daily, long before the encounters. Their religious affiliations are diverse—seven Catholics, three Jews, ten Muslims, three Hindus, six Buddhists, one Unitarian, two Bahai—but many of the individuals claimed no clear religious denomination either before or after the encounter. Spiritual discipline, not religion per se, seems to be the common denominator. Some of the 'encountered'— this is the name the subjects use for themselves—consider the 'Magician' a prophet for the new millennium. Some of them report that the Magician told them he would reveal the complete reason for his presence, and the complete lessons and power of his teachings of 'Union,' sometime soon, to an individual he calls 'a gifted one' and 'the Messenger'—the person whom the Magician has said will carry his full message. This individual's role will be clarified by certain signs. It's amazing, Ben, the detail these 'encountered' can go into about this hallucination."

Mick took a sip of wine. "Seems a lot of these folk believed earlier this year that a guy named Joseph Kader was 'the Messenger.' Kader denies it. But he does have the most comprehensive knowledge of the Magician encounters." I had already noticed Dr. Joseph Kader's name mentioned throughout the file. "He's a Turkish anthropologist and mystic," Mick continued, "turned sixty-five this year. We've got a comprehensive bio on him. A lot of books to his credit, an interesting life, not only in Turkey and Europe but in Africa and Asia. A fascinating character."

I hadn't seen Mick this interested in a project in years. A short, wiry Irish-born American—graying, bow-shouldered and bow-tied—Mick still carried a hint of an Irish accent. Nearly sixty, he had been growing tiny veins, like tiny red snakes, on the end of his nose. His clean-shaven cheeks and broad forehead were cloudy white, and his blond hair almost completely gray, except for his reddish-brown eyebrows.

About three months ago, he had become the supervisor of a project to study the Magician phenomenon funded by a San Francisco foundation devoted to exploring paranormal phenomena. The foundation had become interested in the stories about the Magician a year before, having received a letter from an American Air Force officer stationed in Turkey, Joshua Millicent, that had detailed his experience with the Magician. In the next few months they had been forwarded other accounts that detailed similar experiences. The foundation felt this phenomenon to be important enough to warrant hiring Mick Laur's team at the Institute of Transpersonal Psychology to conduct research into this psychological phenomenon. Mick had come to Paris from California to ask me to go to Turkey and investigate firsthand.

"But I'll tell you, Ben"—Mick bit off a piece of puff pastry—"I think we'd be our own Judas if we came at this phenomenon naive and full of the wrong kind of spit. Something's going on here, of that I'm sure." I agreed it was.

I had set out for Europe more than six months ago to travel and take stock of myself after my master's thesis in transpersonal psychology had died in writer's block. I had wandered the continent, but I hadn't been to Turkey or the Middle East yet. I had paid my way so far with savings and what I made with my magic, juggling, and mime street act. From my father, an off-Broadway director and NYU drama professor, and my uncle, a professional magician, I had learned early how to perform magic tricks. The coincidence—or irony—of my being a magician and the fact that this research project was about someone called "the Magician" was not lost on me—or on Mick.

Mick put both palms on the edge of the table. "Among all my students in thirty years, you more than anyone have underestimated your talents. Life should be lived as a quest, a calling. You so often stand just short of the threshold, yet everyone who knows you knows you are meant for some big song. I knew it when we first met. You haven't worked with a real guru, a real mystic, only with scholars and academic pandits like me. Joseph Kader is a mystic of world repute. This Magician phenomenon—which he, more than anyone, has a sweet handle on—this is up your alley, lad. Even if it turns out, as I suspect it might, to be an induced hallucination. I think you will get some piece of yourself from this."

I grinned. "You always have believed in me, Mick. Thank you."

He flushed with a tinge of embarrassment. "Well, there it is. I can talk, can't I, lad?" He spoke now with the thickest of Irish accents, poking fun at his own gift of gab.

His seriousness and enthusiasm, his words, his very presence after the months of traveling alone—all of it lit me up. It made my chest warm and my feet bounce under the table with excitement.

I sifted through the file for Joseph Kader's biography. No doubt, it would be interesting to meet a spiritual authority from the Mideast. Unfamiliar with the Islamic world, like most Americans, I saw it as an alien place of fanatics, female oppression, violence, and ancient mysticisms that wanted to be Western, on the one hand, and crush Westernism, on the other. Reading about Kader's life, I saw that it had begun in a very "Muslim" way: his father had been an imam, or preacher. Kader had spent his early childhood in the tiny town of Kor, about a hundred miles from Turkey's capital city, Ankara. His father was Turkish-Chinese, his mother Turkish-Russian. His family lived in Ankara and Istanbul during World War II, then moved back to Kor, where his father had become the imam and remained so until retirement. He went to college in Istanbul, then to graduate school at the Sorbonne, Cornell, and Oxford. He obtained a Ph.D. in anthropology at the Sorbonne and returned to Oxford for postgraduate work. After his graduate and postgraduate work, he spent six years in the Belgian Congo among the Kulu natives. He also taught in Central Asia, India, Japan, and France. Writing in Turkish, French, and English, he had published two books in the field of shamanic anthropology and three in the field of mysticism. His work had been translated into eleven languages. His wife was dead. His daughter and her family lived in Paris.

Leaning forward, Mick fingered through the file and pulled out an interview. "Look at how completely even Kader believes in the reality of the Magician phenomenon. He's a devotee—or he's the perpetrator, perpetrating a hallucination for some unknown reason." He passed me an interview with Kader in New World Journal, published by the Noetic Institute of the Americas. Pointing to a place on the page, Mick said, "This is one of the only interviews he's been known to give on the Magician, and even this isn't much, but I guess he and this Sandra Lachey are old friends."

LACHEY: Well, Joseph, as we come to the end of our time together I have to ask about the Magician, the sightings in Turkey, your attempts to understand it all. It's little known, but some people think it's quite important. The *National Enquirer* did a story on it, so that means it has hit the big time!

KADER: God help us!

LACHEY: I know you don't like to talk much about it and I appreciate your reticence, but won't you say something to us now?

KADER: Sandra, I am quiet and protective about this subject, for I know myself to be like a baby in my knowledge. A baby becomes easily jealous of others who want to take away his nourishment before he himself has had enough.

LACHEY: You have insisted that you are not the Messenger who will carry the full story.

KADER: Someone is coming toward the Magician. The Magician has called to this person. The Magician has made it clear that this person will be gifted with "the whole story." Until that time, the rest of us who have encountered the Magician continue, as do you, to wonder over the details.

LACHEY: Would you just tell us if you think the Magician is a bodhisattva, a saint, an alien, an angel, a person, a delusion? A colleague quoted you as saying, "The Magician is a Traveler." By "Traveler," do you mean "Prophet"? Do you believe the Magician is the next great prophet?

KADER: The Magician appears to be the next major evolution of the mystical consciousness, following in a long line of others, such as Moses, Buddha, Jesus, Mohammed, Hildegard, Baha'ullah—he comes with a message of great importance for the twenty-first century. We will have to wait a while longer for that message.

A waiter came with a second puff pastry Mick had ordered. Thanking the waiter in French, Mick pulled his pipe and smoking paraphernalia from his satchel. Beside us a group of young men laughed loudly over some joke.

Mick smiled. "If you get close to Kader," he said, leaning over to leaf for a page, "you'll probably meet Ragip and Sela Metinoğlu, two prominent Turkish psychologists. They are entangled in all this for sure." Mick gripped his pipe in his crooked brown teeth and flipped through clippings till he found an interview with Dr. Ragip Metinoğlu, dated March 1988:

> *I have encountered the Magician three times, once with my wife, Sela, once with Joseph Kader, and once on my own. In each case the experience is similar: he appears in a white robe, his head is bald. His smooth face and fine-boned hands give him a fragile appearance. In his eyes, however, is profound strength. In my clinical experience with eleven of the other encountered, I have yet to see a psychological parallel among us that would explain our need for a hallucination. Three of the eleven experienced profound crisis before the encounter but the other eight did not. In all cases we have left our experience with the Magician as a child leaves his mother's breast—reassured, sated, and enlivened. I suspect that Magician sightings, and perhaps sightings of other Travelers, will become more frequent as our century ends and we recognize our millennial mysticism.*

Travelers? Did Kader and the others think of these Travelers as spirit entities of some kind? "'Millennial mysticism'? 'Travelers'?" I repeated aloud. The words felt exotic, lively, like tiny dancers on the surface of something well hidden.

Mick puffed happily. The pipe was a deep rich wood color, brownish red with a mottled rim. As I smelled the tobacco, I remembered with a wave of emotion how the aroma of pipe tobacco had absorbed onto the walls of Mick's Berkeley office, the articles on his desk, the orderly rows of books on his shelves, the student papers he graded in stacks, the white pipe cleaners like fuzzy wires in his garbage can, a few littering the greenish carpet nearby.

"Ben, it's like this: Kader and a number of these people say that mysticism is back in full force all over the world; that it's the world's most popular spiritual tradition but not recognized, not understood by its own adherents—and not quite a religion per se. Kader talks about it. Let's find the reference." He reached the file, and I relinquished it. He thumbed to another place in the *New World* interview.

KADER: Mysticism means "direct contact with God." Mysticism can
be experienced, disciplined, and practiced by anyone—parent,
priest, prophet, pencil pusher. Millions of people are mystics
these days. Billions of people have mystical experiences. You,
Sandra, are a mystic. I see it in your eyes. Everywhere we turn,
we see mystics on their way to work. You will recognize them
when you recognize that you are one yourself. To be a mystic is
to be religious, if you make that choice, but it is also something
that goes beyond the rules and limitations imposed by a human
religion.

For three millennia, since the beginning of the major world
religions—Judaism, Confucianism, Hinduism, then Christianity, Buddhism, Islam—human spiritual life has moved toward
what is happening around the world right now, as we approach
the year 2000: millennial mysticism. The original energy source
of every known religion—"direct and free contact with God"—
is finally able to emerge in our era now. This merging, this
global mysticism was not possible until religions had done the
job civilization needed them to do—to code moral laws for
civilization building. The encoding and the civilization building
have taken three millennia to form. Religions and traditional
moralities are still essential—they are the building blocks—yet
also consciousness is focused on freeing the spiritual self, expanding its vision into hidden realms of perception. Where before there were a few Meister Eckharts and Teresas of Avila and
Galileos, now there are millions.

"He's very articulate," I said with admiration. "It's part Aldous Huxley,
part Bertrand Russell, part Ken Wilbur—but it's something more, too."

Mick said nothing, puffing his pipe so that the smoke filled the air
around us.

KADER: A millennial mystic is generally a person who discovers that
one religion, one single mythology, doctrine, tradition or prac-

tice—does not satisfy. He or she needs many "ways," pieces of many religions and paths, by which to build energy, awaken soul, gain permission of the dog who guards the mystical doorway, and then move through to walk in enlightenment. Our recent and global diversity of tradition is the energy that has created our millennial mysticism.

LACHEY: And isn't it one of your ideas that the new mysticism is ac-tually the original tradition or meaning of every religion any-way?

KADER: Yes. Each major world religion is rooted in mysticism. Each began because a mystic like Jesus, Moses, or Buddha experienced *direct* contact with God and had a vision rising from that con-tact; subsequently, people with corporate sense created organiza-tional systems, called religions, by which to help the multitudes see the vision the mystic had.

LACHEY: I've often heard you say that America has a unique place in the world culture of mystical awareness. Is America some kind of new Jerusalem?

KADER: American mysticism is, right now, the least tradition-bound form of the millennial mysticism. People in the evolving con-sciousness in your vast culture borrow like millennial scavengers from traditions worldwide: Buddhist, Sufi, Christian, Kabbalic, Taoist, Hindu, Native American, African, Mayan. Your love of "personal growth," shamanism, EST, your Goddess mythologies and Joseph Campbell, on and on the list goes—in your country there is much freedom to pursue the individual quest for spiritual truth.

LACHEY: You're saying that I and so many like me are scavenging through all the different ways of altering consciousness and feel-ing whole in the universe. Does this make me a mystic? I don't know. I want to say Yes! but I feel egotistical saying so.

KADER: If we said mysticism is a religion, would you have more confi-dence to call yourself a mystic?

LACHEY: I guess I would.

KADER: I fear, Sandra, that you will not have the easy path of calling
mysticism a religion and thus gaining your confidence. For a
mystic, the acceptance of his or her identity does not necessarily
depend on joining an organized religion. Mysticism is the ultimate discovery of oneself, alone in the universe and yet at one
with all things.

I reread that last sentence, feeling exuberant. It was as if my brain had
been turned off for a few months and had suddenly, with a few written
words on a page, clicked back on. To accept that one was alone in the universe, yet to feel one with all things—wasn't this the final goal of the human mind?

"You see why I think you're so right to work on this?" Mick asked, his
red-blond eyebrows rising like crooked fingers. "You of all people will
know how to get close to Kader, how to talk to him. You were made for
this, lad!"

All through my life, all through my strange experiences as a child and
young man, and then their disappearance during college and graduate
school, all through my ordinary days of eating and drinking and lovemaking and freedoms and responsibilities, I had always felt alone and yet so
touched by the quick, the transitory breath of something large, something
absolute and complete that finds only those people who know how to be
alone. All through my life, I had known there was much more to being
alive than most people saw, a depth to each atom and an infinitude to each
moment that most people didn't seem to want to know. Yet no matter how
many religions I tried or number of spiritual practices I dedicated myself
to, I could not seem to experience the depth and breadth *fully*. "You're so
wise for your age," people would say. "You're an old soul." Yet I couldn't
break through, I couldn't really understand what I thought I understood. I
could see that Dr. Joseph Kader was the kind of person who really broke
through and understood. Suddenly I wanted to meet him.

Mick put his pipe down, blowing smoke circles into the air. "Tell me
you're ready to go to work, and I'll tell you something very interesting
about you and this Kader fellow, something you could never imagine."

"What are you talking about?"

"You won't believe it."

"What?"

He grinned. "Now I'm off to the rest room. You sit and make your decision." He pushed up out of his chair.

"You're a nut, Mick!" I called to him as he walked off.

I took a last sip of wine and closed my eyes in an impromptu meditation. I sat in the tension between the excitement of a new adventure and my reluctance to let go of the renewed innocence and peace I'd found in Europe. When Mick returned and sat down, I opened my eyes. As he scratched the red snakes on his nose and reported that he had ordered us another round, I said, "All right, Mick, drop the pebble in the pond. What is this bit of information you're holding?"

"Then you're going to go to Turkey, Ben?"

"Yes, I'm going." I smiled. "You must have known I would."

He shrugged slightly. "I wasn't sure. I couldn't have known what you'd been doing over here. But as to the pebble, as you call it, well, it's very simple, and it's quite bizarre." He leaned toward me, picking his pipe up and finding the metal tobacco packer. "Your father knows Joseph Kader. When your father did his guest directing stint here in Paris, he met Kader and they got to know each other."

"My father?"

"Yes, your father."

My father had been in Paris four years ago to direct a play, but he'd never mentioned meeting a guy named Joseph Kader. But then, why would he? He and I didn't talk much, not any more than any other father and son.

Mick nodded. "You remember I said we have to take this thing seriously? This is one of those very interesting things that happen in life."

I thought of my father here in Paris, sitting with Kader years ago.

"You'll want to call old Dad," Mick instructed me, "I have a bit of a plan. I must admit, I feel something like a detective, thinking it up."

"What plan?"

Kader, he said with a conspiratorial smile, would be in Paris for about another month before he returned to Turkey for his annual summer sojourn there. I could meet him here, with my father's innocent help. Kader, a dual citizen of Turkey and France, lived here in Paris most of the year.

I shook myself. Kader lived in Paris? "Mick, why didn't you start out by telling me he lived here?"

"You shouldn't know *everything*, not all at once." He grinned.

"All this is happening so fast. Do I know everything that's going on here, Mick? This is all so—coincidental, so convenient: Kader in Paris, me in Paris; Kader knowing my father."

"Lad, now you know everything I know. This Grant II is a strange grant, I'll admit. And a part of me suspects there's something bigger behind it, something political. But all I know for sure is this: we're academics, probably too naive for our own good, getting paid to do the work we like to do: exploring the edges of human consciousness. Why this phenomenon in Turkey is worth hundreds of thousands of dollars, I don't know. But our steering committee thinks the best chance of unfolding this mystery and fulfilling the grant is to get close to Kader. You are right for the job, and you deserve to have an adventure. That's what I know. But who's running the really big show, well, maybe that's a matter of spiritual discovery."

We lapsed into silence. I pondered the whole thing and thought about what I would tell my father when I called him. I'd learn more about Kader. I'd ask my father how to set up a meeting. I wouldn't tell him the whole story, just that I wanted to meet Kader. This was an adventure I wanted to have, at least for a while, by myself.

Mick offered his hand, imitating Jimmy Cagney. "Shake on it, bub?" He'd always had a terrible penchant for trying to imitate movie stars.

I shook his hand, and he clapped me on the shoulder.

"You'll keep good notes, won't you? That exquisite memory of yours will stand you in good stead, I'm sure." He was referring to my unusual auditory memory. As a kid assisting my uncle, I had been billed as "The Boy with the Magical Memory" because I could listen to people or albums or the radio and repeat what I heard.

"You won't want to tell Kader you're studying the phenomenon," he cautioned. "He'll close you out, I'm sure. But if all goes well, you'll become his pupil and he'll take you to see this Magician hallucination. For your labors, you'll earn a salary of two thousand a month, plus expenses. Sound all right?"

It was more money than I had ever made before.

Mick opened his briefcase and laid out lists, phone numbers, printouts with instructions. For half an hour we worked out logistics; then it was time for me to prepare for my evening street performance. He handed me a thousand dollars as a cash advance. "No need to work tonight," he said with a smile.

As the sun set behind Notre Dame, Mick and I parted company, embracing on the sidewalk. A half hour later I was on the phone to New York, leaving a message with my father's wife for my father to call me back, any time, day or night, in the Hôtel de Seine, where I had decided to splurge on a fancy room for the night.

In an instant, a life changes. First I'm in my *chambre* in Paris, waking up to the sound of sparrows, then I'm at a café near Notre Dame, working out a path of deception. Presumably, soon I would meet a teacher who might introduce me, in a Muslim country I'd never dreamed of visiting, to a phenomenon I had been trained to study. The Buddhists say we are always prepared as we need to be for whatever comes our way, but we can never actually prepare enough. This was how I felt. Most of the path before me was invisible, but I felt ready to walk it. I felt my life had built to it, though I could not even see, at that moment, the true outlines of my future at all.

SECOND ✳ DREAM

Ben Brickman called this second dream "The Assassination of a Prophet." It is the second and last dream in which the life of Nathan imploded in Ben's consciousness.

"Nathan! Oh, my God!"

The man, lying next to the woman on the bed, hears her words before the bullet hits him in the chest. This Nathan has gray-white hair and is powerfully built, more than two hundred pounds, but the bullet doesn't care, squirting his blond chest hair with red.

A man at the door—it must be the shooter—is singing Led Zeppelin in a very high-pitched tenor. I can't see him except in shadow, but I know him from the last dream.

"And when I wind on down the road . . ."

The woman in the bed is not shot, but she's screaming.

Nathan's wound, just to the left of the heart, expands into a red stain. There is darkness, a long tunnel—very quiet, sonorous, a fragrance, perfume. The tunnel leads somewhere, into time itself. He smells lilacs. Like an insect inside a flower, he is enveloped in lilacs. He and the woman are somewhere else now. A hospital?

He hears car horns as if his ears are large. He feels a draft on the skin of his arm like cool foam, as if the ocean is spraying him lightly. He needs water badly; his mouth is dry.

He hears no voices but suspects he is not dead.

What am I? is his first thought. Not Where am I, but What am I?

He feels as if he has been transformed in some way, or soon will be. He has no power over his eyes. He can't open the eyelids—he sees only black.

Yet he senses things. He senses that the woman was not shot. He sees into her mind as she sits next to him in the hospital room. He senses and sees her mood. His sensing is like the sensing of the American man in the cold room in Paris, drugged and able to sense without seeing.

"Don't worry, dear," he murmurs wordlessly, "all will be well."

Then the seeing into her mind is like déjà vu, as if he has been here, exactly, before, lying unawakened, she sitting beside him, a car horn, a lilac, a breeze.

She thinks suddenly of her mother, who died. She recalls cleaning her baby daughter's nose with a paper towel, sitting in the red Camry. She wants to ask, "How can he be in a coma from a chest wound?" She has asked it many times and wants to ask again. She hears the doctor with the thick accent say, "Very unusual, very unusual." She sees in her mind's eye the tall American who gunned Nathan down. He too was shot. Will both men die?

Even now, as he lies in a coma, Nathan reads his wife's mind with a sixth sense. In her mind the doctor says, "If he recovers soon, he will live. If not, I don't know." She is thinking that there must be something in his brain, a splinter of bullet the doctors did not find.

You're right, he tries to tell her, there's a terrible pressure in my head! Tell the doctors. This killer shot something into my head, at the neck, before he shot me, before you woke up. He shot something into my neck from a dart or a needle. Tell the doctors.

Now something happens, a light—a light is starting in the center of the Nothing. Cannot read her mind anymore. Cannot think a thought. Only the light. So beautiful. So complete. What is it?

Now the mind is incorporating. Incorporating everything. Everything is mind. The sense of everything as mind. A million beds—millions of people in beds. Children, flowers, buildings, leaves, voices, everything blending. The mind is mixing with a seventh sense. What is this sense? Pure energy. Seeing the pure energy embodied in everything, everyone. Not seeing—being the seeing. Feeling purely, energy purely. What is this seventh sense? Want more of it.

A million billion stars. Congregations of energy. Clusters of energy. What are they? Who are they? All alive. Incorporation of mind into them, they into mind.

They are all one, yet all individuals. Strings of energy—one string, yet individual points—flying out from the origin of light. Need the seventh sense to see these strings. Mind feels more at home in one string than in any other. Why? It's pure incorporation, so how can there not be equal affection?

The strings of energy are billions of billions of themselves.

Is this dying? Is this death?

---

*W*ide awake in my bed in Paris, I sweated and breathed like a wheezing machine. This was like the dream a few weeks ago! I threw my legs off the bed, wiping my naked chest and my head with the sheet.

I stood up, went to the toilet, stared into the water while I peed. The first dream had come almost a month before, then nothing till now.

I felt strangely as if I were being sent information from somewhere, that it was important I get it just right.

Outside it was near dawn. I pulled out my journal, beginning a page with "The Second Dream." I wondered if there would be more dreams like these—these were as much visions as dreams, like hallucinogenic visions. Yet I had taken no drugs of any kind. At the bottom of a page I wrote, "There will be seven dreams in total. I don't know why I know this."

CHAPTER 2

Meeting the Master

> *The mystic's second task is submission to a master. One cannot know God directly unless one has submitted to a mentor who becomes like God. This mentor humbles you with authority, wisdom, tenderness, and firmness. Always you will prove yourself to the master in some way, and always the master will be proven to you. The master is not the doorway to God; the master is the key.*
>
> *Mystics tire themselves with inquiries: "Who are the masters I should seek? Where are they? How will I know them?" Even searchers of great soul and depth waste their efforts trying to plan the meeting with the master. They look around for masters, try them on like clothes. You do better to ask, "When I meet the master, will I be ready to submit myself?" Humility will be required, or the master will withhold the key to God's doorway.*
>
> *—The Magician*

The morning of the day I met Joseph Kader, it poured rain. About noon, the sky healed—the sun's emergence so bright, people on the streets squinted. By four in the afternoon, I'd done my half-hour magic show twice, performing beside a cherry tree outside the Café du Thé, alongside the Seine. All day my hands had been a little shaky. I was preoccupied with my recent all-too-real dream of the man named Nathan being shot. I was also nervous because I knew that at the end of my performance, Joseph Kader would finally talk to me. I shook hands with a well-wisher and moved toward my favorite table for a postperformance café au lait, carrying my donations cap. In it was one withered cherry blossom, white with browned edges, among the coins and bills.

During the performance, a short, dark-complected, Middle Eastern–looking man had come to watch, a man whom I knew, from his photo, to be Kader. Over the last two weeks he had come to several of my performances, sitting each time against the café's glass windows. Today he sat right up front, at a table adjacent to the one I used to stow my things and gather myself after performing.

For almost a month since my meeting with Mick, I'd honed and savored the deception by which I intended to make Joseph Kader my guide to the Magician. Now, as I was finally about to talk to him, my stomach turned over.

"Don't forget these," Kader offered from his table as I sat down next to him. He tossed his customary two-franc donation into my magic hat. He had a deep, sonorous voice, like a cello, something the file hadn't mentioned.

"Thanks, *merci*," I acknowledged.

At sixty-five, he was bald on top, his shiny brown skull speckled with whitish liver spots. Thin gray hair stuck to the back of his head, but his sideburns, mustache, and beard were a thicker gray. His eyes had a soft wetness about them. Just under five feet tall, he wore a white silk shirt, tan slacks, argyle socks, and brown slip-on shoes. Over the last two weeks, I had seen that, except when he fully concentrated, he wore the eternal smile of the mystic.

Perhaps his most fascinating bodily feature, far more than his dwarflike height or his smile, was his face, which looked smashed in, as if before birth God had reached into the womb and punched, with a balled fist, the front and center of the skull. The face jutted out at the ridged forehead above the eyebrows, then caved in at the eyes, mouth and nose, so that the nose was almost flat, the front of his skull not reemerging again until the chin. His lips were thin and pink, lighter in color than the rest of his brown complexion.

"May I offer you a drink, my friend?" he asked, still smiling. His Middle Eastern accent overlay a British one: formal, careful. I knew from the file that he had learned English in a British-run boarding school in the 1930s.

Trying to appear nonchalant, I thanked him and accepted a café au lait. On the table, just under his right arm, I noticed wrapped packages and books. He gave our order to Luc, the waiter, who already knew what we both liked to drink. As Luc left, Kader and I traded names. His was Yusuf, he said.

"You're from the Middle East, right?" I asked, feigning ignorance.

"My friend," he smiled, "you might say I'm from the center of the world—the country of Turkey."

"Turkey is the center of the world?"

"It is both Europe and the Middle East, the bridge between East and West. You have heard of the Bosphorus, haven't you, a strait in the center of Istanbul that separates Europe and Asia? You should go to Istanbul one day, my friend. I will give you my card. It will tell you who I am. I know who you are, you see. I have watched you with pleasure these days."

From his breast pocket he pulled out a thin gold card case. The fancy case held very simple calling cards, plain white with black lettering. YUSUF KADER in the center, with an Ankara address on the left and a Paris address on the right. Under his name, in small letters, was the word "Anthropologist."

"An anthropologist," I said. In the movies and on television, people make it look easy to deceive others, to act as if they know nothing about a person when in fact they've read a very thick file. It's not easy at all; it takes real concentration. One thing my father had taught me about acting always stuck with me: "If you don't have a script, don't talk much. Ask a lot of questions." I had found this to be good advice throughout my life. "What kind of anthropologist?"

"I've worked mainly in Africa," he replied. "Until recently, that is, when I returned to my Turkey for some important anthropological and spiritual work."

Luc put the drinks in front of us and took Yusuf's francs. I thanked my new friend for his card.

"Look again at the card," Yusuf suggested. "Don't you know me?"

I looked again. "Yusuf Kader," I repeated. "Sorry, it doesn't ring a bell."

"Yusuf," he said, "is another name for Joseph."

In my best pretense of wide-eyed recognition, I laughed, "Ohhh, my Goddd! *Joseph* Kader! You're Dad's friend!"

He let out a loud, giggly laugh. "I have tricked you a bit. Every day has at least one moment of pure delight, and this one now, to see the face on you, my friend, it is wonderful!"

"Geez!" On we went with the farce. I reached my hand out to shake his. "How long have you known—known that I—was me?"

"Oh, I've known for weeks!" he grinned. "I've watched you and known all along! Your father called me a few weeks ago: 'Joseph, have you heard from my son?' I confessed I had not. He told me you had written him that you performed on the street near a little café. What café? He wasn't quite sure. There are thousands in Paris. But he was so energetic about you. 'He is one of a kind, Joseph! You two searchers should connect!'" *Connect*—such a wonderful American use of the word! I thought it a fine idea but had no way of knowing where you were. Then, two nights later, I came to this arrondissement to visit a colleague, as I often do, and passed by the Café du Thé, as I often do. I saw a young magician performing. Voilà! Here we are."

"That's a hell of a coincidence," I said. "How did you know it was me?"

He laughed. "I don't believe in coincidence. I knew it was you."

"And Dad said I was one of a kind?" I wasn't acting now; I felt truly surprised. I felt that feeling of being pulled by nature toward events—being pulled by forces toward Joseph. My father was supposed to tell him I worked at the Café du Thé; I had dropped the hint to him more than once, but he'd obviously forgotten. Yet Kader had found me, and known me.

Leaning forward, Joseph continued, "Harry told me you are a searcher in the old sense of the word. You seek those questions and those answers which are most important not only to yourself, but to all nature and humanity."

These were loving words my generally reticent father had spoken. They caught me off guard.

"I am a searcher too," Joseph said. "A searcher in the old sense of the word. Perhaps we can be of help to each other. The old like young friends, you know."

I lifted my cup, offering a toast. "To Paris!" I clinked it to Joseph's glass. "Where else would people just meet this way?"

"To Paris!" We each took a drink. "So," Joseph said, "tell me who you are, this son of my old friend, this spiritual searcher? What places have you called home? What is your mission in life? What is your quest? Tell me the history of your mind and your soul."

No one had ever asked me so openly and completely about myself.

"Well, I don't know," I temporized, a little embarrassed. "Where do I begin?"

"I will help you." He reached his hand into his breast pocket and pulled out a shiny stone, reddish white quartz of some kind. "Every relationship should begin with a gift. You have given me a gift in your many performances. Let me give you this gift I brought you. It's from a mountain in Central Africa, a place of great power. Touch the stone, will you?"

I took its smoothness into my right hand, cupping it, then kneading it between my thumb and forefinger. Its warmth surprised me.

"Is it warm because it was in your pocket?"

"This stone is naturally warmer than other stones. It is what the African Kulu call a heartstone, for opening the heart to truth and for . . ."

I lost the next words as my body experienced some kind of spark, a jolt of tingling electricity shooting through me. It was invisible, an itching on my skin. What a bizarre feeling! It began somewhere in my groin or lower back, then moved up my spine and central organs, down my legs, up my shoulders, down into my feet, then back upward, swarming into my head.

"Jesus," I muttered, dropping the rock on the table, shaking myself free. "What happened?"

Joseph reached the rock to touch it. "It's very warm now."

"I—I felt so—" I couldn't speak well. I felt warm, clean, inspired, as if I'd just run ten miles. Then I thought: Wait a minute, it's a trick. There has to be something on the stone, some topical stimulant. Or maybe Joseph is doing some kind of hypnosis? Maybe, I suddenly thought, there are tricks on both sides of this conversation.

Before I could get words out to question Joseph, I saw a vivid image in my mind, vivid with the same quality as the dreams, but very quick: my finger touching the soft back of a bumblebee. Where had that come from? Suddenly it was replaced by a quick, vivid image of a black dog in a forest. What was going on? What was on that stone?

I lifted my cup and drank the entire café au lait. "Can I see that stone again?" I asked, taking it from him. It was still warm but this time produced no sensation in me—it was just a stone again.

"In America," I said, "different native peoples have 'power stones' or 'medicine objects.' Is this stone like that?" As I asked the question, I felt a quick mournfulness: the moment of total, almost dreamy connection with life was gone.

"How did the stone affect you, my friend?" Joseph asked.

Should I really say? I wondered. Would being open with him help bring me closer to meeting the Magician? I decided it would.

"It's like the feeling of being everything, not just *me*," I answered. "Joseph, I became a graduate student in transpersonal psychology because I wanted to find out more about all the strange, mystical moments that I had and other people have. Then my thesis project fell apart—Dad probably told you. After six months of wandering, I understand why: it failed because I sense a hidden self, but I can't find it and hold it and keep it. I'm looking for the secrets of the universe. This is more important to me than to just write a thesis on a specific topic. I feel such a pull toward something big. But I don't have the wisdom."

The sweet taste of the café au lait gave me something to hide in for a second as Joseph responded. "That statement in itself is wise. It's difficult to know why a person is unable to let go. Perhaps you have never truly been taught how to do so."

"I know a lot *about* it, but I guess I don't understand *it*." I saw an opening. "I remember Dad once saying you wrote a lot about these sorts of things."

Before answering, he waved at Luc, circling my empty cup and his empty glass with two fingers and mouthing "*S'il vous plaît*." "Yes, Ben, perhaps my best-known books are those that concern my own initiation by the Kulu tribe in Africa and my lifelong study of Sufi mysticism. My *Initi-*

ation into Central African Shamanism, Sufi Mysticism, and *Mysticism for the New Millennium.* You have not heard of them, I'm sure."

I shook my head. "I haven't. I'm sorry." I had, of course, from the file, but I hadn't read them. Mick and I agreed that I shouldn't read Kader's work; if I did, I'd be more likely to slip up.

He chuckled. "My books are hardly best-sellers!" His laugh, his twinkling eyes, his deep breaths, his dwarflike appearance—his whole demeanor—revealed a genuinely happy man. I envied him.

I reached for the stone again, but there was no jolt. I fingered it, thinking: Focus on the plan. Draw him out. Get an invitation to come to Turkey. "Was the initiation by the tribe pretty hard?" I asked. "Are they the ones who taught you how to understand *It,* the letting go?"

"A very difficult initiation, my friend, carried out over a period of years. But without initiation, I must tell you, I was not much of a man, certainly not a man capable of real life. One must be initiated into the mysteries both of adulthood and of adult spiritual life."

He looked at his watch. "I have to be at my daughter's house, yet I do wish to talk with you further. These gifts," he pointed at his parcels, "are for my grandchildren. What about this, my friend, what if—" He paused for an instant, then asked where I was living and what I paid. I told him about the *chambre* I rented. He frowned. "No good, not at all. You're Harry Brickman's son. You will stay with me!"

"No, no," I protested, "I can't do that."

"I insist. Surely people have invited you into their homes as you've traveled?"

"Of course," I agreed. Not in big cities like Paris, but especially in smaller towns, people had invited me to spend the night and speak English with their kids, who were usually learning to speak it in grammar school. "But I can't just impose on you, Joseph." Are you kidding? I admonished myself. Of course you can! This is just what you and Mick hoped for! Don't let this get away.

"It's no imposition, my friend. I do insist. Later tonight, or tomorrow, you can go get your things."

"What if I only stay a day or two," I promised, "if it's no trouble."

"A day or two is fine. Now I think we'll go." He pushed his glass away. I got the rest of my supplies packed. Joseph volunteered to carry one of my smaller bags, but I showed him how everything combined, with the use of Velcro, into a single small pack.

"What the Kulu would have done with Velcro I cannot imagine," he said with a grin. "Had I brought it to them thirty years ago, they would have made me a saint!"

We left the café, found the street corner underground steps, and descended to the Métro. As we stepped onto the train, I congratulated myself on how well my deception had worked thus far. As we sped through tunnels under Paris, we held on to a center pole of the train, the air humming with voices and electrical juice.

"Tell me more about your life, will you?" I asked. "About the initiation?"

"Yes," he said with a nod, stretching his back in and out, in a yoga stance I recognized as "the crane."

I towered over Joseph as he continued talking, his eyes at the level of my chest. "The process of mystical initiation is about merging into the eternal rhythm of life. When one has accomplished all ten tasks of enlightenment, one has accomplished 'second birth.'"

"By 'second birth,' you mean, like the Christians say, being 'born again'?"

"It is the same concept, but regrettably, many evangelical individuals in various religions—Christianity, Islam, all the others—they end up having an experience of divinity that makes them more fearful of society, not less. The mystic, after second birth, has nothing to fear."

Joseph made it sound so simple, or maybe I just heard it that way. During my born-again Christian phase in my late teens, I had felt as if I were "found" for a number of months. But I was actually pretty lost in fear, even of society, and had ended up feeling lost again.

"Joseph," I asked, "the ten tasks—what are they?"

He shook his head. "Now is not the time. Let us just say, my friend, that without full initiation—without the 'second birth'—adulthood is creativity and abstraction without meaning; it is emptiness and the struggle to control life, to control others, and thereby to cover up the emptiness; it is material acquisitions without a sense of purpose; it is psychological childhood without spiritual depth. When the ten tasks are complete, one's spirit has fully adapted to one's body and one's body to one's spirit. This is completion."

"I don't think I'm initiated," I said, "not the way you describe." I really meant that, and it saddened me. My spiritual searches had taken me to many places and into many religions, but I knew I had not experienced the kind of "initiation" he was talking about. If I had, I would have known it in my bones, and I didn't.

"I'm not surprised, my friend," he said sympathetically. "Most people in the modern industrial world are uninitiated into spiritual life; most people don't know the Oneness that comes from the rigors of the mystical life. They try to fix the lack of spirit in their lives through 'believing in God' or through materialism and the glitter of things. But they don't *know* themselves *as* God—they don't know themselves *as* the evolutionary life force of the universe. This single problem is most responsible for the crisis of human civilization as the new millennium approaches. For you see, my friend, each of us has coded into us an instinct to know ourselves as life force. When we do not gain this knowing in adulthood—or when it is crushed out of us by religion or materialism or some other force—we live in immense pain."

The Métro stopped, but Joseph motioned me to stay put. "We will take the Métro farther, into the ninth arrondissement. My flat is in the rue de la Tour des Dames."

"Joseph, I really appreciate your talking to me and letting me sleep over," I said as I felt a stab of guilty conscience. As I shamelessly used him, he generously opened up to me.

The electric doors squeezed shut, and the train lurched mildly, like a bed shifting under us.

"It's my pleasure," he assured me, his smile warm. I looked down at his brown head and gray hair; I felt the pleasure of being in the company of an old man who wants to tell a young man his story.

"How did you meet the Kulu?" I prompted as we began moving forward.

"Well, my friend," he said, clearing his throat, "I went to Rhodesia—

now Zimbabwe—to study the effects of Muslim and Christian missionaries on Central African tribal life. This was my dissertation topic. Even as
a young man, I felt certain that religion would have to transform itself
within a few centuries, and that is what I wanted to study. I wanted to
study those people, the proselytizers and missionaries, who most fear its
disappearance and who, therefore, most vehemently pursue its supremacy.

"From Rhodesia I went into what was then the Belgian Congo. It was
all very fascinating for me, a young teacher about your age. Fascinating, especially, because I began to feel the trance of real consciousness, the
trance of Oneness. I'm sure you have experienced something like the
trance. You studied drama in college, yes?"

"And philosophy, theology, literature, psychology. You name it."

"Did these not 'entrance' you?"

"I guess you could say that."

"You know the edges of the feeling, then. The shamans of the
Kulu, you see, know the trance world well. They *know* spiritual adulthood from the inside out. They can manipulate it with great facil-
ity, the way a good teacher can use knowledge to entrance you. My
teacher, Mwimbo, saw something in me, an openness—and over a
period of a year he and others initiated me in the ritual ways. In 1960,
I spent many weeks in the initiation rituals: fasts, mutilations, mind-
altering herbs, prayer, sweat pits. Oh my, what a trial! I was buried
in the earth with only my head showing! Now I look back in wonder. He who is afraid—he who is without absolute trust and faith in
himself—can never be reborn, can never be free. It took me such a
long time to gain this trust, this *knowing*. Until I gained it, I could
never fully be entranced. This is what I learned, my friend. This was my
initiation."

I had never met anyone quite like this little man. I felt almost as if I
were falling in love with him.

"Ah, let us hold off a minute. There we go, my friend, there's our
stop." He pointed up ahead as the lights and people of the station drew
near.

When the doors opened, I hefted my pack over my shoulder and followed Joseph out and up the Métro steps to the bustling square. "We'll cross here," he directed, fearless of traffic. As we passed a beautiful neighborhood church, I saw the plaque on the side of the corner building: RUE DE LA TOUR DES DAMES. I followed Joseph down the quiet, narrow street. He moved quickly. The houses and apartments were upper middle class— flowers on wrought-iron balconies, stone walls, street lanterns.

"My flat is just up there." He pointed at the second story of a three-story white stone building. "I'll settle you in, then drop these packages at my daughter's flat on the second floor." He pointed at the apartment below his own. I have one daughter and two granddaughters," he explained. "My wife died three years ago." I knew these facts but shook my head and offered my condolences.

He unlocked a large wooden door and we climbed upstairs. His apartment was cooler than the outside, very neat, very small, filled with art, masks, and African sculpture. "There are drinks over there." He pointed to a liquor cart. "Now be comfortable, my friend. I'll return in a sparrow's second." He left with his packages.

I walked to the liquor cart and studied the masks that hung like pictures above it: a lion, a clown, a black female goddess, a bull, a snake-headed man. I poured myself some wine. To my left were glass doors covered with see-through curtains. On the wall to the right stood a small desk with papers and books on it. The glass doors opened onto a small balcony from which I looked down upon the quiet street. Mesmerized by a fancy garden across the way, I barely heard the people come into the room behind me.

"You've found the balcony, I see," Joseph called out. Turning, I saw Joseph, a dark-skinned woman, and two little girls. All of them combined Joseph's features with African features. This startled me for a second. The file hadn't mentioned that Joseph's wife had been African. But then, why would it?

"This is Adrianna," Joseph said, introducing me to his daughter, a woman about my age, then to Hulya, seven, and Lucia, five. Joseph grinned. "They want you to do some of your magic tricks before dinner. Adrianna's husband, Jean-Paul, will return from work, then we'll have dinner with them. Agreed?" None of the kin seemed to speak English. Each had shaken my hand with an *"Enchanté."* I spoke German and Spanish but only the French I'd picked up in the last couple of months.

I smiled. "Okay, sure."

"Come, then," he said, "let's go downstairs."

I grabbed my magic bag and followed his family to the door. Somehow, I thought, I have to get Joseph back to the subject of the Magician.

"My gosh, Joseph," I said, looking at him as if I were puzzled. I put my fork down and wiped my lips with one of Adrianna's white line napkins, "I just realized something. You're the anthropologist who studies that 'Magician' phenomenon, aren't you?" The idea of bringing the Magician up this way had actually occurred to me twenty minutes earlier while I performed a magic trick for the kids called "The Blind Man's Kings." I wear a blindfold but still end up with four kings on the top of the card deck and four aces on the bottom. The secret of the trick is a sheet of paper between the cover deck and the trick deck. The family had been mesmerized, or as Joseph might say, entranced.

Joseph translated my exclamation to his family, prompting a nervous laugh from Adrianna and Jean-Paul. Adrianna said something in French, which Joseph translated: "Adrianna says it is the story of my life, to become famous for things that the scholars I once most admired now shun."

"So it *is* you?" I pressed.

"Oh, yes. It is me. And what have you heard of the Magician phenomenon?"

"I can't even remember what I heard," I lied. "That some people in Turkey have seen a figure called the Magician, and the figure made them feel good. That's it, I guess. It clicked in my head while I was doing my magic tricks. Magic, Magician—" Shut up, an inner assembly of voices muttered, you've said enough. "It just clicked."

Joseph broke off a piece of bread from a long, thin baguette on a wooden board. "It's not something I talk much about, not directly at least, not anymore. It is a phenomenon which, I believe, will change the world. The Magician, I have come to learn, is a divine presence, a Traveler, sent

to bring us to harmony. My public disclosure of this information has created difficulties, so I have stopped writing about it and stopped giving any
interviews. The Magician has made it clear that I am not the one to
speak."

"I won't ask anymore," I said respectfully.

The whole subject seemed to stiffen his family. "Perhaps we will speak
of it later." Joseph frowned. Adrianna said something, and the subject
changed. I had to settle for being lost again in the rush of beautiful French
words. Had I pushed at the wrong moment? I thought not: I had followed
an instinct. Now I'd let it play itself out. My grandfather, Ben, used to say,
"If an old man wants to talk, he'll talk—just wait like a friendly dog, and
he'll get around to you."

Around eleven o'clock we got back to Joseph's apartment. In the living
room, we sat down comfortably sated after a delicious dinner (chicken in
mustard sauce), and dessert (strawberry-filled pastry). He turned on some
oud music—the Turkish oud, he explained, is like a medieval guitar. We
listened to beautiful string sounds, something like sitar sounds, but also
like a lute.

He poured two snifters of cognac and asked about my past. I told him
how my parents had moved a lot, and we had lived all over the world.
Never one to hold back from self-disclosure, I talked about my mother
and my father being distant, preoccupied parents. I talked about good
and bad experiences of boyhood; about my interest in karate and aikido
as a teenager; my spiritual yearnings from the very beginning of my life;
my different experiences as a Jew, a Christian, and a practitioner of Zen. I
almost told him about my sporadic episodes of visionary activity throughout my life and my recent vivid dreams of the future, but I didn't. I held
back.

"Though you have experienced life's joy's and sufferings," he said at
one point during my revelations, "you do not look tortured. Why is that,
do you think?"

I had no answer. I had never really thought of myself in those terms.

Around midnight, when I had nearly given up hope that he'd bring up the Magician, he surprised me. "You have been honest with me, Ben," he said, unaware that behind my candor was concealment. "I will be so with you. I have watched you for days, seeing a glow around you. I want to show you something I have not considered showing anyone in a while. But I think I can trust you with something important." That statement nearly melted me with guilt. At the same time, hiding it well, I inwardly rejoiced.

He went to the antique desk near the balcony door, pulled out a large scrapbook, and opened it—it was filled with clippings—articles in Turkish, French, English, and German. I came beside him on the couch and glanced at the headlines and titles I could understand. I began to read those.

Thanking him for his trust, my forehead, underarms, and chest breaking into a sweat, I flushed with alcohol, shame, and anticipation. A lot of the material in the scrapbook resembled the testimony and vignettes I'd read in the file: interviews with people who had seen the haloed figure in Turkey at various locations. Joseph translated a piece of one article out loud for me; in it, he was questioned by the Turkish Department of the Interior. They wanted him to explain the Magician phenomenon. He insisted he had no explanation. He told them a divine presence from the spirit world was commingling with this world.

He laughed. "A wonderful moment! They had no idea what to do with me." He showed me another article in which the Department of Tourism had undertaken a study of the different "Magician sites" —thirty-eighty places along the coast where the Magician had been seen. A few tourists had started to seek out the sites in hopes of catching a glimpse. So far, the Department of Tourism had learned nothing useful, nor had anyone who had *pursued* a sighting of the Magician ever experienced one. This worried me. The sightings had just sort of happened. What if one did not happen for *me*?

Preparing to build a lie, I inhaled deeply. "Joseph, my God, I just remembered something: in my adolescence I met someone . . . When I was seventeen I did a lot of sweat lodge ceremonies with a southern Ute medicine man named Eagleclaw Simpson. My dad worked on the reservation setting up a theater on an NEH grant. My folks were into every religion around." All this was true so far.

"Native American theology is what got into my heart at that important time of my upbringing. Now I'm talking to you today about the Kulu, and you talk about African sweat pits. It's like the sweat lodge in New Mexico. Suddenly it makes me remember. Eagleclaw said something to me. Jesus, I'm getting chills remembering it." The flesh on my arms, under my jacket, rose in sudden goose bumps. I crossed my arms and rubbed them with my hands.

"What did he say?" Joseph asked.

Now here came the lie. "He told me, 'One day you will meet a man who will know you already. Follow him. He will become your teacher. He will teach you your mission and your destiny.' I remember this seemed like . . . so generalized, you know? So romanticized or something. I was only seventeen."

Joseph leaned back, drawing on his cigar with rounded lips. Exhaling, he said, "In Turkish there is a saying: 'There was bread there for you to eat.' Bread is the staff of life. Some experiences are like doorways into a deep consciousness of life energy and its workings. Perhaps that summer was such a doorway for you. Perhaps this summer is one too."

For a moment, neither of us spoke. Was I reeling him in? I wondered.

Joseph leaned forward and put his cigar out. "Ben, I am inclined to invite you to visit me in Turkey. You and I are carried by an energy greater than ourselves. You are wandering, a spiritual nomad, and I am about to return to my Turkish home for the summer. I will open my home to you if you wish. I have never forgotten, you see, your father's words to me when I knew him here: 'I have never felt even for myself the pride I feel for my son. If only you could meet him, Joseph. He is so gifted!' This your father said to me, and it made me fear you a little. As I watched you performing at the café, my friend, I said to myself, 'What a gift God has given me!' These things are mysterious. People meet. Their destinies link. Your destiny, I sense, is linked now to Turkey. Perhaps in Turkey, we will travel together to some places I know. I don't know what will come of our travels, but I think we are meant to spend some time with one another."

My stomach filled with butterflies. This is what Mick and I had been hoping for! "I'd love to visit Turkey," I said.

"Then we will arrange it. Let us sleep now, shall we?"

I was too excited to sleep, but we set up a bed for me on the couch and said our good nights.

In my journal that night I wrote, "I have met a truly unique and marvelous man, someone capable of innocence and wisdom both, a guide on a journey. It's all working so well—it can't just be because I'm a good actor. What else is happening? I feel something is going that's larger than my deceptions. Or am I just being overly dramatic? Will I ever be able to tell Joseph Kader the truth? He's telling me the truth all the time."

I tried to sleep but couldn't. All I wanted to do was get back into that scrapbook and read more about the Magician. I resisted, worried that Joseph would catch me reading his private papers. Then, around 1:00 A.M., I gave up resisting. Joseph had put the scrapbook back in the little desk by the balcony door. He had locked it with a key but put the key on the top of the desk. Tiptoeing down the hall, I looked under his door and saw that his light was off. Convinced he was sleeping, I went to the desk, opened the drawer, took the scrapbook out, and brought it to the coffee table next to my couch. I thumbed through it, recognizing most of what we'd already looked at. I skimmed a monograph by Joseph in German. He ended it this way:

As we have noted, it is not unusual in the anthropological history of religious experience for the time of a millennium's transition to be marked by the sighting of prophets in holy places. There were an estimated five hundred such prophets preaching on the streets of Jerusalem in the time of Jesus. The presence we have termed "the Magician" comes to his "encountered" toward the end of our own millennium, when millions of people, including the ninety-seven who have sighted the Magician, seek a way of mystical consciousness that is not rigidified by their religions of childhood—a mystical awareness in the new millennium. For them, the Magician appears to be a prophet of their new freedom to feel ecstasy, centeredness, and joy.

I have encountered the Magician myself, as is common knowledge, and I know his presence as, in the Greek, parousia, "the future coming." Jesus Christ was only one of many historical prophets, so the reader should not take my use of parousia to denote "Jesus's second coming." My con-

clusion, from studying many of the encountered, is that the Magician is not a prophet promised by any one religion but a prophet of the universally shared reality we are just now recognizing as "consciousness."

I put the monograph down, breathing in and out quickly, compelled by a strange hot shiver, a tension suddenly so great I could not manage it; I had to expel it. It was like the jolt I'd received at the café table while holding the heartstone. It was as intense as when I had awakened from the future visions. Sweat broke out on my forehead, in my hair, under my arms. I rushed out onto the balcony, letting the breeze flow over me. I found myself mumbling the Hebrew Shema prayer, then singing "Amazing Grace" softly. These felt good, yet still something was happening in my body, something terrifying, like a shock of lightening penetrating deeper and deeper down in my groin.

I moaned and closed my eyes, and then, in a flash of light, I was not there any longer. I stood under the cherry tree by the Café du Thé, blossoms falling around me, Joseph walking up to me, his arms outstretched. All the people around us were frozen in place. I wept and laughed uncontrollably. Joseph embraced and calmed me.

"You're dreaming!" a voice in my head whispered. "You've actually fallen asleep." I heard it while fully cognizant that I was standing on Joseph's balcony. Another voice cried, "The masks and amulets in Joseph's apartment are causing you to be hexed in some way. You're just being affected by black magic." Yet the activity continued at Café du Thé. Joseph let go of me and I let go of him, and he walked away, down the sidewalk along the Seine. The other people unfroze and began to move, as if a director in a film had told them to move. I was again on Joseph's balcony, cold now as the breeze hit my sweat.

"Something has happened," Joseph said, coming onto the balcony, groggy-eyed in his long white nightshirt. "I awoke with a start, feeling pulled toward you. Have you been 'flying'?"

I pulled my T-shirt off, wiping the sweat off me. For a second I couldn't answer. I just had to sit down on the couch. He followed me inside and sat down next to me, watching me.

"I don't know what happened," I said. "It was beautiful. It was terrify-ing. I wasn't here, but I was here. I don't know what happened to me. I felt like a puppet."

"I think you were traveling in your astral body, my friend. Have you ever studied shamanic arts? With Eagleclaw, with anyone else, in India, perhaps?"

"No! I've had esoteric experiences, sure, but never really studied with a shaman or anything." Had Joseph done something to me? Why had he appeared behind me at just that moment? Hypnosis?

"You have many unrealized powers, Ben. Like an Eskimo or Kulu shaman, you are capable of flying. Your cells are trying to realign, to change the container of Self. But your Self is not yet established fully enough, strong enough; it is still weak, and it will not allow the spirit realm to alter its cells. You receive glimpses, little miracles, the brief rise and fall of kundalini or *chi*, but you are not initiated. It is troublesome for you. You are like someone who holds great power but cannot use it."

"Are you doing something to me, Joseph? Did you make that happen?"

He laughed. "Of course not. The powers are in *you*." I forced myself to believe him. And he really did look like someone startled awake from sleep.

"I did have psychic things happen years ago—but not in the last few years, not till . . . well, not till a dream a month ago, and another last night—both about the man named Nathan—and then that stone, that jolt with you, then this thing. But when I was a kid, when I was younger, a few things happened. When I was in my late teens, I left my body and went up a tree. Another time, I dreamt that a friend, who had moved three thousand miles away three years before, had had a baby named Con-stance. I awoke from the dream so startled I called her and said, 'Did you have a baby named Constance?' She'd had the baby the day before and named her Constance. Things like that used to happen to me. They are why I wanted to study transpersonal phenomena." Sweat dripped off my nose. "Jesus, I'm drenched!"

Joseph rose. "I'll get you a towel." When he opened the door of the linen closet in the hall, the creaking of the door's hinge was excruciatingly loud. I covered my ears, and my head filled with a tinny ringing, like after standing near the speakers at a rock concert when I was a teenager.

Joseph handed me a white towel. I could hear the sound of its fabric on my skin, in my chest hairs, under my arms, like a scratching on paper. "Joseph, for two years I've studied extraordinary experiences. While I studied them, I didn't have them myself. But now I'm having very extraordinary experiences. And today, three times in one day."

"What is the tension in you, my friend? There is so much tension in you. It is focused on me. It was present in you when you first saw me almost a month ago at the café." He sat back down on the couch, staring at me. "As a shaman, I am sensitive to the energies people direct at me, especially energies that 'sensitives' like you direct. I sense the energies without fully knowing their content. I sensed when you first saw me that you already possessed a tension concerning me. Ostensibly you didn't know me, and yet you seemed to know me. Would it help you to manage your internal shiftings if you could trust me now by speaking your truth about me?"

I looked into his watery brown eyes and nearly melted. Only a few hours into fulfilling my big plan, I wanted the deception over. For a month I had been setting it up, and now I wanted none of it. He had known there was something wrong from the moment he saw me. What chance did I really have to hide it from him anyway? Neither Mick nor I had realized how alert and attuned Joseph Kader was. He wasn't just a scholar, he was an initiated shaman, for God's sake!

I stood up. I wore only boxers. I reached for my pants. "I have to go," I said. "I don't know what to do. Everything's surprising me too much."

"What has surprised you, my friend?"

"You. You. Everything."

"Come, my friend, wait a moment, sit down. I have something you must see. I took it out of the scrapbook and I have never shared it with anyone. You must see it. Please sit."

"What is it?" I paused, curious.

Joseph headed into his bedroom, where I heard him open a drawer. He returned with a black-bound book. Opening it as he walked, he found the page he wanted and sat down on the couch. I sat down too.

"I wrote this diary entry over a year ago," he said, pointing to an entry in what I assumed to be Turkish. The date was 6/7/87.

"May I translate it for you? It concerns you."

"Me?"

"Yes. It says: 'Dreamt vividly of a young man, 30 or 31, tall, darkish blond and curly hair, dressed in blue blazer, button-down shirt, jeans—American or Canadian? We meet at a café along the Seine. Split souls? Karmic connection? Not clear. He does magic tricks for money. A cherry tree. Everyone sees his magic, only he does not see it. The Magician stands next to him, embracing him. He cannot see. There is severe deceit or trickery arranged by a man with snakes on his face. Hope to dream this again, experience more information about this young man. I have never dreamt the Magician embracing anyone in this way.'"

He looked up from the page. "This is a dream about you, Ben, is it not?"

I put my head in my hands. I had studied precognitive dreams, extrasensory experiences, spiritual hallucinations, mind-altering drugs. I had interviewed many people to whom similar synergetic-coincidental experiences had occurred. Now I was in the middle of one.

Joseph put his hand gently on my shoulder. "My friend, is it not time you tell me your secret? There is a deception, a trick, by which we have met. What is it?"

Before I could think further, it all came tumbling out. I told him who the man with the snakes was, describing Mick's nose and the tiny veins on it. I told him how I'd exploited the coincidence of my father knowing him. I told him how we had set up the meeting with him. I told him my surprise that he hadn't learned the name of the Café du Thé from my father.

"I knew the café, of course, from my dream," Joseph said, "though I did not recognize it until I saw it there, on my evening walk."

"I don't know what to say, how to apologize," I said. "It was work, 'a job,' pure and simple. I didn't know you yet. I guess I was kind of—well—I don't know. I'm sorry. I'll leave right now." I had no idea what I would tell Mick. I would quit. That was all.

Joseph grinned. "Why am I not surprised that trickery lines our meeting like the seam of a garment? What a pleasure to be alive!"

"What?"

"You see, had I not dreamt our meeting, my friend, I could choose to sit with you now and trust nothing about you. I could say to myself, Ah, his confession too is part of their Berkeley plan to invade my life and the Magician's sanctity. But why should I make that choice when I have yearned to meet you as much as you have yearned to meet me? And why make the choice when, throughout the history of mystical search, trickery and deception have been divine tools? Krishna, the great trickster, began his lessons with deceit. If not for Judas's betrayal, would the Christians have a religion? If not for the trick by which Joseph was confined to the pit, would the Jews have their wise prophet? Did you not learn as a boy about how the spider helped Mohammed deceive his oppressors? And now you and I meet through trickery, conceived by a man with snakes on his nose! God bless us!" He clapped his hands loudly.

"But what do we do now?" I asked. "You don't want me to investigate and report on the Magician phenomenon, right? You've made it clear you don't want that."

"I have made it clear that of the three ways of apprehending a prophet—codification by religion, study by empirical science, and spiritual experience by the individual—I will do everything in my power to make sure the Magician experiences as little as possible of the first two. The Magician has made it clear to the encountered that the new message needs to be brought to the world in divinely inspired story. The more he feels either organized religion or organized science embracing him, the more his spirit will recede.

"My friend," he smiled, putting out his hand, "we will become friends, you and I. If you still wish to, you will meet me in Turkey. Do you still wish to do that?"

"God, yes!" I cried.

"I must go to England to give a lecture. We will meet in late July in Istanbul, where I will enjoy your companionship, which is, I'm afraid, quite fated. In Turkey, we will let Fate further unfold. If you give me permission, I will teach you some of what I know about mysticism and shamanism. If the Magician should appear to you, so be it. If not, so be it. Can you live with that?"

I shook his hand firmly. "I can live with that. Thank you. I'll contact

Mick and withdraw from the project." As I shook Joseph's hand, I remembered shaking Mick's hand: two spiritual deals between men, but this one, though I knew Joseph very little, now felt the more profound.

"That would be best, I think," he nodded. "Now I'm tired. Please stop leaving your body, will you?"

Grinning, I asked, "But will you teach me about it?"

He stood up. "I will," he promised, "but do not ask, all right, my friend? Do not pursue the knowledge you seek. Learn simply to accompany the teacher. Can you do that?"

"I can," I agreed, too quickly.

"I will sleep now." He walked back toward his bedroom, taking the scrapbook and his journal with him.

I noticed I was no longer sweating, and the tinny sound no longer filled my head.

It was nearly dawn when I finished a letter to Mick and the institute. As I recall that long night, I recall one of those pivotal moments in a person's life when he risks everything—in my case, job, money, even perhaps Mick's trust and friendship—to seek spiritual liberation. Mustn't every human being, at some point, do his own version of this?

Now I can see I gave up nothing compared with what I found. Joseph had accepted me as a pupil, and I was hungry for the love of God. Little did I know that, at the moment I gained this realization, I had already accomplished two of the tasks of enlightenment. I was already on my way toward myself.

PART TWO

The Doorway

From five sides You move against me,

Hearing, sight, taste, touch, and scent.

To come out is to be caught; I cannot hide from

You.

—JACOPONE DA TODI

Master Tung-kuo asked Chuang-tzu, "This thing
   called the Way—where does it exist?"
Chuang-tzu said, "There's no place it doesn't
   exist."
"Come," said Master Tung-kuo, "you must be
   more specific!"
"It is in the ant."
"As low a thing as that?"

"It is in the panic grass."

"But that's lower still!"

"It is in the tiles and shards."

"How can it be so low?"

"It is in the piss and dung."

— CHUANG-TZU

Rabbi Jacob used to say:

Better a single moment of awakening in this

   world than eternity in the world to come.

Why?

A single moment of awakening in this world is

   eternity in the world to come.

— PIRKE AVOT 4:22

THIRD DREAM

Ben Brickman called this third dream "The Portal." It occurred on an Italian ferry on which he traveled across the Mediterranean to Istanbul, Turkey. This dream is more "normal" than the previous two, less overtly precognitive and predictive of the future. Yet it is compelling in a way very personal to Ben; and it does include an element of the future in the detail of the crippled hand behind the door.

I sit with Mick in a gentle breeze on the terrace of a café near Notre Dame. Around us people chat, drink, and eat. As I reach for my cup, Mick's bow tie flutters—once, twice, three times—and turns into a butterfly. As it flies off, Mick's neck, then head, then torso change into a Japanese maple tree with thin purple leaves. As Mick's face recedes into bark and sap, bees and flies pour out of his eyes as if freed.

I stand up as the butterfly, the bees, and the flies flutter around me. Some land on me, but none stings or bites. Paris recedes—Notre Dame, the street, the cars, the people, all of them melting gradually, calmly, into a meadow, a hill, a forest, deer. I am all that remains of the human realm.

From the trees to my left, a black Labrador, a female, comes toward me, nose to the ground. I understand that she is a guide. Her eyes are gray, hypnotic, like smoke rings spinning inward, one inside another. I feel that she is part of me and I of her. I'm in another world, not just a dream or imaginary world, but another world with a quality all its own.

The dog turns and trots toward the woods. I follow. An archway of trees appears. It dwarfs a tiny doorway, about a foot in diameter—circular, suspended in the air. I bend down on my knees to look at it, touch it. How does it open? I stand up and look into the woods beyond the door. The dog barks. She is warning me that

I mustn't jump over the door or walk around it. I am supposed to go through this foot-wide, foot-high door.

I turn and see my father and Mick Laur coming, following my path. My father gently holds a swaddled baby out to Mick, who takes it lovingly, cuddles it, coos at it. Walking to me, Mick looks up from the baby, tears in his blue eyes. Coming close, he hands the infant to me. I start tearing up as I take the baby. Emotion moves through me—anxiety, nervousness. I feel as if I'm holding stolen property, or failure, or danger.

The dog barks again. I turn toward it, facing the doorway again. I kneel with the baby, and the portal opens. On the other side I see two open hands, brown with black, wiry hair on the wrists and forearms. I cannot see beyond the elbows. On the left hand the ring finger is a stump that ends at the first knuckle. I sense that the finger and arms belong to a real person, that I will meet this man.

I hand the baby to the hands, feeling that I know how to do this from long ago, when I used to live in this place near the archway. Once the baby is through and I pull my hands back, the portal closes. My fear vanishes. I turn back to Mick and my father, but they are gone. The dog barks once more and disappears into mist past the archway.

I feel myself transforming. At first I don't know what I am becoming, and then I see my arms turn into white wings, my feet thin to talons, my upper torso condense, and my stomach bulge out. I become a huge white bird. A melodic voice tells me that I am being reborn and that it will happen not quickly but slowly enough for me to notice the deeper activities of the spirit world. Unafraid, I fly off, up into the trees, and over a lake. Then I'm over the Mediterranean Sea and then back in my seat on the Italian ferry, on my way to Istanbul.

S played out on one of the reclined seats in the aft section, I awakened, the air salty and full of blue sky and the screech of a seagull. My backpack lay beside me and I felt for it, a traveler's instinct. Through dimmed eyes I looked over at a man and a woman in their twenties lying on the deck, backpacks as their pillows, both deep in sleep. I felt extremely groggy, resolving to get up later and write the dream down, sensing very clearly that I would meet the man with the mutilated finger one day in the future.

CHAPTER 3

The
Threshold

The third task of the mystic lies in becoming one with the senses. This is called sensory immersion, or fully occupying one's senses. It comes in the joy of physical activity. It is not hedonism. Rather, it is sensory action that breaks down ego defenses. No one can move into true spiritual clarity who has not learned the fullness of his or her sensual body, for that body is the threshold to the soul.

Some of you choose sexuality as one of your sensual graces, perfecting its pleasure. Others choose the love of food, or athletics and sport, or the care of a garden. Others surround themselves with the great music or the great paintings of the world, immersed in the sensual pleasure of the arts. In the Hindu sacred dance, Bharatha Natyam, the sensuality of the dance consecrates the body. The dancer dissolves her identity into the music; by immersing herself in her sensory body, she becomes a physical medium for spirit. She is fulfilling the third task of enlightenment.

We sometimes hear well-meaning teachers say, "The senses are to be avoided. The senses are just illusion makers; we must crush their appetites!" The Buddha said all this, yes, but only after he completely knew the sensual world.

—The Magician

The boat docked on Istanbul's Asian side, where the stench of fish leavings, sea brine, gasoline, and old city stone greeted hundreds of us as we disembarked. My skin itched, filmed with salt after fifteen hours on the Mediterranean between Parnassus, Greece, and Istanbul. Hair matted and face scratchy with a two-day beard, I wore a dirty blue sports jacket, a white T-shirt, faded blue jeans, and off-white sneakers. The bustle of Turks and tourists carried me off the boat toward a bench near the dock's edge.

As I dumped my pack next to me, my watch read 5:28 P.M. The date: July 7, 1988. Joseph was due to meet me at six o'clock. It had been a month since we had parted in Paris. We were going to travel together from Istanbul to Ankara. I gazed up at two parallel lines of clouds directly above me, almost touching, like the contrails of two jets flying close to each other. The light from the yellow, descending sun reflected off the blue shell of the sky. It delicately hurt my eyes. A slight wind touched my hair, my cheek. Seagulls flew around the dock, screeching, circling, chaotic against the huge stillness of a gigantic mosque to my right.

"Taxi? Taxi, sir? Taxi?"

From a car window, a Turkish face challenged me to use some of the words I'd been studying in this last month of travel toward Asia Minor.

"Hayır, efendim. Teşekkür ederim." No sir, but thank you.

Like most of the Turkish men I'd seen on the ferry, this man had jet black hair, a thick black mustache, dark brown eyes, and olive skin. All around me were dockworkers, family men with kids, street merchants hawking fresh cucumbers with salt. Men walked down the street arm in arm, even hand in hand. I had noted this custom of affection on the ferry. Turkish men in general, it seemed to me, could change their faces from fierceness to a broad grin and back to fierceness effortlessly.

Many of the women on the street wore head scarves, but I could already tell Turkish women from Arab women. The Arab women wore headdresses that covered their hair and faces completely, and only gray or black clothes. Their faces—within cloth frames, their eyes never meeting mine—were hidden almost completely. If a tiny piece of skin showed, it was like a dot on a far wall.

Another yellow-checkered taxi stopped short in front of me, a small boxlike car from Fiat called a Murat, with a sign on the top that read TAKSI. The driver stepped out and came toward me with a smile.

"*Gehen Sie oder kommen Sie?*" the driver asked in German.

"*Nein, ich warte nur. Danke schön,*" I answered. I wasn't surprised to hear him speak German. I had learned in Germany that many Turks lived there and moved back and forth between the two countries.

My watch now showed 5:32 P.M.

Even though Joseph wasn't due, I thought, "He's not coming," and butterflies fluttered through my gut. Why wouldn't he come? Of course he'll come. My thoughts were interrupted as a shadow passed over me and to my right, moving toward the side of the hill. At first I couldn't find the source; then I saw a huge bird like an eagle, white, with a six-foot wingspan, flying toward the top of an old brick smokestack. It was like the bird I had become in my dream! It alighted atop the smokestack and dipped into a large nest, butt out to the world. I watched it feed a tiny chick, then turn around and fly off again. It was not an eagle, nor a heron. What, then? I tracked it with my eyes as it flapped its way up the hillside over the tile-roofed houses, then up along the Bosphorus coastline. I felt drawn to it and watched until it flew out of my vision.

A misty dusk settled over the minarets, houses, and office buildings of Istanbul's city center. Small cars bustled across the Bosphorus bridge. Except for a few nondescript modern skyscrapers, the whole city of Istanbul seemed to consist of white-gray apartment buildings, red tile roofs, and mosques with minarets pointing up like arrows. The red roof tiles, like those in Italian cities, were laid out like rows of red hands cupped over one another. There were TV antennae on nearly every building and people and cars on every street.

Startled by voices in American English, I turned to see a family— mom, dad, three kids—drop down on the bench next to mine.

"Hi," I greeted them simply. A wave of inner emotion, a homesick loneliness, took me almost to tears in a split second. I'd been gone from American childhood for ages.

Startled to be in sudden community with an American, they said "Hi" back almost in unison.

"Doing Europe?" asked the dad, a tall blond man in his forties.

"I was, but I guess we're in Asia now," I quipped. Feeling sponta-
neously connected with them, I smiled at the children. "Here, you want to
see something?" I unzipped my magic bag and pulled out a paneled box,
saying, "I'm a street magician. I'm going to show you a box trick, just for
fun, but before I do, just say any words that come into your mind, okay?
Just start chattering." The youngest child, a seven- or eight-year-old girl,
followed my instructions, saying forty-six words, just stringing them together. To her family's surprise and delight, I repeated them back to her
exactly.

"All right, now, shake this box." She did.

"Now look inside."

She opened it and looked in.

"Nothing, right?" Her older brother peered in over her shoulder.

"Nothing," he agreed.

I took the box back as I removed my watch from my left wrist. Following my gestured instructions, the girl dropped it in the box and shut
the lid.

"Let's shake it all about." I smiled, shaking and shaking. "Okay, now
open it."

No watch! Instead, a doll. Under my sleeve—the watch, right back
where it belonged.

The family giggled and clapped. Some passersby stopped.

The little girl hugged the doll and asked if she could keep it. Usually I
save my props, but I let her. Meeting other Americans here, in my first moments in a new world, seemed like a blessing. So often, doing magic gave
me a sense of participating intimately in other people's lives, as if it
brought them and myself a piece of love. It felt that way now.

As her mother prompted the little girl to thank me, a car pulled up—
a big old American Chevy Caprice. A tall Turkish driver stepped out carefully, unfolding himself like a basketball player. "It's Mehmet!" the girl
cried, and the family embraced him one by one. I stepped aside from the
scene. "You want a lift somewhere?" the father offered, seeing me again.
No, I told them, I was waiting for someone. We shook hands, the car
started up, and soon they headed off into traffic.

Returning to the bench, I got that airport or dockside feeling of being one with every traveler around me, yet utterly alone. For a fleeting moment I wondered what I would do if somehow I had missed Joseph. Then another ferry docked to my left, bumping the mooring and quaking the whole dock. I watched the crowd descend the ramp, each person stepping into a new moment, legs slightly wobbly from the crossing.

Grinning, Joseph walked toward me from the street, a dwarf in the crowd. "It's good to see you, my friend! Welcome to Anatolia!" In his left hand he carried a small suitcase.

I stood up, cried "Hello!" and kissed him on both cheeks, inhaling his cologne. "Istanbul's so incredible!" I exclaimed. In a second, any loneliness in me reversed to love.

"Istanbul is the world's most magical city. Anything can happen here. Come, my friend" —he beckoned—"let us find a taxi and get out of this rush. Here's some water and a snack for you." From the side of his case he pulled a bottle of Perrier and three Turkish delights, rectangular brown candies covered with finely grated coconut, each wrapped in crisp paper. "Eat them all!" he beamed. "I've had some already. I saved the rest for you." I popped all three into my mouth, admiring how casually elegant he always looked, his loafers polished, his slacks pleated, his silk shirt carrying the slight breeze, brightening his dark skin with its blues and greens.

"*Taksi!*" he called to a yellow Murat, reaching for the little magic bag I had detached from my large pack. I hefted the heavier backpack as the cab driver jumped out and greeted us with the informal Turkish hello: "*Merhaba!*"

"Let's put our bags in the boot." Joseph pointed to the trunk. Understanding Joseph's gesture, the driver, a jovial, somewhat rotund man in his fifties, with white hair, a white mustache, and a cigarette hanging from his lips, opened the trunk with his key.

Once we stowed both bags and got into the little cab, the driver, talking steadily in Turkish with Joseph, pulled out in front of traffic; there he received a host of aggressive honks, to which he replied, as if wronged, with his own chorus of honks and curses.

He and Joseph managed instructions and negotiations through all that; then Joseph sat back and turned toward me. "Now tell me how tired you are, my friend. I want to take you to the Blue Mosque, then right away to visit some special friends." When, in Paris last month, we had set this particular meeting date and time, we had done so to take advantage of a whirling dervish rehearsal Joseph wanted me to attend. He told me about a group of dervishes, one of only a few world-recognized original dervish sects, who whirled on hardwood floors for hours and went into mystical trances. They performed their rituals for the public in their home, Konya, a holy city in south central Turkey, in the late fall; but they liked to rehearse in Istanbul in the summer. Joseph and I had agreed that we would take one of the latest buses possible out of Istanbul tonight in order to make it to the dervish rehearsal first.

"Tonight is a rehearsal and then a party," Joseph reminded me, though I needed no reminding.

"They won't mind me coming?" This was just politeness. In Paris, Joseph had said, "There is a unique doorway to divine reality for every unique searcher. Perhaps your doorway is among the Sufis and dervishes. Let us see."

Now he smiled patiently. "They won't mind, Ben."

"Then I have plenty of energy!" I smiled back.

"Enough energy to be remade, my friend?" he quipped.

"Of course!" I quipped back. "I'm always ready for that!"

As we settled into the drive, we moved away from the crowded dock area and into a brief climb. Mosques, houses, and buildings surrounded us, and vegetation too, hillsides of green eucalyptus trees and even a tiny garden behind a house here or there. There was little grass anywhere in this city.

At his request, I gave Joseph a report on Berlin, Zurich, Saint-Moritz, Venice, Athens, and all the other places I'd been since Paris.

"Any places that 'blew you away'?" Joseph asked. In Paris, he had relished the Americanisms of my generation. Once I'd sighed, "Wow, I'm blown away." Joseph loved this. Quick-witted as always, he had replied, "Such enthusiasm and such self-destruction in three words!"

"Florence and Venice blew me away," I confessed, giving him the highlights and finding myself wanting to please him. Our car lurched, jolting the two of us, as the driver cranked it down a gear and we descended a steep hill, passing a horse cart filled with plastic containers, then, a block later, several small groups of fashionable people in professional dress crossing a street.

As we crossed the Bosphorus bridge, moving to Istanbul's European side, Joseph asked, "Now, what have you learned about the Sufis? I am dying to test your knowledge."

He had given me his book on the Sufis, as well as a book of poems by the thirteenth-century Sufi poet Jalāl ad-Dīn ar-Rūmī, both of which I had devoured over the month of travel. In Zurich, I had found other books on Sufism written in German. As so often in my life, a subject of spiritual depth had formed a web around me. It had become me and I it. In the past I had been able to become so immersed in spiritual reading in a particular subject that I would feel as if my heartbeat changed to fit the hidden rhythms of the subject, whether Gnostic Christianity, Kabalistic Judaism, Hinduism, Zen, the writings of Hermann Hesse, or, now, Sufism.

"I've experimented with so many traditions," I said aloud, "and felt passionate about each, and now I wonder if Sufism is my doorway to fully awakened consciousness. I was studying it this last month, thinking: Here, this is *the one*. But then again, I've thought that before."

"What a millennial scavenger you are." Joseph smiled, his eyes twinkling under his thick black eyelashes. When he concentrated, his brow wrinkled, pushing out a huge vein up the center of his forehead. "My friend, mysticism is a universal substance. Each culture gives this substance a unique form. You have experienced many cultural forms of mystical truth but I think not yet the substance itself. Book learning goes only as far as it goes. It takes you to the ocean, but it does not teach you how to swim. Swimming you must learn by *doing*."

He clapped his hands. "Now, having said that, let us hear what you have learned about Sufis. Teach me the ten stations of the Sufi, with both the English and the Arabic words."

I nodded. "The ten Sufi stations, the *tariq*, or path."

First one experiences a call and accepts the mystic's journey, I explained.

Then one meets a *shaikh*, a spiritual master, either in person, or in study, as I had met Joseph.

In *tauba*, repentance, one awakens, sensually and emotionally, wiping clean the haziness of one's past life, entering the journey cleansed.

Tawakkul, surrender to God, occurs next, with the profound realization that there can be no true poverty any longer.

Sabr, endurance, tests one's spiritual will, often through a period of poverty and pain.

Then comes *rida*, a sense of joy even in deep affliction, for one comes to know one's destiny and the soul markings with which one entered the world—soul markings often lost to one because of traumas in childhood and the forgetfulness that comes from busy adult life. When one accomplishes *rida*, when one truly finds spiritual joy, there is no turning back ever again, for the path to real joy becomes destiny, an eternal friend.

Next occurs another descent into darkness, a dark night of the soul, which the Sufis call *gabd*. It reminds one that the ego has been put aside but the full God self, the beloved, has not yet been discovered.

Revelation, or *mahabba*, follows. *Mahabba* means love. *Ma'rifa* means spiritual knowledge. Both, in this station, are the same. When knowledge becomes love, as when a master dies, the soul becomes free.

Full ego annihilation and God self follow. This *fana* is the same as Nirvana or Samadhi. This is the vision of God, of Haqq, the One, accomplished through rigorous discipline.

Then, finally, Baqa, or Beka, the full claiming of divine identity, occurs. The Unity in the Self becomes permanent, as it does in the Jivanmukta of the Vedantic tradition, the "return to the Original" in Zen, or the Shema Union of the Kabalist.

"And which station approximates your place in your spiritual journey?" Joseph asked. "In other words, my bright young friend: What does all this have to do with *you*?"

"I don't know," I answered honestly. "I have been called, I know that. I have met many *shaikhs*, in person, like you, and in books, poems, and prayers. For five years I've repented, in therapy and in personal growth. I've experienced periods of poverty and pain. Beyond the first two the stations seem momentarily familiar but not solid. What stage," I asked, "do *you* think I'm in?"

He closed his eyes, pausing a moment amid the bouncing rhythm of the car. Sunlight caught the driver's mirror and flashed a square of light on the car's ceiling. The *taksi* smelled of cigarette smoke. Opening his eyes, Joseph said, "I have not formed an opinion, my friend. You are both very old and very young. Your mind is very bright and can be quite advanced, yet you are childlike in both your sorrows and your exuberances. I am not sure yet just how to take pulse of your soul. I do know that there will come a moment when intellectual mastery and memory tricks will not be enough for you. I feel certain many things will come clear to you quite soon.

"*Arkadaşim*," Joseph said in Turkish, touching the driver's shoulder. "*Geldi*." By way of instruction, he pointed the driver toward a busy corner ahead and on the right. The driver nodded and pulled abruptly across traffic, angering drivers behind him. Only an hour into Istanbul, I saw that Turkish drivers competed with Italians for being the world's most aggressive! Joseph told me we were not expected at his friends' place until eight o'clock, so we had some time to get dinner.

We had arrived in the Topkapi district of the city, which includes the famous Blue Mosque, the fourth-century Aya Sofya, and the Ottoman Topkapi Palace. The taxi stopped against the curb, and I dug for my wallet as we stepped out.

"You cannot pay," Joseph admonished, stopping my hand. "In Turkey, the host takes care of things."

Thanking Joseph, I put my money away, meanwhile noticing that I felt a little dizzy. "That's the Pudding Shop," I said, pointing at a restaurant. "It's in my Frommer's guide to Istanbul." The driver opened the trunk and we retrieved my luggage. Joseph paid him and thanked him, then I thanked him as well and he thanked me. It almost felt like a Japanese scene to me, our heads moving up and down and hands raised in little waves. "*Çok sağol*," I said, using the casual form of "Thank you."

"Come," Joseph took my arm, "let's get some döner kebab at a quieter spot." I Velcroed the small pack onto the backpack and then we set off.

Was it the talk about mysticism that had made me a little dizzy? How long had it been since I'd eaten any real food? Had I had only candy all day? I hadn't slept much on the boat.

But there was something else too, some other internal experience.

Something made my senses feel so fragile suddenly, the sounds of cars, voices, footsteps floating through me, my skin like a membrane pushed and prodded by the energies of the people all around me. I felt each energy, each footstep, the Turkish couple passing us, caressing my air with theirs, the Japanese tourists coming toward us.

"Yes," I said with relief, "let's go somewhere quiet. I feel tired . . . weird." I sweated, not just from humid Istanbul nor from the backpack, but from the nervous push-pull of myself in the people we passed as we walked. This had come on suddenly, as if I were getting sick. But I didn't feel sick exactly. What about the Turkish delights—something in them? No. I had tried a lot of drugs and could tell when they were in my system. Was I having another shamanic experience of some kind?

"I have to stop for a second, Joseph," I murmured, leaning my pack and myself against a building wall, breathing hard. "I feel like my internal self is all exposed, like my bare tissues are on the outside of my body." We had come to a shop called Salat's Kilim and Halı, a carpet store. Rugs of many colors lay all around in the vestibule and on the sidewalk. I was struck by the brown-and-red one in front of me. Bending on one knee, I ran my right palm across its soft pile. With that small movement, I had a flash of an image: two village girls and a village woman at a loom. I saw them through a translucent vertical membrane of some kind. It was as if they and I were right next to each other, but not in the same world.

"You're tired," Joseph sympathized. "There's hope for me—even the young can tire."

"Joseph, my God, it happened again."

"What happened?"

"The flying!" I described the brief scene—the women at the loom— and the vertical membrane.

"How interesting, my friend." Joseph took my arm. "Kulu shamans in Africa call the membrane between the dimensions of consciousness a 'caul,' like the tissue that surrounds the fetus in the womb. Most shamanic traditions are very clear in their knowledge that we are only thinly separated from each other, from other eras, even other spirits. Those people, for instance, who have encountered the Magician or had other such visions of other Travelers throughout the world can be said to have, if just for a moment, broken through the caul into one of the other realities. It seems you are seeing slightly past the caul into the multidimensionality. Let it happen, my friend. It is a great and rare gift you receive."

"It's taking me by surprise all the time. Why is it suddenly happening now?"

He pointed up the street. "The kebab place is just there and to the right. A good kebab place, with a view of the mosque. Can you make it?"

In answer I hoisted my pack again. He started moving, and I followed. For a small man, he moved like the wind. What the hell was happening to me? Was Joseph doing something shamanic to me? Was this disorientation the realignment of cells shamans talk about—my legs, back, everything so wobbly, my ears ringing and eyes watering? I thought about the caul. I knew from graduate school studies the primitive notion that we can see the spirits of the dead all around us if we just open our eyes to "universal vision." In Malaysia, for instance, natives believe that the distance between the spirits of the living and the dead is not one of miles or even of feet, only of perception. Were the girls and women dead? Was I seeing spirits of the dead? What a strange state to be in on this Istanbul street.

Joseph took us into a little döner fast-food restaurant where we found a small square table. I put my things down beside it.

"Döner kebab," Joseph said wryly, "is the Turkish equivalent of McDonald's." As we moved toward a gray counter to order food, I asked him about my wobbling, lolling body and whether we shouldn't be worried. "You're having many spiritual experiences just now," he replied. "I know you'll be all right. Let yourself observe reality. You will come to no harm, and I will be with you. Try not to think too much!" Easy for him to say!

The restaurant, half full of people, took up about twenty feet by thirty feet, its white walls dirty and the air thick with the aroma of cooked meat. A slab of lamb, two feet high and six inches in diameter, twirled on a vertical skewer behind the counter. One of the men deftly sliced two-inch portions of lamb off it and lay them on plates. I found his movements fascinating, as if he were performing a ritual. Another man put the lamb slices onto long French bread, shoving in a white cucumber-and-yogurt sauce, wrapping the kebab sandwich in opaque wax paper and handing it to a third man, who took our money and handed out glasses for soda. All three men wore white T-shirts, jeans, and white aprons covered with greasy handprints.

The cooking area included a street window for outdoor service. Hungry people stood, walked, squatted outside as they ate their kebab sandwiches. There was no air-conditioning in the place, but two fans kept all of us slightly cooled. Shaking myself, I became aware of my full bladder, looking toward the back for a toilet. The need to defecate had come on suddenly too.

For a month I'd been memorizing Turkish phrases. To the third of the men, the guy counting the money, I called out, "*Pardon efendim, tuvalet nerede?*" He pointed to the back.

With the smell of cooked lamb in my nostrils, I felt a little nauseous now. This too came on suddenly, as if my whole nervous system had speeded up beyond its normal rhythm. Even my heart was beating very fast.

Joseph nodded that he understood my destination, and I headed to the back of the restaurant. At the bathroom door, hearing nothing beyond, I pushed the spring and found myself in a tiny lavatory. There, I nearly vomited from the smell of piss and feces. The toilets in Turkey are "Asian style," also called "elephant toilets." You squat over a hole in the ground with a white porcelain rim, each of your feet on one of the two oversized shoe imprints—elephant's feet—that form the sides of the hole. There's no flushing these toilets.

I pulled my pants down and squatted, muscles tightening in places along thighs and calves I rarely worked. Diarrhea exploded out of me. It had been months since I'd had trouble with my bowels in a new country. Suddenly, in less than an hour, I was dissolving from within.

A metal tube, dribbling water, jutted from the wall, but I saw no toilet paper. A visceral fear shot through me. As if my whole being were composed of brittle glass, the potential shame of a soiled and unwiped ass felt like a terror, a self-destruction. I looked everywhere, mentally searched my pockets, and came up with only one sad option: my handkerchief, an heirloom keepsake of my grandfather.

As I maneuvered to pull it out of my back pants pocket, clarity came: the water tube! The water streaming from it was meant to be used on my ass! Relieved, as if rescued, I cupped the water in my right hand, rinsed and wiped myself over and over, then rinsed my hands and fingers, perhaps ten times, and finally raised my pants. The whole vast effort of using the toilet brought me to tears, a mundane moment in life charged with terror and salvation. Buckling my belt, I checked myself, feeling cool residual wetness at the apex of my legs. What sensations my body suddenly experienced! My God, I thought, even shaking myself sent a shiver of electricity everywhere through me.

"Here you are, my friend." Joseph pointed to my sandwich. "Take a taste of one of Istanbul's treasures."

"Joseph," I asked, "was there something in the candy?"

"What do you mean?"

"Like a mescalate, or a methamphetamine?"

Joseph laughed. "Don't be silly, my friend. Why do you ask that?"

"Nothing. Let's eat." If it wasn't drugs, what then?

Famished after my ordeal, I bit into salty lamb, tangy sauce, fresh, crisp bread. All the tastes swept through my mouth, burning. "Whoa," I exhaled. "What an evening I'm having. This food, it's . . . I don't know . . . it's—"

"Yes." Joseph smiled benignly. "Evenings in Istanbul are magical. And there is nothing like Turkish food." He never spoke with his mouth full. He bit, chewed, swallowed, then spoke; bit, chewed, swallowed, then spoke. Watching him, fascinated, I stopped eating. I must have been staring at him, but he said nothing.

"Thanks for the sandwich," I murmured, closing my eyes and savoring the tastes.

He smiled. "*Recaydim.* It's my pleasure." My eyes still closed, I felt, almost *heard,* his smile. Then I listened to the men behind the counter speaking Turkish, a melodic language, very intense, very fast, and darkly symphonic. I felt the touch of the bread in my palm and the warmth of the leaking sauce on the pores of my fingers.

"Istanbul is a mystical city," I murmured aloud. Taking another bite, I said to Joseph, "It must feel wonderful to *know* yourself as the mystic you really are. I think I feel this, kind of." What was I saying? I sounded like an idiot.

Joseph put his sandwich down. "A mystic asks, 'Have I come to the spiritual doorway and walked through into the arms of God?' Experience teaches the answer. Shall I teach you about the invisible doorway, my friend?"

"Please!" In Paris, we had developed a ritual: he always asked me permission to teach me a lesson, and I always said yes. It was a graceful humility he practiced—he knew himself to be the teacher, yet asked *my* permission. Now I was glad he wanted to teach and talk—it gave me something to concentrate on.

"You see, we all come to the divine doorway at some time in our lives: some of us when we are very young, some of us in the middle of raising children, some of us not until we are very old. Most of us arrive there more than once in our lives. The Magician teaches us to know we have arrived at the doorway because we meet there a teacher who seems to guard it. He or she has knowledge of the magical life and can help us alter our consciousness.

"And the first *conscious* time we come to the doorway, it is this teacher's job to point out that the doorway is a mirror. It is the searcher's job, for a time, to know himself better in the mirror. This is a good thing. But still, it is not the walk through the doorway, is it?

"Many searchers don't get to know themselves fully before they strive, mainly through intellect, to master the techniques of magic. Without going through the doorway themselves, they try to become the teacher, the magic doer." As he paused to take another bite of the sandwich, I got his meaning: he had described me twice. I had spent years looking in the mirror—through therapy, writing about myself, self-searching. Also, I had a big enough intellect and certainly a big enough ego to almost convince myself I was a magician of spirit. In his polite way, Joseph was admonishing me.

"Some others at the doorway look at the teacher and argue with him over the existence of magic itself. 'Is there a God?' they ask. 'What is spirit?' they ask. 'How shall we *know* for sure?' they ask. They are unable to trust what is so very real within and around them.

"Many others come to realize that they know themselves enough, they understand the magical life enough, they need no longer argue its existence—and yet they feel immobilized. They stand at the threshold, learning the rigors required by the other world beyond the door, rigors of prayer and ablution recorded in sacred books. For years these searching people will learn and practice and yet still feel unready to walk beyond the threshold. They'll say in their hearts, 'I can't go through, I have not had a Buddha moment.' The intellect's lack of vision will stun them, the emotions' lack of passion will caution them. Of course, what they truly lack is the Great Intuition at the center of mystical life."

"The Great Intuition?"

"The insight above all insights—that they are soul, energy itself, and that this energy cannot know itself without magic. Without the magical doorway, without the sensation of other worlds, without the vision beyond illusion, without the multidimensional experience, soul is blind. You know this as a magician, do you not? Good magic lights up people's perceptions of the *whole* universe, of the movement of life itself."

"Absolutely."

"Fortunately, these people—of which you are one—do learn after years of self-discovery that they *can* have the insight, the enlightenment, the utter acceptance of self as divine energy. My friend, in those moments, all things change. They understand how to be passionately attached to life's many diverse movements and yet to be utterly still and detached— Unity in Diversity, Oneness in Separateness. They understand this in distinct moments, and it takes them the rest of their lives to really understand. The distinct moments of understanding, we call 'divine moments.'"

Swallowing the rest of my lamb, I said, "Joseph, what you're saying sounds so awesome!" To myself I sounded stoned, overemphasizing superlatives. And I sensed that I understood Joseph's meaning—yet not utterly.

"I enjoy how you say 'great' and 'incredible' and 'awesome' with such generosity. I enjoy the joy in your soul, Ben. Your innate capacity for joy must certainly be one of the markings left on your soul before you were born. Shall we go?" He pushed away from the table, his chair scraping loudly, like rock on rock.

"Markings left on my soul?" I pushed up too, reaching for my bags.

"Excuse me," Joseph said politely, heading back to the toilet without explaining his meaning. Watching his dwarflike body walk away from me, I reflected on the fact that Joseph had just explained the kind of mystical experience I was searching for. The Magician, whom he had quoted so often in the last month, was very wise indeed—whoever or whatever he was.

"Look there at the minarets, my friend." He pointed at the Blue Mosque several blocks ahead of us. "Are they not beautiful?" People jostled us, traffic swirled and honked. The buildings, many of them a dirty gray, crowded in on the narrow street. But above it all the minarets of the mosque—of which we could see four—touched the purple sky.

"They're regal," I offered. Then I noticed that we were passing Salim's carpet store, the place where I had "seen" the village women after touching the carpet. The same Turkish carpets spilled out the doorway. Others hung from the roof's edges. Still others hung bent over wooden racks. I stopped, caught up in all the motion of this multicolored, slow-moving waterfall of hemp and wool spilling, falling, curling over invisible rock.

Joseph stopped with me as I paused to touch the red-and-brown carpet that had triggered the vision earlier. Nothing happened now. A Turkish salesman came out, handsome, dark skinned, and mustached, medium height, dressed in a multicolored silk shirt open to a hirsute chest.

"Welcome, friends, come in and look," he offered, opening his hands to us.

"Let's go in," I pleaded with Joseph. "I've never been in a Turkish carpet shop!"

Joseph honored my request by stepping aside, a gesture the salesman copied, so that I could enter. "*Buyurun*," the salesman said. "You go first, please."

Once we got inside the tiny vestibule, an older man helped me remove my pack.

Farther inside, the store opened to a huge interior space, carpets everywhere—rolled up, hanging, lying in stacks. In the loft above, some Italian tourists negotiated a purchase. A boy of about twelve, dressed like the men in his own colorful silk shirt, pleated pants, and polished shoes, received a verbal instruction from the older man and ran off as we sat down.

"What you want to see, sir?" the salesman asked in clear, accented English.

The colors vibrated around me, shimmered with energy, drawing my energy to them. I wondered how it could be that no one noticed my grin.

"Actually, I don't know if I have the money to buy anything," I told him.

"You'll do some magic on Istanbul's streets, and the money will pour in," Joseph encouraged.

"What's that one?" I asked the carpet seller, pointing to a colorful carpet near us. "Can I just learn?"

"No need to buy," the salesman assured me. "That one you have noticed ... *mihrab* ... from Yahyali region. Prayer carpet, from region in central Turkey. Near Ankara."

He reached as he talked, rolling the carpet open. It was four feet in width and seven feet in length, its base color a rich dark brown. The brown was bordered first by red and green designs. Inside the border were many golden and maroon designs. Within them was smaller, final interior design: a straight line at one end, two straight lines going halfway down the carpet from the initial straightback, then those lines converging into a flowerlike chandelier that came to a point.

I touched it, ran my flat hand over it. "It's so beautiful."

As I spoke, my head again filled with a flash of vision. I was in a village where three girls, in colorful village clothes, helped two older women make this carpet on a huge wooden loom at the back of a large building. I saw a canteen made of metal hanging like a decoration on the wall behind the loom. I saw dyes and water and wads of wool next to a bucket. One older woman pointed to some kind of tool, like a tiny wooden boat, that she slid up and down the wool on the loom. She wanted one of the girls, about ten, to hand her another one.

"Handmade, of course," the salesman explained, "by the girls and women of the village."

As he spoke, the vision ended and the translucent membrane disappeared, leaving me to stare again at the *mihrab* here in the store. For a second, I could see the energy of the female hands shining on the wool. I actually saw it shimmering!

"My God, Joseph," I said, "the strangest thing just happened again."

"You must tell me later," he said.

The salesman continued his explanation: "It is prayer carpet because Muslim sit here"—he pointed to the back line—"hands and head bow here"—he pointed to the front, toward the tip of the chandelier design.

The boy came in with a tray of little glasses. "*Çay geldi!*"

"Ah, tea." Joseph thanked him: "*Teşekkür ederim.*" I too said, "*Teşekkür ederim,*" the polite "Thank you."

"It is nothing, sirs," the boy replied in English. I knew from my Turkish language guide that the Turkish words for "You're welcome" and "gentlemen"—Bir *şey değil,* and *bey efendi*—often got directly translated by Turks to "it's nothing" and "sirs." The boy hovered with the tray as Joseph, the eldest man here, served himself first. He took three sugar cubes on a tiny spoon and dropped them into his little tea glass. The salesman said, "*Buyurun,*" gesturing for me to take sugar next. I took two cubes. Then the salesman took four. The boy, finished with his job, moved to a pile of rugs toward our left and sat down to watch. Impatient, I wanted to tell Joseph about the vision, but he had turned to the salesman and was speaking in Turkish about the carpet.

As soon as I sipped the tea, its flavor exploded in my mouth. I rolled a grain of sugar on my tongue and against my teeth until it dissolved, savoring every morsel of it. Were my cells being realigned? I was in some kind of altered state of consciousness.

The salesman took another sip, then found another carpet he wanted to show me, then another, piling each one onto the Yahyali. At about the seventh, he slapped the pile. "There! For you. From Kars region." It was another *mihrab* design, with contrasting light greens, dark reds, and light blue. It made me think of the bluish rainbow lining of a seashell.

"I want to buy them all," I said grandly. "But I can't."

"One day you come back, sir. You remember me. My card." He walked to a small table to get one.

"Which one did you like best?" I asked Joseph.

"The Yahyali."

"I like the Kars."

He said something to the salesman in Turkish. They laughed. Joseph translated for me. "It is an old Turkish saying: 'Friends should never argue about colors or taste.'" He raised his glass as if in a toast to this wisdom, and I joined him. He downed the last of the sweet tea in our tiny, vaselike tea glasses, leaving only the sediment at the bottom. A young German couple came in.

"Shall we continue our journey?" Joseph asked, his thick gray eyebrows rising like upside-down smiles.

I pushed up and started to don my pack, thanking the salesman, who now handed me his card and assisted me. His name, Sheli, seemed more Iranian than Turkish, I thought. "I'll come back, Sheli Bey," I promised. I gave him my name and offered my hand; we shook, his grip firm.

"I save Yahyali for you," he promised.

I had the feeling he would do just that.

As dusk deepened, we headed north toward the Blue Mosque, which sat in the center of a huge and beautifully tended garden. Walking the two blocks, I felt as if we were gliding. The tea had given me a turbo boost of energy, and I walked as fast as Joseph, eagerly telling him about the village women I'd seen. He agreed that I'd definitely been "flying." Why, and why now, this evening, he didn't know. "A preview, perhaps, of much to come," he pondered aloud.

At the mosque we took our shoes off, leaving them, my pack, and his bag at the entranceway among perhaps a hundred other pairs of shoes and packs. Because cameras were not allowed inside the mosque, thousands of dollars of equipment littered the vestibule, tended only by a young man of about eighteen. Leaving all my things there, everything I owned, sent me into a momentary internal frenzy, as if I were leaving my whole life behind to be stolen. Steal it all! I thought silently, melodramatically. I'll start over!

Like Joseph, I took a pair of black, backless slippers from a bin that held hundreds. Once inside the mosque, Joseph did not get on his knees, bow, and gesture as the other Muslims did, so I, too, remained upright. Following his gaze, I looked up in awe at the blue-tiled, domed ceiling many hundreds of feet above me. Everywhere I saw carefully wrought tile in perhaps twenty different shades of blue. The light of dusk shone through the stained glass, red on blue, coloring the dust motes purple.

First in silence, then with whispered explanations, Joseph led me around the mosque. In this, the first mosque I had ever entered, my cultural bias told me to beware this alien place, yet my soul felt right at home.

Peripatetic, Joseph explained that the Blue Mosque, built between 1609 and 1616, was the only one in Turkey with six minarets. "There in the forecourt," he pointed, "is the famous marble ablutions fountain. My father preached here in the early 1950s. He stood . . . there." Joseph pointed to the east side of the mosque, beside a stack of prayer carpets.

"That must have been an incredible honor!" I exclaimed.

"Just so." He became silent again, closing his eyes. Amid the sounds of voices around us, there was an immense quietness in the mosque, a sense of peace that seemed to yearn for us to breath it in. The place was alive with hidden, invisible energies communicating freely with us. Taking a deep breath, Joseph moved to the place where his father had preached. He knelt on the floor. I sat down next to him, crossing my legs in a lotus position. People looked at us, but I did not feel self-conscious. I felt free and easy, as if I were, for moments, no longer a creature of society.

"My father was a brilliant imam, a brilliant preacher," Joseph mused, his eyes moving gently over the vistas of the past. "Through his orator's gift, he taught his congregants how to love. I watched him do it, right here in this place. All divine speakers can do that." Joseph turned to me. "I watched him and learned what it means to respect an elder. When Mwimbo, my African elder, entered my consciousness in his village, I knew how to become an organ in his body because I had learned how to become an organ in my father's body. Because I trusted my father, I trusted all other men. When Mwimbo told me how to fast and for how long, when he showed me what herbs and plants to eat for hallucination, when he used his hypnotic powers to help me discover my visions—I respected him and thus was able to learn from him. All this because I trusted my father. Do you understand, my friend?"

"I don't really trust my father," I admitted. He had been a man preoccupied with his own concerns, a man who had never quite known how to love his son.

Joseph heard me but did not respond. His eyes seemed a little watery now. Why had Joseph brought me here? I wondered. Why, specifically? Something about my father? His? Despite its attraction to the tourist in me, the mosque held some other significance—what?

"Let us stand," Joseph suggested. We did and then moved to our right, past a family of Arab tourists. Some scaffolding, partially covered with plastic sheets, blocked most of our path. As we found a small space by which to walk around it, we saw artisans painstakingly repairing tiny, chipped blue tiles on the walls.

Just as I was about to say something, Joseph suggested we stop and close our eyes. "Let your thoughts clear, Ben."

I did that, leaning with him against the clammy mosque walls. Time passed and people walked by us, murmuring, talking. We took in the huge expanse of the interior mosque, breathing in centuries of energy. I again found the quiet I knew from years of meditating. It happened quickly for me, as it usually did.

In the quiet, a shot of light exploded and a tunnel revealed itself, long and dark. A figure, robed in black, floated toward me. I sensed immediately that it was a hallucination of the angel of death. In the hallucination I stood, utterly naked, to confront the figure. The ceiling of the tunnel opened. Death pointed, and I, like his puppet, began to float upward, toward the moon, then past it on toward the sun, the light of the sun blinding me, the heat enveloping me. Once I moved past the ceiling portal, I began to change from a naked man into something else, a transformation that was complete as I merged into the sun. I became the huge white bird, like the one I'd seen in my dream and seen again landing on its nest near the dock.

"Jesus Christ!" I muttered. Joseph and I both opened our eyes as I spoke.

"What is it?" he asked.

"I was floating through the ceiling, then flying up to the sun." I de-

scribed the tunnel, the figure, the bird in the vision, and my dream on the
boat of the dog and the portal. "Joseph, I'm having some *incredible* experiences!"

"You're very gifted," Joseph said. "Very gifted."

"What's going on?" I pleaded.

"I don't know," he murmured. "Let us be patient. My Sufi friends will
be so glad to meet you." Maybe they would have information or answers, I
thought. Joseph, for his part, seemed satisfied to just collect the bits of my
strange experiences this evening. It was frustrating to me that he seemed
so sanguine, but who was I to reprimand him? I felt as if I were dissolving—it was frightening, but it wasn't; it felt so good, too.

Joseph moved and I followed. We walked out the mosque door and
put our shoes back on. The inside of the mosque had been so cool that Istanbul's humidity broke a new layer of sweat on me.

"Joseph," I said, "I don't know if this will sound weird, but I think being with you is affecting me. It's scary, but I like it. I feel like I'm totally
with myself, not trying to be other than myself. Thank you for this."

He put his arm around my waist. "Young man, my gratitude is equal to
yours. You let me teach you a lifework. By taking my gifts, you give me
back the gift of love."

I squeezed him tight. I embraced women all the time but rarely men.
In Turkey, with all the men arm in arm, holding Joseph in public felt normal. My body knew how to embrace men; ancient in its blood, it felt completely at home in a man's grasp.

Listening to Joseph give the *taksi* driver directions, I sensed that no
matter what Joseph said or withheld, he was doing something to me.
Maybe he was trusting me with some very intense, age-old shamanic experience. It was something I didn't want to startle with either nervousness
or suspiciousness.

The driver properly briefed, the car in gear, Joseph sat back and closed
his eyes. Sitting beside him, closing my own in exhaustion, I savored the
trust I felt for Joseph. I thought it was possible that I trusted him in some
way I had never trusted anyone else before. I thought I trusted him in ways
I could not trust my own parents.

With each turn of the car's tires, the world hummed around me. The breath of sleep drifted through me. I opened my eyes again, closed them, opened them, closed them. Drifting in that altered state of consciousness, I thought I saw Joseph raise his hands, as if swaying them at me, like a magician, and, with a murmur, willing me into unconsciousness.

FOURTH DREAM

Ben Brickman called this fourth dream "The River of Life," noting that this dream depicts the reality our souls exist in during the transitional time just before we are born into our bodies. In discussing this dream with me, he also noted that he had the pervasive feeling of having come into the land of the unborn not from the past but from the future. "I have the sense," he said, "that I was someone or many people in future centuries *before* I came into this life in the late twentieth century." Only when time is understood as nonlinear, he said, can one be born into the past from the future.

I am in the same tunnel as the one I saw in the mosque. In the mosque I have gone through a doorway, and now I am a child in an intermediate world, before my birth into this world of my present body, "Ben Brickman."

I am pure spirit here, pure energy. I hang with other energies from a huge tree next to a river so vast it appears to be a million oceans in one long stream of being.

We hang in clusters from the huge tree, watching the suns and moons and planets push and pull at one another playfully through the sky. Then it is as if the eye of God fills the sky and glares at them firmly, and they all pop back into their ordered places. From out of their order come flying energies, like dragon-birds, that dive at us on the tree, grabbing at us with their beaks. They think we are fruit; and we are. One of them grabs at my energy cluster, pulling off one of the spirit children and tossing her into the river. I yearn to follow.

"It is time to be born," I hear. I look around me at the clusters of energies and accept blessings from relatives and ancestors. "You will do well," they say, "you have a mission in the world. Never lose sight of it, find us throughout the world, for we will be embodied and helpful to you. You will always recognize us by the love you see in our eyes."

"It is time to see beyond the horizon," I hear another ancestor say. I look far off toward the many horizons. Forms come at me. The dragons, as well as new birds, and then tiny insects and many bees, swarm around me now, attaching themselves to me, picking at me, chewing at the cocoon of my spiritual skin.

"These are your soul markings," an ancestor explains. I watch a bumblebee chewing me and see the skin of my soul marked so that I will later, in the new world, remember and recognize myself, and remember this world, where we stay for a time in detached observation, gathering energy, before making the river journey to a world where love is a choice, not breath itself.

I hear music like trees creaking in the wind. I am swatted into the mouth of a large white dragon bird that catches me, carries me, and then drops me into the river of horizons. This is the beginning of my separation. Choice enters me, a burden of freedom, and I struggle on the surface of the river toward somewhere I cannot see. The current of the river scares me at first, and I yearn for the great tree. I look at the marks all over my body from the beaks and stings. I stop struggling on the river. I hear myself say, "You must remember, you must remember where these marks are."

I am tossed in the belly of the river, looking upward toward the fading tree and approaching another tunnel, aware that I must develop in myself some immense internal power by which to get back to the great tree and the paradise of its world. I want to feel that paradise in the new world I am moving toward. The river carries me, and I know it is not done with me.

I opened my eyes, feeling dazed but relaxed. For a while, as the car moved, it felt as if I were still on the river, flowing through unseen air.

CHAPTER 4

The Divine Moment

The fourth task of the mystic is to become one with the emotions. To accomplish this task, you must experience emotional immersion, the breakdown of emotional defenses. Accomplishing this immersion, this surrender, this union with feelings, may require many decades of practice. When you become a full sensual and emotional being, you discover the freedom inherent in embodied life; you transcend the defenses of the body. Often, from unseen quarters, help comes to you.

As with all breakthroughs, the moments of the fourth task are laden with visionary experience. Often, while learning the fourth task, you feel you have accomplished enlightenment, the full second birth; you feel that emotional expression is all a person needs for completeness of life. You have not completed all ten tasks, but so full of energy and electricity is the emotional vulnerability of the fourth task, so overwhelming the divine moment that emotional immersion creates, so completely do you feel the currents of divine energy running through your sense- and feeling-cleansed self, it is no wonder you think you have arrived at the ultimate promised land. This illusion, too, is part of the journey.

— The Magician

*T*he car lurched to a stop at a red light. Our engine purred next to a loud, people-packed city bus whose exhaust smelled like rotted food. As the light changed, our *taksi* regained speed, and we cruised along dusky, red-drenched roads. We were headed toward Taksim Square, the center of a famous part of Istanbul I'd read about that is up on a hill from the Bosphorus. The sunset glided over the rooftops, giving them the sheen of red light on water. I blinked my eyes like a camera shutter, apprehending glowing light-and-patchwork shadows, each one a separate spirit interconnected by consciousness. Emerging from my river dream, I felt intensely alive.

"Joseph," I murmured, "in my dreams, it's all so beautiful." I told him about Nathan, about the portal and the dog; then I told him about the river and the clusters of energy, how sure I was that the river really existed.

"My friend," he grinned, "I think this river dream is a Bardo dream. You have been given an experience of the dimension from which we come."

"You think I was really experiencing what it's like to be an unborn spirit?"

"Perhaps. The energy clusters, the soul markings—shamans and mystics see these in many world cultures. Think of the mark of Cain. Mystics say this is a soul marking the ancestors gave Cain. Think of your family members and those who love you. Mystics say these are the same souls you have always been and will always be clustered with throughout the many lifetimes. Energy is attracted to other energies in the same way people are attracted to other people. We want to spend our time with the people we like, and we do spend time with them. We are energy. Even without bodies, we act the same way, clustering with energies we have affinity for.

"And you saw the great Tree of Life, the great River of Life—the energy field that is the root of creation. You were given a vision of how energy exists when it is just getting ready to find a container, a body. It seems to make a relatively simple journey."

"It was so real."

"You are on an amazing trip, one like the great prophets went on. Your consciousness—the use of your brain—is expanding at a fast rate. Your gifts show through in this . . . let us say . . . this shamanic journey." I could see in his eyes that he harbored no worries about me, just fascination, as well as some other thinking process going on in his mind he wasn't sharing with me.

We came to another stoplight and pulled up beside another taxi. Seven college-age people were packed into it, laughing and talking. Our taxi driver threw his arm over his seat, turned his head toward us, and asked Joseph, "*Yabancı nerele acabı?*" "Where is the foreigner from?"

"*Amerikalı,*" Joseph replied. "He's an American." The driver spoke again in Turkish, then Joseph translated: "Our friend the driver wants to know what you do, Ben, and why you're here in Turkey."

"Tell him I used to be asleep but now I'm waking up."

Joseph must have relayed my message verbatim because the driver looked confused. Out of politeness, as if dismissed, he turned his attention back to the road. The light turned green. We drove around a statue of a man on horseback spotlighted in the center of Taksim Square.

"I'm sorry," I said to Joseph. "Did I offend him?"

"No, no, of course not."

The driver, his black beard shining red in the sunset light, examined me in the rearview mirror. I met his eyes, and this brought not shyness from him but a wide smile. Are you happy, I wanted to ask him? You look so happy.

"Joseph, are you unhappy anymore?" I blurted out. "Are you happy since you . . . awakened? Is that an inane, childish question?"

"Not at all, my friend."

"You must get unhappy still, right?"

Joseph smiled, pulling out a cigarette. "Ah yes, you wonder if I know the great remedy for suffering." He lit the cigarette and puffed out a little cloud of smoke. I stared at the glow of the cigarette as if in za-Zen, open-eyed meditation.

"The Magician once gave me a useful image," Joseph reflected. "Shall I give it to you?"

"Please." I sat back and relaxed, again awaiting the soothing pleasure his words would give me.

"Picture yourself swimming out from the safe shore toward the dangerous currents at the center of a river." He pointed down at the snaking water of the Bosphorus. "There is someone on the other side, someone whose identity is not clear to you through the foam and mist of rushing water but who attracts you enough to make you try to swim across to him. At first your swim toward him is easy, but soon you reach hard currents— their tug is strong, their danger more threatening than you expected. They pull you under, and you become afraid. You call out to the person on the far shore. Help! But he does not move to save you. You paddle and stroke with all your strength, but the water is so rough you can't even see the direction you're headed. You feel the angel of death coming for you.

"In this situation, what do you do, my friend?"

For a moment we were silent. I had to open my eyes.

"I don't know. Swim harder?"

"You cannot. You're exhausted."

"Swim back to the beach?"

"The current grips you."

"Just drown then," I said, surprising myself. "Let myself drown in this river. It will be all right."

"Exactly, my friend! There is no real death in the river of God's love. You will go under for a time and then reemerge into safer water and a whole new life. If you will let go, let yourself be swept under for that terrible time of little death, you will be reborn, you will become enlightened. You will 'suffer' in life like a floating body suffers its bruises against rocks and fallen trees; but also you will experience the cessation of suffering because you have already experienced death."

We stopped at another traffic light. I looked at cars all around me, people coming away from work toward the next phase of their day, intense faces, beautiful faces, troubled faces—men, women, children, busloads, taxi loads, pedestrians, variety, diversity everywhere, all of them together forming a river of energy in which I was only one small body.

"I haven't let go yet," I admitted. "I'm a struggler. I haven't let myself drown in life itself. I've been blocked, I guess. Or I've blocked myself."

"And how beautiful and true the struggle feels. But then you realize that your life has been worry and desperation merely interspersed with periods of salvation. You want more."

"Yes," I admitted.

"When, in the dangerous current, you are afraid, even spiritual quests exist as mere responses and fear. At first, you cannot see that they are another form of the insane desire to control your life. One day you will let go of fear, Ben, I am sure of that. You will die-in-life. You will hear a music that guides, and you will drown in it, find the stillness that is its creative source. Suffering as you know it now—ghost sufferings that haunt you or even the half-shaped sufferings of spiritual desire—will end."

I did not really understand him, not fully, and not yet, for instead of letting myself drown, I said "But when do you know, Joseph? When do you know you've suffered enough to *deserve* the letting go?"

"You will know." He smiled, puffing at the cigarette and unleashing another billow of white-blue smoke.

I opened my window to let clean air in.

Joseph pointed. "There's the hotel." He spoke in Turkish to the driver, who acknowledged his directions, pulling over to the left.

On both sides of our street now were a number of lit-up hotel signs, many with English names such as Sheraton. We had come to the Hotel Kennedy, a tall building with a vertical neon sign advertising its name. The second neon white "N" in KENNEDY remained unlit, its bulbs burned out.

I shook myself, rubbed my eyes, looked around at the hotel vestibule, focusing on a mother and two children standing just outside the glass doors. I was feeling a little more grounded now than I had upon first waking up. The mother handed her daughter a piece of a sandwich, and they walked down the sidewalk. I saw the name of the hotel painted on the glass.

"Hotel Kennedy," I read aloud. "Is that Kennedy as in JFK?"

"Your John Fitzgerald Kennedy was a great hero in Turkey," Joseph nodded. "Though we are of Ottoman descent, we love Camelot."

First Joseph then I stepped out of the cab. He paid the driver, who stepped out with us, opening the trunk.

"*Teşekkür ederim,*" I said to the smiling driver. He saluted graciously, saying, "*Allahaısmaladık.*" I felt both respect and affection for this stranger, as if he were no stranger and reached my hand out to shake his.

"*Güle güle,*" I said.

In Turkey, the person leaving says, "Go with God," and the one staying says, "Go smilingly."

A teenage bellboy emerged from within the glass doors and picked up Joseph's bag and my backpack, welcoming us. As we walked inside, Joseph told me, "Saadet Hanım and Unal Bey are the proprietors of the hotel. They are mystics, very nice people. And both have encountered the Magician. Long before those encounters, they began hosting the dervish rehearsal. Engin Bey, the director of the group, insists their ballroom has the best acoustics in Istanbul. I will introduce you to all of these mystics."

We walked into a simple lobby: reception desk to the left, phones to the right, then a hall, perhaps twenty feet wide, opening into a larger room. On the far side of this room were huge windows that overlooked the lights of Istanbul and the water. In our taxi, we had climbed to a higher altitude than I'd realized. I wanted to move to the window and the panoramic view, but Joseph greeted a middle-aged woman and man, both well dressed. With them was a very large man, maybe four hundred pounds. They all offered Joseph their hands to shake and exchange the customary kiss on both cheeks, not even pausing in their verbal greetings while they kissed. I had noticed already that in Turkey the kiss was often more a caress of cheeks while lips still moved in talk.

"And this is my friend from America, Ben Brickman. I knew his father, as I mentioned to you. Our friend Ben is a magician."

"This is Engin Bey," Joseph said, and I shook hands with the big man. Turks are formal people and put "Bey" after men's first names and "Hanım" after women's first names, the equivalent of "Mr." or "Mrs." Joseph continued, "And Unal Bey and Saadet Hanım." I shook hands with them too.

"A magician," Saadet Hanım repeated. "I'll resist the impulse to ask you for some tricks. Joseph had said you might come by. I feel like we've waited a long time for your visit."

"So we have," Unal Bey agreed.

Turks were so dramatic in their politeness.

"Your view is magical," I smiled, gesturing to the windows. I managed to remain pretty calm, despite feeling pulled toward the rich golds of the lights on the faraway water.

"Yes." Unal Bey pointed. "Let us look at the view." The bellhop, on instructions from Saadet Hanım, had taken my pack for storage somewhere to our left.

Engin Bey bowed slightly. "I must go sing now. I will see all of you soon. It is so good to meet you after all this time, my young friend, good to see you in the flesh." He smiled. The others bowed their heads slightly to him as he left, so I did too.

"Who is he?" I asked Joseph as we followed Unal Bey across the room. "And what did you tell them about me? They act like they know me."

"Engin Bey is the leader of the musicians. He is a very holy man to the dervishes. He is also one of the Magician's most learned and respected pupils."

Unal Bey opened balcony doors and the cool evening breezed in, the sunset reds becoming grays and blacks mottled by the lights of the city. As we walked the brief distance across the concrete to the balcony's edge, I asked for a visual tour of Istanbul and Unal Bey obliged.

"Over there is the Golden Horn"—he pointed toward the famous stretch of water where pirates had sold their wares centuries before—"and that is where my father started his first hotel, and there is a Russian ship coming down the Bosphorus from the Black Sea. . . ."

Above us, from another balcony, exotic music rang out of windows and doors.

Joseph smiled. "The rehearsal is in progress already."

The music combined drones of chanting voices with drums and other instruments that sounded like flutes, mandolins, violins. "It's awesome," I murmured. My elder companions smiled at my innocent delight.

"Come," Saadet Hanım offered, "before they finish without us!"

Unal Bey leaned toward me. "The Sufi music works fully as spiritual, or cosmic, vibration. It is much like pure spirit. The Sufis, as the Greeks, and so many other mystical peoples, know that certain music, just like certain words or images, vibrates more harmonically and resonantly than others, creating electromagnetic power that opens a doorway, as it were, between this and other dimensions of consciousness. You will see."

As we walked toward the elevators, Joseph said to his friends, "Ben and I have talked a great deal about mystical consciousness. He's very wise, this young man, very sensitive, very sharp. He knows of yours and

mine and Engin Bey's encounters with the Magician. We need not hold
anything back."

"Really. Does he know everything?" Saadet Hanım asked Joseph.

"Everything?" Joseph laughed. "Not even our young friend knows
that." It seemed to me that something was going on between the lines.

Saadet Hanım took my arm. "Let me tell you a little about what you
might experience this evening, Ben. You will see and hear a *nefir*—this is
a special horn—a *rebap*—this is a three-stringed violin with a small body
made of coconut shell. You will see the *ney*, a reed flute, said to hold in its
sound the window to the gods. We have two *hafızlar* with us tonight: Engin Bey, whom you just met, and the famous blind poet Cula Khan. A
hafız. you see, is one who has memorized the whole Koran."

"With his memory,"—Joseph smiled, pointing to me—"our friend
here might have been a *hafız* in another life."

"Ah, perhaps he will yet become one in this life," Unal Bey offered.
"Perhaps there is a new Koran for him to memorize."

They all laughed as we got into a creaky elevator. Unal Bey, Saadet
Hanım, and Joseph carried on a sudden, brief conversation in Turkish. I
couldn't even understand pieces of it. I was sure it concerned me, yet it
seemed paranoid to think so.

"The chanting tonight," Saadet Hanım continued in English as the
elevator climbed slowly, "will come from the Koran and the Mesnevi. The
Mesnevi portions will be the poet Rūmī's verse. The dance is the Sema,
the whirling dance.

"Notice, if you will, how the dervishes' hands look: one hand's palm
open up to heaven, the other downward to earth. This is a beautiful idea,
you see. God's love comes in one hand from heaven, moves through the
body and comes out the other hand to earth, and moves out of earth upward to heaven, an eternal cycle of energy using the dervish as its prism.
So it is that the dervish dancer, in the ecstatic whirling, lives as the vital
connection between all realms. He is a model of what each of us can be in
our everyday lives of love and service: vehicles for connecting heaven and
earth in the dance of life."

We stepped out of the elevator and walked a few steps to outside a

closed ballroom door, the music like a roaring ocean behind it. I thought
of the doorway Joseph and I had talked about, and the threshold. I felt
tingly. Wasn't this doorway at this hotel as real as any other way of passing
through the doorway to the infinite?

"Your presence is most welcome," Saadet Hanım called out to me.
"May you find in Turkey your *mejerel bahreyn*. We all hope this is your
fate."

"Thank you!" I called back, frowning my incomprehension to Joseph.
As she pushed the doors open, Joseph translated *mejerel bahreyn*: "union of
the two oceans." I'd just had the mental image of an ocean roaring behind
the door—coincidence? Or part of an immense simplicity in which I
found myself? "Stop thinking!" I told myself. "Just experience."

As we entered the rehearsal room and its sea of music, I walked on the
floor, socially adept enough to smile and nod with these new people, yet
who floated, like a low swan, just above myself. We moved to a table
against the far wall, the sound of flutes, violinlike strokes, a singing tenor,
and a harmonizing bass, all enveloping us. We passed an open balcony
door, the night breeze coming in, and sat down in chairs next to Turkish
women and men who watched, whispered among themselves, and drank.
Unal Bey poured ice water for each of us from one of three pitchers on the
table. A waiter walked around, filling drink orders. Clearly, for some of the
people, this spiritual evening was also some sort of annual or biannual social time. There were about forty people in the audience, twenty dancers
waiting against a wall, a dozen musicians playing instruments mainly exotic and foreign to me.

Engin Bey sat just in front of the little orchestra. Another man,
dressed in black and about as large as Engin Bey, swayed with the music,
his hands folded in front of him. He seemed about to sing, then laughed to
himself, niggling his finger at the orchestra. He had apparently missed a
cue. Even in the dimmed lights of this ballroom, he wore black sunglasses.
He would be the blind *hafız* Cula Bey, I realized, thinking suddenly of Ray
Charles's black sunglasses.

I giggled, then caught myself; no one at my table seemed put off by my giggle. In fact, I thought I saw some people at the other end of our long table talking about me, but in some sort of admiring way, as if they'd heard about me. They pointed at me, if not with fingers, then eyes.

The blind man finished his instruction to the orchestra, then sang again, mesmerizing me with thick, rich Arabic. I closed my eyes, listening to words I could not understand, but understanding that it spoke to me nonetheless.

Suddenly Cula Bey's voice and the music stopped. He gave some new instruction to the *ney* player, who nodded, licked his lips, and resumed playing. The other instruments joined in; then Cula Bey sang again, his renewed voice filling me with relief. I closed my eyes, concentrating on each sound of each instrument, eventually settling on one, the blind man's chant. There were three tones in a single note of his chant! It was amazing: three tiers of sounds coming from one mouth! Do, mi, and sol in one tone. I closed my eyes and floated in the sound. Engin Bey rose from his metal folding chair, moving to stand next to the blind man, and joined the chant, chanting in words and then in droning tones, like the Sanskrit "Oooommm" with which I was familiar, but different too. And now the sound of the *ney* got stronger. Engin Bey gestured to the *ney* player as a conductor gestures to a violinist when he wants more, and the instrument's volume increased. Even those people who had been chatting sotto voce grew quiet and focused on the scene. Something was happening, something so beautiful it mesmerized us all.

Engin Bey and the *ney* player held the notes for a long time, like an endless note, with the blind man quieter in his multitones, the string instruments providing a bed of sound, the drums giving it a heartbeat, the horns silent.

I felt a warmth rising from the base of my back up my spine. My mouth dried out, and I took a drink of ice water. The rising warmth, unabated by the water, gave my stomach intense butterflies, then started to constrict my esophagus. I swallowed hard again. It was the jolt again: physical, very physical, like the nausea—but warm, pleasurable, as if my body were trying to tell me something I couldn't quite understand.

Engin Bey droned like the earth speaking, and the *ney* called out like a flying sound for some kind of recognition; the drone responded, and I was caught in it. Engin Bey began to sing words, words some people recognized, for they sighed and nodded, as people do when they hear a tune so familiar their souls can never get enough of it. Engin Bey sang a whole song of some kind, his voice substituting for the *ney*, the reed flute dissipating. And then, just when I was sad that it was ending, the *ney* came back, and Engin Bey drew his breath. I felt my body embrace the sound of the *ney* like embracing a lover. How long had I been hearing it now, ten, fifteen minutes? But with each tone I heard something different in it.

As I watched Engin Bey's huge body breathe, something exploded in me and my mind—my observing mind—shut off altogether. My best memory is that my body felt like exploding light and my skeleton dissolved, limp, so that I couldn't reach my glass for water. I tingled with a hot liquid self—the music seemed to be living energy. The drone chant became a harmony of light and dark between Engin Bey and the blind man; the pure sound of the *ney* disappeared in their chant for a moment, then reappeared, very loud.

"Ben, my friend." Joseph leaned toward me. "Are you all right?"

I couldn't speak. The big men chanted, "Hu, Hu, Hu," the word for all Gods, in a drone that pulled me out of myself. I wanted to leave myself fully, I wanted to let go completely into the sound—but I returned to my body, to memory and real time, not fully letting go. I saw at once my Jewish history and my Western culture crying, "No! Don't let the chant of a passionate God take you! Stay louder than God, especially this Muslim God." The *ney*'s cry patiently urged me to awaken, to walk through the doorway. I followed it, grasped it, and at that moment it disappeared again into the chant of "Hu, Hu, Hu," then "Allah, Allah, Allah"—as all the names of God and the Muslin name of God took the *ney*'s cry, embracing it, embracing me. "Allah! Allah! Allah! *Allahhu ekbar!*" God is great! Engin Bey chanted the Arabic like an opera singer. Then I knew I wasn't "converting to Islam"—this incredible feeling, the voice in me, the *ney* singing like my own soul—this wasn't like when I'd seen Jesus in my friends' church, so lonely and depressed, and converted to "born-again" Christianity on the spot. Islam wasn't drawing my soul into its religion—God, here in Turkey, in a hotel ballroom, drew my soul into the Universal.

It was stimulated by beautiful religious words and sounds, but somehow more than religion. Only the universal energy mattered, the droning voice God chanting for millions of years in all languages:

"I am God.

"I am God.

"I am God."

Could I sing it too? In what language? How?

At that moment Engin Bey looked at me directly. Joseph, Unal Bey, and Saadet Hanım seemed surprised, looking at me too. Why was everyone looking at me? Other people started looking at me too. What was going on?

I had risen from my chair—that's what was going on. I swayed my arms, within myself but moving outside myself, watching myself in my blue jacket, my jeans, my tennis shoes, swaying there, my chair pushed back, aware that I shouldn't be so conspicuous, but conspicuous as a volcano. No one else swayed as if possessed: just me.

As the high-pitched *ney* sound crescendoed and I stood swaying in the ballroom, my eyes closed, I saw the membrane, the vertical wall of mind, form again. I saw the tree from my dream—the huge world tree—on the other side of the membrane. Hanging from it was a jewel—hanging in the middle of the ballroom like a chandelier—a huge diamond, as big as a room, shaped like a human tear. I was in this ballroom but in another reality too. I saw the sound of the *ney* splitting into its own atoms as it shot through the membrane, then through the jeweled tear, the tear a prism. I saw that my body, my whole existence, was this prism. The breathing celebration of the reed sound shot through me, weeping in atoms.

I.

Am.

God.

I.

Am.

God.

That is the great faith—to say it, and to know it.

The membrane disappeared. Then the vision disappeared as well and my floating self reentered my swaying body. I fell back into my chair. In front of our table an old man wearing a conical *kulah* headdress—the dervish *arif* or *fakir*, the *shaikh* leader of the dance—drifted onto the ballroom floor, moving to the middle as if stage-directed with a masking tape X at his feet. But he needed no X on the floor; his eyes weren't even open, yet he moved to the exact spot he wanted. The drumbeat began, wrenching at my heartbeat as he padded to the spot. The drumbeat caressed my aorta, my ventricles. Visions came again, now in the form of memories, flooding me.

I was on a mountaintop in Germany. I was in India, in Benares, a child at a festival. I was a teen praying in Eagleclaw's sweat lodge. I was in synagogue at nineteen, learning Hebrew. I was in the Baptist church at twenty-two. I saw them all, all memories, and I saw something I had never seen, that I *was* the church, I melded to it, I breathed it. I *was* the mountaintop. I *was* the Torah, the heat of me leaving my body and drifting into the Hebrew parchment. The visions receded. More dancers began moving onto the floor, each whirling toward the *shaikh*, receiving his blessing before whirling away to their own places. Some of them whirled slowly at first; others started out fast, like fire. The whirling was like a magic show. Each dancer held one palm up, one down, as Saadet Hanım had described.

All of a sudden I was overwhelmed. I had to get out. Too much stimulation! I couldn't handle it. I pushed up out of my chair, went for the balcony, the air. "Ben, are you all right?" Joseph called after me, but he received no answer, for I barely heard—the music was so loud! City lights blinded me with their variety and beauty. I fell into a balcony chair. Joseph followed me. "Are you all right?" he asked louder. My mouth was so dry. "I need some water," I murmured. He went back in and got my glass for me. I drank the whole thing in a gulp. "What's happening?" Joseph asked. It was too difficult for me to talk. The music inside kept me shimmering. Istanbul's cool night air wanted me. I was ready to fly away.

"Joseph, I don't know what's happening to me."

"Tell me."

I told him what I could: the membrane, the diamond tear, the sound of the *ney*, the sense of being a membrane myself, a prism that converted energy, then the sound of my own soul, the sudden memories of my past. While I talked in fits and starts, the music stopped. There was clapping, indicating a break in the rehearsal.

"Speak to Engin Bey," Joseph suggested. "I will get him. You have had a divine moment."

I stayed on the chair, watching him go inside. I could hear movement, voices in conversation, clinking glasses, coughs, the sounds of human life. Engin Bey came out with Joseph, who must have been telling him what I'd experienced, because Engin Bey immediately asked me to open my eyes. As he peered into them, he asked me about whether I'd experienced a warmth, a tingling.

"Yes," I said, "yes."

"From the base of your spine?" he asked.

"Yes!" I cried.

"Kundalini, then" he said to Joseph. They talked some more in rapid Turkish, Joseph probably explaining more of what I'd said. I knew what kundalini was, of course, the Sanskrit word for energy that rose and fell through the seven chakras of the body.

"It's all gone," I said aloud. "It was there, and now it's gone. All my life, these 'moments' occur but it's so frustrating—nothing stays!"

"Ah, the power of the divine." Engin Bey sighed, dropping heavily into the chair beside me. "It can seem never to satisfy." I noticed that Joseph had gone back into the ballroom. Why? I wanted to call him back. I felt so small, like an abandoned child. Don't leave me alone with Engin Bey! Who is Engin Bey? The ecstasy had turned to pain so quickly.

"My song," Engin Bey said, "was Rūmī's. You know Rūmī, the greatest mystical poet of all time? His song has entered your soul." He wiped his sweating forehead with a white handkerchief. Because of his huge girth, for Engin Bey breathing and talking in tandem came with difficulty. He wiped sweat from his cheeks with the handkerchief.

Rūmī, I knew, was a thirteenth-century mystical poet who went into trances and wrote ecstatic poetry.

"Rūmī," he sighed, holding the wet handkerchief to his right cheek, "describes in poetry that the self is a circle around a zero. Can you picture it in your mind?" He made a circle of his thumb and forefinger. "Any circle has within it the space, the space inside. The line of the circle holds the space inside. Rūmī said, 'Uncurl the line of the circle from around the space. Uncurl it and let the space, the zero, meld with the All.' I was

singing about doing this, about how difficult it is to do this, about how
beautiful it is to do this."

"I felt something, something like that."

"Yes. I have wondered if the Magician is not, in fact, Rūmī, returned
to us as a Traveler. Both teach that when we achieve Beka, when we give
up the circle around the zero, the soul is freed, it joins with the All, it is
liberated. Perhaps this has happened to you this evening, perhaps a moment of this, what the Buddhists mean by Samadhi, and the Hindus, Nirvana, and our Beka. Perhaps for you." Returning our eyes to his curled
thumb and forefinger, he now opened his fingers and blew breath at them,
like setting free a leaf or a butterfly.

"I'm looking, I'm looking so hard for myself. How can I uncurl the circle, how can I give up the self when I don't have it, don't know it? God!
It's so . . . it's so . . . I don't know. One minute I feel so free. Then we're
talking about it. Why am I talking about it? Nothing ever happens when I
talk about it. I think too much, that's my trouble."

"You don't trust life, my friend, that is your trouble. You just don't yet
trust life. You are a little bit angry, still frightened of living fully. The membrane you saw, is it not a doorway? To pass through, you must learn to live,
fully, no games, no fear, just the truth of the experience itself."

Angry? I focused on that. I never enjoyed it when people told me I was
angry. "Angry? At this moment I'm angry, yes. But not generally. I'm not
an angry person, Engin Bey."

"Are you not a very angry person? You don't trust life when it tells you
every moment of your existence that you are soul, soul that is one with all
souls, with All-Soul. Every moment, life teaches you this ultimate love.
But you cannot unwrap the ego from around the soul in order to hear this
lesson. Even you, who have, I am sure, a very intense and busy and well-
practiced spiritual life—even you cannot unfold the lesson. To unfold the
lesson—this is why any spiritual practice exists. It is why the dervishes
dance. The dance unwraps the circle from around the soul and sets it free
to join the All. Do you have a way of dancing in life this lovingly?"

Every teacher had taken me to this kind of place, but no one ever took
me past it. Every tradition had its Beka, and I never really got it.

I wanted to yell, "Tell me the secret! Tell me how!" Desperate, I asked,

"You say, to trust enough to unwrap the ego from around the soul I must first unwrap the ego from around the soul! It's the chicken and the egg."

"Yes, you do think too much, my friend. Stop thinking. Jump into the All." He gestured toward the view. "There is Istanbul, there is the city. City of God. Come, we will jump together." He pushed himself up out of the chair.

"What!"

He put out his hand. "Take it."

The balcony's rail was three feet in front of us.

"What?" another lesson? He couldn't be serious about jumping!

"Come to the balcony." He held out his hand.

I took his bulbous, pudgy, sweaty hand.

"Come on," I said. "I know you're not serious." But I moved with him. Our abdomens touched the railing.

"What do you see?" he asked, looking down.

"The night. A dirty street lit by a streetlight. Those apartments. A woman doing laundry. A man in his underwear. A TV on, lots of antennas, minarets."

"What do you *feel?*"

I measured answers in a millisecond. What was I supposed to feel just now? "To be honest," I said, "I feel silly holding your hand."

As he laughed, his belly and chest moved like water in a container. Letting go of my hand, he said, "You are terrified, you are angry. You are angry with yourself and with the divine—you are angry for all the hurts you have experienced in life. I hope soon you will plumb the source of your anger—to the shame you keep hidden deep in your heart. You are not honest yet, not fully so, and thus you cannot find Paradise." He spread an arm out over the city. "You have the potential to be an *âşık,* one who is enraptured by divine mystery. I see it in your eyes, your energy. It has been predicted. You felt it tonight, the pure possibility of rapture—you danced.

"But you cannot give in to it. You falter. How painful for you. The liberation from yourself you want so desperately terrifies you desperately. Is this not so, my friend?"

In that second, I hated him. I ground my teeth and looked at a ship out on the Bosphorus. Its lights gave the water around it a yellowish color. On it I saw the tiny movements of men as they folded a tarp under a flight-deck light. How easy Engin Bey made it all sound! But his truth did not liberate me. It left me feeling empty, inadequate and incapable.

He was right. I couldn't let go. I just couldn't.

"Maybe I'll jump," I said with bravado, tossing my right foot over the railing. "That would be liberating." I moved and spoke but felt stupid, so sad, like a little boy who had fallen into a well, terrified and lonely. I was the dork, melodramatic. But I was doing it, my one leg over the rail, then the other. I gripped the railing behind my back, my heels holding on to the edge of the balcony.

He made no move to stop me. "My friend, destroying your body is not liberation. It is just evidence of self-hatred. It will not unwrap the circle from around the zero. Your energy will return again, into another life wherein it must find the pathway to compassion for itself. To destroy this body is not Beka. To confuse the literal with the metaphysical is to fear real love. You already know this."

I clung to a three-inch railing, one hundred feet above a dirt pile that sat in the backyard of a small apartment building. I thought of the swimmer Joseph had described who struggled against the current, the one who must let go, let himself nearly die, risk death itself. I teetered on the brink, filled first with mischief but now with a real desire to fall, a desire so quick in coming, I could barely stop it; I wanted to reach out into the huge dark hand, borne on a night breeze, that beckoned me to clasp it.

What was I doing in Istanbul? Weren't these Magician lovers a cult? Who was Engin Bey really? Why was I alive?

With a surge of energy, tears welled up out of me, unstoppable tears. Usually, my self-protection was good—usually I was an even-tempered, contained person, in control; now I felt like melting wax. I started to cry.

"My friend," Engin Bey sighed, bear hugging me from behind. "Oh, my friend." He held me so tight, so tight in sudden love; I sobbed, and he held me tight.

I was scared. The whole otherwordly nature of being in Turkey—all the strange and exotic and intensely physical aspects of the day—swept through my mind. I had cried in therapy—good tears, real tears, but tears that now seemed only like practice for this bizarre night of feeling nakedly human and alive. I wept in the arms of a stranger.

"Engin Bey. Please. Help me."

He pulled me back over the rail, lifting me easily and lowering me down onto the wood of the balcony floor.

"Integration," he murmured. "Liberation. Freedom. Let it be so." He started praying in Arabic as he held me. I felt the puffs of his breath on the back of my neck. I wiped my eyes and nose and mouth with my sleeves, sucked in, breathed hard, finding my way back to familiar ground. Was he the Magician? Were they all magicians, Joseph, Engin Bey, Saadet Hanım? He sent light all through me with his praying and holding me. He was healing me.

I lay back into it, closed my eyes, let the tears flow, let him engulf me fully in his love. It was all I could do; it was everything at the moment. I became aware of Joseph coming out to the balcony, asking after me. I heard Joseph and Engin Bey talking about me in Turkish. I just let myself go, murmuring "I. Am. God," murmuring, "Hu, Hu, Hu," correcting, for that moment, my world. Saadet Hanım and Unal Bey came out too. I heard their voices through my tears. "He is the special soul," Saadet Hanım said in English to Engin Bey, who agreed. I started to come out of my trance of tears and saw around me four Turkish people whom I really did not know well. Yet I felt somehow that they knew me better than I knew myself, as if they gazed at me with ancient, ancestral eyes.

We spent another ten minutes on the balcony, talking, drinking water, looking out at the city. Engin Bey went back inside, and a few minutes later, when the rehearsal started again, we followed.

I whispered to Joseph as we entered the room, "I'm different tonight, I'm changing at an incredibly fast pace, hour by hour."

He put his hand on my head, as if to hug and bless my mind.

I embraced him for the second time that night, feeling again, after the cleansing of tears, that my life was blessed.

"Joseph?" I whispered as we sat again. "Why do these people look at me so much? Why do Engin Bey and Saadet Hanım say things like 'It was foretold' or 'He's the special soul'"?

He smiled. "My friend, the Magician told some of us—myself, Engin, Saadet, Unal, Sela, and Ragip, whom you'll meet in Ankara, and others here tonight—that someone would come to be the Messenger of the Magician's whole vision. Because you are a magician by trade, some think you might be that someone."

Joseph laughed disarmingly. "Think little of these outward things, my friend. Concentrate on *your* inward journey. The Magician will make everything clear."

What a strange, even pleasant thing to think about. Yet I couldn't help thinking, "If they only knew what kind of person they were confusing with a messenger of God—we'd all have a laugh!"

The rehearsal continued and I listened, letting the *ney* sound entrance me again, but I did not fall utterly into it this time. I had no visions. But I had a gentle awareness of peace. When had I felt peace before? I wondered. This was a kind of peace I could not even put into words. I simply relaxed and sat there enjoying it for as long as I could.

As the rehearsal ended, Engin Bey and some others came to our table. He asked after me and I thanked him for being so kind. I asked how I could return his kindness. He acted insulted by the idea of a debt, but then, with a glint in his eye, he asked that I do some magic tricks. Everyone else there joined in the request and agreed I must entertain them. I was glad they had asked.

So I did some magic tricks, entertaining my new friends. Because not all spoke English, rapid translation of my patter occurred among many of the twenty or so people. For my memory trick, I asked Engin Bey to repeat the whole Rūmī poem in Turkish. I listened in my memorizing trance, then repeated the poem in Turkish. I could sense myself making a few mistakes, which often happened when I repeated remembered words in another language; yet I must have done well enough—there was enthusiastic applause from the small after-hours crowd.

"Perhaps he is capable of remembering all of history," Engin Bey said with a smile.

"What a gift he has," Unal Bey agreed.

We drank and talked until four in the morning. Then Unal Bey drove us to the bus station, where we waited for the 4:45 bus marked ANKARA.

"Find your destiny." Unal Bey smiled as he said good-bye. "Let tonight be merely a beginning."

"I will," I promised.

"Notice, wherever you go, the love that surrounds you. Will you do that? Everywhere, people strive to love you. Will you pay attention? That is all you have to do. It is the universal way of becoming a servant of love."

"I will."

"Then may your two seas unite." He pulled away, leaving us in the crowded bus station.

"What a night, yes?" Joseph said, lighting a cigarette.

"Such a night of love!" I cried out, raising my arms like an athlete who has just won a race. People around us glanced at the crazy foreigner.

"Yes, a night of love," Joseph agreed. "A night drinking love in, drinking in the source and composition of all vibrations. You drank the original wine tonight, my friend."

"Yes." I grinned, putting on a smiling clown face of my own. "Well, at least nothing else can happen tonight, right? We'll rest on the bus," I reassured myself. "I haven't slept well in a few nights now. The benches on the boat for two nights. Now it's after four A.M. Let's just sleep."

"Sleep would be fine. If it is to be."

"What do you mean?" I challenged.

"On the bus I must tell you a secret, my friend," Joseph said above the crowd noise.

"What secret? You can't tell me now?"

"Let's get settled on the bus."

Everyone who ever guided me had tried to teach me patience.

Joseph picked up his small carry bag, leaving me to my larger pack. "There's our bus. Let's get on and see if the night has finished with us." Brakes squealed as the blue-and-white bus pulled into our stall, number 11. We got into line, waiting for the door to open and passengers to file out. As they passed, I found my eyes closing while I stood there; as my forehead felt the caress of a breeze from a passing bus, I disappeared, as if asleep, and left the clamor around me behind. I thought I heard Joseph murmur, "Happy travels!" as if he were sending me off. Awake enough to shuffle behind Joseph onto the bus, I fell completely asleep almost the instant we settled in the seats.

PART THREE

The
Self

You thought yourself a part, small

Whereas in you there is a universe.

— HAZRETI ALI

Great blessings come by way of madness,

indeed madness that is heaven sent.

— SOCRATES

FIFTH ✳ DREAM

This fifth dream finishes the vision of the world of the unborn. Ben Brickman called it "The Creation," for in it the unborn soul appears to move
into creation, leaving behind the intermediate world in which the soul
markings occurred and finding the self now emergent into "life on Earth."

---

*The horizon lies before me, waves of light and darkness infinitely expanding and con-
tracting as I journey to them on the water and then slide effortlessly through them. I
hear the sound not only of wind but of the Void itself, the original sound of nature that
creates all other sounds. In this I float, recognizing that soon I will lose my memory of
this place. I will have to barter it away in order to gain the world of born experience.*

*I get closer and closer to the source of the great roaring sound now; then I am
in it, like being in an explosion of the Void. I'm tossed like an insect in a sandstorm.
I'm raised and whirled in a terrifying catastrophe that also feels like a grand dance.*

*The movement stops and I fall, landing not back in the water but in sand and
dirt. I sense that I've been to this land before. It's a well-known place of some kind.
It's a place where people believe the water will disappear one day. In this interim
world, all woe and pleasure are dependent on the water, on whether one has water or
not. Some of the people here form into shapes and containers that can hold the water.
Others fight to protect the water or take it from the people who have saved it in forms.*

*I am weeping tears of grief at the privation and aggression here. People come
with cups and try to catch my tears. They attack me and wound me with knives
made of their own tears. I cannot fight them all off, so I close my eyes and wait for
them to destroy me.*

*When I open my eyes, I find myself in a place of trees where a horde of spirits
is imprisoned in a cage, waiting for me to free them. "Your mission," a voice says
from the trees, "will be to free your people." My breathing feels heavy to me. I real-*

ize I am breathing water. I am in a place where air is water. I realize that I have been on the tree and then in the river and through the tunnel and now will leave here to enter a water-holding form called a "body," which is so delicate it can breathe only the thinnest of waters, called air. It cannot breathe the water it came from until it dies again, in the many ways it will die during and after its embodied lifetime. I re-alize that if it chooses, it will be able to die a little bit every day of its life, and thus be able to breathe the water for a few moments every day. Learning how to do this will be the same as learning to be free from the cage. I realize I am supposed to teach it how to do that. I say to the spirits, "I can't free you here, but I will free you when I get a body. Be patient." They stare at me, frightening me with their empty eyes. "Be afraid," they say like a chorus. "Be afraid to go to the place where you cannot breathe the water."

Their empty stares frighten me. "I am not afraid to go to the place where I can-not breathe the water," I whisper. "I want to go there." As if it had waited for the appropriate signal of creation, now the loud, original sound of water rushing, the im-mense thunder of explosion overwhelms me, and I am shot through another tunnel. The wind in the tunnel pulls me through toward the new world, where my family of clustered energies yearns to care for me again and yearns in their new bodies and forms, for my care. Darkness explodes into light, and I shoot through the light.

I woke up on the bus to the smell of cigarette smoke and the whir of tires on asphalt. Some people chatted behind and in front of us. We had not left the city yet; we were still surrounded by lights from the build-ings and streets. It was not yet 5:00 A.M. Outside my window other cars, smaller than our bus, strived to speed past along the narrow streets, honk-ing and receiving honks from our driver. Joseph's eyes were closed. I closed my eyes again, just for a few moments. I was wide awake, though. There was no somnolence in me, as there had been earlier when I'd dreamt the river; now there was just alertness. I searched in my jacket for my little pocket notebook. Finding it, I began to write down everything I could about the amazing experiences of this night in Istanbul.

CHAPTER 5

The Atonement

> The fifth task of the mystic is to become one with suffering, for suffering is the origin of compassion. You must become immersed in the sicknesses and pains of the world, and you must heal them. The world is at once an ecstatic contemplation of God's navel and a grotesque experience of God's bowels. The mystic's life vacillates between these extremes of experience. The point of the vacillation is for the growing soul to experience its responsibility in all good and all ill that transpires in life.
>
> Where there is forgiveness, there is God without end. Once you have moved through the doorway of senses and emotions, the spirits will, through the experience of atonement, help you alter the very cells of your consciousness. Do not be surprised if you feel, at times, eaten by dogs, and wish to flee these fierce, loving dogs forever.
>
> —The Magician

The bus driver revved the engine of the clean, almost new Mercedes bus. Since Turkey is considered a "developing country," I had expected much more poverty and perhaps dirty buses crowded with goats or squawking chickens—a Third World stereotype. But most people on this bus were nicely dressed: men in jackets and ties, women in modest skirts. And there were no animals. Above me was a light I had switched on in order to be able to see my writing in the darkness of predawn.

As the driver waited impatiently at a streetlight, I looked up to see red lights snaking ahead of us: we sat behind a long line of cars headed toward a tunnel that cut through a low mountain.

Joseph awoke. He did not interrupt my writing, but as I had nearly finished I said, "I had that dream again, a continuation of it. I've written it down. Do you want to read it?"

He did, accepting the notebook. The driver honked as we moved slowly.

When Joseph finished, he handed the notebook back to me. The huge vertical vein on his forehead pulsed, his dark eyes looked off for a moment into the middle distance. Then he said, "My friend, you have seen the Creation in your own way. You have seen the way the energy of our spirits operates. We are composed of energy, and that energy exists 'before' we contain it in these particular physical bodies. One of the greatest spiritual questions has always been 'What happens after we die, what happens before we're born?' You are seeing a piece of this puzzle."

"Could that really be?"

"I have absolute faith, yes. I think the Magician is already working with you, giving you gifts for our new millennium. And it is time I tell you a little secret."

"A secret?"

"Let me close my eyes for just a moment, my friend, and gather my energy." We fell silent, and I lay my head back on the headrest. The bus rolled on through the darkness of the tunnel. On the other side, as we left Istanbul, I turned and watched the lights of the city behind us, resolving to come back to this city to explore its depths. But at the same time, I felt overwhelmed by the urgency of my desire to go anywhere Joseph took me.

Soon we headed over the Bosphorus bridge, becoming pilgrims who left Europe and ventured into Asia. We would arrive in Kor, Joseph's ancestral village, just after dawn. Kor lay two hours from Ankara, which was our destination for the day after. I closed my eyes, smelling, hearing, tasting—cigarette smoke, lulled voices, my own salty lips.

The taste of my lips suddenly triggered a flash of memory, from when I was seventeen. I felt a sudden nausea too. My mind filled with a huge, brutal scene and experience I had long forgotten. My lips had been salty then too. I shivered visibly at the memory, turning to Joseph, who, noting my shiver and loud sigh, now studied me.

"You are cold, my friend?" It was warm on the bus, enough to glisten our foreheads with a slight sweat that cooled as the air conditioner blew on it.

Instead of answering him directly, I turned back to the black bus window. "Joseph, I just received the clearest flash of memory. Man, it was like I was there." I stopped talking, and he waited. "Joseph, what if you think you don't deserve the chance to walk through the magical doorway? The memory is of a thing I did, a terrible thing, when I was a kid." I shook my head. A realization shook me. "Can a person be unworthy of . . . of succeeding . . . of learning the truth . . . of being . . . free?"

"You have done something of which you are deeply ashamed?"

"Yes." I turned to him.

He pondered me a moment. "Everyone deserves the chance to swim in the second sea. But not everyone gets to its shore. There can be obstacles."

What I had done at seventeen, in July 1975, was as evil as evil could get. In my exhaustion now, and following a beautiful time of divine connection, I saw a terrible shadow.

Joseph blew out cigarette smoke. "Often a searcher finds himself at the doorway to full reality, but the self is not quite ready, not quite strong enough, too weighted down to pass through. Perhaps you are weighted down."

"Yes. I think I feel like I've messed up too seriously in the past and I don't deserve happiness. I think I've felt this for a long time, but I never fully *got* that I felt it until just now. I don't know. Joseph, how strange that I should remember that terrible time so clearly, just now, and . . ." I trailed off, unsure how to proceed.

Gently he asked, "To what exactly are you referring, my friend? What did you do?"

I looked out the window, pausing to consider how to tell the story. Around us was night, the black thick of night. We sped through a dark road and landscape. My sinuses burst with the cigarette smoke. It seemed as if every Turkish man, and even many women, smoked cigarettes including Joseph himself, who was smoking a Marlboro he had bummed off the passenger across the aisle.

"*Pardon efendim,*" we heard, and looked up to see a young Turkish man holding out a bottle for our inspection. I was startled to find out that in Turkey the buses have young male attendants. The smell of lemon cologne wafted powerfully from the bottle. Joseph reached his hands out, palms up, receiving drops of the cologne and rubbing his hands together. I held my hands out too, then thanked the teen.

"You American?" he asked in a thick accent.

"Yes, I am."

"Best country! I go there some time."

I smiled back. "I hope so. I hope America will be as friendly to you as Turks have been to me."

He beamed and moved on to the next passenger.

Joseph put his cigarette out in the aluminum foldout ashtray in the back of the seat in front of him. He turned to me, reaching upward to click the light on. "May I look at your eyes?"

"Sure," I said. "What for?" Engin Bey had done this too.

Joseph peered at me like a doctor, pulling my eyelids up with his fingers and staring directly into my pupils, first into my left, then my right. Nodding, he pulled back and reached up to turn off the obnoxious light.

"It's time for me to tell you my secret. Please be open-minded as I speak." He took in a deep breath, then exhaled heavily. A thin filament of smoke, residue from the cigarette, drifted up from his nose. "I confess, my friend, to having helped alter your consciousness. The candies I gave you, do you remember?"

"Sure."

"I injected Kulu-ander into them. It is a South African methamphetamine, like mescaline, a tribal initiation herb. It is not dangerous."

"You drugged me?" I had asked him, and he'd denied it. "Jesus, I was right! I thought there was something . . . Joseph," I lamented, "you lied to me!"

He grinned. "Well, not quite. When you asked me if I had given you drugs, I did not lie. I deflected your question. I did not deny it."

That was true. I remembered him saying, "Why do you ask that?" a question I hadn't answered.

"But that's a . . . a technicality! Why would you do that to me?"

"I will explain. Through your father, and in the days I spent with you in Paris, I learned you were a young man rich in gifts, a special soul, a searcher. I knew you also to be an advanced consciousness, yet still insecure and resistant to your own senses, resistant, in your heart, to the special destiny of every searcher—the destiny of liberation, of Oneness with universal energy. I needed to see how your body and spirit would respond to the rush of total altered consciousness. I did not look forward to investing time and energy in you if your spiritual searching was really a pretense. I hope you will pardon my bluntness and my unorthodox ways."

"It's kind of hard for me to be pissed off," I admitted, "since I deceived you first." I pondered his words. "So how did I do? Did I pass?" I was disappointed to think that my incredible journey of the last few hours had been brought on by artificial stimulation. This realization was somehow more upsetting to me than the fact that I'd been dosed.

"You passed with flying colors. You surrendered, you trusted. Though others in your life and past had not been trustworthy, you decided to trust your teacher. No one moves through the doorway without learning to trust his teacher. No one. And you had a divine moment tonight, which is a rare occurrence for anyone who takes Kula-ander for the first time."

"So all that really *did* happen tonight, even though you drugged me?"

"It all happened, quite clearly."

"Tell me the component specifics of Kulu-ander. It's unique in my experience, better concealed than anything I've ever taken. I've experimented with peyote, ololiuqui, soma, sativa, LSD. This one felt different. I knew something was going on, but I couldn't *feel* the drug like I always can. There was no smell, no taste."

"Kulu-ander is called 'the quiet song' by the Kulu—very difficult to detect." He described some of the chemical components—some familiar to me, some not. "I do not have to tell someone of your experience that Kulu-ander, like most tribal initiation mescalates or methamphetamines, is not meant to be used frequently." He lifted his palms to his face, smelling his scented hands before continuing. "Once a year or so, it provides the self with a model for how liberation can feel. Those model feelings help the mystic achieve and sustain liberation the rest of the year. So it should be with peyote and other spiritual hallucinogens."

"You gave me a *taste* of the truth. I understand." Then I thought suddenly: What about other side affects? I asked Joseph, and he nodded.

"There will be one. You will experience it sometime in the next hour or two: you will feel very sick. Or to put sickness another way: You will feel the weight of your material world in you, and you will be able to throw off that weight only by atonement and repentance. As the drug passes through and out of your body, you'll develop a fever, both physical and emotional."

"That's something to look forward to," I teased.

"Please. Don't feel condescended to or experimented upon, my friend. In giving you Kulu-ander I hoped you would gain an inner virtue. But had I not given you the Kulu-ander, what happened might not have occurred, at least not when it did. Kulu-ander tends to speed up a process that might take much longer without it. Had I told you what you were taking, I think you would have invaded your own experience with too much self-consciousness."

He was right, of course. If he'd told me, I would have been watching myself every moment. Without the Kulu-ander, I wouldn't have had the sudden and immense moment of divine reality, a moment different in some way I couldn't yet fathom from all the hallucinatory or visionary moments I'd had during my graduate school research. In a way, I felt honored that Joseph had done what he'd done. I couldn't remember anyone—a college teacher, a parent, a friend, even Mick—treating me quite as Joseph did. In his presence, my life seemed to matter a great deal.

I asked, more a musing than a question, "Joseph, why do you think I'm here with you? I've become your student."

"It is our destiny," he agreed. "You have been brought to me, and I to you. You are raw, but you are meant for something very important in the evolving spirit of the world. Perhaps I can help you find it."

"I'm meant for something important," I repeated. "Like being this Messenger?"

"Perhaps, my friend, though if not that, something else. Everyone born is meant for something holy, some profound purpose. There are no accidents of birth, and there are no 'unnecessary' or 'unimportant' people. We are all essential in our own way to the progress of the universe. Jesus,

Saint Catherine of Siena, the Buddha—all were ordinary searchers called to learn their purpose, and to live it. Each met the call, and thus gained a formidable importance in the world's eye. But these were simply ordinary people. In their lives, as in every mystic's life, there were oppression and confusion and brutality. No life is immune to these."

We fell silent a moment as the bus slowed, moving up a steep hill. Joseph had just hinted for me to tell my story, but again I hesitated. All around us, people were beginning to doze off. Joseph said, "My friend, do not be surprised if, for a time now, you are on edge. Often, a divine moment is followed by a very conscious sense of fragmentation—anger, guilt, shame. You came to the doorway, and you are moving through it. Have you had any sense of fever yet? You shivered earlier."

"I don't think that was from fever."

"Be ready. And remember this: the fever is a path to healing, as sickness so often is in people's lives. It is sacred. As you know, the Hindus speak of kundalini awakening. Their terms are different from mine, or from your American therapy, but their content is similar. As the kundalini rises, they speak of *kriya* emerging—you know of *kriya?*"

I nodded, telling him what I knew: when the Hindu version of cell restructuring occurs, millions of tiny, often unexpected *kriya*—"little sufferings"—can occur, often in startling memories which the kundalini energy is trying to purge from the energy centers of the Self.

"Yes," he agreed, "a self perpetually unhealed cannot fully channel the power of God's pure love. Instead, God's energy may channel into ego aggressions or depressions rather than compassion. The self must move through all atonements and be healed so that the life of compassion can be lived."

"But we're never really healed. We always have issues to work through." I heard myself sounding like a therapist.

"That is a perspective Western psychology has made popular. However, from a spiritual perspective, a different perspective emerges: a person can *finish* with the emotional and behavioral impact of past traumas and experiences. In fact, one must."

Western psychology had not taught me this at all. And I did not immediately understand Joseph. The field of psychology had taught me that the wounds of the past are always "patterns" or "pathologies" we can regress into if we get stressed or don't "keep working on them."

"With intense work of spiritual practice," Joseph continued, "with spiritual initation and God's embrace, and in fulfilling the many tasks of mystical life, one is able to heal the wounded self. This is the spiritual promise of mysticism. If the mystic does not seek this healing, he will hold up his wounds as his only jewels. He will not inspire and serve others and God; rather, he will constantly 'work out his stuff,' as you Americans say. This is like the goat that prefers to ram his head against the fence rather than care for his young. It is an adoration of one's own woundedness. Do you understand what I mean, my friend?"

I nodded. I had always defined myself to people I had tried to love, especially women, by pointing them toward my open wounds. Being honest about who I was—for instance, on a first date—meant being vulnerable, which meant telling my life story, which meant telling what kind of family I'd come from, what wounds I'd suffered, what my path to healing had been so far, and what work I still needed. My wounds were my jewels; I asked lovers to help polish them, to help heal me. Joseph wasn't saying that doing this was wrong; what he was saying was that there was another step beyond this awaiting the searcher.

"The spirits are working on you, my friend," Joseph continued. "Become very aware of what the fever wants to teach you as the Kulu-ander gives you its last blessing. Will you do this?"

I nodded. "I will."

We rode on in silence for a while. Then the bus slowed, approaching what appeared to be a well-lit Turkish truck stop: cars and buses parked in front of a broad, gray, one-story building, people milling around. I looked at my watch: 5:45 A.M.

"We're stopping?"

"Yes. We will have tea. It is the custom. At intervals our buses stop for tea, sweets, and rest room." Though quite modern, the Turkish bus did not have a rest room in the back.

I yawned, then exercised my face and jaw, opening my mouth and eyes wide against the smoke-thick air. As we pulled to a stop, bodies rose and stretched and shuffled toward the door. A small stream of souls, we moved through the little parking lot and into the brightly lit çay house. I went quickly to the rest room, where many of us stood peeing together against the porcelain urinal wall. The stench forced me to breathe through my mouth.

The eating area of the çay house was a huge room with numerous tables, a little sturdier than card tables, folding chairs around them; posters, calendars, and portraits of politicians on the wall; and glass display cases full of candy. An aroma of freshly baked bread and pastries wafted from the kitchen. Men carrying çay trays circulated among the bus passengers. Most passengers sat at the tables, but some stood or squatted outside.

When I came back from the rest room, I found Joseph seated alone, facing into the room smoking a cigarette, two tea glasses in front of him on the table. I dropped two sugars into my glass—Turkish tea glasses look like miniature vases—and quipped, "Did you put anything in this I should know about?"

He smiled. "I assure you, my friend, I did not."

The first sip burned my tongue. After blowing on it, I took a second. When it hit my stomach, I felt a sharp twinge, like a bite inside my gut by a bee or a snake. From the bite rose a burning, like heartburn, up into my esophagus. I swallowed hard as the burning continued up through my esophagus into my throat.

I winced. Joseph leaned forward, regarding me. Then I put my glass down with a bang, grabbed my chest, and began breathing hard. The burning moved into my mouth, then my jaw, attacking my cheeks like the shock of blowing up a balloon. The burning moved through my shoulders, down my arms. I broke out in a sweat, my mouth becoming dry and salty.

"Jesus," I said aloud, looking Joseph in the eye, "I'm having a heart attack."

"You'll be all right," Joseph assured me. "Ride it out, my friend. It is not a heart attack. It is the fever, and I am here with you."

The burning became a kind of achiness in my back, like a flu. Dizzy, I leaned my head forward. My elbows rested on my knees, my heavy head bobbing at the end of my neck like a bowling ball hanging off a flower stem. I licked my lips, leaning farther forward until my forehead touched my folded hands on the tabletop.

"The dizziness is normal," Joseph said. "Have no fear."

I don't know how long I sat with my head against the table, but now I heard men's voices, one of them Joseph's, speaking in Turkish. I heard words like *arkadaşim* and *hastalık*: "my friend," "sick." Joseph reassured the inquiring men, but two of them sat down with us, continuing their conversation about me. I opened my eyes to look at the men—one dark-haired, dark-mustached. The other, younger, most probably his son, was dark-pigmented also, but blond-haired. On his blond hair and in his young face I saw someone else, someone from my past. It was a feverish hallucination, and I knew I was projecting it, but I couldn't stop it. Shaking in the fever, sweating, I saw Allen Tremmel from that summer back in 1975, in Durango, Colorado, when I was seventeen.

I must have been staring at him because Joseph said, "My friend, what do you see?" He had requested cold water from the waiter and now received it, handing me the glass. I downed it, trying to regain control over my mind. "This Turkish kid is *not* Allen!" I told myself, but in my mind he had the same gaunt face, blue eyes, small nose, chiseled cheeks, and mean look. Allen Tremmel had been a brutal teenage peer of mine in Durango, Colorado. He had brought the worst—the Devil—out of me.

"Please," I managed to say to Joseph, "please tell this guy that I'm sorry, he just reminds me of someone, something. A hallucination. I'm sorry. I don't mean to stare."

"*Pardon efendim,*" I said to the father and son.

Joseph spoke to the men. They smiled, making gestures that it was no big deal.

"I'm burning up," I said to Joseph. "Jesus, am I burning up!"

"Let us go into the fresh air," he suggested. "You are having a strong reaction in Kulu-ander's last phase." He helped me up, and I wobbled, like someone injured or drunk.

"This isn't gonna end," I moaned. "I'm going to die."

"Immerse yourself in it, my friend. Don't resist the pain." He sat me down on the concrete steps in front of the *çay* house. Someone had turned the television on inside. Its voices, in Turkish, resounded in my head.

Some men squatted near us and watched me. Joseph explained to them that I was an American and I was sick. He put his arm around me and spoke softly into my ear: "My friend, let yourself go. Let go of all self-consciousness in your pain. Let there be no spectator to your pain. Think only of the river. You will not die of drowning. This sickness is every sickness, every suffering, every pain. Let it be your teacher now."

On and on he muttered. "Shut up!" I wanted to yell at him. "Shut up! I can't! I can't do the spiritual thing right now! I feel like shit!" Only some great respect for him, or fear of making a scene, kept me from yelling at him.

He held me tight, as Engin Bey had, in his smaller arms.

I closed my eyes, shutting out all the people who were watching me, my head bobbing forward again. I let the dizziness come like a flood; I fell into it, surrendered to it, moaning, letting myself moan, right there in public. The pain was too much, and I wailed like an infant.

"It's okay," Joseph soothed. "Yes." At that moment, as if I'd found the cure, the fever began to pass. The burning subsided. The achiness began to dissipate, the change more sudden than I had ever experienced a healing before. And suddenly I had to pee! "Joseph, I have to go, have to go." I stood up, then ran to the bathroom. He followed me into the restaurant and to the back, waiting at the bathroom door while I relieved myself. Now another memory flooded my brain. It was Dr. Francis, the psychiatrist who had forced sex on me when I was ten. Standing at this Turkish urinal, I saw myself peeing in the older man's bathroom. "Jesus!" I hissed under my breath; then the memory left.

I washed my hands and face at the sink and looked in the mirror. My hands shook and my face was pale. What the hell had just happened to me? This was like therapy, but thirty sessions in one.

"I've never experienced anything like this," I said to Joseph. Hadn't I despised him seconds before? Like an ever-present spirit, he just stood, his arms folded, within my reach.

"My friend," he said, "I must tell you, it is rare for someone to pass through the sickness so quickly. You have a great deal of defensive power. There may be more coming."

The burning had all but subsided. Peeing had helped immensely, as if

I'd passed not a kidney stone but a—what should I call it—a sickness stone, and now I felt great relief. The cold water helped. I bent to cup my hand and drink the tap water, then thought better of it. I'd go get bottled water from the cafeteria.

The bus honked twice, indicating we should get back on quickly.

"I need some drinking water," I said to Joseph. "But I think the spell is done."

"On the bus our young attendant will give you some water. Come now."

When we came out of the bathroom, we joined the line filing onto the bus. Grinning, I raised my arms sheepishly to everyone. In English I said, "I'm okay, I'm okay." There were laughs of good cheer all around, and I felt strangely unembarrassed. What had Unal Bey said? Learn that everywhere people strive to love you?"

The driver said something to me in fast Turkish.

"I'm okay," I responded, "okay," opening my arms like a proud bird, showing off my health.

Once we were back in our seats, Joseph asked for a bottle of water and received it from the attendant. The bus moved beneath us again, out of the parking lot, back onto the asphalt road.

I laughed. "All I can say is 'Wow!'" Now I felt not only unfeverish but in fact elated, as if I had defeated cancer. I looked at my watch. Twenty minutes had passed since we'd gotten off the bus.

As I glanced at the watch, it started happening again.

"Oh, my God," I moaned. This time the burning began in my brain and skull. It fanned downward from there. "Oh no, Joseph." I clamped my head between my hands.

"Tell me what's happening. Name it." He touched the back of my head with his palm.

"My head's exploding!" I lay back, closed my eyes. "What the hell is going on?" I cried. "Jesus, my head!"

"What is in you, what penitence? What is the *kriya*, my friend? Tell me. It is so strong in you. It floods the fever and makes it burn. It wants to move. What are the memories? What is the evil? What is the pain?"

"Oh Joseph," I moaned, "it was so sick."

"Tell me, my friend. What is your burden?"

I rocked in my seat, my hands now clamping my chest. I saw love in his face, compassion in his eyes. "I was in bad shape, just after my folks separated that time. They sent me to a psychiatrist. He—I can say it, I've been in therapy, so much woundedness. There's a bee in my hair. Is there a bee in my hair?" I felt a bug in my hair, pushed through my hair with my fingers, my hair and fingers wet with sweat.

"Go on."

"That guy in there, he looked like Allen Tremmel, not really, but to me, that teenager in the çay house. No bee? Nothing in my hair? You sure?"

"There's no bee in your hair. Who is Allen Tremmel?"

"I had this friend. In Durango, Colorado. That's where we lived for a while. I was seventeen years old. This neighbor guy, David McConnell and I, we became buds, best friends. One night I told him about Dr. Francis, the psychiatrist, making me . . . have oral sex with him . . . then . . . well . . . you know . . . having sex inside me . . . intercourse . . . up my . . . when I was ten. Six months Dr. Francis did me. Not the worst sexual abuse story, right? But enough. David was the first real friend I'd had in years, and I tell him about Dr. Francis, and I figure that's it, it's over. He'll think I'm fucked up, and that's that. But then David tells me about Allen, Allen Tremmel, this Durango bully, the things Allen did to him, beating him—fucking him up like I was fucked up. You know? Sorry about the language."

"Go on, my friend."

"It's like David and I were brothers in everything. Boy, this is weird, telling you. I've been in therapy so long—but it's so hard."

"Speak more of Allen Tremmel," Joseph pressed.

"Joseph, it was the worst moment in my life, worse than getting corn-holed. I became a demon that night, that summer, in Durango. David and I—we became evil. I was already into high school drama, you know? Into acting. I'd been in three plays already. So I convinced David what we'd do. We'd put on KKK sheets. Pretend we were the Klan. We did a whole elaborate plan. We got Allen to an old mill barn out of town. We told him to strip naked, and we made him jerk off—you know, masturbate himself. My dad had a gun, and we made Allen do everything at gunpoint. Shot at him to terrify him into submission. Jesus, it's so bad. I've never really told any-one *everything* about this. Not even my therapists."

Memories of the scene enveloped me, strings in my brain, in my skin, my hands; every part of my body I had used that night seemed to still carry a demon.

"Let it out, my friend, let it pass through. What happened? It was one night. It is not you—let it out of you."

"It was one night. Yes. Let it pass through." Those words helped. Let it pass through. All of it. "We beat him to a pulp. I remember how I loved the violence—I remember how I was all sweaty and how salty my lips were.

"I held the gun, and David beat Allen's naked body, then David held the gun and I beat him. We beat him with a two-by-two. We shot right be-side him into the ground. We made him . . . we made him piss himself, we made him jerk off—masturbate. It's too gross. I can't trust you. I'm too afraid to say."

"Trust. Now. Trust. Let go. Say it. You have a destiny to know yourself fully as God, a destiny so powerful one night cannot keep you back."

"I shoved the gun—loaded—up his ass. Okay? Like Dr. Francis shoved his . . . penis up mine. You see? *I* did that. I with the destiny, *I* the spiritual searcher, don't you see? I shoved a gun up a guy's ass! I destroyed Allen just like I had been destroyed. David and I both hurt him, but I was the leader. I planned it out. I was the sick one. David was afraid through-out most of it. He was only fifteen, I was seventeen. *I* did it."

My head throbbed behind the right eye, my teeth chattered, sweat poured off me. I wasn't in tears—this realization struck me. Why was I not crying? This was a different sort of catharsis.

"The point is," I finished numbly, calming down, "you see, the point is—Allen joined the Marines right after that incident. He didn't finish high school. He surprised everyone by just quitting, boom! And he joined up, and two months later, he died in a jeep accident in Vietnam. I think about this all the time, even when I'm not thinking about it. It's been fif-teen years."

The shivers began to recede. Joseph looked at me intently. Was he right? Would this confession, this speaking the full memory aloud here, on this bus, change my energy? Did it realign my cells? Could this really be so? Often I had spoken my pain and gotten a certain amount of relief; yet this time I had finally spoken my worst pain and not been destroyed.

"You have held on to this for so long," Joseph said. "And now what is left for you to do?"

"I don't know," I answered honestly. "I forgave Allen years ago. But not myself. I can't forgive myself."

"When will you do so?" he asked. "When, my friend?"

"Forgive myself? I don't think I can." Would he and I have to part company now, now that he knew my worst secret?

"When will you forgive yourself?" he asked again. "Tell me."

"I don't know," I responded, searching his eyes.

"If you do not forgive yourself, you say to the world, 'Come, world, hurt me as I have hurt others, for I know no other way to do penance but to be in misery for my sins.' Don't you see, my friend? You are saying, 'When you hurt me as badly as I hurt Allen, only *then* can I forgive myself.' But you will never feel hurt enough. You will keep receiving pain and wanting more—no matter the good faces you put on. Ultimately, you will learn emptiness, power struggle, insecurity, distrust. You will marry these and sire these. But I think these are not your destiny. Do you think they are?"

The shivers had disappeared. The throbbing was ebbing too. I downed my water. "I don't know, Joseph." Was forgiveness of myself really possible? I glimpsed the idea, felt a glimmer of hope, even felt barriers trying to dissolve.

Joseph smiled. "You do know, my friend. You know I speak the truth. I suspect you have confessed, repented, and atoned over and over. Now you must take the next step in the process of atonement: you must completely forgive."

I sat back, closed my eyes. I saw David McConnell, the tall, gangly friend I had left behind in Durango. I saw the old barn, the sawdust on the floor, the sawdust on Allen's sweaty body as he writhed from the beatings. I saw the white sheets we wore, the hoods, the gun in my hand. I smelled

Allen's anus, his urine, his fear, my own sick rage. I saw it all without flinching. I watched it. For the first time, I saw myself there but knew myself now as different from that boy I had been.

Inside my closed eyes I felt Joseph next to me, an eternal presence, the first ally in my healing who hadn't said, "Don't blame yourself, Ben, you were the first victim, remember, you were the victim in all that abuse"— the first healer I had opened my guts to who had seen me for what I had been—sick and brutal—and made no excuse for me, explaining instead the possibility of forgiveness, of rising out of shame, of having a real choice and a task I must accomplish.

"Forgive myself," I murmured. "Joseph, what a thing that would be." I held the thought inside me like something sacred, a jewel in my hand.

"You will do it," Joseph assured me, leaning back and away. He put his hand on my wrist for just a second. "Soon it will come. You are capable of more courage than you realize, my friend. To forgive oneself, to fully atone and do penance, takes more courage than anything else. I know, I have learned it." He pulled his hand off my wrist. "Atonement is a kind of magic, alchemical and transformative in its power. You are a magician, my friend. Everyone is a magician when it comes to the world of suffering. We are all capable of the magic of healing."

"I feel physically better. The fever—it's passing, I think."

"The drug is finished with you. You've sweated it out. What is left in dilution will not affect you much. It has given you many gifts, hasn't it?"

"Yes." I felt tears of sweetness coming to my eyes. "I've been more emotional in eight hours than I've been in years."

"When you wish," he offered, "we will talk more of your past. As you wish it, and if you wish it. It is yours. Your history, the well you drink from. When you offer a cup of it to me, I will drink with you, but only then. There is a beginning, a middle, and an end to everything, even your historical pains. Each of them is a story. Once it has been told, it joins the ethers. Until it does, all your actions are clouded by it.

"Now, I am an old man, my friend. I must sleep. We will be in Kor quite soon. We will end our talking for now."

"Of course. Thanks, Joseph. Thanks for everything!" I'd been so focused on myself for—well, for hours, ever since I'd stepped off the ferry—

that I hadn't really noticed how tired Joseph must be getting. As he was able to do everything else, he was able to switch moods and consciousness in seconds. Two minutes ago he had helped me look into the abyss. Now his eyes closed and he relaxed into sleep.

But I couldn't sleep. I put my head back, imagining forgiveness as something akin to the bread of life. I only needed the courage to eat it. Having a friend and teacher show me the way to it was a blessing, a gift. Could I fully eat it?

Joseph snored lightly beside me. I stared at the window, watching the beginnings of dawn with its blues and whites. I won't sleep now, I thought, I'm feeling so much space open up inside me, so much time inside me becoming light. . . . But sleep did come, just as dawn began to spread. As I relaxed into the vibration of the wheels on the road, sleep came like a hum, a warmth in and through my body, an embrace of unconditional love as sleep can often be in a moving car or bus.

I dreamt. I was in the house of my childhood, before my parents' divorce, in Westchester County, just outside New York City. I was in my room, my bed unmade, the closet a mess, pictures slanted on walls. I reached up and straightened the pictures. I opened the curtains. I cleaned up the closet, then made the bed.

It was a strange, sweet, and simple dream, a moment of immense self-love. As I started to walk out of the cleaned room, I heard a sound behind me and turned. There, on a wall, was the small doorway again and the injured, waiting, olive-skinned hands with the missing finger reaching out as if for a bundle.

I drifted back to wakefulness, heard the hum of the tires and noted the light that was filling the sky, then fell back asleep. Deeply asleep. And I dreamed again.

SIXTH ✳ DREAM

The sixth dream, "The Wall of Time," yet again exposes Ben Brickman's ability to apprehend strings of experience from different planes of temporality. Ben has posited that within a few centuries all humans will be capable of "traveling" as he does in his dreams, and capable of doing so even more completely. Our frustration will not be that we wake up before we make any progress through the curves of time. Our frustration will come from the stress and overstimulation of breaking down the boundaries and barriers of normal perception. We will have to rethink what a human is, for humans will no longer be bound by a tiny span of time.

I am standing naked on a beach, facing the ocean. Behind me are a small shelter and a dying fire. To my left looms a vertical, brown, oozing membrane, connecting earth to sky. I walk to it and raise my hand. It ripples at my touch. I poke my fingers through it. It feels like Jell-o softly embracing my finger. I close my eyes and put my head through. I can tell from the touch of the membrane on the nerve endings of my facial skin that this is an ocean, not just a thin sheet—a vertical ocean stretching far beyond the initial translucence. I open my eyes inside it. I can see, in the slightly murky way one sees underwater. I try to see something in particular but can make out only brackish, backlit water. There is an immense light source far back in the ocean, but I cannot see it. I want to walk into the vertical ocean but am afraid to commit my whole body.

I call out for help. The call doesn't get far in the thick ocean. But then in a flash I see an old woman's face. She is about seventy, with long gray hair parted in the middle, eyes close together, thin-boned cheeks and a straight chin, and a dot on her forehead as if she is a Hindu. She's dressed in strange clothing. On her long shirt is sewn the word "Sandal." Behind her I can see spaceships and lines of cars floating in the air between city skyscrapers. In a second I understand that she is an inhabitant from the future, trying to communicate something to me. This vertical ocean makes the possibility of communication across time possible in some way.

Her lips are moving. She is talking in heavily accented English. I can pick out something like "twenty-four," then the words "He searches for you." She points to her head, then mouths the words "Travel without machine" then "You must come." She gestures with her arms for me to come to her but then she turns furtively to one side. Before she can look back at me, she fades away. I keep looking, but now there's just the brackishness. Where has she gone? Why has she gone? Will she come back? I wait. Nothing happens.

I close my eyes now, my head still in the vertical ocean. From inside my closed eyes I sense movement in the light, and so I open them; nothing. I close my eyes again, see light moving from inside the membrane of my eyelids, open my eyes quickly, but again nothing. Am I imagining the movement in the light? I realize there is no way to find out except to walk in all the way.

I place my right foot forward, through the membrane, then my left, then my torso. I'm in the ocean now, surrounded and embraced by a wetness that isn't wet.

I open my eyes.

And I wake up.

━━━━━━━━━━━━━━━━━━━━━━━━━━━━━━━━━━━━━

A terrible frustration swelled in me as I awoke on the bus next to the sleepers around me. I had almost stepped through a membrane of time. I knew that very clearly, though I couldn't say that anything except pure intuition gave me such certainty. I felt that I had been pushing and prodding the normal boundaries of perception in these dreams and never fully being allowed—or finding my way—through. Through to what? I didn't know. But in all cases there had been some kind of overt or covert sense of being asked into the future or into the unborn past. I was dreaming in ways that crossed the limits of life, but I could never fully penetrate.

Still half asleep, I pulled out my little pocket notebook and my pen

and wrote what I could. In the inverted bowl of the dawn sky, pinks, purples, and blues were reflected against one another. It was shockingly beautiful. Despite my frustration, I felt the immense safety a person can feel in
the lull of early morning, the warmth of my coat over my chest, the whispers around me of others gradually awakening. I yearned to slip back into
sleep, into that cozy secure morning calm, into the strange dream. Yet I
had to be satisfied simply to write down that while I had glimpsed the future, I had not been able to go there. Yet I sensed that in time I would. I
truly felt, at that moment of dawn, that nothing was impossible.

CHAPTER 6

The Hidden Map

> *Your sixth task as a mystic lies in discovering the story you are liv-*
>
> *ing. This discovery takes place in relationships with others, whose in-*
>
> *tuitions are a mirror for you. Your life story, the mythic journey you*
>
> *are living, clarifies like divine revelation. You feel and are the hero*
>
> *and the heroine. Your importance transcends you. You realize that*
>
> *now you know why you are here, embodied, on this earth.*
>
> *To open yourself to revelations, and thus the resolution of the*
>
> *sixth task, you must begin with full understanding of this: The*
>
> *breath of life that gives the form of your body its life carries with it a*
>
> *cosmic memory of who you are, in the same way that genes and cells*
>
> *remember what to do and how to do it. The cell knows what it is, and*
>
> *so do you.*
>
> *— The Magician*

Joseph opened his eyes and smiled at me. The white hair and side-burn on his right side were matted against his temple, shining with grease. We were pulling into the tiny town of Kor. Two seats behind me, an infant awoke with a squall, its mother's voice quickly soothing. It was 7:40 A.M., the street quiet, shops still closed up tight. The squat concrete buildings, gray in color, provided a bland contrast to the dawn sky.

The bus sighed to a stop at the station, and any serenity shattered in a commotion of humanity. Passengers greeted loved ones and gathered up luggage. Joseph immediately found us a taxi and asked to be taken to a small hotel, the Oteli Baş. As we drove, he explained to me that we would visit his relatives and friends, but first we would sleep and shower. The taxi sped along dusty, quiet roads to the hotel. We checked in, got a room with two beds, stripped to our underwear, and fell sound asleep at once.

I dreamt again. The dream of the island and the membrane returned, in more detail. Again I stood on the beach, wearing my brown bathing trunks by my small shelter and glowing fire. To my left was the vertical brown membrane. I walked to it and raised my hand. My finger rippled the sheet. I put my finger through it. I put my head through, closing my eyes at first, then opening them inside the ocean. Now through the membrane I did not see Sandal, the old woman; I saw myself lying back in the hotel room, sleeping in my boxers, here in Kor.

I pulled my head out of the ocean and pushed it back in—again the same scene. I was looking down on the hotel room as if hovering near the ceiling and watching myself and Joseph breathe in sleep. I was two selves in two worlds. I wanted to walk all the way into the oceanic wall, but again I felt paralyzed with fear. I pulled back out of the brown ocean onto the beach. I stared at a huge, unlimited wall. How, I wondered, could it remain so invisible to everyone in the "real world" when it was so obvious to me here? And where, I wondered, is this sandy island I'm on?

Dropping to my knees, I reached into the red coals of the fire. My hands felt the heat, but my skin did not burn. I stood up and looked out at the blue sea that separated this island from the shore. On the shore, about a mile away, was a seaside village. I walked into the low, lapping foam and on into the water as if toward that far shore. I felt afraid of walking into the vertical ocean, but not into this one. The water chilled me, though not severely. I walked forward till the water was up to my chest. I stood still for a moment. Then I turned back to my island shore, emboldened somehow, ready now to walk into the vertical ocean of hidden time and space.

But it was gone. All I saw was the island, the bivouac, the fire, cliffs behind.

I had again been afraid to enter the new world, and my fear had again cost me. Frustrated, I yelled out at the world and awoke in my hotel bed. My body sweated and shivered simultaneously, and it tingled as if a thousand insects were crawling on me.

"I'm losing it," I muttered, sitting up. "The damn Kulu-ander is still doing something." Scratching my arms and shoulders, I got out of bed and jostled Joseph awake.

"There's something still going on!" I cried. "Look at me. Are there insects on me? I can't see them." I had the light on by now, and he reached for his glasses as he blinked himself awake.

"What is it, my friend?" he murmured. "What has happened?"

I told him about the dream. The tingly feeling kept on as I talked, though lessening. I scratched myself as Joseph, at my insistence, searched my back for bugs. He found none, saying, "Perhaps they are spirits helping you." By the time my rush of words subsided, the itching began to subside also. He seemed to know the island and the village I spoke about.

"When you saw the village," he clarified, "did you see a water tower and a mosque next to it?"

In my mind's eye, I reviewed the scene from the dream. Yes, just as Joseph said—there was a water tower and mosque.

"How interesting. It is Kadı Kalesi, I believe."

"You know this place?" I asked.

He nodded. "It is a place at which the Magician has revealed himself to at least eleven of us."

"Is it near here?"

Instead of answering, he said, "You are flying again, between dimensions. You left your body during sleep. You went to a place the Magician finds comfortable. You are continually being inspired by visions from the near and far future. I do not understand yet why this is. You are seeing through an elemental form of time itself. The way this is happening to you—it goes even beyond anything I am familiar with."

"It felt like I was seeing something that is actually all around us at all times. It seems so real, the membrane . . ."

"There are many dimensions of experience existing at once, separated only by separation itself. All arguments about whether one or another is real or not real—these are the separation itself, the separation built into the human personality. When the arguing within the personality stops, we discover the elemental connection that makes up all things. You have slipped past the inherent separation of embodied life and glimpsed what most mystics sense but still don't quite see. One has to believe that Jesus and Moses and Buddha, and the other prophets of legend and history, have done this in their way. Now you are doing it in your way, a somewhat new way . . ."

He reached for the lamp. "Now it's time for us to get some more rest." As he clicked off the lamp, he said, "Later, tonight, with Sevda Hanım, many things will become clear." He had mentioned her already on the taxi ride to the hotel. I understood that she was a shaman and storyteller. "The feeling of insects," he pondered, as he settled back into his bed. "This is what the Hindus call *prana*, the vital life force. It is moving in your body, from your spine outward, and re-creating your cells, one by one. The hot and the cold are manifestations in the body of the cells restructuring. Many of the most powerful shamanic and spiritual rituals around the world, like sweat pits, sweat lodges, and *kwadi* rites, are based on sweating in heat and then jumping into cold. They do this because the contrast of hot and cold melds and molds our cells. Your emotions, your immune system, your mental capacities will all flex and flow at times uncontrollably over the next few days. Do not be surprised by sudden feelings, by fevers, by visions.

"My friend," he said in the dark, "let us go back to sleep. No more talk now."

He said it with firmness. I half thought he would interrupt his own silence with more words, but he did not. So I just said goodnight.

Lying awake in the dark, I thought about cell restructuring. Part of me wanted to measure what was happening. In my LSD and mescaline research we had been able to detect neurotransmitter alteration, some of it permanent. We had never measured changes in other cells of the body, but we had always assumed that if there were permanent neurotransmission alteration, the rest of the human being would gradually alter. Was this happening to me?

Around noon I awoke, hungry. Joseph had awakened first, showered, and gone downstairs to a little store, where he bought goat cheese, wrinkled black olives, and crackers. By the time I awoke, he had set them on the little hotel room table with napkins for plates. We feasted on these.

Then it was my turn to shower. When I got out I was refreshed but as exhausted and tired as ever. I didn't want to miss a second of whatever Joseph had planned; nonetheless I said honestly, "Joseph, I'm worn out. Do I have time to just lie down again?" In fact, he did have some things to do and people to see without me. "The drug itself is quite potent," he added. "Some people have been known to sleep on and off for twenty-four hours after taking it. Go back to sleep now. This evening we have friends to meet, and then we will take the overnight bus to Ankara."

So it was that I did not see Joseph until evening. I had planned to get up in midafternoon and wander about the small town, but I slept until he woke me at 5:30 P.M. I hadn't slept through the afternoon like this in years.

Joseph said his cousin Mehmet was due at six with his car, and we would eat at his aunt and uncle's house. From there we would walk to Sevda Hanım's house, on the outskirts of the little town.

We waited in front of the hotel for Mehmet to pull up. A big, jovial man, he was about ten years younger than Joseph, darker-skinned, with a decisive Asian slant to his eyes. He spoke no English and only a little German. When we got to his parents' home, there were greetings, kisses, and hugs. Mehmet's parents, in their eighties, both looking as much Chinese as Middle Eastern, were bent and feeble but very gracious; they laid out a banquet for us, most of it prepared by Mehmet's mother, a tiny woman Joseph referred to as Auntie Necla.

There were at least ten *mezeler*, appetizers served on little metal plates: oysters, bean salad, tiny fish, olives, cheeses. Then Auntie Necla and her niece brought out something called *mantı*, a food like ravioli but smaller, rounder, crusted from frying and served in a yogurt-and-tomato soup. I leaned over to Joseph during an ebb in their rapid Turkish conversation: "This is the best food I've ever had!" Joseph translated, and Auntie Necla, immensely delighted, gave me a hug. I thanked her in the bit of Turkish I knew. Joseph invited me to learn a more idiomatic expression: "When we like someone's cooking, we say '*Eline sağlık,*' 'Health to your hands.'"

I spoke the words and she beamed, responding. "*Afiyet olsun,*" or, as Joseph translated, "*Bon appétit.*"

She grinned. *Çok güzel Türkçe konuşiorsunuz.*" Joseph translated: "You speak very good Turkish." I understood now, realizing that she had used the respectful, formal ending to the verb *konuşmak,* "to speak." If she were treating me like a kid, which she had a right to do—I was fifty years younger—she would have said, "*konuşiorsun,*" addressing me in the equivalent of *tu* in Spanish or *du* in German. But she addressed me in the *Usted* or *Sie* form of her language, giving me the respect due a fully grown man.

The later courses of her meal involved lamb dishes with mint leaves, fruit plates, fish, another soup, and two exotic salads. We ate elaborately and richly in the way I recognize now to be part of the mystical approach to life. For those people, at that moment of human communion, eating was a doorway to soul.

Afterward the women cleaned up, with the help of a neighbor girl who came over. The women refused my help. I asked Joseph to explain that in America I had been brought up to help clear the table and do the dishes. Joseph obliged, but the women laughed. Joseph escorted me into a small living room filled with old furniture of an Ottoman flavor—the floor covered with two layers of Turkish carpets, the walls filled with miniature scenes painted on flattened bone. In what was clearly an after-dinner ritual, Joseph, Mehmet, and I each smoked a cigarette. I didn't usually smoke, but the room was so small that it was either smoke one or swim around lost in their secondhand smoke.

Over the next hour many different people came over, all of them somehow Joseph's relatives or friends, or congregants who remembered Joseph's father. Some of the younger people spoke a little English and directed me toward the TV set, where *Dallas* flickered. Listening to JR and the other southerners in dubbed Turkish was as shocking as it was funny. I tried to explain how bizarre this seemed to me, with little success. Then a man about forty, who had just come back from Germany, joined the group, giving me a conversational companion.

At nearly ten o'clock, some people began to leave and Joseph announced that we would now visit Sevda Hanım. Though it had been two years since the people around us had seen Joseph, their native son, they let go of him without much fuss. I gathered from their tones of voice and nods of approval that Sevda Hanım's name carried a great deal of weight. The man who spoke German confirmed my suspicion: "If Jusuf Bey has brought you here to meet Sevda Hanım, it is a great honor. He must think highly of you."

We said our many good-byes and gave our many thanks. Cradled in the food, good humor, and nurturing love of these relatives and friends of Joseph, I experienced a much-needed respite from the constant and relentless spiritual experiences of the last twenty-four hours. We set out from the house on foot down a dirt street that led us onto a paved main road. Joseph suggested we stop at Evran Pasha Camii mosque in the center of town.

Except for lights emanating from within houses, the streets were dark. There were family noises everywhere, kids talking, two adults yelling. On the street a block ahead, some boys kicked a soccer ball in the dimness.

Both Joseph and I felt enlivened as we walked, happy to be out in the night. "There"—Joseph pointed toward a street—"I believe that is the place where the horse . . . yes. I will tell you, my friend, a story of my mother. Shall I tell you of my mother?"

"I'd like that," I said. Joseph never stopped asking my permission. It was like Necla using the formal form of the verb—I felt respected in a way I hadn't back in America. There I was just an average guy that no one paid much attention to. In the last couple of days, here, people measured me by my highest, not my lowest, common denominator.

We came to a row of closed shops that offered metal goods. Copper bowls and trays filled the windows. Behind the buildings someone must have been working, for we could hear a rhythmic banging of hammer on metal.

"Mother was a pretty woman," Joseph recalled, "with black hair and dark brown eyes, very short but very powerful. As boys will do, I loved her with an ardor I could not describe. Always I knew that when God did not relinquish an answer to a question of the heart my mother could. Often I went to her after spending hours as a student in my father's study or after hours with my friend Celi in the market. I'd find her supervising the girls at prayer or speaking in her quiet, respected tone with congregants' wives over tea. I watched her and felt both awe and empthy, for I did not think her altogether happy and I did not know why, not then, as a boy, living in the spell of family life. Once I asked her about her sadness. She called me dear but wrong. Once I asked my father. He said, 'God restricts every life. Your mother is a free spirit. Her life is too restricted in my shadow. Yet we do God's will, for the greater good. My son,' he said, 'you can do no better than to love her as you love God.'"

Joseph's brown eyes watered a little more than usual, glistening in the moonlight. We had stopped walking now, and he looked around at the street corner.

"The morning I remember occurred in my eleventh year, just here." He pointed down at the dusty sidewalk. "I walked back home after prayer, just past Sali Bey's metal shop, where I discovered three men beating a fourth with sticks and feet. The horse of the beaten man snorted to get free of the reins that held her to a post—just there." He was seeing it all again as he talked to me. "The mare's eyes, a deep brown like my mother's, caught mine in silent pleading. Its legs kicked up as if seeing me had inspired it, and it broke the reins and attacked one of the aggressing men. The men turned on it, but only briefly, for the beast was more powerful. Running away, they crossed the dirt street and ran past the mosque. I calmed the horse and helped the injured man to my mother's care. Others had come out by now to help us. The man lived, and for three days I tended to the mare. My mother called me the Protector, a great blessing to me. It is so good to be named well for one's good deeds."

Joseph nodded us to move forward. "Look there, past that corner, that is where Celi lived. Let's look. These would be his relations, there at the television." We peeked in a window and saw people watching an old black-and-white. "I think we won't stop. It will take so long. But Celi, I will tell you about him, my best friend as a young boy. Now he has moved to Antalya." We walked a block or so, turning a corner. "Being with you, my friend, has inspired my memory.

"I remember so vividly the morning before Celi's *sünnet*, the ritual circumcision. He and I were both seven. There was a garden there." Two flat gray houses stood in the space he pointed to. "I came upon him that morning and saw my friend intent on a budding lilac bush. He kissed the unopened buds of the bush and ran his face among the buds and smelled them and kissed them again, and then, moving to the bud of a lilac at the tip of all other buds, he kissed it, his eyes closed, as if kissing a lover, but with a look of grief on his face too, like he would lose this lover. I turned away and met him later for the *sünnet*, where he succumbed to the ritual knife, and in his cry of pain, when he lost the bud off his penis, I saw why Celi had kissed the buds with his look of loss. We were the kind of friends that happen only a few times in a life: we were each other's spirit tenders.

"There, you see the minaret?"

I followed his finger to a minaret two blocks away, the mosque itself still hidden from view behind buildings. It must have been a small mosque, for it had only one minaret.

"Come," he said, "let's cross the street." We waited for a car to go by. He took my elbow, acting for a second not like his usual confident self but like an invalid old man who needed help.

"I will tell you, Ben, it was here on this street I lost my spiritual innocence." We had gotten to the other side and now had a clearer view of the mosque up the street. Joseph stopped, pointing to the pavement. "It was here I, just nine years old, walked with my father. Shall I tell you? An old man can bore the world with his story."

"No. Please tell me."

He considered something for a moment, then continued. "I had just listened to my father preach and became filled with a sudden misgiving, a distrust of the father. You see, I heard him preach that morning from An-Nur, Surah twenty-four, the Light Surah. In this section of the Koran, which emphasizes how the light of God is revealed in the homes of believers, the Koran seems also to reveal male domination over the female. I heard him call this domination a pillar of our faith, yet the night before, he had expressed, in our home, another view, a view more like an ocean than a pillar. When, after the preaching, I was alone with my father, walking home, and right here at this spot, I explained my confusion: 'Father, I did not understand.' I think I wanted to say, 'Father, I'm afraid,' for I was a very sensitive boy. My father said to me, 'Don't be afraid of my uncertainty, my son. When I am uncertain of what to teach the flock, I teach tradition. Tradition is the gift of our people from our ancestors. Not all things can be clear to the teacher at all moments. So we have our traditions to guide us. Perhaps you will see better than these traditions, but I cannot.'

"I said, 'But, Father, if *you* don't know what is *your* truth about something, how can you teach anything?'

"He liked my questioning. He smiled as we walked. 'My son,' he asked, 'must I know *every* truth in order to teach *the* truth?'

"I said nothing, letting his question, which was more complex, I sensed, than at first hearing, wash through my mind and into my soul. There, in my magic boyish soul, my answer came; 'Yes, you must.' It was the first answer from my boyhood that opposed my father. I realized at that moment—though it was not clear to me until years later—that a suspiciousness of organized religion is essential, for religion is not a perfection, and God and religion are often not the same thing.

"I said, 'Father, I am not at peace with what we have said.'

"He embraced me, here on this street corner, he embraced me, and years later, myself a father, I realized what he had seen in his mind's eye during that embrace: he saw his son's path, which would be one of rigorous learning and some confusion. He murmured so I could hear him, 'Allahu ekbar, God is great,' murmuring into my churning thoughts the best secret he knew."

Joseph touched my shoulder gently. "We'll glance into the mosque and then find Sevda Hanım."

The small mosque was just ahead of us now, a dome and a minaret.

"Your father sounds like a very wise man," I said. Though of a different land and different generation, Joseph's father sounded a little like mine: smart, sensitive, dwelling in the worlds of intellect and spirit, a man who loved his son as best he could.

"Yes," Joseph agreed. "He understood energies and the life of the soul, though his views became too orthodox for me, and increasingly less open, as he got older."

Unlike you, Joseph, I thought silently.

Joseph didn't strike me as a rigid man. In his sixties, he was more intellectually relaxed than I. I felt a surge of delight, a surge like light moving through me, as I glimpsed myself at Joseph's age, ageless.

"When did your dad die?" I asked out of curiosity. The mosque was a one-dome structure, dirty tan in color, the usual loudspeaker like a black nest halfway up the minaret, the front door illuminating seven or eight men taking off their shoes.

"In 1944. He predicted my meeting with the Magician. I will tell you. I was there with my father on his deathbed to receive his blessing, as children and loved ones will do: an important day for me, at twenty years of age. I had returned home, on leave from my military service, to be there. I cannot forget, even now, his words to me." He trailed off, remembering, eyes far away.

"My father called me close. 'My son, you must find a way to be both a creator, full of passion, and a monk, your soul at peace. Look for someone to teach you this way. I,' he said, 'I have been torn between the agitation of creativity and the search for calm bliss, the two polar paths of the mystic. I see that you too choose every day between action and contemplation and feel pulled by the one not chosen. I hope for you that you end the choosing and find a way to unite both. The path of this unity, I see now on my deathbed, is the path of creating not images but light itself. You will meet the keeper of the light, my son, and learn to create the light itself in all things you do, no matter how mundane. This, I think, is your destiny.'

"Though I could not fully understand his meaning—'create light itself'—I kissed his hand, as is our custom, and then he mine, and we wept. Then he turned to my sister. I listened to the blessings he gave all our family, my heart aching with death. Ben, I must confess I am only now, forty years later, coming to understand what he meant, how to move beyond the contradiction between being and doing. At the moment of blessing, I yearned to cry, 'Father, don't go yet, teach me *how* to bring together the hermit and the soldier, the creator and the monk. Oh, my yearning at that moment! Thank God I realized before my words escaped that I must not ask my father any more questions. My father had taught me all that he knew. It was my time now. It was my world now.

"I clutched his hand in the lonely nights. Two days later, he died. He left me in the great paradox of the mystic: how can a spirit-driven person be both utterly creative, like God at the tumult of creation, enamored of His diversities and yet utterly harmonious, like the quiet breath of a sleeping child, complete in unity?"

"Yes," I breathed. "How?"

We had come to the mosque. I wondered about my father, where he was right now, how he was. I yearned to hold his hand when he lay on his deathbed. Scenes flashed: he and I fishing at a beaver pond in Wyoming, he driving our family to the Adirondacks, he on a stage directing actors, he clipping the hedges in our backyard in North Carolina. I felt loving toward him, very forgiving.

"Thank you," I murmured to Joseph, under my breath, "for the gift of that story."

Joseph braced himself on my shoulder with a stiff arm while he changed his shoes and put on mosque sandals. When he was done, I sat on the step and took my tennis shoes off. Slipping on sandals, I stood back from Joseph as he spoke vibrantly, but in a low voice, to an old acquaintance he met just inside. The man wore a very long beard, a turban, and some kind of religious garment like a caftan in gray and black layers. Joseph introduced me in Turkish. I shook the man's hand, murmuring polite greetings. Following their example, I picked a small prayer rug from a stack near a pillar and carried it to an empty spot on the floor between other congregants, who bowed in prayer. The man laid his small rug down, Joseph laid his beside his friend's, and I lay mine next to Joseph's.

To Joseph I whispered, "I've never prayed like a Muslim before."

"Please do not," he said firmly. "You do not know the gestures and the meanings. Just sit on your knees and watch."

I did as asked, and for the first time I noticed the immense variety and complexity of Muslim gestures: lips kissed the carpet, arms came out, hands opened, palms upward, then closed, faces touched carpet again. The repetition and variety, an oceanic rhythm of a hundred synchronized bod-

ies, pulled at my soul. Though Joseph had admonished me not to partici-
pate I felt pulled to experience some of the gestures. I bent forward, my
face to the carpet, and kissed it in a humility of spirit like a bird dipping
into its nest to feed its young. I raised back up, sat on my knees aikido
style, and closed my eyes, listening to sighs, breath, the tiny snap of earth
kisses, and garments that moved like the sound of paper.

When I opened my eyes again, I saw that Joseph had finished. The service continued, but he rose, pulled up his prayer rug, and replaced it in the
stack against the wall. I followed him and did the same but found that I did
not want to go. The energy of the little mosque had welcomed me with
open arms. Had I become a Muslim for a moment? I had felt completely at
home among the turbaned men, kissing the ground. I had felt pure love
like this in churches, near rivers, in temples, in basement meeting houses,
and now in a mosque. It was the openness of the heart, the return for an
hour of the human soul to the place of its origin.

Joseph had trouble getting away from the mosque: a man recognized him
and wanted to talk. When we finally set out again on foot, I told Joseph
how good the Muslim prayer had felt. "You will feel at home wherever divine moments can occur," he smiled. "You are mystic, my friend. You are
being transformed into a butterfly." He grinned at this radiant little
metaphor.

"Look there"—he pointed—"there's Ahmet Bey's son. Let us get a
ride from him. Must a mystic always walk?"

We laughed together, jogging across the street to talk to a village man
about my age. Once Joseph told him what we needed, we jumped into the
man's very run-down, smelly Ford Galaxy. All over Turkey I had noticed
big American cars from the late sixties and seventies. The rear shocks in
this Ford were, in a word, shot. We bounced in potholes and then turned
out of the town, driving through a field. Ahmet, a tall, mustached man,
talked nonstop with Joseph in rapid Turkish, with words from something
else, Arabic or Persian or maybe Kurdish, thrown in.

I noticed the half-moon and bright stars as we bounced along toward
our destination. Bathed in moonlight, we arrived at the outskirts of town

and lurched to a stop outside what I presumed to be our driver's house. He invited us in, but Joseph politely refused, and we walked up a village street. The driver, or someone else in his house, must have recently journeyed to Mecca, for the door was painted green, the sign of a return from a successful pilgrimage. We walked past other such doors.

Throughout this villagey part of town, the houses were mostly low, one-story, concrete with some kind of adobe finish, colored gray or white. There were no streetlights. Through one open window I saw a young woman walking into a back room, an older woman teaching a girl to do embroidery. We avoided mud in the road and walked past what Joseph said was a schoolhouse. Light emanated from behind its thinly curtained window.

In a doorway, some children squatted with their mother and older sister. I greeted them in Turkish, prompting the children to follow us, tossing questions at us and making gestures like pushing a camera shutter. Joseph explained to them that I had no camera, but they did not lose interest. We passed boys playing soccer in the moonlight with a half-flat basketball. They paused to talk about us. To our left we passed an open tavern, a television mounted on a shelf near the ceiling. *Dynasty,* dubbed into Turkish as *Dallas* had been earlier, entertained the men. It was smoke-filled, crowded, and loud, with backgammon and other games going on at tables and drinks, mainly milky *rakı,* going down throats. The huge hall held what seemed to be every man in the village. Cars pulled up front as men arrived from the mosque service, now gathering in community here at the meeting house. It seemed like a fun, raucous place, and I wanted to stop there, but we had another destination: the world of women.

Sevda Hanım was tiny and very old. She sat near a stove with a small group of village women and children around her in a small room. Paint peeled where chairs had scraped the walls. Couches, hard chairs, and floor cushions filled the room.

For a moment I became the center of the scene, Joseph answering questions about me. Like the village boys up the street, some of the young girls here asked if I had a camera. Villagers, Joseph explained, have no cameras; they love tourists taking their pictures. Polaroids especially. I apologized for not having brought a camera with me tonight. I wished Joseph had told me to bring one. Photography was an easy magic to prac- tice here. Instead, I did two quick magic tricks for the small crowd: a coin- and-tissue trick, using my own handkerchief, and a coin-and-cup trick, using a small coffee cup that sat on a table. The kids loved these and sat fascinated while Joseph took a quiet moment to get reacquainted with the adults. One of the older girls tried out her halting English on me, asking me to teach her how to do the coin-and-cup trick. I told her a magician must never reveal his secrets, and she hid her disappointment well, saying something to the other girls with a mischievous look that made them all giggle wildly.

Most of the women wore colorful village clothing, and all wore head scarves that showed hair and face. I knew that because the scarves didn't cover all the facial features and hair, these weren't very orthodox people— traditional, but not religiously orthodox. They sat knitting, sewing, talk- ing, drinking tea, the children, except when distracted by me, doing similar tasks as the adults.

Sevda Hanım's eyes were grainy, nose flat, lips skinny and pale, body emaciated, wrists bony. As she and Joseph exchanged comments and laughs about my tricks, I asked the girl who spoke a little English to get me some thread. She got some from an old woman near her, and I did a hand- string trick called "The Web" just for her. She beamed. Then Sevda Hanım said something to her, which she acknowledged by standing up and relinquishing her chair to me. Joseph sat next to Sevda Hanım and I next to him. These chairs stood to her left, so that the chairs in the room were all in a kind of circle, but I had the feeling our chairs were now like chairs sat in by guests of honor.

The chatting died down as attention turned to Sevda Hanım, who said something in Turkish that brought seriousness to the crowd. Two older girls brought us tea, and Sevda Hanım obviously asked Joseph to say some things to me, because Joseph acknowledged her comments with a nod, then turned to me. He told me to remember that Sevda Hanım was a holy woman, a shaman. People came from the city to see her for astro-

logical advice, psychic readings, and storytelling—she could divine a person's destiny. "She'll reveal it in a story," he explained. "She takes a measure of who you are, using a valuable item you will give her, an item that
has been touching your skin and therefore your energy, for a long time.
Then she tells the story she sees." She sounded to me like psychics I'd
gone to over the years. Very few of them had helped me in more than general ways.

"We shall have a story tonight," she said, "a story to celebrate your
coming, young brother." Joseph translated, and I thanked her politely. Her
bony hand came out, palm up, as if she wanted money. "Give her something you cherish," Joseph instructed. "She will return it if you wish. Most
people, however, do not wish the item returned."

I had money, credit cards, that kind of thing. It didn't seem right to
give her those. Joseph confirmed that it must be more personal. "Watch
her eyes," he told me. Indeed, she looked me over. She seemed to look especially at my hands, folded on my lap. She must be looking at my ring, I
realized, the simple turquoise-on-silver my mother had given me. How
could I give her that? But then her eyes moved to my wrist. She was eye-
ing my watch, a Seiko my father had given me for my eighteenth birthday,
a graduation present.

"Joseph, I can't give her that," I said emphatically. "My father gave it
to me over a decade ago."

"Trust that your father will bless the use of his gift this way. Every father wants his son to learn the map of his destiny."

I took the watch off my wrist and handed it to her, bowing a little. She
thanked me, clasped it between her palms, let them settle into her skinny
lap, and closed her eyes.

Everyone joined her in silence, as at a Quaker service on a Sunday
morning. Even the dog just sat. I bowed my head awaiting whatever would
happen next.

After about two minutes she began to chant, a droning chant without
words. Then she began to speak, a kind of invocation that seemed to mark
the beginning of the "reading." Joseph translated: "My young brother, I see
into your soul with my eyes. If you wish, I shall tell you the story that
I see."

"Please tell the story," I replied respectfully.

"My brother, I see that there are an apple farmer and his wife, unhappy with each other. The wife gave birth to five sons, the fifth a special boy they called Keloğlan, 'the bald boy,' for he came out of the womb bald and was already wise.

"As he grew up, he was smarter and wiser than his fellows. His father chose to live in a hut far away in the orchard, and his mother spun a web of violence and affection for her son. Her rages were famous in every valley and mountaintop. Even the trees became quiet when she wielded her whips and her sticks. She attacked her youngest son, for a time, more than all others, so great was her love of him and therefore her fear of him.

"But Keloğlan was blessed and watched by the angels. Even when his parents sent him to a soul doctor, who, filled with spooks, tried to drown his soul in liquids of the flesh, still the angels watched over the boy."

This old woman was telling my life story! From touching my watch! I couldn't believe it. My violent mother, my parents' divorce, Dr. Francis. I wanted to say something to Joseph but stopped myself from interrupting the flow.

Why five brothers, though? I didn't have five brothers.

"One day when Keloğlan was twelve, all the older brothers had gone into the far orchard to tend the apples; their mother remained behind with Keloğlan, very tired; she said to him, 'My son, you will be a man in a few more years. Learn what it is to be a woman first, so that you will always respect all women, unlike what so many men do.'

"'Mother,' he replied, 'how shall I learn this?'

"'Grow inside yourself a womb, grow it there.' She touched his stomach with her finger, and he felt the womb growing inside.

"'İçime kürt dusdu!' he said with a delighted laugh, for he felt a worm growing inside his womb, and it tickled him there."

What was this about? What worm had I grown inside me?

"The years went by. The mother and father died. Keloğlan became an apple farmer. Keloğlan coupled with many women, but always the couplings were difficult, for always between them was a bulging, this womb inside him. As he came closer and closer to his woman, the bulge grew, making their lives difficult. They were unable to make a soul together, they had no children. Keloğlan was often sick to his stomach, feeling the pangs come from the womb in his stomach, as if it wished to give birth."

Not only had I had many unfulfilling relationships with lovers, I had suffered from lactose intolerance that had kept me constantly sick and in gut pain through my mid- to late twenties. I had only identified and treated it at twenty-eight, just a couple of years back.

"One day Keloğlan found a soul doctor who helped him give birth to the child that was in the womb. The child was his mother, curled up in there, dead." The soul doctor must be my therapist, Andy Helt, who had shown me that I must resolve my hatred and fear of my mother.

Now Sevda Hanım paused for about three minutes. Again no one said anything. I leaned to Joseph and whispered, "She's really right about a lot!" He didn't look at me and only acknowledged this with a smile, holding himself in a state of stillness like hers. A little embarrassed, I closed my eyes.

"One night," Sevda Hanım continued, "the Dark Goddess came to Keloğlan in a dream. She wore the face of his mother. She said, 'You must dig and burrow. Go and find the castle.'

"One day soon after, Keloğlan discovered that something was eating his apples during the night. He hid behind a tree in order to watch and saw a giant come to his orchard. Keloğlan followed it as it left his orchard at dawn. He followed it to a faraway castle. Inside this castle the giant disappeared into a hole, and Keloğlan decided to follow it down. Too late he realized that the sides of the hole were slippery, easy to slide down but impossible to climb up. Too late, he realized he was stuck underground forever. He found himself at the bottom of the hole, in the dark, wandering toward a giant's dangerous lair.

"But Keloğlan had courage. And he was protected by angels. He crept into the lair and found himself in the center of a cave, where a torch lit the darkness. In the light he saw the giant working at a table on the far wall. Nearer to him, chained to the wall of the cave, was a beautiful young woman, the beloved Light Goddess, Serpil.

"'I have been in this hole a long time,' she whispered to him, 'waiting for you to free me. I have learned how to kill the giant, but I cannot do it while bound in these chains. Here is what you must do: take your knife and cut off his ankles, then his knees, then his waist, then he will come down to your level. Then you cut off his head. To kill him you must cut off his head. In his head, you will find another being.'

"Because Keloğlan had grown a womb inside him, he knew the power of woman, and he did not, from male pride, resist Serpil's wise in-struction.

"Like a silent stalker, he crept up behind the giant and lashed at the huge ankles from behind, slicing through them. Then he quickly severed the knees. The bellowing, wounded giant swatted the bald boy, bruised him, broke his bones, but Keloğlan kept cutting until he had cut off the head. Inside the head he found the dark Goddess, who thanked him for liberating her and rose upward into the rock ceiling and disappeared."

What the hell was that all about? The story was getting too far out, but she continued.

"Keloğlan had only enough strength to unchain Serpil, who then nursed his wounds. For days, they drank from an underwater spring and ate the meat of the giant's body. When Keloğlan had recovered, he and Serpil made their way back to the bottom of the hole that had led them into the cave. Looking upward, they saw light and in that light the moving shadow of a huge white bird, a stork."

A stork! That's what the bird on the tower in Istanbul had been—a stork!

"Keloğlan and Serpil called up to the wise bird for help. The bird flew down the deep well hole and spoke to them. 'I will help you,' the magical bird promised. 'I will carry you on my back. You must feed me meat when I yell "Gaaak" and water when I yell "Geeek," for you are heavy and the flight is difficult, and the magic has its price.'

"Serpil drew water from the giant's cave into a gourd, and Keloğlan shoved meat from the giant's body into a bag. The two lovers mounted the bird. 'Geeeek,' it yelled as it flew, and Serpil gave it water; 'Gaaak,' and Keloğlan gave it food. Just near the top of the hole, they ran out of water and meat. 'Geeeek!' came the cry. Serpil cut her arm and gave the bird her blood. 'Gaaaak!' came the cry. Keloğlan cut his leg and gave the bird his flesh and muscle.

"When they came up out of the hole, the stork said, 'You have proven yourselves. You have given of yourself for the common good.' He pulled back from his throat Serpil's blood and Keloğlan's flesh and returned these to the lovers' bodies. 'You, Keloğlan, are one with Serpil. You are the gifted one, the Messenger.' "

There were nods and murmurs among the women in the little room. Everyone looked at me. They did not seem surprised by what Sevda had just said.

"It's the next sign," Joseph murmured. "I'm not surprised."

"He is the Messenger," Sevda Hanım repeated. "*O Haberci olior.* You told me you might be bringing the Messenger to my house, Joseph Abi, and you were right."

"It's too much," I said to Joseph. "She's talking about 'the Messenger,' right?"

"Quite clearly, my friend."

"Wow," was all I could say. I looked into his eyes and realized I had known this was coming. The amazing dreams I'd been having, the quickness with which Joseph and the others in Istanbul had accepted me, the hints about my having a destiny, the connection of my magic with the Magician, the audiographic memory I had—hinted at in Istanbul when Unal and Engin and Saadet had suggested that there was some holy text or words I would have to remember—all this pointed to my being the messenger. I resisted the idea not only because it seemed so egotistical of me— after all, I was clearly no "wise man"—but also because it felt so weird, so cultish. I hadn't encountered the Magician, and I had enough "science" in me to feel that it was all some sort of hallucination in which I was embroiled. But I had trusted Joseph and the feeling that something unusual was unfolding. The experiences I'd had in the last few days had been amazing. I trusted the feeling that whatever this unfolding Magician story was, I had an important part to play.

Everyone looked at me in silence, waiting for me to speak. I told Joseph what I had been thinking just now, and he translated. Sevda Hanım got quite a bit of delight from my face, which must have shown a combination of confusion, resignation, and, still, some suspicion. Her small body vibrated, and her face lit up.

She looked at me in a grandmotherly way and finished her story. "Keloğlan offered the stork safekeeping: 'My family lives close to here. Please come with us.'

"The stork said he could not remain just now but would return. Before he flew off he said, 'As I am the bringer of the unborn to the born world, I will be your magic animal and aid you in your destiny, which is to help other humans accomplish enlightenment, the second birth.' Bathed in light, the stork flew off.

"Keloğlan and Serpil returned to his orchard. Keloğlan and Serpil decided to marry. A village grew up around the orchard. Keloğlan and Serpil lived joyfully. As promised, the stork came again to Keloğlan and taught him the principles of magical life, so that Keloğlan could teach them to others."

Finished with her story, Sevda Hanım smiled and put the watch on her bony wrist, where it dangled more like a bracelet than a timepiece. One of the other women rose, then another, to bring us more tea. There was an energy of both admiration and tension in the room.

I said, "Joseph, when did you think I was . . . well . . . you know—supposed to be more than just a traveling son of your friend Harry?"

"Since I saw you at the Café du Thé I think I knew, my friend. But then, one must wait to really know."

Sevda Hanım started talking again, and I saw that she was touching the watch again on her wrist. Joseph translated.

"Your father gave you this watch at a place in your country where the buttes are high and the sand is red. You came to this place in a green car shaped like a box. You did not wear the spectacles you wear now. Your father wore these spectacles. Your father gave you the watch and the car. You embraced. This was a rare embrace between you. Below you were three boys climbing the butte in their shirt sleeves."

She had an amazing gift! My father and I had indeed driven on a Sunday in northern New Mexico toward the southern Ute reservation in his green 1967 Chevy Nova. He had gold wire-rimmed glasses like the ones I wore now when I wasn't wearing contacts. There were three boys climbing up the butte too.

"She's completely accurate," I said to Joseph.

"Once she touches that watch," said Joseph, "seeing into your life is not difficult. Listen carefully to her interpretation of how you and Keloğlan are the same map of energy. She has said to you an important thing today, my friend, by naming you the messenger."

Sevda Hanım began again in her creaky, droning voice. "You have rich gifts, young brother, but you have not understood their use. You guard yourself too closely, convinced you have no people, no tribe. This is the malady of your generation. It is also the doorway to the vast human future.

"Throughout your life you have met strangers who help you. You are the kind of man strangers want to teach and to love. In your own hidden way, you fear this. You think not strangers but family should help you. Go out, find strangers, and make them your family. You are a Wanderer, but know that you are a magnet for Travelers, spirits of great power who inspire you.

"You are watched over by the spirit in the stork, the magical bird who brings life. This bird has the longest memory among the birds.

"Now we will stop, and I will enjoy the gift of time you have given me. The door of pure energy is closing. I wish you well, Messenger. All will become clear."

She closed her eyes and relaxed, closing off her mind. I didn't understand everything she had said and meant, but I felt moved by her concentration, her vision of me. I thanked her and asked Joseph if I could shake her hand. He nodded, and I stood up in the middle of the roomful of women and shook her ancient, bony hand. She surprised me by embracing me, her face, like Joseph's, only coming to about my chest.

We sat back down as more tea came in. "Joseph," I said with a laugh, almost giddy. "What an amazing journey I'm having!"

"Yes, you are," he agreed. "Everyone in their lives is a messenger of love. But not everyone gets the chance you are getting, to reach so deeply into the heart of the human community."

Trays of cookies were now being put out on a wooden table. I reached for one—curious to experience yet another exquisite new taste—when the front door opened. One of the women who had been knitting, a tall, skinny grandmother, hustled in a young woman about eighteen years old, who held a crying baby. Following behind her were another woman and a man, who guided his son into the room in a makeshift wheelchair, hand-made from bicycle wheels and wooden crates.

Joseph understood what was happening before I did and immediately engaged the newcomers in a heated dispute. I understood none of it, only that the people pointed to me. Now a middle-aged woman came in the door with a teenage girl. Her name, Büna, appeared in the conversation a number of times as her mother pointed her finger at the girl. By now the room had become crowded and tense. Büna just stared at me, forcing my eyes away.

"*Tamam! Bitti!*" Sevda Hanım yelled into the fray. She spoke to Joseph in a commanding tone. He argued a little but then seemed to resign himself. When they had worked something out between them, he turned to me.

"Ben, do you know what is happening?" he asked.

"I don't. Is something wrong? The girl, Büna, keeps staring at me."

"Büna is an autistic child. The boy, Efram, is paralyzed on his right side—his right leg gave out about six months ago, according to his father. There is little medical help for either of them. The baby is colicky and never sleeps more than an hour at a time. Each of these families has come to you now because they believe that there is a chance that you, the Messenger, can heal their children. You see, the word has spread about you already."

"Are you serious?"

"Very serious. I have told them you should not embark on anything of that kind for months at least, and certainly not until your ritual initiation is complete and the Magician has come to you. But these people are desperate, as any parent would be. Sevda Hanım believes you should lay your hands on the children to satisfy the people, even if no healing occurs now. Will you please do it, as a hopeful act, if nothing else?"

I had no idea what to think. "Should I?" I asked, feeling like a boy asking his father's advice.

"Yes. Try it. Empty your mind, take your time, close your eyes if you wish. Move your hands along the surface of the child's body, just above the clothes. Feel the body as if you are listening for something like a bulge of sound, a place of unrest. When you feel it, touch your fingers to it, place your palm on it. As you mentally step aside to let divine healing move through you, the work will be done through you by the eternal energy of healing that is everywhere. You may feel heat in your hands. Just do as you are moved to do."

"Have you done this before? How do you know about it?"

"I have been involved in healings. Yes. Your power to heal is, however, far greater than mine, I think."

"But Joseph, what if nothing happens? I feel like I'm sinking in quicksand here!"

"There is nothing to be done except what will be done. These people are fatalists, Ben, they will accept fate. But at least you will have tried."

As I had listened to him, my body had heated up with embarrassment. I tried to smile at the newcomers, who saw me as some sort of doctor or healer. If only you knew! I wanted to cry out.

Sevda Hanım said something that prompted the woman carrying the baby to come up to me. I moved to her as well, passing instantly into an aikido trance just to stay calm. I reached my hands out toward the baby, whose crying was irritating us all. "Feel the baby," Joseph reminded me, "use your hands like an artist's hands."

I put my open palms toward the baby's swaddled feet. Closing my eyes, I slowly moved my hands upward. I felt nothing out of the ordinary, just my own severe self-consciousness. My palms moved along the baby toward its chest: still nothing. Up to its head: still nothing. But now the baby whimpered, not a full cry. I opened my eyes to look at it. Its eyes had opened. The mother looked down at its face, smiling. That's why it stopped crying, I thought, because its mother's there. But the tiny black eyes stared up at *me* from a gaunt brown face. I was aware of an invisible mesh over the baby's face, a mesh of heat, not something literally there, but something just between my palms, a membrane between the baby and me, like wrinkles of heat that rise off a desert road.

Now something was definitely happening. I moved my palms around the baby's head, watching the heat mesh that surrounded the skull like a plaster mask. The baby, curious, did not cry now. The room around me was utterly silent except for human breathing. Indeed, as Joseph had indicated, I felt heat now, no bulge of sound or cacophony but definitely heat, all around the head. I sensed I had to cool the head. I was the one sensing this yet it wasn't me. I was in service of some larger, fuller force of energy. As if this larger force suddenly turned my inner furnace off, I felt myself cooling down, my hands cooling down, my palms touching the face now and cooling it.

As I touched the face, I felt a bulge of sound. It was somewhere behind the left eye, a bulging I could not feel physically, like a lump on skin, but a bulging like a bubble on the membrane of air or a thin wave of sound. It was there a second, then gone. To the woman I said in English, "I think there's something behind his left eye, a cyst or tumor." Joseph translated immediately. The room seemed to pause for breath, and then the mother asked me questions in fast Turkish. Joseph translated, but I could answer none of them: Can you heal it, *Habercı* (Messenger)? Where did it come from? Can you tell Allah to take it away? The moment definitely ended for me as the talking began. Joseph gave the woman instructions about what to do now, or something along that line; she thanked him, bowed to me, and backed against the wall with her grandmother while the wheelchair was rolled up to me. I followed the baby with my gaze, astounded that it had stopped crying, that I had felt something invisible. I felt sad that I couldn't heal the tumor myself.

Joseph directed me to the boy in the wheelchair. Now I felt less resistant, less strange. I was relaxing into the feeling of being almost taken over by a large, calm power. I felt myself in a trance and self-consciousness dissipated as I focused on him, moving my palms along his whole body, starting at his head and moving down to his leg. My palms stopped at his thigh, but I sensed something missing. There was something on his back. I motioned for him to stand up. His father helped him, and the mother pulled the chair away. I moved behind him, touching him at the top of his ragged jeans and feeling, as with the baby, something wrong under the belt. Into my mind's eye came an image. Through Joseph's translation, I told the family what I saw: a spiderweb inside the boy's vertebrae. Heal it, they begged me. Without confidence, I put my hands above his belt. I left them there for some time—Joseph later told me I had focused there for at least five minutes. In the hush of the healing, I did not sense that I did anything for the boy. When I lifted my hands, he tried to stand on the bad leg but buckled, and I had to catch him. He got back into the chair, and I apologized, through Joseph, for being ineffectual. As Joseph promised, the people harbored no ill will, though I thought the father might have been a little angry.

But his feelings did not disturb my concentration as Joseph walked me over to the autistic teenager, Büna. Touching her with my palms, I saw mainly black in a kind of aura around her, then white quivering inside it. Strangely, I saw a tunnel of white revealed in the quivering. This was different from the boy and the baby. This "healing" filled my head with images—no bulge in the flesh anywhere, just images of tunnels, whiteness, blackness. Where was the color?

"Joseph," I said, "I see no color in her." He translated for the family and then asked me, "Can you help her colors awaken?" I closed my eyes and tried to see color in her colorless world. I couldn't do anything. It was as if a wall existed. I felt powerless.

When I stepped back, exhausted, Joseph helped me sit down. "I tried," I said, disappointed. "I tried with her, but I don't know if anything happened."

Joseph translated, and people could tell I felt drained. An old woman brought me a drink of water. I watched people watching me and then watched them begin to talk to one another again. I felt the trance leaving and me returning to my imperfect, fragmented self. Famished, I wolfed down five or six cookies. Whatever I had just been through had eaten up a lot of my energy. I replenished it fast, even though I should have been full from the huge dinner. Joseph told me this was to be expected.

Some people tried to talk to me, women, men, kids. I used sign language to communicate, trying to release Joseph from the compulsion to translate. Clearly, both the adults and kids talked about me among themselves, not bothering to hide their admiration and curiosity about the Messenger. The families of the sick kids talked to me, thanking me. I must have said, "Recaydim" (it's my pleasure) some thirty times.

As I tried to listen to the low tone conversations directed at me, I discerned the Turkish word for messenger, *haberci*, countless times. How far I had come from a research institute in a university!

A few minutes later, Joseph indicated that we should go, and Sevda Hanım's friend, the woman who had made the tea, suggested we find Hakan, her son, a few doors down. We said our good-byes as if we were leaving. I went to Sevda Hanım last and said in Turkish, "Thank you for your great teaching." It was all I could say. I wanted to ask her a hundred questions about what had happened in her house that night, but I just thanked her. I felt completely opened up, calmed, awakened—and overwhelmed.

We stepped out of the house, where Joseph found Hakan, who drove us back to the mosque. Joseph wanted to walk from there.

As we made our way along the quiet streets, Joseph told me he understood, after hearing the story from Sevda and watching the healing, where my ritual initiation would take place. "Did I really heal anyone?" I asked. "Frankly," Joseph said, "I think you probably did. If not, you did diagnose what seem to be two tumors in two children. You have immense powers, my friend.

"In Istanbul," he went on, "I received a letter from the daughter of a dear friend, Aykut. Aykut has been dying for some time. Selay writes that he will go soon—prostate cancer. After a visit to Ankara, I will go see him at his summer house, which is near mine, in Kadı Kalesi. This is a village on the Aegean coast, near Bodrum." Bodrum, I knew from tourist brochures, was a castle city on the southwestern tip of the country.

"The castle city?" I asked.

"Yes," he nodded. "Sevda was seeing it, I think."

"Why not just go straight to there?" I asked. "Why do we have to go to Ankara?"

"Important adventures await us in Ankara. Someone in particular awaits us, someone you must meet. You will see." I knew better than to push for more details. Whenever he said things like "You will see," or "It will become clear," I knew he would force me simply to wait for the experience itself. I was glad, actually. As an American, so used to quick gratification, I welcomed Joseph's rhythm.

"Earlier today, my friend, you dreamt of an island from whose shore you saw Kadı Kalesi—the water tower and mosque. Tonight you and I heard of such a place in the story from Sevda Hanım. The island of Lobos, just offshore from Kadı Kalesi, is known as the "island of storks." It is clear to me that you must spend time on Lobos, where your destiny, your meeting with God, awaits you."

"My 'meeting with God'? Will I meet the Magician? Is that what you mean?"

"God wishes to speak to you clearly. I believe the Magician will be the voice that speaks to you. But also, other things must happen in your ritual initiation. You have healing powers that must be refined. In some inward way, you will die on the island—the giant, the hole, all will make sense there. The rituals will clarify things. When, in the story of Jesus, John the Baptist led Jesus through the ritual initiation of baptism, so much was clarified for Jesus, the young messenger of God. The life of Jesus is a model for all our lives. Once baptized, Jesus knew himself as a mystic from then on. This is the ultimate duty of ritual initiation: to take the journeyer, the searcher, from fragmented spiritual self-knowledge to full and whole self-knowledge.

"Hopefully, after your ritual initiation, you will fully know yourself as a mystic, a searcher who has discovered full and absolute faith in the Cosmos."

"How amazing that would feel," I said. "It's what I think I've always tried to find, in all my experiments with different ways of knowing God."

"Yes. Everyone has a journey, and everyone has an island of truth. It is your fate to learn ultimate faith. I truly believe this now."

"To really do it," I said to Joseph. "This is kind of . . . scary. Sevda Hanım said that thing about me not feeling like I have a people. It's true, I don't. I'm a Jew by background, but I don't feel Jewish per se. I wasn't bar mitzvahed, my parents were atheist when I was thirteen. I really have no preset tribe of people. I'm like she said, a wanderer. I'm a little piece of every group. I always thought that meant I could never be fully initiated. But you say I'll experience a full initiation. I just hope so, I really do. I've been getting ready for it for many years now, haven't I? This is what you're saying."

He nodded. "Life has been initiating you. Your boyhood initiated you. College and graduate school initiated you. Love and loss initiated you. The mud roads of a village initiate you. Life is always initiating us into new consciousness. Sevda Hanım was saying that, in fact, you have fought the giant already; you just don't realize it in your deepest core. Like everyone, you are always actually further along in your initiation than you think. Also, like every searcher, you must find a place and time that we call "ritual initiation" in which to *fully* understand and accept your destiny. You chose long ago to seek understanding, and your life journey has brought you a lot of it. But now Lobos is the place of full understanding."

"Will I really 'get it' on Lobos? Will I really understand?"

"If you do, you will have reached enlightenment. Enlightenment is complete understanding of one's place in the flow of universal energy. The Magician has helped approximately a hundred people reach this enlightenment. Maybe you will be one of these." Joseph went silent for a moment. "I don't exactly know yet what we shall do on the island—how we shall seek to stimulate your state of grace. I have some ideas—some energies—that will not materialize fully until we get there. The Magician will teach me what I need to know. I have initiated many young people in ritual ways. The answers will come to me. One thing you must do soon is to write a list of all the strange experiences you've had since you and I met. These are 'signs' I referred to with Sevda Hanım. Make a list, and don't show me. You will be amazed, soon, by many coincidences. Will you please do this upon our returning to the hotel?"

I said I would.

"It will be very hard for you on the island. Your ordeals will be great. And before the island, in Kadı Kalesi, I will need your support as I visit my dying friend. This may prove difficult for you. The sitting and waiting may prove boring."

I laughed. "Nothing with you is *ever* boring."

As we approached the Oteli Baş, I marveled at my life and appreciated the day, this little town, its quiet street, cars parked on each side, low buildings in the moonlight. "Thank you for everything, Joseph," I said turning to him.

Like a good Turk he answered, "It is nothing, my friend."

S E V E N T H ❊ D R E A M

In this seventh dream, "The Visitors," Ben Brickman experienced a nearly complete association of his personality with that of another person, a woman named Beth. From her vantage point, he participated in a spiritually significant incident in 1994—six years after he dreamt it—among people he had never met. In discussing this seventh dream with me, Ben confessed that he was not clear on how he could so clearly "become" another person. Even his "becoming" Nathan had not been as complete as his becoming Beth. He theorized that Beth and he were "soul mates" or "split souls," not only energy strings of the same cluster but actually the same string itself.

In rendering the dream here, I have exactly duplicated Ben's writing. In it, he began the dream in complete union with Beth but soon experienced a separation from her. "Both Nathan and Beth are real people," he told me. "Of that I am sure. There is far more going on in the spiritual physics of this universe than my brain can explain in human terms. This is ultimately what these dreams taught me."

I am a woman of around thirty years old—large, about 220 pounds, but only about 5'4"—sitting beside an elderly woman—small and very thin—on lounge chairs in a backyard overlooking a river. There are pine trees all around. The older woman has wispy gray hair and wears a cardigan sweater and jeans. I am disheveled—I've been camping down at the riverbank. My medium-length brown hair is uncombed, falling over both shoulders, my black-rimmed glasses a little askew. My white blouse and jeans are dirty with spots of loam and dust.

I am looking to my right, toward the next house and yard, drawn to something there, even while talking to my elderly friend. In the adjacent yard I see a very old man and woman standing in the yard, watching another elderly man mowing his lawn. The man mowing wears brown golf slacks and a polo shirt. The two elderly people watching him are unclearly dressed—as if not dressed at all, but cocooned in a whitish glow tinted with blue.

"Beth, what do you see?" the old woman in the lounge chair asks me, raising a glass of iced tea to her lips.

I don't really answer, just murmur something, and stand up, leaving behind my own iced-tea glass on the grass next to my chair. I am mesmerized by the glowing figures in the yard. They call to me somehow, call to me to help them speak to the man who has been mowing the lawn. He has finished, the noise of the mower finished. He has wheeled it toward his garage. I can hear the water flowing in the river to my left, and I see a big house across the river. I walk toward two elderly figures who seem to be glowing.

"Are you spirits?" I ask. As soon as I hear my own voice, I the dreamer, Ben Brickman, experience a separation from Beth, with whom I have been so comfortably connected. I recognize that this is the voice of someone other than I, yet I move only a few feet away, watching, as if I am indeed an invisible, but necessary, part of the scene, and not disconnected at all.

"We are Harold's father and mother," the male figure says. Indeed, they look a little like the old man with the mower, Harold. As Beth speaks to the spirits, Harold sees her. Now, from outside her, I can see that she has a face that naturally wants to smile but always ends up serious instead. This expression greets Harold, as well as a kind of fidgety nervousness. "I don't know how to say this, Harold," she temporizes, "but there are two people . . . two spirits . . . here . . . right here . . . who want to talk to you. I sense they want me to help."

Dumbfounded, Harold frowns, looking about; not for a sight of the spirits, but to see if this insane woman has brought insane friends with her. His neighbor, the old woman in the next yard, waves a hello. Besides her, there's no one else about.

"I know it sounds weird," Beth says, "but it's true. They've been standing here awhile. They know you are about to get a phone call and want to talk to you about it."

"It sounds very weird," Harold says. "I don't know how you knew about the phone call, but yes, we are waiting for one."

"Your mother and father want me to help you see that they are here. They have asked me to tell you that you will turn seventy-seven in ten days, you were born in Rochester, New York, in 1917, your mother called you 'Goopy' when you were a baby because it was the first thing you said after 'dada,' and you said it while you were looking in a mirror on your hands and knees. She says she can see everything and everything is going to be fine. You shouldn't worry."

Harold looks shocked. "Beth, how did you know my mother called me 'Goopy'? And the mirror? How did you know about that?"

Now another elderly woman comes out of the house to join Harold. "Laura, Laura." He turns to her. He pulls at the sleeve of his yellow golf shirt nervously, so that his arm crosses over his chest to pull at the seam of the short sleeve. "Beth is talking in a very peculiar way."

"Hello, Beth," Laura says politely, coming up to Harold's right side. She wears a tan shirt and black slacks and black pumps without socks. Around her neck is a thin necklace with a pearl dangling across the space of her heart, her V-neck shirt just allowing it to show.

"Laura," Beth says to her, pointing just to the right of her husband, "Harold's parents have come to talk to him. It seems to be about a phone call you're about to get. I know it sounds strange, but I have been having a very strange day at the river. Something is going on, some kind of awakening. Spirits are showing up all around. Two have shown up here. They know about the phone call you're going to get. You're going to get a phone call, right? I mean, am I just going nuts, or is this really happening?"

Beth seems to be new to whatever is her power or gift. She seems genuinely confused yet clearly sees what she sees and hears what she hears.

"We're getting a phone call today, yes," Laura says calmly, gripping her husband's arm. He seems territorial, animalistic in his confusion, as if when a younger man he would have pounced on Beth.

"Harold's mother says her name is Victoria. Her mother's name is Harriet. She is saying other things about Harold when he was a boy. Harold's father says he *wishes Harold would cock his arm back better when he throws the fly, and he has to quicken his wrist, or the fly won't catch the water right. Harold's mother says she lost a baby just before Harold was born and another just after, and she knows he used to make up names for them even though they never lived."*

Harold is wide-eyed and speechless. Laura looks at Beth, then at Harold.

"Does any of this ring a bell?" Beth asks.

"She couldn't have known these things," Laura murmurs to her husband.

"Are my parents really here?" Harold asks, standing more erect and breathing in deeply.

Beth nods. "They are here. Do you want to say something to them?"

"I . . . this is so . . . well, I mean . . . are they all right?"

Beth pauses only an instant, then speaks. Her eyes are a little glazed, yet she seems very alert. "Each of them is happy with their death but had distinct regrets about their lives and have remained available in order to shepherd new life. Harold, your mother is saying they had to finish something, and it's about the phone call, and it's going to be fine, and when it's done they'll feel they've finished their jobs.

"You're both glowing, you know? Laura, Harold, you're glowing. It's not just the glow from your parents, it's your own."

"Glowing?" Laura murmurs.

"You're glowing, like the sun is rising behind you." Beth bows her head, then holds it with her hands. "I don't know what's happening to me. I'm doing and seeing things today I've never done before."

Laura comes away from her husband and over to Beth, touching her shoulder with her right hand. Beth looks up at Laura, smiles wanly, then looks over at the two spirits. It seems as if she's hoping they're gone. But they're not. They're still there, waiting for her to listen again.

I woke up to the sound of the bus tires on the road. We were on the road to Ankara, in the middle of the night. It took me a second to realize I was not in the backyard by the river in whatever that pine-treed city was. The year must be 1994, I realized—Harold was born in 1917. He wouldn't be seventy-seven for six more years. Would I meet these people? Hadn't I somehow done so already?

Joseph sat beside me, awake, smoking the end of a cigarette. "My God, I've just had another incredible dream," I told him, describing everything I could. He listened carefully, then suggested I write everything down in my notebook.

"I suspect that's the last of these wondrous dreams you shall have for a while," he said enigmatically.

"Why," I asked.

"It's just a suspicion. I've never met anyone quite like you," he smiled. "We're going places!" This was a new phrase I had taught him. "Yes, we're going places!" He giggled and finished his cigarette. By the time I finished writing, he had begun to doze off. I did not believe him at that moment, but in fact he turned out to be quite correct. I had no other dreams like the one involving Nathan in Paris and the other on the ferry, and then the five within a few hours of one another here in Turkey. These seven dreams were unique in their texture and content.

"Have these seven dreams been predicted?" I wanted to ask Joseph, but I let him rest. We were both worn out and needed sleep. Laying my head back, I suspected Joseph did, as usual, know more about my experiences than he shared. I didn't mind being kept in the dark. It felt like a gentle surrender of control.

CHAPTER 7

The Beloved

The seventh task of the mystic is to become one with the Beloved. This is perhaps the most-discussed task in human literature — in it is the discovery not only of a beloved companion but of the Self.

Some mystics embrace the Beloved in a series of marriages. Others mature their love in one lifelong marital friendship. Others never wed but nonetheless find the Beloved. No matter your choice in a particular lifetime, you will be hurt in your search for the Beloved, you will be accepted and rejected, you will feel ecstacy. Through each participation in an activity of love, however confusing, you meet the hidden force of energy that guides the universe.

The mystic acts with passion and commitment until Love and Self merge and then become the Infinite Love that has always been yearned for. The seventh task is the one most discussed by humanity, for love of another and love of self are like dreams, and humans are great dreamers. But love is never an orderly dream, and the Beloved appears often in unexpected places.

— The Magician

Ankara, the modern progeny of the classical city of Angora, had been built up in the early twentieth century to become the capital of Turkey and house 500,000 people. By the time Joseph and I arrived, it was a teeming city of more than 3 million. Businesses and homes alike still burned coal for fuel so that, as our bus pulled in, a smoky fog made the air grainy.

The bus station was the busiest, loudest, most crowded place I'd ever been in—talking, yelling, running, bumping, crying, laughing, breathing. A colorfully dressed village family with bundles on their backs scurried across the paths of honking vehicles just beside us, only to discover that the bus to their village had already left. Businessmen in suits and with briefcases maneuvered through the melee. Families were strewn about everywhere. The smell of exhaust consumed the station, a heavy morning cologne.

We made our way through it all and out to the city street in front. There we hailed a cab from rows of about fifty. Our driver was a friendly, loud Turk who smoked one cigarette after another. He drove us through a maze of city streets toward a neighborhood called Asağı Ayrancı, the region of the city where Joseph lived. Joseph pointed out government and military buildings, Atatürk monuments, consulates of foreign governments. He remarked that his own apartment building stood just six buildings down from the Russian consulate and residence.

Most of Ankara's buildings were of 1940s and 1950s architecture— three to five stories high, rectangular, no frills, colored gray, white, or tan. Joseph's building turned out to be a five-story tan box with twenty apartments. Each apartment had a serviceable balcony off the living room, but the building possessed no elevator, so we carried our bags up four flights of stone stairs.

Joseph had decorated his Ankara apartment similarly to his Parisian one: African objects nicely arranged on shelves, Turkish carpets on the floor, masks and pictures on the walls. Someone must have known of Joseph's arrival date; the place seemed cleaned and recently dusted, and the refrigerator, which Joseph went to immediately, was stocked with goat cheese, milk, and olives.

Once Joseph showed me my room, I lay down on the bed to rest a bit. I heard him stowing the contents of his little carry bag, opening windows, making the place home again.

As I rose to hang up my jacket, I heard him laugh. When I opened the closet door, the smell of mothballs spilled out into the bedroom. I decided to avoid the closet and closed the door. We'd be leaving in a day anyway for the trip to Bodrum, Kadı Kalesi, and the island of Lobos.

Joseph laughed again. Curious, I walked out of my bedroom into the living room.

He looked up from his mail and invited me to come closer: "I have received a wonderful letter from Alfred Hecht, a millennial mystic and great friend from America, a psychiatrist and professor. You must meet him some day. I will give you his address for your time back in America. He survived the Nazis, fled to Israel, became a hero there, married an American, and ended up in America. I met him in Oxford in the forties. A great old friend.

"He has written me a letter that I think you must read. You of all people will appreciate it. It is about your generation, my friend."

I took some typed pages out of his hands—pages three through five. He didn't give me the front pages, so I saw no letterhead or date. Joseph had been gone from Ankara for three months. The stack of mail before him was at least knee high, stowed in a fruit box. This letter could have come anytime in the last few months.

I read:

What is it, I wonder, when I amble to the river for my solitary walks—how can the young people of this generation, children of a fruitful America, their whole lives before them, seem to believe so completely in their own worthlessness? Why do they wander about telling their whole life stories, their family secrets, their sexual exploits, their intimate neuroses to anyone at all who will listen? Everywhere I turn is an advisee, student, or group in conversation for whom the great topic is not the history of ideas nor the wealth of poetry nor the journey to God, but instead, the human individual's daily tribulations. They have no real sense of history itself, only a sense that they have lost their own personal histories to "painful childhoods." They have little sense of the great wheel of time.

Do I sound like I'm just complaining to hear myself talk? I sometimes doubt, Joseph, that these young people will do what we have striven for in

our time—to ferret out the sickness of the generation, heal it, and free the
human soul from it. Could they truly be exempt from the mission of all the
most gifted of any time to speak out loud the life of the evolving soul?
If only, if only, I could see a way to help them better.
I do wish I had seen you in Paris this year. Best.

"What do you think of our Alfred Hecht?" Joseph asked.

"I think he's right."

"Perhaps you will meet Alfred one day."

"Millennial mystics," I said. "In colleges, in businesses, in churches. People like him, and you, are all around?"

"And people like you," Joseph reminded me. "It is not a religion—it is a spiritual identity." He swept his hand over the mail. "I have hundreds of letters here from colleagues in this identity. Take a look."

There were return addresses from Singapore, Australia, Czechoslovakia, Brazil. "And most people write you in English?"

"Just as it is the world language for business, it is the world language for the mystical work. Some of the letters come in other languages, often French, for instance. But for the most part, English is the vibratory conduit of energy for our time as once Sanskrit, Persian, and Hebrew were conduits of this energy for their time and place. What effect global information systems will have on the language of mysticism is yet to be seen fully. English is now a convenience for many of us. I have a colleague in Argentina, a musician, who argues that by the twenty-first century, music will become the universal language of mystical searchers."

The morning passed gently. I meditated for thirty minutes, then did thirty minutes of aikido. Later I dozed off again. Joseph told me we were to have lunch with his good friends two floors down. He told me the woman, Birtane, kept his apartment up. "Birtane and Ahmet have a beautiful daughter," Joseph quipped. "She might be an angel or a Serpil: beware." I sloughed this off as a joke between men. "She is immensely gifted, too," he said more seriously. "She has been having some amazing visions. She is the primary reason we are here."

At 11:30, I put my jacket on and went downstairs with him. The day had become hot, and my underarms already sweated. We arrived at apartment 204B, where a middle-aged Turkish woman answered the buzzer. After kissing Birtane Hanım, Joseph introduced me to her, a short, bubbly woman with gray hair and glasses hanging on her chest. We entered her vestibule, and the apartment unfolded to reveal her husband, Ahmet Bey, short like his wife, stocky, with white hair; their son just back from America, Haydar; and their daughter, a stunningly beautiful woman of twenty-four, educated in England, Feza, who was dressed in a white silk blouse and Levi's.

When Feza saw me, her eyes both lit up and became afraid at once. She was beautiful in the exotic way that Middle Eastern women are beautiful: flowing black hair, a classically chiseled face, olive skin, deep brown eyes, moist red lips, a natural sensuality in her body. As the small group around us played out greetings and chatter, she raised her eyes and searched mine. When I shook her hand, I asked boldly, "Do we know each other? You look like you know me." Her handshake, soft and warm, seemed at odds with her wary eyes.

In English she said to Joseph, "It's him. As you thought it would be." To me, she said, "It is you. Yes. I know you, in a way." She took two steps back, toward the corner of the wall, where a large blue circle with a black dot in the middle hung like a painting. I recognized it as the Turkish *nazar*, or "evil eye," a symbolic blue-and-black circle found in nearly every Turkish house and shop. I'd read in my Frommer's guide that it supposedly looked the Devil's eye in the eye and offset any evildoings if one touched it, sort of like a rabbit's foot in America. Feza bit her lip as she looked at me and touched it. In Turkish she said something to her family about me that startled them.

Birtane, her mother, spoke quickly in Turkish to Joseph and her husband. Joseph put his hands up, quieting her anxiety. Though I didn't understand everything, I did hear Sevda Hanım's name and the Turkish word for "messenger," *haberci*, and also the word *seyyah*, which I knew to mean "traveler." Out of respect I didn't cry out what I wanted so much to: "Feza, what do you mean, I'm the one you saw?" The whole family, having received the explanation from Joseph, looked at me as the families who wanted healing the night before had done—as if I had transformed, before their eyes, into something more like a mountain than a man. Finally Joseph told me the story.

Over a period of a year, Feza had had visions in which I and a few other people appeared recurringly. She had been diagnosed as schizophrenic and treated with antipsycotics, psychotherapy, and naturopathic experiments. "You came to her in her dreams, Ben. These were recurring dreams during her mental illness, involving not only you but some others as well. As her psychologists will tell you later, Feza is one of those people rich in mental gifts whose psychic structure cannot handle the richness; that structure collapsed when she became visionary." She had dreamt about me the way I was dreaming about others! I shivered for a second, wondering if I too would become mentally ill, but I banished this thought.

Recently, Joseph continued, she had shown marked improvement; she was able to think about working again, able to sleep again, able to function again. Without telling me, Joseph had called Feza a few days ago, describing me and warning her that he would bring me by. He said he'd realized back in Paris that I was one of the people from her hallucinations.

Listening to Joseph explain, watching Feza's eyes, her crossed legs in the chair, her gaze, I felt an attraction to this beautiful woman. Perhaps I should have been wary, given her previous mental illness. Instead, I couldn't take my eyes off her.

"This raises very important questions," Joseph was saying. "Now that it has been confirmed, many new possibilities emerge."

"What are we talking about?" I asked. "Please be specific."

Birtane started speaking again. She clearly didn't want her daughter upset. She seemed to resent the fact that Joseph had put Feza's mental health at risk by surprising her with my arrival. Of course, Feza wasn't surprised; Joseph had called her ahead of time. But Feza had not told Birtane or anyone else. The family had been caught off guard.

"Birtane would rather we do not discuss it now," Joseph translated. "I promise you, Ben, it will all become clear later. We will visit the psychologists who treated Feza. She has given them permission to talk to you. It is important they do so. There is more here than you know at this point. I will simply ask you to be patient."

I looked at Feza for confirmation. "I'm sorry to have invaded your life," I said, unsure what to say.

"My doctors will talk to you," she said. "Let us have lunch and not speak of these things now."

Here it was again, a lesson in patience.

"I'd love lunch," I replied, mystified.

Sitting beside Feza at the table, I swore to myself that Joseph was one of the Greek gods, planning everything out, including my erotic desires. I wanted Feza: an aching want in the loins. Was this a test Joseph was putting me through? I sat at lunch, my reptilian brain wondering how to woo and love this woman while my abstract mind kept asking: What should a mystic believe about lust? Is lust okay just before a ritual initiation? By the time the lunch of *meze*, fish, and baklava ended, I just knew I was in love. I didn't just want "sex" with Feza. I didn't just want a "relationship" with her. No, this was *the one*. I wanted the life of the soul with her. This is why I had met Joseph, I thought: in order to meet Feza. Now I could leave Joseph behind! My mind was washed over by an ocean of desire more powerful, at least at that moment, than even Joseph's mysticism.

Feza had shopping to do in the Ulus district, and I volunteered to accompany her. At first her mother hated the idea, but Feza promised she wouldn't discuss the hallucinations and I promised not to ask, though I desperately wanted to. Feza spoke English with an accent similar to Joseph's. Throughout the walk to her car, then in her car, then throughout our time in Ulus, I stuck to my promise. Meanwhile, I planned strategies of lust like a general. It was as if I had taken another drug; if I had been an old-fashioned, John Wayne kind of man, I'd have said, "She's cast a spell on me." I thought back to what Joseph had given me to eat thus far today. No Turkish delights. Had he slipped some herb into something else? I didn't feel drugged; though somewhere in the midst of my desire I reminded myself that hormones are indeed drugs.

Throughout our excursion into Ankara's old town, Feza and I flirted. When the sun hit her eyes just right, I told her so. When her eyelids flickered, I admired them aloud. Obviously a little smitten with me as well, she touched my hand as we walked, stood in the doorway of a shop so I had to brush against her on my way out. It was a time of pure, unadulterated pleasure between two potential lovers in full flush.

Then, strangely, after about three hours of this lust, something happened inside me, like the breaking of a stick, almost a snapping sound: my perspective returned. I recall the moment I saw it clearly. Feza and I had shopped for a couple of hours and now sat in a little teahouse, our packages around us. I raised my tea glass to my lips and saw Feza sitting there in front of me. Light came through a window, touching wisps of her hair on her temple. She brushed the hair back, turning her head slightly, showing a tiny blemish in her skin, just under the wisps, where she'd perhaps had chicken pox as a child and scratched too hard, leaving a crater.

In an instant, repelled by the flaw, my lust dissolved. I saw the real person. She was beautiful, yes, but where the hell had I gone the last few hours? It happened as simply as that.

I sat back in wonder. Something must truly be happening to my cells, my nerve endings. Transformations manifested in crazy engrossments and detachments like this one. I was in a kind of hypersensitivity; it let things into me, sudden things, insights, lusts, love. Feza was attractive, yes; I wanted her, yes; and if I were a different kind of man, if my respect for Joseph and his world had been less, if I had been in my own culture and world, I would have tried to seduce her. But I was more interested in the changes within me during this strange journey with Joseph than I was in trying to seduce this woman. That in itself indicated a sea change in me.

Leaning forward, I did something that totally flabbergasted me. "Feza," I said, "can I tell you something that's been happening the last few hours?" She'd been in therapy and would understand a psychological conversation, I assumed. In fact, she said she'd be very pleased to listen, and so I told her exactly how I had been feeling. I told her about the last few days, and about the Magician, and about having been named "the Messenger." I apologized to her for having lustful thoughts about her and said I felt especially strange about them since other people were seeing me in a context of a large, unfolding spiritual event.

She, in her soulful beauty, was flattered, not embarrassed. She accepted my vulnerability with an emotional effortlessness that made us friends.

"You are a student of Joseph's," she said with a smile. "His students always search for the joyful life." She said it a little enviously, I thought. "I wish I could have encountered this Magician I hear spoken of in such quiet voices. My own journey has been more complicated. Now I'm glad I don't meet the Magician. I think it would affect me with problems. But I wish I was not prone to the mental illness."

"I'm sorry," I said sympathetically. "And let me tell you, Feza, I don't usually feel so much for a woman in a few hours, then end up being so honest with her! I'm usually more withdrawn about what I'm *really* feeling."

She smiled, her eyes twinkling, her lips red. "I'm glad we met. You have a certain sweetness to you. I will never forget this moment." We both breathed in deeply and touched each other with grins. I was aware of holding in my energy, my vibrations, so she could have an opportunity to guide us. She guided by looking away, toward the middle distance, then turning back to my eyes. "I wish," she said, "you stayed in Ankara longer. I do not meet men like you, so smart, so handsome, so mystical."

"Maybe I'll leave Joseph," I said, "and you and I can elope."

Our laughter pierced the drone of café conversation around us. Simultaneously, as if we had closed the world off but now, in our releasing laugh, we had opened ourselves again, the young waiter came over, asking if he could bring us anything. We realized we had better go, so we lifted ourselves and headed out into the sunny afternoon.

On the way back to Feza's apartment, I promised her a magic act. On her balcony now, I did tricks with water, string, handkerchiefs. Joseph had gone off to see some friends and wouldn't return for about an hour. I thoroughly savored the chance to show Feza my magic.

Toward dinnertime I began to look for Joseph. Feza and I knew where he was going to take me: to a neighborhood called Gazi Osman Pasha to meet two psychologists, Ragıp and Sela Aytur, Feza's therapists. When I'd heard their names I remembered them from the Magician file I'd examined in Paris.

Toward dusk Joseph got out of a cab below us. I finished a trick for Feza that I call "The Rainbow Chain," involving yellow, green, blue, and red handkerchiefs. Her vast capacity for delight made my job easy. When the handkerchief came out green and I let it drift over her hands folded on her lap, she didn't grab at it or crumple it. She just let the cloth cover her hands like silky water. She turned her hands to the silk, opening her palms as if cupping water. As carefully as she watched my every move, I watched hers. The intense watching was like a lovemaking between us. I saw, as I often had seen, that magic had the elemental power to remind a person of the great hidden mysteries. One can always see it in peoples' eyes as they watch a magic trick. Feza's eyes sparkled with the energy of wonder, surprise, and joy.

"Yusuf Bey!" I heard Birtane greet Joseph from inside the apartment. Before other energies invaded, I bent down to retrieve my cloth and kissed Feza on the lips. Just as our lips touched, I felt her breath exhale on my cheek. She let the kiss flow, wanting me. When we released, sensing and hearing the elders coming, we were flushed, my face was hot, her neck red like a cardinal's.

"You've been struck by Feza's presence, haven't you, my friend?" Joseph observed in the taxi.

I sighed with love. "Her eyes sparkle—they tremble, they twinkle. I wish I could stay here in Ankara and be with her, Joseph. I even confessed to her I was lusting for her, and she embraced my confession!"

"You will follow your energy. Perhaps you will choose not to go to Kadı Kalesi. Perhaps you'll choose against your ritual initiation on Lobos."

"No, no," I assured him. "I want to go. I have to go." My eyes lit up suddenly with an idea. "What if she comes with us?" Then as I exhaled, I saw the words disappear into my own resounding No.

"She leaves in two days with her family to go to their summer house in Marmaris. Maybe later you can meet her there."

"Maybe," I said, watching cars and buildings whiz by. "You're a big-time shaman, Joseph," I quipped, turning and looking him in the eye. "You even make love happen on call."

He laughed. "Hardly." He was about to light a cigarette, then decided not to, shoving it back into the Marlboro box. "Why has instantaneous love of a beloved woman come to you just now in your journey, bringing all its gifts? That is an interesting question. I suspect, though I cannot see it fully at this time, that you are being guided to live a journey in which all the keys to the opening of the divine doorway are displayed. I myself am a guide to some things, but we are both guided by larger forces. In this larger guidance, there is a design to the appearance of the Beloved at just this stage of your journey. Perhaps it will all become clear, and others will look back at your journey, seeing in it the meanings that give it its ultimate sense. Of at least this much I am certain: Feza's affection, at just this time, is significant, and your feelings are obviously wonderful for you."

"I'm feeling so open, Joseph. I feel very opened up the last few days. Maybe my love of Feza would come to anyone every day, if everyone were as open as I am now."

Joseph rested his head back on the seat, closing his eyes, obviously a little tired. We had crammed so much into a couple days, and were running on as much adrenaline. "Yes," he said with a smile, "so true. What a strange effect that would have on society! Everyone loving each other so often and quickly. It will be a long time before we're ready for that."

"How far till we get to Gazi Osman Pasha?" I asked. "Do you want to rest?"

"Oh, no." He opened his eyes. "We'll be there soon." He pointed to the northeast. The cab climbed with traffic up the side of the city toward a high plateau. Folding his hands on his lap, he said, "I closed my eyes a moment and remembered my beloved Nura, when we were young and courting. I remembered our joy."

I saw Feza's hands, the silk on them. I felt her breath on my face.

"Will you teach me about joy?" I asked.

"Joy," he sighed. "Yes."

My heart felt light. I never wanted to sleep again. "When I'm in love," I said, "I feel light, very light, like a feather. That must be joy."

"Yes, love takes an orphan out of his loneliness and fear—love gives him a home. Most of what people mean when they speak of love is really joy. How I do wish more people spent more time experiencing and confessing their joy. Then they would learn the great secret at the center of living. But how can they? So much human self-loathing blocks the joy. So much rage of broken hearts and souls. The great secret remains unrevealed.

"*Abi,*" he said to the driver. "*Geldi.*" He pointed toward an apartment building. We had arrived.

"Joseph, what do you mean, 'the great secret'?"

He cut me off, waving me out of the car. "We'll talk further of these things. Let us meet Ragıp and Sela."

"Tell Ragıp and Sela about Sevda's story," Joseph instructed me as we walked up to the apartment building. "They know her well. See what insights they have. They are two of the most celebrated minds in Turkey, to say nothing of their intimacy with the Magician."

Ragıp turned out to be a tall, skinny man with a harelip and balding head, perhaps seventy. His wife, ten years younger, was short and quite round. He was dressed in a gray suit with white shirt and gray socks, which hardly distinguished him from any of a number of other older Turkish men I'd seen. She wore lots of gold jewelry around neck and wrists, and an ankle-length, unbelted cotton dress, very colorful, under which her rotund body undulated.

Ragıp and Sela—they insisted I delete the "Bey" and "Hanım"—wanted to know about me, about my life, and ultimately about the story Sevda had told. From the moment I met them, Ragıp and Sela treated me with affection, Ragıp clapping me on the shoulder, Sela touching my knee, as if they knew me.

They asked me what I thought Sevda Hanım's story meant at its core levels. I thought carefully before I answered; then I answered honestly, "The essence of the story for me is that I may not know what joy and ecstasy are. When I do feel somewhat okay in my life, it's like I see a torch light up." I put my glass of wine down on the coffee table and leaned forward. "Okay, here's what it's like for me. I think: Wow, I'm feeling great, it must be the torch that makes me feel great. So I grab the torch"—I lifted my glass again, holding it out, gesturing with the deep red wine as if it were my guiding light—"and then it's as if, well, I have the torch, so I guess I should go explore a dark place. Oh, okay, I see it, there it is, a dark cave, let's go in there. Let's follow the giant in there, into that darkness and pain. The torch makes this journey possible.

"So I go deeper and deeper into the cave, more and more into the dark. The thing is, the torch, the light that could bring me joy and ecstacy, I take it into the dark, sad cave. What this means to me is that I feel more and more like a failure, an impostor, worthless, afraid. Demons and more demons come, their eyes are images of my failure, deprivations, emotional poverties, times of self-destruction. That's what's in the cave. They all emerge into the torchlight, I go deeper, fall farther, fall into the pit, get to the bottom, the center of the cave—now we're talking two, three days or two weeks into a failure episode, a meaninglessness cycle—and poof, the torch goes out. Just when I get to the center, it goes out. I'm left there, alone, in the dark, and the giant's coming. His footsteps are so loud. Everything trembles.

"So I guess, you know, instead of ascending, I always descend, and I always end up alone. At least that's how it's been. Until . . . this last month . . . the Magician . . . I'm changing, I'm molting somehow. Now I'm afraid, sure, because it's dark in the depths, but somehow I'm not afraid. That's what's so weird. I'm not afraid. It's as if now I'm used to it here in the clammy dark where the demons and giants are. I know I'll wake up soon. I recognize the smells, the sounds of a stream down here. It's as if there's even a sacredness here in the aloneness, the pain, the times of momentary loss of meaning."

"Yes," Ragıp answered, as if we were old friends. "Perhaps a year ago, I would have seen in you the need still to plumb meaninglessness. From what you've said, meaninglessness was certainly your doorway into the search for joy, as it is for many deep-thinking young people. But in your heart and soul you are a mystic, and all mystics are ultimately joy seekers. You seek a self strong enough to both descend and ascend as spirit requires you to do. The mystic seeks to make every moment like the moment of birth. Thus every moment must combine ecstacy and pain. I should think you will discover, in your lifetime, your own ability to alter consciousness toward this end.

"He's a special soul," Ragıp said to Joseph. "How much does he know?"

Joseph patted my knee. "Yes, he is special. He has been exposed to some of his destiny. He is anxious to learn many things tonight."

"Very anxious," I agreed. "I'm on a wave of energy, and I'm ready to ride it wherever it takes me."

Sela's face, olive-colored, mottled, her eyes deep brown and radiant, showed maternal concentration. "By now Joseph has probably asked you to make a list of your unusual experiences. Everyone, no matter their particular destiny, has the same *universal* destiny, to find the portal to God. In their clear journey to the goal, they will experience things and see signs they need help in interpreting. Do you have your own particular list of signs?"

"I didn't bring it," I replied. "I didn't know I was supposed to. But I remember what I wrote down. I have a good memory."

"Of course you do," she said. "Ragıp will get you some paper," she added, and her lanky husband stood up, went to a table where the phone was, and brought back a pad. "Write down your list," Sela instructed, "paying special attention to any dreams you've had. I will get the list of the signs of the Messenger we were given by the Magician."

As I wrote, she stood up, went into a bedroom, and returned with an elegant photo-and-notes album, black with a gold rim. I jotted down a number of things that had happened over the days—the vision of the village weavers in the Istanbul shop, "flying" in Joseph's apartment, the vision with the dervishes—and I remembered her instruction about the dreams, listing the two Nathan dreams, the two spirit journey dreams, the dream about the membrane, the dream about the large woman seeing the dead people, the dream about the tiny portal and the dog.

Joseph, Sela, and Ragıp waited patiently for me, assuring me, each time when I looked up self-consciously, that I should take my time. Finally, I held out my finished list to Sela.

"Why don't you read your description of your dreams aloud?" she invited.

"Okay.

"I had a vision of a man being trained to assassinate another man.

"I had a vision of the man actually getting shot.

"I dreamt that I was like a baby being passed through a tiny portal.

"I dreamt that I was living a life in between lives, hooked into a kind of energy group of some kind on what I think is the Tree of Life.

"Then I dreamt I fell from the Tree of Life into the water, picked off by storks or a big bird, then made a journey into birth.

"I dreamt about a kind of vertical ocean, like another world that exists invisibly in this world.

"I dreamt about a woman who could see spirits, like a psychic or healer, who helped some people talk to the spirits."

Those had been my most significant dreams, those seven. "There was other stuff. I had a vision of a diamond tear, huge, with light flying through it.

"I do this 'flying,' where, for instance, I was in Paris by the Café du Thé at the same time I was in Joseph's flat.

"My body has been going haywire, hot and cold, up and down my back especially."

Looking up from the list, I said, "Then there have been a lot of bizarre coincidences, like my dad knowing Joseph, and Joseph dreaming about me, and Feza seeing me in her visions.

"There's more. Should I go on?"

"I shall read the dreams that the Magician gave us as signs," Sela offered, picking up reading glasses from the coffee table. "You can judge whether they match."

By this point I assumed they would match, yet I felt nervous as she began to read:

"Previous Messengers in human form have lived similar lives to this Messenger, but records of their lives are scarce. This Messenger's awakening shall be well recorded. He himself will provide much of the record in his own words.

"This Messenger will encounter seven dreams in a short period by which you will know him. These dreams will provide the people with past, present, and future discoveries. Many of these discoveries, and much of the material in the dreams, will not be clear to the Messenger or the people at the time of dreaming but will become clear over a period of many years.

"I will inspire the Messenger with these dreams in this order:

"Of a decision to destroy a scientist whose discovery will alter human consciousness.

"Of the assassination attempt and the scientist's unfolding within it.

"Of the portal by which the Messenger shall engage in his second birth. The hands that reach out for the Messenger in his birth dream belong to an individual spirit the Messenger will meet in this lifetime, a spirit whose journey will link with the Messenger's.

"Of the movements through realities by which a spirit engages and unfolds between lifetimes.

"Of a prophet whose abilities will surpass her contemporaries'. She will become essential to the evolution of consciousness known as *Homo infiniens*.

"By these dreams you will know the Messenger, and by them he will have found some of his allies in his search to unfold human consciousness."

Sela looked over at me. "There's certainly no doubt, is there?"

"Wow!"

Ragıp nodded. "In a word."

I turned to Joseph. "Has everything been planned? Have you taken me to specific places, like to Sevda Hanım and Feza and here to these people, according to some kind of instruction book?"

"No manual," he responded. "I have followed my intuitions. All the Magician gave us were these signs. It seems clear that some things, like the dream of the psychic woman, will lead you places in the future. They are like invitations. I would suspect some won't even enter your life for many years."

"Our role," Ragıp added, "is to help you as we can during your journey of initiation into the mystical life. There is a message about evolving consciousness that this 'presence' that calls itself the Magician is preparing to give to the world. The Magician is preparing you for the 'job' of receiving the message that will lead the people into new life. The Magician's presence, and other presences like it, have prepared other evolutionary voices in our culture over the millennia. Now you are becoming an evolutionary voice for this age. We will do what we can, with the wisdom we possess, to make your life more capable of realizing this."

"Have we explained what we understand about this well enough?" Ragıp asked his wife.

"I think so," said Sela. "Though it is fair and useful that we reveal what Feza has told us we may reveal. The Magician was clear that Feza's experiences are an important part of the moment of human evolution we call *Homo infiniens*.

"Yes," I begged, "please tell me what that's about."

"It would be our pleasure, Ben," Sela said. These people were peering into my soul and the very soul of the world, but always so politely. Sela looked to Ragıp, who loosened his tie, sipped his tea, cleared his throat, and began.

"Feza came to us as a patient. She presented with insomnia, depression, and hallucinations. She had taken LSD with a friend in England, Stevenson, a chap from a wealthy family in the north. He and Feza were like brother and sister—nothing romantic, as he was gay. One day he came to her, telling her what brutal cads some of his mates could be; he wanted to take LSD but not with them, so would she join him in it and make sure he didn't make a fool of himself. After only a bit of apprehension, her curiosity won out, and she obliged, without really considering the consequences.

"Feza, you see, had quite an active precognitive life as a child, precognitive dreams, ESP, that sort of thing. Because none of the psychic activity had continued past puberty—it is quite common, actually, among both girls and boys for early gifts to go underground at puberty—she had nearly forgotten about it all and certainly never thought the LSD could bring her highly antipsycholytic effects.

"So Feza and her friend ingested the LSD—in Feza's words, 'just a tiny bit,' though it must certainly have been a large quantity, perhaps more than seven hundred micrograms. At first she became more jovial than ever, laughing and talking in dialogue with a fireplace in the Stevenson's guest house in Cambridge. Stevenson, in Feza's words, 'became quite silly in a beautiful way, like his soul had gotten free of its chains.'" Ragıp smiled at the typical acid melodramatization. "Feza and Stevenson danced and sang and, again in her words, 'leapt into the world of color.'"

I grinned. "I've felt the same way on acid myself. I've taken mescaline, peyote, and LSD," I added more seriously, "and I understand what you're referring to."

Sela continued the story. "The incident that relates to you, Ben, occurred four hours into Feza's experience." As Sela told the rest of the story, this elderly psychiatrist seemed to do so with an appropriate clinical distance, yet with something else in her eyes, a loving and caring regard for Feza.

"Four hours into the LSD trip, Feza felt nauseous and went to the bathroom. She crouched over the bowl, thinking she would vomit. Nothing came. She stood up, immediately became light-headed, and heard a voice—soft, sullen, and male. At first its words were unintelligible. Looking around, she saw nothing peculiar, certainly no man near her. Towel, towel rack, shower curtain, toilet, sink—all normal, and Stevenson himself somewhere at the other end of the house. Again came the voice, this time with distinguishable words, in an accent unfamiliar to her: 'I am the Karver.' These words meant nothing to Feza, and she had the sense to assume she was simply having a very lucid hallucination. She covered the toilet bowl and sat down, hoping the voice would pass. She didn't want to go back out to Stevenson and confess a crazy hallucination.

"But the voice came eight times in the next three hours, no matter whether she stayed in the bathroom or went out into the other rooms or the garden. By the fourth time she realized it was not 'I am the Karver,' but 'I am Karver,' as if indicating a name. Frightened for her mental health, she sat under a tree, trying to avoid Stevenson. The voice kept saying things to her, things too thick and garbled to understand. She had never heard this voice before nor been more sure someone was communicating with her from somewhere else. In her words: 'It was as if my brain was a satellite in space or radio receiver picking up a garbled signal.' She developed a terrible headache, moaning in the garden. Stevenson came to her, promised to call an ambulance, and had to be talked out of it. Feza feared an ambulance would lead to a mental hospital. She took aspirin and cried in Stevenson's arms more than once, and he apologized profusely for getting her into this mess.

"After about nine hours of 'experience,' she felt finished, numb, bloated, and sad, her headache diminishing. The voice had gone 'like a radio had been turned off.'

"Feza never took any drugs again and gradually forced the episode out of her mind. Once she put a few weeks behind herself and the strange voice, she decided it was an acid-induced hallucination, no more."

As I listened to Sela and Ragıp tell the story, I recalled hallucinations of my own during altered states. None had affected me so powerfully, but then again, I had never taken a dose as high as Sela and Ragıp thought she had.

"Nothing in the same vein occurred in Feza's life until over a year later," Sela continued. "By now Feza had graduated from Cambridge and returned to Ankara to begin work as a travel agent. It was summer, two years ago. The date of the return of the auditory hallucination was July 22, 1986. At a beach bonfire near Marmaris, a vacation city on the Turkish Mediterranean, she had a flashback—full, clear, all-consuming. She left the bonfire to go into her family's summer beach cottage to use the toilet. As she entered the bathroom, she heard the voice, exactly the same in tone, timbre, and accent as the Karver voice in Cambridge. She saw a face now, too: a young man, perhaps her own age, but with completely white hair, beard, and mustache. He seemed very distressed. He seemed to want something of her. His face came at her from behind prison bars.

Recalling that there had been fire in both of Feza's environments, I wondered out loud, "Do you think the fire was the trigger for the hallucinations?"

"Yes," Ragıp responded. "We used candle and fire in our treatment, in fact."

Sela continued. Over the next six months, Feza's mind had been invaded by the image of the white-haired youth, as well as the voice and its production of lists of disjointed words. This mental state affected her sleep, job performance, and relationships. Finally, she told her parents her secret. Afraid for her, they kept it from everyone else. One day, drunk, she told a friend, who started rumors at work. When confronted by her manager, she admitted to having hallucinations, was put on disability leave, and received a visit from a psychiatric consultant.

"By the time we met Feza," Sela continued, "she had become an inpatient at Ankara Psychiatric. She couldn't sleep from the visions, voices, and vulnerability to hallucination. She was on Haldol and an accompanying dose of Librium. She had been diagnosed as a late onset schizophrenic. We saw no reason, in our specialist consultations, to disagree with this diagnosis. With the medication, she stabilized and was released from the hospital to our care. Now let us show you something, something that connects all this to you personally, Ben."

As Ragıp reached for something out of Feza's thick file, I thought about the Feza whose wrist my magic handkerchief had touched, the Feza so easy to talk to, the Feza so beautiful—I saw her locked up and medicated.

Ragıp handed me several laminated sheets of paper. "Feza developed an incredibly well structured hallucination that introduces a truly interesting phenomenon and theory, one that we as clinicians know to be an extension of insanity, yet one that we as mystics know to be laced with elements of truth. Read this, if you will. Feza has permitted us to show this piece to you, so feel no compunction in that regard, Ben. I have translated these paragraphs into English for you."

I took the sheets and read:

I went into one of the trances again. An entity calling herself Rachel, and "Traveler," has spoken to me of Karver, who speaks to me sometimes from the future. The Traveler told me she is not a spirit like Jesus, Mohammed, Buddha, or Teresa—these are messengers—she is among others unembodied who travel between dimensions to keep spiritual inspiration and balance in human consciousness. These Travelers are energy bursts like an earthquake or meteor is an energy burst.

*Karver is an important person in the year 2411 who wants to com-
municate to us in this time, for reasons I have not yet learned. I know only
that it has to do with different people who are also Travelers and Messengers. Messengers assist Travelers in some way I have not found yet. I have
found out that very soon I will meet one Messenger who works with stone
or brick and is named in eight letters but prefers to be named in three.
When I think of this Messenger, I think of a clock. I can see the clock. I
also see his face. The hair is blond, the beard and mustache blond but the
eyes are brown. The face is long and thin. Karver and an old woman, his
friend, seeks this messenger among others.*

*Karver uses me in this seeking because I have a mind sensitive to
transtemporal communication, the temporal vibrations and vibrational fre-
quencies on the time-space continuum that others do not consciously feel.
Physical time travel is still impossible in his century, but through altered
consciousness of transpersonal experience, with certain very sensitive individuals such as myself, telepathic time travel is possible. This is a process of
mind-to-mind conversation through time. I do not understand it all yet.*

The translation ended there. Lifting my eyes from the page, I said,
"This is way out! Telepathic time travel?" Yet she had clearly described me
and actually seen me in her vision. I repeated her description: "A man
'who works with stone or brick' must refer to my name, 'Brickman.' And
my name, Benjamin, has eight letters but I prefer to be called by Ben,
three letters. Okay. And then my looks. They all fit. The clock? What's
the clock?"

"We assume it to refer to the clock in London, Big Ben. She was fond
of sitting near it when she went to London. It became associated in her
mind."

"Jesus, this is too much!" Suddenly I remembered a piece of the dream
I'd had about the vertical ocean. There was an old woman mouthing
"Twenty-four," pointing at me, and mouthing "Travel without machines."
Had I dreamt, or hallucinated, something connected to Feza's vision? Some-
thing about Karver's friend, an old woman, and 2411, and time travel? It
seemed so surreal, yet my gut told me there was something going on here.

What if Feza were right about somehow communicating with the future? What about all the dreams I'd been having in the last few days? Most of those had involved the future.

Sela smiled. "This is the great difficulty with Feza's case. This matter of time traveling and so on must be a hallucination. Yet these other elements appear so clearly valid. Our thought is that she is a psychic but was also insane. We strive to continue studying her very unique case, but, as you Americans like to say, we've shot ourselves in the foot, in that regard." She laughed, but my face showed noncomprehension.

"What she means," Ragıp explained, "is that we have all but cured Feza, cutting off our own studies. You see, in the beginning of our time with her, we used LSD psychotherapy, consulting with Stanislav Grof. We took her fully into the hallucinations, extending them, fleshing them out, as it were. Giving Feza the full flow of her insanity seemed the best course, and indeed it relieved her troubles for a time. But then the incidents returned as dreams rather than waking hallucinations. This development regenerated the insomnia. I will never forget the sympathy I felt for her when she told me that she felt like a woman in an underground prison with an animal trying to burst out of her. She became suicidal from the pressure.

"During this next phase of treatment, we discovered Feingold's research on food allergies. Have you heard of Feingold, Ben?"

"No," I admitted.

"He's an American. He cured one third of the schizophrenics in one of his studies by deleting wheat and all gluten products from their diet. This deletion did not affect the remaining two thirds, so it is hardly a panacea, but we had nothing to lose in suggesting this course as an augmentation to Feza's medication. We have never been averse to naturopathic solutions. Her hallucinations, auditory and visual, as well as the attendant disturbances of sleep, mood, and appetite, dissipated within one month and vanished within three."

"Are you serious? From not eating wheat anymore?"

"Quite serious. We wrote to Feingold to report our success and have in fact begun a rich correspondence with him. Many factors probably helped Feza, from medication to therapy to dietary changes. If you found her ret-

icent to talk about her hallucinations, you'll know that she does not want
to go back to the way it was. She's just preparing to return to her work in
the travel agency her uncle owns.

"But we are left with no more insanity in Feza and thus no more material to continue our fascinating search, as mystics, for the deeper truths
that lie within it."

"Insanity," I agreed, "is a natural altered state. In fact, maybe she's
right about *all* of it!" I quipped. "Even the time travel."

Ragıp smiled, and Sela laughed. "Ah, Ben, if only we could show you
her whole file. Some of the crazy things she said. Quite a bit much, quite
a bit."

They talked about her like a specimen, and for a second it sent a dark
chill through me, a desire to protect her. Earlier, all I had wanted to do was
get Ragıp and Sela to talk about her. Now I didn't like them peeling back
her mental skin.

Diverting their attention back to myself, I asked, "And how does all
this relate to me? What's my next step?"

Sela answered for the three of them: "No matter what in her hallucinations is not at this time provable, Ragıp and I and many others know
that the existence of the embodied life force we call the Magician is very
real. And we know—as you must now, having matched the list of signs
with us—that you are the Messenger he predicted would come to him. You
are now in the process of being initiated into a self capable of intense
prophetic vision.

"What is your next step in this initiation? Perhaps to put it in terms
that you, as a magician and illusion maker can understand: In your first
thirty years of life you have mastered the art of psychological illusion. You
learned early, because of family traumas, to mask life's natural joy with
masks of fear and woundedness, loneliness and pain. More recently, you
have awakened; you are seeing past illusions to the ecstasy that waits behind suffering. You are seeing, more clearly, the Beloved."

"The great irony about suffering," Ragıp joined in, "is that unless
your suffering brings you closer to God it is not, in the mystical sense, real.
All energy seeks to come closer to the full embrace of God. Often I work
with patients who suffer and suffer and suffer, victims all, and never come

closer to insight, growth, or God. They feel pain, but they don't fully suffer. They mask their actual pain in things like blame, criticism, victimol-
ogy.

"The next step for you, if I may be so bold, is to strip away the mask,
the illusion, and notice that joy is the untapped force of love in the personal universe. Joy, the magic of the stork, is the primal force that gives
your life its origin, its bearing, and its destination. Over the last decade,
perhaps, you have played tricks with light, you have wrestled with your
demons, but now, in your present journey, you are wrestling with the angel and thus becoming light itself."

"You all talk," I said, a little impatiently, "like there's a manual somewhere, some abstruse tome or mystical playbook, that explains all this."

Sela reached over and squeezed my hand. "Again, Ben, there is no
specific instruction book. Just thousands of years of mysticism. Every generation, in its own way, experiencing the same joys and sufferings. A simplicity of archetypes. When the heart has opened and the self has emerged
through the doorway, as yours must have for Sevda Hanım to see your
story so clearly, then it takes no genius for Joseph or Ragıp or me to know
your next step. This knowing is, in fact, the job of your mentors and teachers. The human soul is living a journey that makes great sense to those
that befriend it. Joseph, as he has done already, has been your able guide
on your journey east, and he will now take you west again, a step closer to
the Magician."

Ragıp nodded. "Do not underestimate, by the way, the effect on your
emotions of the shock of understanding, over the last few days, that you
are a Messenger. You, like everyone who encounters his destiny, will become somewhat labile. This is necessary so that you can release your deep
anger at yourself, your deep self-hatred. I would think this work is coming
soon. Don't you, Sela?"

There it was again, that thing Joseph kept saying about my anger.
"Joseph says that too," I protested. "But I don't feel it. I don't feel angry."

"Ah, the illusions. Yes. you are the master of illusions."

They clearly didn't believe me and regarded me as if I were a specimen. I felt a sudden great distance from them, as if a wind had blown me
across the ocean from them. The teacups, the cakes, the Turkish carpets,

the Ottoman coffee table, everything was right there next to me, but far away and I was alone. I realized I was very angry. My blood had begun to heat, my face was hot. I felt a breath rise in me. I wanted to say, "Yes! I feel it. You want me to feel angry? Okay, I feel it! I'm angry!" Though the words did not come, more anger came, more and more of it—directed at the three old people.

Through gritted teeth I scolded them: "I'm just not an angry person. You all think you know me, but you've got this wrong."

"So be it," Sela nodded. "I'll just bring more baklava, yes?" Ragıp liked the idea. She stood up and waddled out.

My stomach had knotted up. "What's the music we're listening to?" I asked Ragıp. The exotic music came from a cassette tape deck in the back corner—sensuous, undulating, with quiet wails, flutes, low drums.

"It is *qawwali*, Sufi ecstatic music," Ragıp answered. "This particular group comes from Pakistan."

I imagined myself simply standing up and walking out of the apartment. Why not do it? Why not? Well, how would I explain it? But what was I doing here instead of being with Feza? I wanted to be with Feza! Yet this was impulsive anger talking. I dropped my head into my hands, trying to hold my anger in. It was as if Ragıp and Sela were trying to make me angry and succeeding.

Sela returned with a little silver tray on which small square baklava sat on tiny china plates. The forks were tiny too, like little corn on the cob forks. She set the tray on the coffee table and handed out plates. She seemed to me to be moving in slow motion. It seemed as if she put immense care into the small act of putting the plates in front of me and Joseph, on the coffee table, handing Ragıp his, then sitting back and holding hers near her chest. Watching her take her first bite, I felt myself becoming distant from my bitterness, a smile coming to my face, one that might have looked false, like a mask, but from inside it felt as if my face were vibrating with both anger and admiration, both bitterness and pensiveness, both defensiveness and openness.

It felt like a moment of enlightenment, one in which I suddenly realized that I had never consciously felt two so different emotions simultaneously. I felt as if, in my emotional life, I was in two dimensions at once. I stayed frozen in my pose, not wanting to move, wondering what would happen. Sela saw me looking at her and smiled back politely.

Ragıp interrupted the moment by asking, "Will you have some of Sela's baklava? It is, as you might say, 'the best in town.'" I turned to his smile, and the moment of multidimensional emotion continued. I said aloud, "I'm having the strangest emotional experience. It's nothing like I've ever had before. I'm feeling two—two contrary emotions at the same time, and I'm really conscious of both, as if I can choose between them. They're just sitting in me, waiting for me, for my . . . higher self . . . to make the choice. How bizarre."

"Tell us more," Sela invited, leaning forward.

I leaned forward too, picking up the baklava in front of me, wondering if eating it would shut down my emotional state. "I feel heaviness and lightness both." Now I felt flushed in the face but cool in the abdomen, groin, and legs. "My body just shivered a little, and I'm hot and cold both. It's like I can see into the very heart of the emotions to the essential elements of emotion . . . no, I don't know . . . words don't work. Sometimes there are no words. It's like trying to tell the person you love how you really feel. There are no words. You just feel so . . . complete . . . so . . . alive."

Suddenly, in my mind's eye, I saw snow falling. It was a strong image, snow falling on mounds of snow and trees.

"I just saw snow! Snow." I looked for more, but then it was gone.

"You are vibrating, my friend," Joseph said with a smile, nodding slightly as if he understood. "You are vibrating in at least two dimensions, *and* you are aware of the vibrations in each. So gifted, my friend, you are so gifted. I did not think in my life I would meet one like you. Prepare yourself, my friend, for another significant vibration now."

Sela and Ragıp nodded agreement. I felt a wonderful peace come into me, flowing like warm water over all my other emotions. It did not remove them; it joined them all into one! It was amazing. "It is wholeness," I said aloud. "I've just felt completely whole and loved."

"The encounter with the Beloved is multifaceted," Joseph said, "a psychological encounter with self, a freeing—wholeness is the result."

"Yes, forgiveness and integration," Sela agreed.

I saw the image again. Sudden, clear. Snow, a car, a street. I was a little boy.

The image left as Sela said, "You are an impressive young man, and I thank you from the bottom of my heart for your presence in my home." She pushed the plate of baklava toward me along the coffee table. Moments ago I had been angry at her, but not now. Now her words moved me. The kind of formal acceptance these people vibrated around me, the kind of acceptance everyone on this mystical journey seemed to have—it touched my soul, here in Sela's kindness. My eyes watered. I took another bite of the very sweet baklava, tasting not only the syrup but also the tiny grains of pistachio nuts. "This is incredibly tasty," I said.

Sela smiled. "I'm so pleased you like it. How are you doing now?"

As if not quite myself, I said, "When we admit our own imperfection we have forgiven ourselves—we know that sweet imperfection as our soul marking, our invitation to call for God's help. The person who achieves enlightenment has forgiven himself like the sand is forgiven by the eye it irritates, or the wind is forgiven by the tree it breaks, or the beloved is forgiven by the lover."

Joseph started to say something, when a memory suddenly filled my mind—me crying tears as a little boy, three years old, in piles and piles of snow. It was Milwaukee—my father a graduate assistant at the university, our family living in faculty housing apartments next to a huge vacant lot. Clothed in huge snowsuits, gloves, face masks, we kids played in snow tunnels. This year, the snow had risen to the rooftops. I was a tiny boy, as small as a stone, sitting alone in the center of a huge snow tunnel. Two other boys, my friends, jumped on top of my tunnel. Their jumping crushed in the ceiling, burying me in a deep crush of snow. I was panicked, the snow burying me in whiteness, my arms stuck to my sides, my face and head covered, my breath buried, as if there were a huge clamp on my mouth and nose, stopping my breath, ending me in white death. I screamed, but nothing came out. I had no voice. It was as if I were dead, looking out into white, cold cotton that suffocated me. I was buried, unable to move.

"What has happened?" Joseph asked.

"There's my father," I said. "And my mother. What a memory!" There they were, clawing at the snow, clawing me out of there, and other elders too, and the two boys crying, and me falling into blackness. Then there they were again, with me in the hospital, my mother weeping for joy that I had awakened, my father clawing his big hand through his hair in relief. There were hugs, kisses. There was snow falling outside the hospital window, now seeming so friendly, twinkling in the sunlight.

"I'm sorry," I said to Sela and the others as I began to cry. In that moment I loved my mother utterly. I loved my father. I saw them as energies in my soul cluster as in my tree dream, allies whom I had known for eons. I reached out and embraced them, reaching across time to kiss the bodies that had brought me into the world and touch the souls I had forgotten how to love because their parenting had destroyed my innocence as much as protected it.

"It was *prana*," I said to the others, "very beautiful. Just now." As tears rolled down my cheeks, I wiped my face with a napkin. "I had forgotten, until this moment, how that had happened. It's like I've had amnesia. I almost died when I was three, in a snow tunnel collapse. I remember it now. And this time I remembered it with such love. No fear—just love. Think what my parents must have felt. Think how frightened they were. I think every mystic, to have direct contact with God, must forgive his parents."

"Yes. And they did love you utterly, didn't they, even if they didn't quite know *how* to love you?" Sela asked gently.

I nodded. "And I did love them."

"Perhaps your vision begs you to return to innocence, so that you can fully receive the message of the cosmos. If any walls exist, if there are any people you have not forgiven, if there are any you do not love, how can you act as an enlightened one? You must love even those who have hurt you. You have understood that now."

"I was such an innocent little boy, sitting in that tunnel, crying for my friends. I was so loving, so capable of pure love. I remember it in my body. How beautiful."

We all sat in silence for a moment.

Then Joseph said to his friends, "I think Ben and I should get some sleep. We have early travel tomorrow. We will go find Aykut."

Sela nodded. "Yes, I still hope we can meet you in Kadı Kalesi later this week." She took my hand and squeezed it. Then, on an impulse, she leaned over and kissed my cheek. "I think you are the best student Joseph has ever had."

"He is that," Joseph agreed.

"You are the Messenger, my dear," Sela smiled, mirroring what was now a beaming smile of gratitude on my face. "We will see you soon, I think. Even if we don't, will you stay in touch?" she asked. "We'd like that."

Ragıp nodded. "Absolutely. We must hear of your exploits, your life, no matter where it takes you. You will always have our support."

I thanked both of them. "I'll stay in touch," I promised.

We were all exhausted, perhaps no one more than Joseph, whose eyes were filmed with sleepiness. As we stood at the door shaking hands, Ragıp stopped us in our tracks: "Wait, let me give you something." He went to the tape player and pulled out the *qawwali* music, handing the tape to me. I refused it at first, as was polite, but realized that I wanted to accept it, not only to receive it as a gift but also because I wanted to give Sela something. I pulled my mother's ring from my pinkie finger. I told Sela that Mom had given it to me and that I wanted to let it go, to give it to Sela in exchange for her help. At first she refused, but in the end she accepted. She thanked me, hugged me, and said, "Well, now, perhaps, you have left something here, a piece of your soul, that you will have to retrieve some day. We will most certainly see you again." I bent and kissed her soft brown cheek.

Ragıp and Sela closed their door, and Joseph and I walked down the stairs, then out to the sidewalk. I paused to look up into the sky. I saw the Big Dipper and the North Star. Joseph kept walking, but I stopped, bent my head back completely, rotating to see Orion. There were no clouds, and despite the bowl of light reflected upward by the city, a twinkling sea of stars was visible, spread out above us in the velvet black sky. I remembered nights as a kid, a teenager, college nights, nights after work, lying on the hood of a car or in a sleeping bag, or on the grass with a girl I'd made love to, admiring the stars.

I remembered lying with my friend Jeremy at fifteen after my parents had divorced, saying passionately about his recent born-again Christianity, "I wish I could be like you, Jeremy, I wish I could be saved and reborn like you." All he had talked about in those days was how he'd been baptized in the spirit in a ceremony at his mother's new church, how he'd found Jesus, how he'd found God, how he felt like a star, radiant, bursting, how he felt as if he had just been planted by God, like wheat. Years later I would go through my own born-again Christian phase, but at that moment I had known only envy of his starlit certainty.

Standing in Ankara, I said to the sky, "I've been like a seed, hard. I don't open year after year. But now I'm growing. I'm through the doorway."

Joseph couldn't hear my muttering, but he saw that I had stopped in my tracks to look upward. He came back to me.

"What do you see?" he asked.

"Everything's so intense, Joseph."

"It is always thus when God decides to come for you. It will become even more intense before you're through. You will learn, and you will teach. And you must always expect the unexpected."

We both looked upward for a few more seconds. Then, as we dropped our heads, Joseph started walking and I followed, feeling at peace and yet simultaneously a little in shock, as I began to really wonder what being the Messenger would turn out to be. What would happen next? I could not know, and for a moment I did not feel my usual impatience to know.

At Joseph's instigation, we continued down the walk and toward a *taksi* that sped us toward Joseph's flat, where we had left our bags. We asked the *taksi* to wait while we went upstairs, got our bags, and locked Joseph's flat. Before us lay the bus journey west to Bodrum, then to Kadı Kalesi and the island of Lobos.

That night, on the bus, I did not dream. I wrote Feza a letter, telling her how much I'd enjoyed meeting her and thanking her for letting Ragıp and Sela tell me about her. I told her that their story had only made me feel closer to her. I promised to contact her again. I sealed the letter, then wrote what I could in my journal.

Then I turned off the little overhead light and, along the drone of the bus's motion, fell asleep. It was a gracious and peaceful sleep, uninterrupted by any visions. The seven dreams were, as predicted, complete. I think when I awoke in the middle of the night to go into the teahouse for the usual *çay*, I felt almost a sense of grief—for the end of the dreams, or perhaps for the end of my previous life.

PART FOUR

The Initiation

A disciple came to his master and asked, "It is terribly hot, and how shall we escape the heat?" At once the answer came: "Let us go down to the bottom of the furnace." So the perplexed disciple asked again, "But in the furnace, how shall we escape the scorching fire?" To which he received the surprising reply "There, no further pains will harass you."

— ZEN STORY

The fair tree of enlightenment
Spreads through all the worlds.
It bears the flower and fruit of Compassion
And its name is service of others.

— SARAHA

CHAPTER 8

The Blessing

The eighth task of the mystic is to become one with nothingness and death. It is by embracing death and nothingness that you proceed beyond the illusion of the finite. You learn that the process of living, the journey itself, is the destination. You recognize that emptiness is equal to fullness in the life process. The eighth task of enlightenment is accomplished when you understand, to its depths, that the inner treasure of reality cannot wither and decay, for it is not.

Generally it takes the mystic a lifetime to embrace death, nothingness, and the void. Often it takes many lifetimes for you to learn that life is an infinite journey. What you need, you are given. Thus you are given many lifetimes, and each is completed by death.

— The Magician

Shamans and mystics have said that the universe is like a huge drum, in which energies bounce and echo to create the appearance of coincidence. So it was the next day: one of the most amazing coincidences occurred.

We arrived after the overnight bus ride in the castle city of Bodrum. From there we took a *dolmuş*, a shared cab, to the seaside town of Turgut Reís, and from there a Murat cab to Kadı Kalesi, the village where Joseph's childhood friend, Aykut Bey, was lying near death. When I went over to his bed, the first thing I noticed was that the ring finger on his right hand was missing! His brown, wiry-haired hand was the one I'd seen in my dream a few nights ago, reaching through the tiny portal for the baby!

I reeled back with surprise. Joseph gave me his kind, all-knowing look. He, of course, had suspected from my description of the dream that it was Aykut's hand that had appeared. "It's him!" I cried, excited despite our finding that Aykut was very ill. Joseph said something in response which I did not understand until days later: "My friend, I think someone in your energy cluster must die so that you can be fully born."

Aykut Bey had been Joseph's friend since they served in the military together back in the late 1940s. They were young educated men, captains, and served in the days when NATO had begun, then served again during the Korean War. It was during the war that Aykut's hand had been injured. Joseph and Aykut had remained friends as Joseph had become an anthropologist and Aykut a poet and philosopher. In the 1960s, when both men had had young families, they had built summer cottages side by side, here in the seaside village of Kadı Kalesi.

Earlier that morning, about 10:00 A.M., before I knew anything about Aykut Bey, Joseph and I stepped out of our cab next to a general store and cafe in the center of town. In Turkish, kadı kalesi means "the castle of the judge," Joseph explained, pointing to the ruins of a stone house on the hill to the east of the village. The ancient ruins reminded me of the castle that Sevda Hanım's story conjured in my mind. Joseph recalled that a very rich provincial judge had lived in the castle two hundred years before, overlooking the ocean and, a half mile offshore, the island of Lobos.

"So that's Lobos," I said aloud. To talk together, we had to raise our voices over the din of construction. There was a large building going up next to the café.

"Do you see the stork flying?" Joseph asked, pointing toward the island.

I could barely make out the flight of a huge bird flying out there. My stomach quivered with anticipation. If things went as Joseph thought they were meant to go, my quest would take me out there. I would be tested there, matured there, changed there. I might meet the Magician on that island; at least, that had been the Magician's prediction.

An old woman and a young man walked from around the construction to greet us. They were Aykut Bey's sister and nephew, now Aykut Bey's caregivers. Between Joseph and the two came the usual kisses of greeting, then introductions involving me, and then anxious conversation between Joseph and his friends as we walked along the beach toward Joseph's cottage and Aykut Bey's, next door.

The young man, about nineteen, named Hamit, talked to me in Turkish but saw that I couldn't understand him. Both of us were burdened by bags, so we lagged behind the elders in silence.

We passed chickens and roosters roaming behind cottages. We walked through low palm trees, village kids peering at us, shrubs that bloomed a white flower like honeysuckle. As we came to a stucco cottage, Joseph told me this was his place and I should make myself comfortable there—Hamit would show me around. Joseph pointed to an identical stucco cottage next door, saying I could join him in that one to meet Aykut Bey when I was ready.

The old aunt started talking to me in heavily accented Turkish. Joseph translated: "We are honored to have the Messenger with us. Thank you for coming." For hours at a time I would forget I was supposed to be "the Messenger." I saw something akin to supplication in her eyes and gestures, and I was sternly reminded of the gravity of my role. Putting my hand out to shake hers, I said, "I am honored to be in your village. Thank you for your kindness." She just nodded, smiled, and turned with Joseph to go to her family cottage.

Aykut Bey was dying much faster than Joseph had expected. I could see it in Joseph's face as he greeted me an hour later at the door of his friend's cottage. "He drifts in and out of consciousness," Joseph said. "He is going very fast."

Aykut Bey was only a few years older than Joseph but looked twenty years older, lying on the bed, emaciated, with a bald head, skinny arms, skinny legs, almost no eyebrows, the injured hand. He was awake, and our eyes met.

"*Erkek kim o?*" I heard him ask Joseph in Turkish, referring to me. "Who is this man?"

"*Amerikalı arkadaşim,*" Joseph answered. "My American friend. *Habercı.*" Aykut immediately recognized me by that name.

I gave Aykut my American name, using all the polite Turkish phrases I had learned for first meetings. Even dying, a Turk seemed to have patience for them, perhaps even a yearning for them.

Joseph told Aykut about my journey. He spoke quickly in Turkish—I could pick up only words, phrases. My comprehension of Turkish was rapidly improving, but not enough for me to hear more than " . . . his father . . . my companion . . . a few weeks . . . Paris . . . the Magician."

Aykut chuckled. "*Her şey bilior mı?*" he asked Joseph.

"*Bilior.*" Joseph answered affirmatively. "Yes," he was saying to Aykut, "yes, my young friend knows all about the Magician and the Messenger." When I heard Joseph say "*Lobos Ada,*" Aykut sighed, nodding, and murmured something to Joseph, who understood and stepped away from the bed.

Aykut turned to me, speaking English. "My young friend, make Joseph be honest about the island. It was I who showed it to him."

"I'll be honest, Aykut Abi," Joseph smiled.

"It is a good place for setting out on new paths. It is a good place to receive the cosmic gift. Come, my friend, let me feel your hand."

I put my right hand in his, so we were shaking hands like businessmen. In his fragile grip I felt acutely how he was the dying clasping hands with the living.

"It's my time to go," he said to me. "Look after Yusuf. He will appear to look after you, but be his friend. He's an adventurer—but no matter what brave face he puts on it, losing me will not be easy for him."

"You talk like you're going today," Joseph complained. "Leave it be."

"Yusuf Abi, you are shocked at how advanced is my condition. You thought you would come here and we would have weeks together. It is not to be. I have done here what I came for. I have left enough of my soul here in this lifetime to return for it in a future life. It is time for me to go. Let this young man carry your burden."

Joseph said nothing. He seemed embarrassed by all this. He feared death too, like me, like everyone—not as much, but he was still afraid. Realizing this quieted the anxiety that was building in me as Aykut Bey held my hand.

"Do you remember how your wife loved me?" he asked Joseph.

"*Tabîî, tabîî*," Joseph answered. "Of course."

"She thought you would go first among our group—now you are the last."

The two began speaking in Turkish, and Aykut let go of me. I stepped back, Joseph coming forward to take my place. A few minutes passed. The two old men talked. I went out into the living room, then out the door toward the beach.

"I'm sorry, my friend," Joseph said, walking toward me with a book in hand two hours later. "He is much more ill than I suspected. Our plans for your ritual initiation will not change too much, but I must be with him now— a day, two days, I think no more."

"Tell me what I can do."

"Nothing for now."

He had found me sitting at a metal table on the beach. Sitting across from me, he placed the book between us and opened a bottled apricot drink called *meyva suyu*.

He needed to talk. "Aykut has always been a free thinker. Even as a soldier in Korea, he read, searched, wrote poetry, philosophy. He turned out to be one of Turkey's finest poets and thinkers. Now he journeys toward nothingness. He seems prepared. I hope so. I will tend to him as one tends a child. As you are born into your new life, he will pass through the doorway and be born into his newest death."

"I'll do anything I can to help."

"I know you will. But your destiny awaits you, and so you must understand what is written here." Joseph put down his bottle and picked up the book, pulling out a sheaf of folded papers and a stapled monograph in German entitled *Das Nichtsein und die Entstehung des Bewusstseins*—"Nothingness and the Birth of Consciousness." Or, in a more literal translation, "Nonbeing and the Emergence of Conscious Being." He flipped through the pages of the book itself: they were all blank.

"The monograph is a German translation of one of Aykut's philosophical journal entries. Please translate it into English and then memorize it. I will not tell you what to do with the blank book. It will come to you later.

"When you write of your journey, it will be by divine inspiration. So it is with Aykut in these passages. Through Aykut, the evolutionary energy of the universe speaks clearly. It has spoken especially in his journals, which are his unique way of doing philosophy. It is time now for you to learn, through Aykut's thinking, how energy inhales Nothingness and exhales Being, by this method transforming itself. In order to find access to this process, my friend, you must examine the mystery of nothingness, first through your cognition, then later . . . well, you will see.

"Take these papers. They are brief but potent. When you need something, Hamit will help you, with food, and so on. Swim, lie in the sun, work on these papers. Your mission among them will clarify itself."

The next twenty-four hours passed quietly. I slept, I swam in the bay, I offered to sit vigilantly, like the others, by Aykut's bedside, but Joseph, Hamit, and Auntie Fusun refused my help.

At midday, I walked up the hill to the castle of the judge, wandered the limestone ruins, then descended and swam in the warm Aegean. I pondered the island of Lobos offshore, settling finally on the beach below the castle to translate Aykut's writing. From the biography at the beginning of the monograph, I learned that Aykut had a big following in Germany, where he had taught at the university in Cologne for ten years. This monograph had been published in a popular philosophy journal in October 1986.

The monograph itself began with a reference to the Magician:

On the island of Lobos, off the coast of my native Turkey, I encountered a presence called the Magician, a white-robed figure of light. I learned that he was an entity we might call a Traveler, a spirit who travels between dimensions, a Wise One in our dimension. Let us consider this figure a hallucination, to save ourselves the trouble of arguing over its existence. Let us consider the whole multidimensional concept, including the notion of Travelers, our little hallucination.

Following my hallucination, I experienced a vision that I wrote, as follows, in the kind of white heat experienced when the scholar relinquishes his scholarly distance and melds thought with Thought.

I translated the vision directly into my journal:

"Tonight everything I have searched to understand makes perfect cosmic sense because tonight a Traveler has taught me how *nothing* makes sense. Here I am, old, cancerous, beginning my journey toward death, and only now I understand nothingness. How silly to have waited so long.

"Nothingness, I see, is the parent of Being. Nothingness sought to love itself, and thus created Being. Love is the force of nothingness knowing itself. Anything, even nothingness, when it finally, fully knows itself becomes love.

"The universe—i.e., life as we know it, the Big Bang, Creation— occurred because Nothingness knew itself utterly, and in that moment love sprang forth from this creative force into being.

"Why was there the original Nothingness?

"That is like Russell's idea that to say, 'God exists' is redundant.

"There is no Why question about Nothingness. Nothingness is the primal state of absence, which is the most powerful creative motivation imaginable. Without absence of motion is there need for motion?

"There is no word for what Nothingness was and is except the Word. There can be no word. There can only be a full logos for God, i.e., for Love. This is the best language can do, for language is a form of love, not Nothingness.

"When a person seeks to grow, to become powerful, to find truth, he does so because he is faced with Nothingness—the inchoate lack that is our companion throughout life and compels us to fill life with activity. Any new thing is possible, there are no limits, there is only infinite potential—why? Not because all is already done but because of what has not been done. The Void is the impulse of creation and the seat of our ambition.

"When we lose a loved one to death, or feel utter meaninglessness in daily life, or fall in love and are rejected, we human animals feel the essential and original Nothingness from which the human species sprang. In these instances, as in instances of failure, abandonment, regret, we feel the Nothingness that is exactly the same non-Being, the same Void, which scientists say existed before the Big Bang. Nothingness is present as much as past.

"So we can say that we understand why suffering exists: suffering makes sure Nothingness—absence—is always present, so that change can always be present as well.

"After encountering the Magician, I fell into Nothingness. It was ecstasy. I surrendered to it, lost myself in it, and then came out of it like light. This is the way of the spirit in the human, to fall into the dark and rise into the light. This is the way of death: through death, to touch the eye of God. Death is detachment and always comes at the right time.

"The spiritual child will ask, 'How do you know when it's right for someone to die? How do you know when an attachment is saturated with materialized energy and it is time to let go? I'm scared of death, so I must avoid it.'

"This is not the mystic's course. When energy reaches its saturation in a body or in a relationship, it seeks to leave the form that the 'body' or 'relationship' is; it wants new form, having filled the old form too much.

"'It hurts so much!' the spiritual child cries, feeling tears rise. 'It's so scary for me to be around death like this. I'm afraid to lose the body! Why can't *this* form live forever?'

"There is a survival instinct that pushes our minds to think of ourselves as mainly Body. Thinking this, how can we not fear the loss of Body? We think of ourselves as a delicate glass vase for whom the great challenge is to keep ourselves from breaking.

"We forget that we are eternal light itself. Without the glass the light is never refracted, it can't spread *throughout* the dark—we need the glass, this body. But our light is not limited to one glass vase. We will flower elsewhere as well. We will, when we must, surrender this glass, letting it break, so that we can continue our cosmic journey.

"In my vision, I have seen myself. My Word has been accepted by the Silence.

"Now I am free."

After I had finished my rough translation, I reread and revised and reread, passionately. I felt palpable spaces of nothingness around my mind as I strived to understand everything he wrote.

I jumped into the ocean, letting the coolness cleanse me. Coming back to shore, I dried myself, picked up my things, and set off back toward the cottages. I had questions to ask.

I began to suspect that something strange was happening when I passed the café and saw a group of tourists there, most of them staring at me. As I continued along the beach, some followed. When I got back to the cottages, there were more tourists there, some elderly, some middle-aged, some young, some with children. Some people were setting up tents on the beach. Several cars pulled up behind the bungalows. People were crowded in front of Aykut's cottage.

"What's going on?" I asked Joseph as soon as I could find him, keeping my head down as I walked past the people.

"These are individuals and families who have encountered the Magician. They've heard that the Messenger has been identified. Ragıp, Sela, Mehmet, Fusun, and others on your journey have called to these people. They have come here to support you and be with you. They will also pay their respects to Aykut. Everyone will wait for you to receive the message and bring it back to us from the island."

I looked out the window at them all. They hugged and greeted each other, chatted, helped each other. Some of the Kadı Kalesi villagers helped the newcomers get settled; others looked somewhat irritated by the huge influx of people and all the commotion.

"Joseph, look there!" I exclaimed. It was the people from Sevda Hanım's house, the ones I had tried to heal. They unloaded Ahmet's huge old Ford Galaxy. The boy with the leg problem still sat in the wheelchair; the woman with the baby held her child, who was not crying. I did not see Büna or her family.

"I wanted to ask you and Aykut questions about Aykut's words," I said to Joseph, curious to talk to the families from Kor. Were the kids any better?

"Aykut will be gone soon. Your questions may have to wait to be asked of the source, the Magician himself. For now, your learning is out there. Go and talk to these people. Enjoy being among so many enlightened people."

He turned back into the corridor and toward Aykut's room. I put the book and papers up on a bookshelf, put on a T-shirt, wrapped my towel tightly around my waist over my swim trunks, and walked outside. A tall Turkish man came up to me, speaking in German. I learned that he was from Istanbul, a technician in a lab at a hospital. I told him I had attempted to heal a few of these people and asked if he would translate for me. Through him I asked the Kor villagers about the healings. The baby did not cry as much, the mother said. The boy's leg felt better, the father said. Both families were going to Ankara in a few days to have the lumps I'd felt tested at the hospital. Through the Istanbul translator, they thanked me much too much. As they did so, I thought I felt heat rising in my hands again.

An hour later, Fusun Hanım came out of Aykut's door and called one of the group of five people with whom I was now in conversation, a middle-aged woman from Izmir, Farrukan Hanım. My anxiety at being the center of attention had lessened over conversations, fruit juice, unpacking, tea.

The gestures and conversation between Fusun Hanım and Farrukan Hanım quickened. Farrukan Hanım broke off, coming back toward me. I had their eye most of the way; once Farrukan Hanım saw this, she gestured for me to come. Excusing myself, I broke away from a small group around me.

"What is it?" I asked.

"Aykut Abi will die very soon. He gives blessings. You will come."

This seemed to be a very important tradition among these people—to bless family and friends before dying. During the last few days and the last hour, I'd heard conversations—some sad, some joyful—about Aykut's death: people recalling deaths among their own family and friends, people recalling dead ancestors, tragic deaths, funny deaths, debates over life after death, prayers for the living and dying. Aykut's death seemed to furnish the town with a focus, a portal, a source of memory, anticipation, love. I was not surprised that Aykut knew he would now die and was calling intimates around him. Many mystics did this. In India I'd learned that anyone, if he or she could get past the fear and denial of death, could feel its approach.

We walked into the house, where I saw about fifteen people around Aykut's bed. Fusun, Joseph, Aykut's eldest daughter, and two children stood on one side and other people I didn't know on the other. Aykut held his other daughter's hand and spoke to her in Turkish. There were tears in nearly all the women's eyes, and some in the men's too. I immediately felt my own eyes water. Through the tears, I felt some other emotion than pain—an undercurrent of a calmness. The reeds and the wind were in it. The ocean and the birds and the clouds and the seeds were in it. Aykut was not just a dying body surrounded by other bodies. Spirits congregated around us to welcome Aykut's soul. Their energy darted among our bodies.

"*Haberci*, come," Aykut whispered to me. The daughter stepped away, and I moved to Aykut's side. Tears welled up in me again, clouding my eyes.

"It is time for me to die," Aykut said. "I will ask you to help me die. Will you help me?"

"Yes," I whispered.

"If it is in your power," he continued, "wherever you go on this earth, let no one die alone who has not chosen to die alone. Will you become a friend to all the dying you meet?"

"Yes," I promised in a choking voice.

"Give me your hand." I put my trembling hand in his cold, bony hand, and a chill moved through me, quivering my skin.

"You are special," he said. "You have been given the power to feel more clearly and quickly what all people can potentially feel. In the pres-

ence of the Magician, you will find out what you must know of your destiny. Until then, you have only the facts, not the reasons. Often it is only
the facts we have—impatient for reasons, we make them up. Do not be
this kind of impatient person. Learn the patience of the dying, who are in
no rush."

I nodded. "I will."

"You are blessed, *Habercı*. Your energy, like the energy of every awakened soul, will become a well from which many people around the world
shall drink. Learn that the well of soul is always full. Help people learn
that the well is always full. You are worthy. Will you always remember this
blessing?"

"Yes," I said quietly, "I will remember."

"Now, *Habercı*, it is an honor to give you my love before I die. When
my mother died years ago, I had the chance to look her in the eyes. She
begged me to do so, but fear stopped me. And I have regretted it. And so
my last gift to you, and everyone present, is my eyes. Look into my
eyes . . ." Movement erupted as people responded to the invitation, moving in closer, pushing against me and against the bed, encircling Aykut on
all sides. "Look me in the eyes, please, my friends, look into the eyes of
death, be not afraid as I am not afraid." His eyes slowly swept across the
faces pressing in around him. He moved his head slightly to try to see
everyone.

When his head settled again, I, his eldest daughter, Joseph, and Fusun
Hanım were best in his view and so I looked into his deep brown eyes
through the pupils, further into a whiteness, a hidden light circle inside,
then further still into a blackness within the light, into a hole in the center of being.

He blinked his eyes and whispered, "Be afraid no longer," murmuring
now more to himself than to us, for I could sense a part of him, the instinct
to fear death, rising in the last moments. There was pain in everyone as we
all stiffened to keep looking into his eyes. I felt a shot of pain in my head,
toward the very top, my crown.

Aykut Bey blinked, looking at his eldest daughter, who fell onto her
knees near his shoulder, weeping. He reached a hand to her, and his eyes

found mine. I did not turn away. At the moment when I thought it was too much, his eyes softened and began to drift, the eyelids beginning to close.

Then his eyes closed, closing off the portal. There were sobs, hands clutching, wailing, and then awareness of myself weeping and hurting, and suddenly, from the crown of my head downward, a searing bolt of pain. I grabbed my head and moaned. Falling back out of the crowd, I moved out the back door of the cottage toward a chicken pen ten feet away, where I sank to the ground and huddled in a corner, cold, as if too much of me had gone into the hole with Aykut.

About fifteen minutes later, Joseph found me. He dropped down next to me, onto a piece of plywood. A hen pecked at seeds on the ground near my foot. The rest of the chickens were wandering out near the houses. I saw from Joseph's face that he had been crying. A tear had dried and stained a runnel from his left eye down to his chin. His eyes, red, moist, and puffy, looked sad, yet there was something else in them, a lightness, a joy—agony and ecstasy in the same face.

"He's gone, isn't he?" I said. "And you two were so close."

Joseph took my hand, squeezed it, nodded, and turned away from the chicken pen, out toward the sea, which lay about fifty feet from us. "He's gone. Yes. I have cried myself out at the location of his body. Now I seek the courage to free his soul from any grasp I may have on it.

"If I did not have faith in God, my friend, faith in the infinite, a mystical faith, that I am one with All, I could not survive the end of attachments, so many attachments, my attachment to my own boyhood, to my parents, to friendships that end, to love, to passionate life with Nura, her death, the children growing up, now Aykut's death. Every attachment reaches a saturation point—its death point—and we need so much courage to let it go, as I need courage now."

"Yes," I murmured, my head still hurting and my body beginning to ache. Was this aching experience in my body related to Aykut's death process? Saturation? Attachment? Was I holding Aykut somehow?

"When I was a young man, maybe twenty-five," said Joseph, "I realized I could not relate well to a lover because I was still too attached to my mother. What an immense confusion I felt. I did not want to fully grow up.

I did not want to give up my romantic adoration of my mother. Even my mother wanted me to give it up, but I could not. Because I could not let go of it—because I could not see and respect my mother as a woman, rather than my boyhood love—I could not grow up. Freud turned over in his grave when he watched me as a young man!

"In a mystic's terms, my childhood attachment to my mother had reached saturation, but I was desperate to keep it. I wanted more of it, more." He clenched his fist as his body remembered the grasping. "A teacher of mine, with whom I played backgammon incessantly, told me I had to let go, construct my own identity, understand that only one attachment is infinitely permanent, the attachment to God. For years I tried. Not until I was about your age, with the Kulu, did I feel my cells realigned, my psyche restructured, my Self fully enlivened. Yet knowing how to let go does not mute the grief. That in itself is a great joy, isn't it, my friend?" He turned to me. "To grieve is one of life's greatest joys. Aykut knew this, didn't he, my friend?"

"I hope I can be that way," I said.

"Yes. Now, with your memory you will calm yourself and calm me in my grief by recalling what Aykut wrote—about the glass, my friend. What was he saying?"

"He said the problem is when you become like a piece of glass for whom the great challenge is to keep yourself safe from breaking. You forget that you are light, eternal life, eternal light itself. The glass effect is an illusion, but what a challenge it is, what a piece of work because without the glass the light is never refracted, it can't spread *throughout* the dark. We need the glass, this body. But most important, we need to surrender to God so the glass can do its job. Like death is a surrendering."

Joseph smiled, watery-eyed as I was. "Yes, my friend. Let us be grateful, now, my friend, for Aykut's life. Let us go and do our duty to Aykut and to everyone. Come, let us send our friend homeward."

We helped each other up, both of us smelling a little like the chicken pen. My head throbbed as we walked back toward the house where death lay. We had a great deal of work to do to help one body die, setting to that work in a community of like-minded people, all in some pain but all aware that Aykut's energy was free now. We wrapped Aykut in ceremonial Muslim fashion, then recited many prayers I did not understand. Then we all ate and talked well into the night. Ceremonies, prayers in many languages, and ritual wailing filled the village.

Throughout this time, my body felt like a volcano building toward eruption. There were tiny explosions of gas and pain, spasms of sneezes and spittle. I became pale, tried to be social, tried to talk, tried to understand the languages spoken around me; every hour, I became less able to keep up, less capable of holding myself back from some terrible sickness that came at me. About midnight I realized I had a bad fever. About one o'clock I got someone to help me back into Joseph's house, and I fell onto my sleep cushion there. I tried to fall asleep, hoping for a cure, sure now that my sickness and Aykut's death were connected, an idea both thrilling and frightening. I tried to talk to Joseph about a death and a life working in tandem, of spirit and body communicating through my cells—but I could not articulate. As the night waned, I became delirious, and I slipped into a fitful sleep.

CHAPTER 9

The Ordeals

The ninth task of the mystic is the ritual initiation. Every mystic
must be baptized in the fires and the waters of personal transforma-
tion. While everyday life initiates the mystic all the time —every cer-
emony, every birth, every marriage, every trial and joy an initiation
into cosmic consciousness —still there must be in the mystic's life cer-
tain rites of passage through whose ordeals, ceremonies, and visions
the mystic returns utterly to the Source. In these the mystic is to be
tested, cleansed, and pulled out of the everyday self; like dying more
than once in life, and being reborn.

—The Magician

*I*t was 3:00 A.M. when I awoke on fire, exploding with achiness and
trembling, sun and moon whirling inside me, heat and cold circling
and crashing and leaving me with nothing left but moans, cries, a raging
fever, and a terrible cough.

A woman I hadn't met, who was dozing in the living room, came running in. She helped me stand up, but I crumpled onto the floor. She ran
out to get help. Joseph and Fusun Hanım came, along with others who
blurred in my vision.

"The sickness isn't going away," I murmured, as if no one could see it.
"I'm okay, I'm okay, but I'm sick." Just getting the words out felt like
climbing a mountain. Joseph and Fusun helped me back onto the cushions; meanwhile, there was a lot of talking, someone running for cold
water, a rag, then the rag on me, Joseph talking. I slipped into unconsciousness again.

"Is this doubt?" What a strange thought. Where was I? Daylight filled the room, sun shining through a window without a curtain, my body gutted, my brain gutted. I was waking up, my body still on fire. Three words kept replaying inside me: "Everything is bullshit. Everything is bullshit." I felt nothing . . . nothing inside myself; in my sickness, this nothing felt like doubt. The Magician, the idea of the Messenger, Sevda's story, Joseph's teachings, Ragıp, Sela, Engin, my seven dreams, my "flying": bullshit! I hated it all. It had caused my sickness, I was dying, wasn't I? Aykut taking me with him. Dying because of a quest for a hallucination, a conspiracy of fantasy mystics who *want* there to be a God. I shivered and sweated in a brain-burning fever; no "force" could save me, no "Being."

"No!" I groaned at myself. "What's happening to you? Your faith can be so fragile?" I talked to myself, rationalized. Even in my fever, clutching myself and sweating, couldn't I remember feeling Energy, Force, Power, God? The whole amazing manifesting world and all of human civilization had to begin in some kind of unified, evolutionary energy. I knew if I could keep talking, keep debating myself, I wouldn't die. You have known God too often, too deeply. Fight this doubt, this hatred, this sickness. Fight it!

But I felt a doubt like a craving, and I knew even if there were a God, there was no path to God except just breathing itself, everything else a fantasy. No Travelers. No Magician. No Messenger. I would never achieve "enlightenment." There was no "magic."

I felt empty of God, and I hated God for the void in me.

I drifted to sleep and dreamt I became a minuscule ball and flew into the center of a Turkish lira coin, got trapped in it, consumed by the metal and minerals, everything dark in there, me bouncing around in a pocket, in the air, skidding on a gambling table or grocery checkout counter.

I drifted awake to feel Fusun putting a damp, cool cloth on my chest. "Is love real?" I asked her. She understood nothing, just smiled. "Is love the absolute energy? Or is it all instinct, just instinct, and everything else is bullshit?" And I became unconscious again. It isn't doubt, I thought in a dream, I'm going insane. I'm becoming Feza.

I awakened again as the doctor who had tended Aykut gave me a shot.

He wore khaki shorts and a short-sleeved white button-down shirt, sweat wet in the armpits. He told me my temperature was 105 degrees and would have to be broken; I would have to get into an ice bath. Joseph helped me strip my underwear off, and then he and the doctor lowered me into a tub of cold water. I screamed. Time sped up and slowed down. I faded in and out, freezing and sweating at once.

"There's nothing!" I yelled at Joseph. "It's all crap!" He spoke to me in low tones. Hands lifted me, ending my stay in the icy cold pool. Back in bed, in my boxers, the fever down for a while, I whispered to Joseph, "Aykut's dead and I'm troubling everyone. I'm so sorry."

"It's nothing," Joseph assured me.

For four days I had a fever above 103 degrees. During my sickness, Joseph and the others performed a final service for Aykut and sent his body back to Ankara, where it would be buried.

Ice baths became a routine for me. My cries, heard throughout the village, were a matter of laughter. "The young prophet is awakening," I heard the doctor say to a German follower. I hated the doctor as a soldier hates a drill sergeant.

On the morning of the fifth day the fever passed, and my whole being cleared, as if an evil spirit had been expelled. My overwhelming doubt had vanished. Remembering my rantings, I felt silly. Throughout the rest of that day I improved; the next day too. People, even children, brought in gifts of food, knit shirts, a new pair of shoes.

"Please tell them to stop," I begged Joseph. But the little gifts kept coming.

During my fever, Sela and Ragıp came from Ankara. They visited with me a number of times during my recovery. Sela spoke for many, it seemed, when she said, "You have faced the evil, the doubt, and the darkness. It is the first of many ordeals for your initiation here. We are proud of you. You inspire all of us to face our destinies."

To Joseph I said, "Teach me about destiny," wanting to hear the timbre of his voice, the richness of his teaching.

He handed me an herbal drink that tasted like ocean brine.

"You know of destiny, I think," he demurred.

"I don't know. I just want to listen."

He lit a cigarette and looked into the middle distance. "I think everyone is born with a spiritual mission instructed by the divine life energy that is uniquely his. Everyone has a destiny that, once enacted, will connect him utterly with God, despite the limits of the body. This destiny, this mission: it is many in one, like a plant that bears many flowers, over many years. But it is one plant."

"What is your destiny, Joseph?"

He didn't even pause to think. "My destiny has felt different at different times of my life, but I see now that all stages of it have carried the same thread—to teach. For this stage of my life, as an elder, it is my destiny is to guide young searchers to clear, courageous paths of enlightenment and service."

He knew his destiny simply, almost in one sentence. This seemed beautiful to me.

"When the destiny is finished, its mission completed, the person dies. Death, in this context, is not a tragedy, only a time limit. Aykut Bey had fulfilled his destiny. And he died.

"You have a destiny. I and many others who care about you can sense some of its nature, but I can't know your destiny. Only you can know it. All I can do is to help you. You must discover who you are and why you are here on this earth. You must leave behind the comfort of being a stranger to yourself."

"A stranger to myself," I repeated.

"You are very close to knowing yourself. Your confidence, your fragility, they will come into balance soon. Yet I still smell in you the odor of terror. You are still a stranger. Spiritual fear of this kind does not exist when you know yourself, when you know yourself as one with the All. So I concluded you do not fully know yourself yet."

"But I will. I know I will."

"Yes. You will have the vision. You have had many already, but you must have One. God must speak to you. Now that the fever has passed, it is time, my friend, to clearly and purely experience God, the pure evolutionary energy of the universe—to close your eyes and see the world through God's eyes. You are ready for the island."

Lobos. It had become THE ISLAND in capital letters in my mind—a sacred place, the place where I would be reborn. I knew it was possible the island would turn out for me to be just like every other place of importance, every other church, synagogue, holy ground—each moved me to the soul, then I moved on, as if nothing had really happened, storing up wisdom and guidance, surely, but not really coming to the center.

I said to Joseph, "I've always felt like as soon as I mastered something, I had to move on to some new thing. I haven't been able to settle. I want to learn Buddhism, so I do, but then I want to become a Quaker, so I do. Then I study and practice Native American animal powers, then aikido. I used to think this was because I got bored or had some kind of pathological compulsion to disequilibrate whenever I found fulfillment—a typical modern human. But sometimes I think this wandering is my destiny—to keep looking, keep awakening in new spiritual paths, never to settle. Is that wrong?"

"Ben, I have been like you. You are young, after all; you must move like a bee from flower to flower. Soon, I think, you will come to find the commonality, the mystical essence, and you will ride its energy no matter the form it manifests itself in. One day you will notice that what has been constant in your life, what all the other flowers have had in common, is the bee itself.

"You have been fulfilling a large part of your destiny in all your searching through the many forms by which spirit is manifested in our cultures and civilizations. Especially now, as the millennium gathers to make its turn, that is our human way, to experience all we can, to be young searchers scavenging, collecting, expanding. So many traditions vibrate nowadays with mystical energy that a sensitive person such as yourself will respond to the call of the vibrations and be drawn here and there, willy-nilly. Many of us are drawn out and challenged to grow beyond, when necessary, the dogmas that no longer serve the human quest. As we journey into this 'beyond,' we sometimes fear we have lost the foundational Self, the traditional Way. What could be more frightening?

"Yet we have not lost, we have gained. We have found a freedom we must now ground in 'spiritual destiny.' In the end, there is nowhere to go to seek a destiny—an intuitive grounding for one's personal responsibility—but deep within. This is the lesson—the lesson of Jesus and all the mystics. It is the lesson our consciousness has only now evolved enough for us to learn."

"This is millennial mysticism, then," I realized aloud.

"Yes. It is what we settle in."

I watched the smoke from his cigarette rise above him and smelled the burning tobacco as he spoke.

"But settling is for the initiated, my friend. You are not initiated, not fully. You have not been attached, by your community, to the All. You cannot settle yet. Even if you mated now and had children, these would 'settle you down,' but without a total immersion of spiritual initiation, without a second birth, your soul could never fully settle into *You*. The Kulu have a wonderful way of teaching this: without second birth, the soul wanders into and out of us, seeking its true body. Until we are initiated, until we accomplish the second birth, the soul does not feel completely at home. This is why so many searching people wander into and out of attachments, even marriages, without clarity. They seek second birth but do not accomplish it, and so never align soul and body completely. In the next days we will work to initiate you, to settle the soul in you."

"I'm ready, Joseph."

"I know you are, my friend."

I felt much better over the next twenty-four hours, and Joseph set about telling me what we would take to the island, how I would fast, when we would begin. I would have to wait at least two more days he said, to fully recover from the fever. My body would be stressed again by many trials, including fasts. In order to flourish in the hardships ahead, I would need to get my strength back.

For two days we puttered around, packing, socializing. I was asked to perform more healings, which I attempted with humility. Sometimes I felt the heat in my hands, sometimes I did not. Joseph monitored my activities carefully, telling people, even the needy and sick, that I must not be utilized too exhaustingly right now.

On the second day, I began to fast in the Muslim way, which is to eat before dawn and then not again until after dusk. I was allowed to drink only water during the day, in measured portions.

On the third day, we packed anything and everything of importance to me.

This confused me. "So much?" I asked.

Joseph smiled. "Of course! Pack it all!" So I slowly filled my large and small packs with all my magic gear and clothes, and we loaded them into a small boat in the town harbor.

We packed food parcels, but nothing with synthetic chemicals, no food with additives, no sunblock or insect repellent. We packed matches and sleeping gear.

That night I was given a big send-off party. Many people got drunk on raki, beer, and wine. I drank no alcohol.

The sun rose around 5:00 and so did Joseph and I, after only two hours' sleep. We ate and then, about 5:30 A.M., started off to the island in a little motorboat donated by the owner of the grocery store. In the blue sky above us were high cirrus clouds and one huge cumulus cloud shaped like a mountain. As we moved away from shore, people waved on the beach; after a few more minutes, the white stucco houses blended in with the dry white hills. Far to the south, along the beach, we could see the town of Turgut Reis. To the north was the peninsula of hilly land on which we saw, high up, the ruined castle of the judge.

The motorboat was loud, so we didn't talk much. Despite the din, I felt pristine here. I felt myself drifting into the ocean blueness and the misty horizon. After half an hour, the island loomed before us. What looked at first to be a beach turned out to be more rock than sand. In fact, the entire shore of this side of the island was cliff and rock. I thought we would nonetheless try to land, but Joseph motored alongside the island instead. It was the other side we wanted, he yelled, from which I would see only horizon, no shore, on which was a real beach where I would camp, and above which were sheer cliffs. On the tops of the cliffs lived the storks we could always see from the mainland, flying like specks over the sea, now larger than specks as they, with their six-foot wingspan, flew over us.

We pulled up through gently breaking waves onto a white sandy beach. The sandy area had formed inside a small lagoon: the square footage about thirty feet square, sand turning to dirt, then dirt to talus. In the talus and cliff walls were only a few shrubs and trees, growing out of cracks. The tops of the cliffs were at least a football field's length up. Seagulls populated the cliffs. Storks nested in tall trees far up on the top of the island, beyond the cliffs. There were far more seagulls than storks, but the few storks flew more majestically on the high currents.

We unloaded everything and piled it near an old fire pit. Joseph told me to gather wood. Driftwood wasn't exactly prevalent, but with some walking, I found enough for a fire. I brought it back to find that Joseph had laid out my sleeping gear, some tools, including a small shovel and hammer and nails, and a tarpaulin. He had begun building a small bivouac—which we continued to build together—into the face of the rock. It was like the one in my island dream, six feet long and about three wide, with a tarp roof and two poles in the sand. Rain wasn't expected for weeks, but the sun, I knew by now, could destroy a person by midday. The beach area would not always be shaded, as it was now, by the cliffs high above.

Since we used some of my driftwood for the bivouac legs, Joseph sent me out for more. The ebbing tide left rock pools to the east of our camp. Bending for a piece of driftwood near one pool, I saw a bee drowning in the water. I had the strangest moment of indecision: Should I save it, or should I assume its destiny to be death and let it drown? My body told me I had to rescue the bee. I stuck a piece of driftwood into the water next to it so it could climb up. By the time I carried the wood back to the camp, the bee had dried enough to fly off.

As morning progressed, Joseph sent me out for wood over and over again. He seemed to be planning quite a fire. After five loads, he seemed satisfied. He suggested I generally get to know the island during the afternoon, meditate, and sleep. We were both tired from the very late night celebration. I did as he suggested, wandering gently around this new world I would live in during the coming days. Around midafternoon, he and I lay down on the beach and slept.

When I awoke, I saw that Joseph had laid out some simple clothes for me, as well as the rest of our food and water. He had also taken my journal, the blank maroon-covered book he'd given me, and two pencils out of my pack, and laid them out. Everything else was in my packs.

"What are you doing with those things?" I asked.

Instead of answering, he instructed me to light a fire. Using dead, dried shrubs from around us as initial firewood and picking a spot toward the shore just beyond my packs, I lit the fire and nursed its flames. Joseph said he wanted the fire quite big, so we threw more and more wood on. Dusk moved downward toward us now, but the air was still hot. Watching the quick-start fire, we stood in our swim trunks and T-shirts, moving back from the flames as their heat filled the air.

"It's a good fire," Joseph said, "but it can be better. My friend, it is time for you to decide whether you can leave behind the person you were and become the person you are destined to be. Are you ready to make this decision?"

"Sure," I agreed naively.

"I have taken your wallet, your journal, and other essentials from your pack. They are there, in the bivouac. Dig a hole with the shovel in the back of the bivouac and bury them."

Nodding, I moved toward the shelter, grabbing the shovel on the way. I buried my essentials about a foot down. Interesting, I thought. A neat gesture.

Returning to the fireside, I brushed sand off my knees.

"Good," he said. "Now take your packs and throw them into the fire."

"What?"

"You may take jewelry out of them, if you have any, or family heirlooms. Otherwise, the packs are filled with the paraphernalia of your present self: clothes, magician's equipment and props, books, scraps of paper about the Magician. All of it must be burned."

"Are you serious?"

He was quite serious. "Your goal in initiation is to find yourself. Only then can you *feel* the truth of what you do. Only then can you *know* where you fit and who you are. Until you know yourself, you do not know your-self as divine, you know yourself only by your paraphernalia. Until you know yourself, you cannot be sure of anything except the most material instincts. In my initiation as a young man, I did just what I am asking you to do—I destroyed the accoutrements, the paraphernalia. Do it here, *now*. It is a symbolic but potent gesture. I ask you to go through your pack item by item and gently, consciously, surrender your past to the fire. Throw each item one by one and watch the smoke of each rise to heaven."

It was too much to take in. All my magician's props? All my clothes? My Walkman, my tapes, my hairbrush, my toothbrush? "I can't do it," I said.

"Open the magician pack first," he suggested. "Look in it. What can you burn?"

I opened it, looking in at the juggling pins, handkerchief rolls, decks of cards, magic box. It's all replaceable, I thought to myself. I can buy new ones. But dammit, each brought back memories. I knew the feel of each one. It takes a magician years to get the feel of his equipment, to become one with it.

I looked up at Joseph. "But if I'm supposed to learn about energy and how it vibrates, why must I get rid of all these things? Everything I own, everything I'm attached to has vibrations for me, memories, energy."

"Yes," Joseph smiled, "that is a very wise argument, my friend. Each one does. But now you are challenged to feel safe enough to give even these up. In doing so, you invite the flood of God's love. This is a defining moment of your life, Ben. Do you have the courage to let go of yourself so that you may give birth to your Self?"

"You're saying that if I burn all of this, I'm destroying my attachment to these things, and this will open me up to utterly new experience."

"In simple terms, yes. You're inside the paradox. You must be capable of giving up everything in order to become One with all things."

"I've read about this in so many books," I said, "but I never thought I'd really have to do it. I thought I could just imagine it, and I'd be a new man."

"Some things," he said, "you must do."

I was afraid. Why? Everything I looked at seemed replaceable. Even the Magician scrapbook, I knew, could be re-created. Why was I so afraid? I had no answer. I almost asked Joseph, but I didn't really want him to answer. I wanted to know the answer myself.

I sat on my knees, surrounded by my paraphernalia, and heard snippets of wisdom flood my brain: "Because the attachments are hard to let go of . . ." "Because you are a child of materialism . . ." "Because you are afraid to let go, truly let go . . ." They all seemed true. Then, at some point, none of them seemed to matter anymore. A thought flashed into my mind: "The plastics won't burn well, plus they're bad for the ozone layer." I laughed to myself. The point was, I realized, I had no intellectual answer to my fear. To Joseph, I said, "How simple. At some point, intellectual mastery is not enough." He did not respond.

Was I really going to do this? Could I?

Picking up my magician's deck out of my pack, I began to deal the cards one by one into the fire. Each one took a second to ignite. Next I took my juggling pins out and threw them in. Their paint pealed up into oranges, blues, greens, every color of the rainbow as the different chemicals burned. I threw my scarves in, then my magic box. As it began to burn, I felt a terrible urge to grab it, rescue it. Instead, I threw the rest of my magic act into the fire. Joseph and I moved back again as the flames got higher and hotter.

Wordlessly, I threw the pack itself into the fire. It did not burn as easily as the wood and papers, but finally it did catch. I started into my other pack, pulling out everything from toothbrushes to clothes. One by one I threw underwear, socks, shirts into the flames. The individual gestures of letting go felt immense; the fear was still present, but the immensity of carelessness, the immensity of risk and detaching, much more profound. A great deal of time passed in the silence by the fire. Finally, I threw in the pack itself. The flames spit and clawed at the plastic.

"I did it," I whispered reverently. "I did it."

"Yes, you did," Joseph laughed. "Yes, you did, you stupid fool! You have become naked. And a fool!"

I felt stung. "Why do you call me a fool?" Was this a trick? Had I fallen for something?

He grinned, embracing me. "Only a fool would burn what he holds dear. Only a fool, a nut, a madman would do it—yet you did. You trusted. You had the courage only the trusting fool has. You are regaining your innocence, my friend. Yes, you are!"

The next forty-eight hours or so were spent in fasting, praying, talking, and silence. Joseph pointed to the stork nests on the trees far up on the pillar cliffs; he said that before the Magician came, I'd figure out a way to get up to them. He led me in a number of what he called "small rituals," promising a major initiation ritual soon. I couldn't think what ritual could be much more major than burning up my whole life. He told me he did not want me writing in my journal for now. I left it buried. I asked him why he hadn't asked me to burn it. "You will know later" was his only reply.

As the attachments of my life gradually receded into the fire bed, I shared with Joseph fond memories that arose from my staring into the flames late at night and then, in the morning, at the ashes. After listening attentively, Joseph suggested it was time to throw even the ashes of my old life to the wind. He instructed me to put the unburned plastic of the backpacks in a sack he'd brought. He would take it into the village and dispose of it. Once the plastic was stored, I took the remaining ashes from the fire bed in my hands and threw them toward the ocean. Before long, I myself was covered in ash. Diving into the water, I washed it away.

The lack of food got to me, bringing back memories of other fasts I had done in which I had suffered from headaches early on and become weak. It happened again this time, but it felt different; I was different, utterly involved in every moment of this initiation, utterly focused. There is a cliché that we can do something a hundred times but not until we're ready for it to work does it really work. During a particularly Hindu period, I had fasted because "it was something to try," faking my surrender to its process, and somehow my intuitions or even my biology had resisted it, making me weak and sick. Now my physical weakness and headaches moved through me quickly, and I felt centered, alive, devoted, and cleansed.

There was also a giddiness in me, a carelessness, a disheveledness, a sense of not being a part of the world and never caring if I were again. I became very funny, Joseph said, as he laughed often at my gestures, my silly comments, and my comedianlike imitations of all the people we'd met.

On the night of the second day, Joseph went back to the village, saying he would return the next, third day. He instructed me to stay awake all night and listen to the sounds of the night. In the embrace of those sounds, I should pull my journal notebook back out of the earth and write all the questions I wanted to ask the Magician when I met him.

That night was one of the most beautiful I have ever spent. For the most part, in the dark, there was only water. I went and lay in it for minutes. I lay near it, my ear to the sand. I let the crabs scuttle around me. I had long ago let the fire go out completely, so there was not even the sound of wood cooking. I sat on a rock away from the crabs, just listening to the water, imagining my own center, my own soul, as this water, making these sounds, if only I could hear it, every moment. I was lost in the lapping, the gurgling, the foaming, the singing of waves in the dark.

When Joseph returned late the next day, I lay asleep in the tent, having dozed off and on during the day. He shook me awake and laughed. "Oh, if you could look in the mirror! In a few days, you will barely recognize yourself!"

He asked me for a report on the night. I told him about the water, my oneness with it. He said, "Do you know the Latin derivation of the word 'conspire'?"

I did not.

"To conspire is to 'breathe together.' Last night you conspired with the water. You breathed together with it. In your attachments from now on in life, you must search for that measure of conspiracy. In all of them—whether with a mate, children, a job, even an attachment to a favorite fishing rod or a baseball bat—ask yourself whether you are 'breathing together' with the person or object. That is the lesson of the water, the womb from which your body came, its first habitat.

"Now let me ask you: Have you rested enough to move into the next, perhaps the hardest stage of your initiation?"

This must be it, I thought—what he had called the "major ritual."

"I'm as ready as I'll ever be," I responded.

"Then we will begin."

"Will this ritual bring the Magician to me?"

"You're still impatient, aren't you?"

"I'm impatient," I admitted.

"Well, my friend, then perhaps you need some work to do. Dig a hole there." He pointed to a spot near the center of our little camp. "You'll find sand on the surface, then dirt. Dig a deep hole."

"Just dig a hole? Is this part of the ritual?"

"Oh, yes. Make it two meters deep and three fourths of a meter in diameter. Can you do that with that shovel?"

"I guess so," I judged, looking at the small shovel and the sand.

"I will return in the morning, and we will continue."

"Joseph," I asked almost pleadingly, "is that all? Just dig a hole?" I had admitted impatience to him. Was he now going to test my patience?

"For now that's all. I'll be back tomorrow."

I wanted to ask more, but once again we said our good-byes and I settled in to wait for the passing of dusk and the coming of night. Once the sun had fully set, I could eat my night ration: a can of sardines and a package of crackers. I opened them but did not eat yet. In the light of the descending sun, I did my aikido katas. Then I meditated. Still it was not sunset, so I started digging the rather large hole, looking longingly at the already opened fish.

To accomplish the task Joseph had given me, I had to dig an incline along the ground that then allowed me to dig the hole he wanted: approximately six feet by two feet. If I didn't dig the incline, I would have difficulty getting the sand and dirt out of the bottom of the six-foot hole— two feet of diameter wouldn't allow bending down and shoveling out. So I dug the trench incline, then mastered the hole, then filled in the trench. This work was hard but enjoyable and took two hours. Night had come. I ate ravenously and fell asleep as soon as my head hit the sand.

When I awoke, I mumbled angrily at missing the dawn. How had I slept through the stork calls? Now I would have to go the whole day without food. Jumping into the ocean, I cried out with the cold of the water, but it woke all my cells like a shock. Back on shore, admiring the hole, I saw in my mind a bad kung fu movie where the old master tells the kid to just fill it in again, then dig it, then fill it in.

I looked up at the cliff trees where the storks perched. Would I get up there today? I was aware of the instinctual intensity of my fear of the rock face. Joseph had assured me there was a safe way up, but I couldn't yet see it.

An hour or so later, the morning still young, Joseph arrived, the motorboat sliding smoothly up onto the beach. As he got out, I saw that he carried with him a thick white linen cloth.

"What's that for?" I asked. After a lonely night, human contact invigorated me.

"In this next ordeal, you will encounter evil and your fear of evil."

"Evil," I repeated, waiting. "How?"

"You will see, my friend. You will feel the evil. Be patient. You are still impatient for the Magician to come, my friend?"

"No, I'm all right," I lied. He looked at me knowingly.

"Okay, yes," I said frankly. "But don't make me fill up the hole again. Please."

He laughed. "Oh, no, not that. Please now, take off your swim trunks so you are naked, and then get into the hole you have dug."

"What?"

"You will be in the hole a long time. You will urinate and perhaps defecate in it. You will not want your only pair of shorts dirtied."

"Oh, man!" I exhaled. Now I remembered, in Paris, his comment about his own ritual initiation in Africa; he had been buried for days. I froze, looking at the hole. A stork let out a croaking call above us. Joseph peered up toward its shadow on the cliff wall, then toward the bird itself.

"If you hesitate out of modesty," he said, returning his eyes from the sky to me, "you must tell me."

I frowned. "You know it's not that. I couldn't care less whether you see me naked. I'm just—" I was going to say "curious" but knew it was a lie. More honestly, I said, "I'm scared, dammit. You want me to get buried in that hole, right?"

"Yes, up to your chin."

"For how long?"

"We shall see. For as long as it takes."

"To do what?"

"It will become clear. Take your time considering this new course. I will wander around the island and return in a while."

He dropped the white cloth and walked off along the beach, disappearing beyond the rock parapet and leaving me to my feelings. You knew you'd have to do something bizarre and scary, I reasoned with myself. You knew, so what's the problem? I remembered the Lakota Indians when I was a boy, how we had driven to the reservation and watched them shove metal prongs into their skin—piercing themselves—and dance the Sun Dance. I thought of the yogi in Madras who had sat in one position, on ten nails, meditating, for twenty-four hours. I thought of boys going to war and living through Hell. I thought of a woman giving birth. What ordeal had I ever undergone, really, that was like these? Here was one I should do.

Standing there, looking at the hole, I remembered also that the first man, besides my father, I could recall asking me to strip naked was the doctor who had raped me. Slivers of that memory coursed through me— the heavy breathing, the feeling of his penis up my anus, the flight of my mind from my body. Hadn't that been an ordeal enough, dammit? Hadn't six months of that, at ten years old, been more than enough? It had taken me a decade of therapy just to feel like a normal human being, not just a shame-filled victim. What's all this bullshit about ordeals anyway? And initiation—hadn't my life been enough of a damn painful initiation?

"Okay," I murmured aloud, "you're scared. Let it come at you. I'm scared," I said aloud, "it's okay to be scared. I've been scared before."

Admitting the fear felt good. It was an instant of altered consciousness, a moment of healing.

I breathed deeply, opening my eyes and looking at the hole again. I imagined my body enveloped by the earth.

"The earth," I said aloud, thinking: Earth. Then: Earth, Air, Fire, Wa-

ter. These were base components of any authentic initiation. Fire had
been the burning of my past; Water, my night vigil? Air? Was Air the
storks or something yet to come? And now Earth? Return to the womb
now, at my second birth? Feel the earth vibrate around my body like a
mother?

As if coming out of a trance, I noticed insects coming at me. On this
island I'd already experienced gnats and flies during my first day. A few had
bitten me on and off so that I was used to them. The gnats hadn't swarmed
me yet. Now, as I stood at the hole, a swarm of the gnats found me, circling
mainly my head and shoulders. A bee seemed to come with them, finding
my stomach. Some flies and horseflies came too. This was a very strange
assault upon me, a strange sudden attraction of them to me. They landed
on me more in these few seconds than they had in two days. What the hell
was that about?

I swung my arms wildly, swatted, twisted, murmured. Aloud I said,
"What in God's name—" I ran toward the water, plunged in, went under,
getting relief. Under the water's surface I felt safe. Raising my head, I saw
no insects. At first this seemed fine; or they'd gone away. But then, as I
studied the water's surface, I noticed few insects there. Most had flown off
me before I'd hit the water. Damn! I couldn't see them swarming onshore,
but they must be. Where? How the hell could I stay buried in a hole, only
my head above, and survive the insects, the itching, the attack, my hands
trapped and unable to help me swat them? Impossible!

I rose up out of the water, salty now, and dropped onto the sandy
shore. I watched a fly light on my wet leg, then another, felt a horsefly on
my back, then another. I swatted at them, but they immediately came
back, reattaching to the curly brown hair of my legs, arms, and torso.
Stings and irritations bulbed up, and I scratched. A black butterfly with
two gold eyes on each wing poked at the flesh over my stomach. I watched,
wanting to repel the insects but mesmerized, too, by the little black antennae near my belly button, antennae that looked just like two of my
own hairs. While I watched, more insects came, the flying horde of gnats,
returning for more of me. I felt the urge to jump up again, like a swelling
of a cough or sneeze inside me.

But I caught some other signal, a soulful feeling. It sent a flash of electricity through me that exploded in every piece of my body, with strange tinglings like a million tiny bee stings, freezing me there in its tingling, not hurting me, not stinging, but as if bees were pollinating every cell of my body from within. I felt lit up inside, as if my inner cells were somehow making a quilt of connection and communication with these insects on my skin.

For I don't know how long, maybe just a few seconds, I could no longer feel insects bothering me. Either they had stopped or I was so stimulated by the tingling inside that I could not feel them. My eyes were closed and there was no itching on me, no flies sucking salt off my dropleted skin. I felt no fear, no fear of the little intrusions because I felt no separation. Was that it? Yes, that felt like it, no separation, no difference. It was like flying, it was Union, I saw the insects not as attackers but as lovers. They were loving me; they were letting me feed them. They loved me as they ate my bits of flesh, loving me because I and they were one in the larger Union. I was the host to life. Everything fit together as the quilt of tingling, a gift from God, kept me from having to scratch and run.

I knew this moment of grace to be an altered state, for when it passed, I saw all over my skin welts from the stings of gnats, horseflies, and bees. On my arms rose three, four welts, on my legs the same; my neck, my chest, my back were also scathed. After the minutes of altered consciousness passed, intense pain invaded. I swatted, itched, jumped up and into the water, wanting relief; now completely gone was the altered state that had controlled my motor reactions to skin irritation and pain. The water relieved the pains, but the salt made them worse. I came out of the water, swatting at another bug on me, groaning.

I had been pollinated. At the time, it had been painless. Now it had finished, and I was in pain. I dropped onto the sand, rolling in it, knowing from having lived in Hawaii as a kid that on the beach, sand was the best way to nullify the pain of insect bites.

Despite my discomfort, I wore a smile from ear to ear. "Thank you," I said aloud, nearly in tears from the altered state and the pain. The insects moved away from me, finished with me, enabled to continue on their way.

To encourage them on their journey, I picked up the linen cloth and used it as a fan.

I sat alone a long time, meditating, desperately trying to stifle the urge to scratch all the stings. "Joseph!" I called out. He wasn't near, so I stood up and set off on foot to find him, still covered in sand and welts.

"You've done it, my friend!" He delighted in my description of the ordeal.

"Was it the Magician doing it, not me? How did I have the power to do that with the insects? Did *you* make it happen? I mean, the pain of the stings—I barely felt it. I was in an altered state. The itching, it was terrible, yet freeing—so alive, so full of embrace, painful embrace, like the yogi lying on a bed of nails. He embraces the pain. That's what he does. I understand how he does it."

"Yes," he agreed. "And perhaps in your particular biology there is something in your sweat that attracts insects."

"I'm ready for the hole now," I said, scratching myself. "Is the cloth to cover my head from insects?" We had walked back to the bivouac, where I pulled off my shorts. He picked up the shovel.

"Also the sun," he explained. "During the daylight hours I will stay with you and guard you from sun and bugs. I remember once in the initiation ground near Kulu, both the initiate and the initiator fell asleep and a poisoned mosquito bit the initiate near the eye, infecting it. He lost his eye. I do not wish this for you."

Joseph instructed me to try to urinate, and I did, in the ocean, emptying my bladder. I came back and dropped down into the hole, finding that it came only to my shoulders, not reaching my head. Joseph helped me out and held my legs as I went face first into it with the shovel, bringing up more dirt from the bottom. A few minutes later, I dropped in again, the hole just right. Joseph began filling the dirt in around me.

"You will be in this hole for many hours," Joseph said. "The cloth will protect you during the hours of sun. You will enter different kinds of wakefulness and sleep. The earth will be your teacher. The sound of the ocean will be your lullaby. You and I will not speak. At night I will sleep nearby, keeping the fire. Crabs may want to come at you in the night, but the fire, the smell of its smoke, will deter them. I will sleep not in long passes but in short bursts. I will guard your body so that your spirit can be liberated. This is my duty now."

As he talked and shoveled, the sand slapped at my flesh like cold hands. It didn't take long for him to finish burying me in the clammy earth. Patting the dirt down around my neck, he said, "I will not speak for some time. Be well, my friend."

"Thank you for everything, Joseph," I said and closed my eyes, resolving not to speak again until he did.

To be embraced by the earth is an indescribable feeling—like a satin robe, immensely tight. Once the earth, after an hour or so of my twistings and Joseph's last pats, settled completely around me, I could manage no movement of feet, hands, anything. At first I thought I couldn't breathe, the earth was so tight across my lungs. I flailed as best I could. "Quiet your breath," Joseph whispered. I wriggled more in the vice, my body strong enough to cause some cracks in the sand up by the neck but not strong enough to free me. "Quiet your breathing." I moaned in fear but did finally slow my breathing. Yet over the first hours, even with my breathing in place, I continued to experience instinctual recoils. I felt irritability rise, I begged Joseph to let me out, I yelled at him. He did not respond, and again I quieted myself. Joseph worked at building a stick scaffolding for the white cloth, silently working around my head. By the time the sun became uncomfortable, the scaffolding was done, my head protected.

By that time, too, my waves of anxiety had passed. There was, in the end, just the cool smoothness of the earth's skin tight around me, and I a tiny being, held by that skin, ready to stay. My face was at ground and ocean level and adjusted to it; my eyes watched the tops of waves. I heard slurps and insect buzzings. Joseph swished a fan of white cloth around my head, warding off bugs. The itching on my face was miserable for a time, my hands frantic at first to scratch all over me. But even that passed, and the earth itself healed the itchings on my torso, arms, and legs.

Under the hot noon sky, I felt myself drifting into the ocean, like a wave. Shadows of storks swathed the ocean's surface. Stork croaks entered my head like a language I thought I knew from another place. I closed my eyes in meditation, seeking the center of myself in the unfamiliar world of motionlessness, carried on the laments of waves lapping onto shore.

The many hours I spent enfolded in the earth were some of the most grueling and ecstatic in my life. Joseph cared for me as he promised, and tears come to my eyes as I remember his silent, able presence during those forty hours. I ate nothing. I drank only the water Joseph held to my lips every few hours. I exploded with visions and dreams, wanting to write them down, speak them, remember them—but remained immobile, so many insights fading into oblivion, unrecorded, lost. I came to a time when I experienced the blending of self with Nothingness. I came to a time when I saw myself blended with Everything. Both experiences were, in pure feeling form, the same ecstasy.

After about a day in the ground, I found myself climbing the rock face to the stork's nest. I was aware of my soul leaving my body and climbing. I was aware that it was a dream, but I was also aware of climbing. It was a hallucination, altogether real. I climbed impossible, mossy sides of rock, came to a huge tree, and climbed up it to a nest of eggs. The storks attacked me but never touched me. They fought their own instincts, wanting to keep me away from their eggs, yet holding back from a full attack on me, as if some higher self in them knew I was meant to touch, even bless, their progeny. I held one egg in my hand for days, motionless, patient. In its hatching, I became the father of a squeaking bird child. Leaving the bird there to its own species, I climbed back down the rock face almost effortlessly.

Later I saw back into my past—bits of childhood, images from college, my midtwenties. I flew through scenes of places, parents, friends.

In the middle of the second night, I found myself wandering far into the human past, into another man's life centuries ago that felt as if I, or a close friend, were living it. In this life I had a wife and children; my wife's name was Gabriella. I walked on a pilgrimage from Istanbul to Ankara; a man of faith and a scholar of some kind, definitely a Muslim.

While I and an entourage of people, followers of mine, lay sleeping, bandits attacked us. Though a spiritual man, I was tough, my hands made for more than praying; I fought the bandits with my big hands. There was a teenage girl whose legs were pried open by a huge bandit rapist. Like a lion I charged the beast on her, knocking her free from him. With my fists I raged at his filthy hard cock. He groaned as his manhood was pulverized. My rage was like nothing anyone had ever seen in me.

I seized the rapist's sword and prepared to cut off his genitals, feeling in my adrenaline like a hero of the flesh. But something in his moaning stopped me, his voice the moral breath of God. Realizing myself again, I rushed to the girl, who cried, "Imam, imam, watch out!" Behind me came three of the bandits. I couldn't fight them. They pinned me down, one of them hissing in my ear. "Are you an imam? Are you?" I answered yes as the girl ran free. I fought the men but then was hit on the head and fell into darkness.

When I awoke I lay tied by hands and ankles, on a horse's back, my head facing down to the moving earth. We rode deep into the forest. I descended again into sleep and reawakened in an encampment where I lay on a bed, in a tent, lit by candlelight, among riches, beside a man of some social stature attended by his warriors. The man was huge, tall, and imposing. He already had about him so much of death, the warriors of the flesh could do his soul no good.

I learned quickly why my life had been spared and why I was here. This dying man, a chieftain of outlaws, had in his throat a growth so large—as big as an orange—that he could hardly speak. Feverish, he had been crying for a healer with divine powers. When his warriors heard the girl call me imam, they had thought that their master's prayer was answered and brought me to the encampment. Here I stayed for days, ministering to this dying man, whose name was, I learned, Sultan ibn Yusus, not of Turkish but of Arabic origin; I learned that he was a man of the desert, clearly a brutal man. Even in his dying, he asked his warriors for an exact counting of the dead and the raped. I wanted to kill him, but I had to do what a holy man did. He wanted spiritual conversation and salvation from me. As I gave it, I asked for my books, so I could read to him. It turned out that everything had been burned. I had only myself to rely on with the evil soul.

I talked to him, trying to think of a way to outwit his group and get away. During my time with him herbs, leeches, bleedings were all admin-

istered by a doctor whom his warriors had captured from a caravan and
whose ministrations were not successful. Neither of us was allowed more
than a few steps from the tent. A stream talked to me from behind a bank
of trees, but I never got close enough to touch it or bathe in it. I became
the dirtiness of their world.

"Quote for me the Second Surah, you piece of shit!" Yusus would
order, croaking words, terrified by his own helplessness, enraged by his terror, and then becoming apologetic for his flashes of disrespect. I wanted
desperately not to quote any of God's words to him, not a syllable. But
really, I had no choice. In flashes I would see humanity in Yusus, and I
must try to teach him. Then the flashes would disappear, and I would con-
template ways to kill him. In those moments I saw myself as an agent of
civilization, removing from the town square a predator who menaces the
children of civilization. But then I realized that if I killed him I would
never see my wife and child again, for I myself would be killed. I came to
feel utterly powerless. All I could do was just keep doing.

One morning, the doctor-healer came in with his head dragging
down. He knew he must tell the outlaw chieftain of death's imminence,
but he also knew if he did, the outlaw would need him no longer and
would kill him. He brought the sultan the morning's usual poultice and
herbs and administered them to the huge man. Just before he left, I said,
"Sultan ibn Yusus, I have made a decision. It has come time for you to
speak to God. You desire salvation, but it will not come if you die unwit-
ting, or without the proper preparation. So you must admit you are dying
and die a good death—not a flight from death, not a false hope. You must
face death, for you are not one to be consumed in fear. Isn't that right?
Aren't you fearless?"

Yes, he said, he was fearless.

"Then a holy man must kill you and a healer must assist. This is what
I have dreamt. God has spoken to me. The doctor has hidden the close-
ness of your demise from you to save his life. You must ask the doctor to
tell the truth."

The doctor shuddered, thinking I had doomed him.

"Yes," he admitted, "you will die today or tomorrow or the next day.
Your bladder, your spleen, your liver, all have stopped."

Before ibn Yusus had time to think, I said, "Your course is clear." The
sultan began coughing up a red, muddy stream. While the doctor tended
him, I said, "Call your finest man, tell him he must spare our lives and return us to whence we came and must not punish us for taking your life. Explain to him it is your will to die now, in God's grace, rather than later, at
the door to Hell. I will then slit your throat; the doctor will assist me. Recall that though you have been many bad things in your life, one thing you
have always been that is glory to God's sight, and that is fearless."

Ibn Yusus thought for what seemed an eternity, weighing his whole
life in those moments. Then he called his guard to find his lieutenant. He
told me to explain. Wide-eyed and suspicious, the lieutenant argued
against the plan, but ibn Yusus exercised his ultimate authority. His decision was final, he croaked. It was God's will. With the angry but compliant
lieutenant in the room, I led ibn Yusus in prayers, and then, as if I were
made for it, I slit his throat. The cancer was revealed, and I slit that open
too, like a rotten fruit. When I had slit to its center, devils swarmed out,
and I screamed.

Joseph awakened with my scream. He came over and looked into my eyes,
but said nothing. I started to talk, but he turned his back. I was afraid, the
night all around me, the dreaming so vivid, so intense. I watched water
lapping onto the shore, relieving myself in the earth, feeling my own urine
against me, tight, warm on my midsection. I tried to talk to Joseph again,
but he walked away. He disappeared, and I worried he would never come
back. I cried for him. Night was dark, forever, and I kept staring into the
maw of the dying outlaw. If you have never seen devils and demons face to
face, you have not really felt your inborn human fear. I struggled to get free
of the earth, shaking and wriggling myself inside it, rocking and pushing
back and forth, side to side. Though my efforts exhausted me, I managed
to open perhaps a centimeter around my neck, no more. I screamed with
claustrophobia, screamed with the darkness of my vision, the pain of it,
the darkness of the night. I railed at Joseph, calling him a son of a bitch.

Time passed, probably hours, and I realized that I understood finally
something Joseph had said to me back in Paris: "Women give birth—it is

a physical suffering like no other. Every man must at some time suffer pain equal to the woman's in her birth throes if he is to know he is a man." I closed my eyes, tasting my own salty lips as if they were food, and they were my only food.

When I slept again, I entered the world of hallucinations again. This time I lay in a coffin. The world became very dark, and I rose up beyond my dead body into the air above a road. Around me I saw trees, buildings, clouds, birds, all of them in spirit form. It was a congregation of angel spirits, each a pulse of light. A tunnel emerged in sky, utterly dark, and I entered it. There was the angel of death in black robes, holding her hand out to me. I clasped her hand, happy to find it, and we floated down the tunnel. We came to a wall of light, shot through it, and entered the wall of ocean I had seen in one of my seven dreams. Passing through it, we came to a huge tree that rose from earth to heaven, like a cross. It was like the Tree of Life in my other dream. All the planets circled it, moon and sun and stars, and there were sounds all around of thunder and flashes of light.

"I'm flying," I said, "I'm flying." The angel of death was gone. There was just me. And I had become me, really me, again, flying through a world of ocean, like a dream-fish, gods and spirits all around me. I came to a pillar from an old Greek ruin. On the pillar was a stork's nest. I landed on the nest, sat on the eggs. I had become a stork! I had died and become a white bird, like an angel, sitting on a nest in which one egg begged to be born. Then there came up at me a man, myself, climbing up to my nest. I flew up, circled, cried, called, brandishing my authority at the man, but he sat so serenely with my egg, he sat so much himself like one of us, like a spirit, seeming so deserving of touching my egg. I attacked him, but I did not touch him; I raged, but I did not kill him. I wanted him to bless the egg. He held my egg for the longest time, and I saw that it was not my egg he held but God's, and at that moment it cracked, and the baby came out, and the man blessed it and then went away, climbing back down the side of the pillar, to his human world, and I realized I would miss him terribly, and I called to him.

The man looked back up at me, as if he understood. I hoped he understood. I hoped that my dying and his living could become one. I hoped he realized that he would always have on this side of the wall his other

half, me, who searched for him, and for his blessings, as excitedly and fear-
fully and hopefully as he had searched for me and for my nest.

I opened my eyes into the dark of the Lobos night. Joseph lay sleeping by
the fire. I felt no need to wake him, to call out to him. I had seen beyond
the wall of human vision into the other world, where I had a companion.

"It is time," Joseph said as dawn rose. "Wake up, my friend."

Joseph squatted at my right side. He had not spoken in days, so he had
to clear his throat to be heard.

I tried my own voice, saying nothing at first except his name.

He smiled, lifting the shovel.

I murmured, "I've seen something. I've been somewhere. Freedom is
possible."

As his shovel hit the earth and I, from within it, felt earth shiver, I
talked a blue streak, laughing at myself as I did, telling him everything I remembered.

Soon I was out of the hole. He told me to go into the ocean and clean
off. I did it and came back and, in a fit of adrenaline finished telling him
everything I remembered: the stork egg, ibn Yusus and the outlaws, everything. He suggested various interpretations, all of which made sense to
me. The outlaw chieftain was a past-life episode, remembered vividly.
Joseph said that he himself had gone through a similar kind of dreaming
and hallucination when he was in the ground during his early years of initiation. The stork egg was a gift to my future life, in which I would be a fertile father, he suggested. I had held one egg, so he thought I would have
one child. "Your death and rebirth into a stork is no surprise," he suggested. "Like the stork, you are the bringer of new life to the people. In
the stork, you have found your companion spirit, this mirror self, who is
always near to help. In your time in the earth, you have experienced
spiritual liberation. You are a new person now, my friend. You will notice
it gradually."

"Thank you," I said, tears coming to my eyes. We embraced each other firmly.

"Now, my friend, the Magician will be here very soon. So I must leave you to your encounter. You will sleep off your exhaustion so you can be ready. You will continue to fast. Your mind will need to be sharp and pure, your memory capacity in full bloom. It is one of the reasons you've been chosen as the messenger, so you must be ready."

"I feel ready," I said to him. I felt utterly open to life.

"Do you feel worthy of vision," he asked, "worthy of seeing beyond what anyone before you has seen?"

"Yes, I do. But beyond anyone else? I don't know. Am I more worthy than anyone else? I can't see why I would be."

"You are not more worthy than anyone else. Anyone's vision is potentially the next step in our spiritual evolution. You are here, however, and the Magician is coming. Are you worthy?"

"Yes," I said quietly, "I am."

"Do you feel worthy of God's love?"

"Yes, I do."

"I have done what I can to prepare you for your destiny. I will leave you."

We talked more but mainly because I couldn't bear to part with him. When he finally did leave, I fell into a sweet loneliness. I wandered the island, I slept, I wrote in my journal, recording everything I could of my experience over the last days. I felt compelled to record it *now*, as if I were about to risk death. I wrote furiously, some moments like a poet, others like a scientist.

During this time I experienced many small ecstasies. The ocean spoke to me. I slept some more. I talked to the storks. I became a child of my surroundings, losing my human form, spending lots of time on hands and knees, smelling briny sand or swimming in the sea. I looked into the fire, remembering the vignettes of Joshua Millicent's encounter with the Magician, the Urdu encounter, Ragıp's encounter, remembering so many and wondering how mine would go. I realized in remembering their encounters what a long way I had come toward my own. What had each of them gone through, equivalent to my two months since that moment with Mick Laur, to prepare them for their encounters?

I thought that what had happened so far on the island was immense and beautiful in its own right. Even if the Magician never came; even if he, and the Travelers, and the whole thing turned out to be, in scientific terms, a hallucination that a hundred people had experienced due to food or drugs, I had already received more gifts than one could expect in a lifetime.

Toward evening of the next day, Joseph came out to see how I was doing. By the time I saw him, my moment of completion the day before had gone. I was impatient. I wanted the Magician! My own fickleness, rather than filling me with shame as it might have even a few months before, entertained me. I told Joseph about it and confessed the real truth. "My impatience doesn't go away!" I complained. "Even after all my incredible experiences. I'm going to be enlightened one day and still impatient! That's just how I am."

Joseph smiled. "Yes, that is your life burden, to learn patience. Be patient, my friend. What you want will happen. The Magician will come."

I'd been away from the town for almost five days, but he said most of the people were still there, camping, waiting; in fact, more had arrived. Joseph and I talked a little while; then he left, and dusk burned red on the horizon. I slept well during that night and awoke to find a bumblebee lying, quite dead, on my naked chest, above my heart. I stared at it for a long time, then rolled left, catching the bee in my hand as it fell off me. I stroked its soft back with my finger, touching it as I had seen myself do back in Paris, in a split second of déjà vu.

CHAPTER 10

The Message

The tenth task of the mystic lies in accomplishing illumination itself. Illumination is not merely a matter of "seeing the light," it is a matter of becoming the light. It is not merely a matter of "having a few ecstatic days of union with God," it is a matter of becoming God for good. Illumination is the full understanding of oneself as One.

The Travelers have always directed the people through the first nine tasks of enlightenment to the tenth and final task: absolute faith. The ultimate sense of interconnectedness is called faith, and gaining it is more difficult than any other matter. The mystic becomes the light by becoming fully a person of faith. You know people who have accomplished the tenth task when you meet them. Their faith is a rock that cannot be shattered. Their service to their loved ones and to the world is the foundation on which life rests.

—The Magician

*L*ight began to form on the ocean's surface. Feeling like a feather floating on an invisible current of air, I sat near dusk the next day and watched the light grow some fifty feet out on the sea. I had spent the day naked, swimming, waiting, my impatience passing into solitude. All day I had felt love for myself, for the salty air, for the smell of brine, for the stork dropping or scuttling crab, for the bug bite or fresh breeze, all of it was love to me and of me, an incandescence everywhere of myself and yet not myself, a flickering of flame in every thing and every mood. I had come to the end of myself, like coming to the edge of a world. There was no more I could do except get out of the way and let the ocean of air take me, float me, wherever it would.

A thought flickered by—"You've annihilated the ego"—and another—"You're in the next world, you're in a totally altered state, this is a shaman's journey." But these seemed irrelevant and I was happy to let them go, so tired of naming and defining, so ready to embrace a long, long forgetting that became alternately repentance, apology, ecstasy, humility, pure gratitude.

"You're coming," I heard myself murmur. "I feel you. I feel you coming."

Light flew at me like a stork low on the water, as if it were a stork made of glass, picking up the sun's light and flying to me. I blinked, and it was a stork. I blinked, and it was pure light. It kept coming at me, moving along the air above the soft waves, expanding as it got closer. I was aware of myself, naked, sitting on the sand, watching light fly over the ocean. Without thinking, I curled my legs under me and got on my knees. As the bird of light came floating at me, expanding into human form, I bowed, like a praying Muslim. I raised my head and saw the Magician before me, white light in a tall body, the bald head, the robe.

"I am the Magician," the figure said—ghost, spirit, hallucination, light emanation, Traveler, God? Speechless, I stared. It was actually happening to me—what had happened to the other hundred people was happening to me! The Magician had finally come, and I, like a supplicant, swayed and rocked and stared wide-eyed in the presence. Throughout my body I felt drenched in the joyful light that emanated from him. All resistances in me, then even my sense of my own body around me, dissolved.

The Magician's face was a smiling one, every feature white—eyes, hair, eyebrows, lips—and everything lit from inside, as if his skin were translucent and thin, a membrane barely able to contain the immense glow that washed the world with love. I realized in an instant that I had never felt love like this—unobstructed, unentangled by its own actions and relationships. This was pure love.

"You are the Messenger chosen to carry lessons for the world," he intoned. "I am the spirit who will provide them to you. I bring to you the first of seven messages for the new millennium. Others will receive the subsequent six messages at a later time. Are you ready to receive the first message?"

"You're so beautiful," I whispered. "You're so alive, so real. I've never experienced reality like this before. This is what's real, isn't it? The mystics are right. All the rest is illusion."

"No," he corrected me, his voice moderate to low in pitch, almost whispery. "There is not one reality and the rest illusion. There are many layers of infinite Being. Your world of breath and bone is not mere illusion, as so many teachers have taught. It is *a* reality. I gave you glimpses into some of the other realities in your seven dreams. At this moment in time, you are experiencing me in the fourth reality, to which you have come like a wanderer.

"Your human brain, when it is stimulated and utilized most fully, is capable of understanding, experiencing and harnessing the power of five of the realities. You are with me now in this fourth reality in order to play your part in the evolution of consciousness. Your brain is presently incapable of finding the other three realities. Your memory is very fine, as have been the memories of many of your messengers, known as prophets, throughout the last three thousand years. Your memory is one of the reasons I have chosen you as the Messenger. Remember what I say."

My brain had a question every millisecond—What are the realities? Where do the spirits live? Are you God?—yet my brain simultaneously calmed itself. I breathed.

"Your race is evolving from the ascent of intelligence, which for two million years you have experienced, to the embrace of the spiritual mind, capable of many dimensions of experience. A few among you, shamans and legendary prophets and great thinkers and teachers, these beings of great compassion, have always been able to travel among the dimensions. Now many more than a few of you are becoming capable of this compassion. It has made your race mad with frenzies of technological creation and confusions of love and hate. Such is the fate of a race now evolving from what your people have called *Homo sapiens* to what you will call *homo infiniens*. A time of transition is always frenetic.

"Now I suggest you ask me the questions *you* were born to ask."

Like a chant, I recited the questions Joseph had suggested I prepare.

How was the world created?

Why are humans on this earth?

What is a soul?

I asked many questions like these. When I was done, he said, "I will present ten spiritual principles now. They will answer many of your questions. These are the primary principles of mystical intelligence. On these, the new human bases the life journey."

"Principle 1. All Creation evolves from the Void.

"Young Messenger, I can recall when the darkness was All, its evolutionary energy immutable but unmoving, a stillness unborn. It lacked power to know itself as All; thus it did not move, for all movement is knowledge, all energy exists toward one end, to know itself.

"To fully understand these things, you must gain access to the sixth reality, which is beyond creative process, a reality your brain cannot discover except in symbols of a story of sudden explosion. In that sudden explosion began the Creation. That sudden explosion itself was and is what you call God. What is God? God is the evolutionary energy of the universe. God exploded within the nothingness that is the basis of all things and began a spiral path to you, to this moment.

"Principle 2. Love is the reason for existence.

"The original energy of all things is Nothingness. The evolutionary energy of all things is Love. Let us speak of love, for love is the reason you have your first reality to live in.

"Once God exploded from the Nothingness, mystical evolution began. It began with one purpose and one purpose only, to know itself. That purpose has one longing within it, and one only, to be compassionate to itself. And so God created oppositions with attractions—stars, animals, plants, humans—so that never again could Nothingness occupy all of time and space. The oppositions are forms of consciousness. Consciousness moves in all realities, seeking love. One of its highest forms is the human form. The ability of human consciousness to experience love and compassion on a cosmic scale is the human being's great blessing but is also, at present, still confusing to the human, causing crises of attachment and detachment, as well as misunderstood sickness and pain.

"Principle 3. Crisis is as essential for the development of consciousness as is quiescence.

"Neither sick nor well is a 'better' state of consciousness, but in the well state, suffering is experienced as a part of abundance; in the sick state, it is experienced as alienation. In the evolution of consciousness, sickness would not feel painful except that Nothingness is ever present and finds a home in sickness, returning the sick being to evolution's original stasis in the Void. Thus, just as a child is born in pain, pain is the original state of being, the stasis from which God, or consciousness, or the Great Potential and the Great Opportunity, exploded, and explodes and evolves in all things, including you, the human consciousness. Without the crisis or sickness, consciousness would not be motivated to evolve.

"Principle 4. Human consciousness is a unique and discrete form of energy.

"Human consciousness is one with all other forms of consciousness, plant, animal, spirit, and spook. The ego religions have forgotten this fact and have imagined a human place that is superior in the moral realm to other forms of consciousness. This is the primary source of danger in your world at this time. There is no moral superiority between forms of energy.

"Human consciousness is, however, particular in the self-consciousness of its knowing. For trillions of your years, there was evolution of consciousness but no conscious reciprocal activity between creator and created. All creatures know how to pray, but with the human brain came prayer that crossed over from the first reality all the way through to the second, then after many years of development, to the third, then more recently to the fourth.

"God in youthful creativity created beings evolving in space but without the capacity to cross time. But the human brain communicates as God in God with God of God through both space and time.

"So the evolutionary energy, which first exploded from Nothingness, exploded again when your brains learned to see, two million years ago. But your brains were afraid, so new was their power, so new were they to the self-consciousness that is God before your eyes, in mystical connection. So afraid are they of the freedom that the brain allows, the freedom to discover the many realities.

"Your brains became afraid and developed ways of ego, including a passion for material goods, yet these have not freed the brain, and the brain is feeling trapped.

"Your brains became afraid especially of their own dying. This is to be expected, but now your civilization must study dying. It takes little intuition to notice that this is a course you have already decided upon in a joyless way as you accomplish the extinction of species and perhaps your own life on your planet. However, you will soon find another course of deepening compassion and consciousness and freedom that will allow you to experience death without either nuclear explosion or gradual degradation of your planet and its billions of conscious beings.

"Principle 5. Human consciousness is evolving from what you have called *Homo sapiens* to *homo infiniens*, capable not only of wise intellect but of seeing in many dimensions.

"The evolutionary energy explodes with compassion, and in this explosion, which is creation, it seeks to know itself. Knowing oneself is compassion, in the same way that in your experience compassion for another person begins in knowing that the other is really you. So with the evolutionary energy: God creates and in creating created a human creature capable of knowing itself as God, and this was compassion incarnate, consciousness in its most intense form. To be compassionate with God, the Whole of all dimensions, is the goal of *Homo infiniens*.

"As the new millennium arrives, you feel that the human race is becoming less compassionate rather than more; you feel you are on the brink of destroying life on your planet. It seems that when consciousness existed in single-celled organisms there was less danger than exists now in multi-celled humans.

"Have no fear, you humans cannot destroy life. You have power only to increase or decrease alienation and loneliness.

"Principle 6. Depth of relationship is the ultimate prize of human life, for relationality is consciousness.

"Beware those who struggle to save every single human life as if the primary spiritual concern of the human is the physical existence of a single human life. Fight for the decrease of human alienation, the decrease of loneliness; make this struggle more important to you than the saving of a single life, even your own. Know that populating the earth with more and more human forms does not in itself decrease alienation and can increase it. Know that there are as many reasons to die as to live.

"All teachers are now called to guide your people toward consciousness of love. When millions among you live in alienation, that consciousness is not evolved by the action of humans bearing more children than they need. Beware, your earth has too many children.

"The existence of a single human life is not necessarily love itself, for the human life exists in the other realities already, well beloved, and does not need your world for its only fruition. It is more essential to give love and compassion to those who live in loneliness.

"Principle 7. The human soul, or psyche, reflects the glory of God.

"What your people call 'psychology' is the reflection of the organizational system by which an individual human organism holds in its material container the evolutionary journey of the universe. Now I will teach you the mechanism of human consciousness detailed in the brain, which will become technologically clear to scientists, like the Nathan of your dream visions, in the next decades, but which the mystic has known for all time. It is through the psychological structure of the human brain that

God evolves in the human consciousness and can find constant activity in the human life span should the individual human, constructed of God, utilize free will to activate the mystical mechanisms of the Self.

"This teaching is the metapsychology of Self that your human brain has been clarifying in story and science over the last millennia, and with great fervor in the last two hundred years. This psychology pivots on the power of intuition, though the simplicity of this pivot has not been clarified previously to the extent we will clarify it at this time.

"There are four layers of human consciousness: Soul, Self, Ego, and Instinct.

"The central layer, at the core of human consciousness, is called Soul. This is energy with soul markings, like personality and mission, that indicate its fate and destiny in your body.

"The bridge layer, the second layer of consciousness, is called Self. It is the membrane between God's pure love and human suffering; through it, recognition of love occurs in you. The Soul is the energy Self works to guide in this physical existence of body.

"The social layer, the third layer of consciousness, is called Ego. It attracts suffering. Were the world not a world of lack and Ego not the receptacle of lack, compassion would have no template by which to learn itself.

"There is great confusion in human consciousness between the Ego realm and the Self realm of the psychological mechanism. Words such as 'self-esteem,' 'self-fulfillment,' 'self-realization,' and 'self-actualization' are often actually masks for Ego esteem.

"Beware the confusion of Ego and Self and teach a spiritual solution to it so that spiritual clarity can guide human consciousness. Self-esteem that rises from outward approval is Ego esteem. Self-esteem rising from the search for soul is Self-esteem. Self-realization that rises from the material mechanisms of society—money, social power, and other manipulations of psyche—is Ego realization. A person who pursues spiritual clarity searches for treasure in the realm of Self. A person who pursues 'self-fulfillment' for its own sake seeks to resolve pains in the realm of Ego.

"The fourth layer of consciousness is Instinct. In this layer of consciousness, the human is most able to feel his body comradeship with all living things. So it is that often this layer is called the 'animal' layer of the human.

"Principle 8. Intuition is a growing power open to human consciousness.

"The knowledge humans now possess—the information, data, historical perspective, and analysis—has reached a threshold of completeness that now allows human intuition to flourish in ways it could not before. Move your hand to the sand, and it will draw in the sand."

Reaching out, I found my hand drawing circles automatically. I found it frustrating, though, because I kept wanting to draw three-dimensionally on the sand and couldn't. Feeling my frustration, the Magician said, "Stand up, and draw on the air." I stood and began drawing holographically. As I drew, the Magician said, "Human consciousness has evolved to the point of paradigm integration, and so divine consciousness provides that integrating paradigm to you now."

Led by a greater hand, I drew a three-dimensional diamond and, within it, a multilayered set of three-dimensional circles. I was drawing the diamond tear I'd seen in Istanbul, during the dervish music! Now I drew circles inside.

The Magician said, "You have drawn a jeweled tear, representing the Cosmos, and within it four concentric spheres, representing a human consciousness within the Cosmos. The jewel is the ocean of Being in which consciousness floats. A human consciousness seeks to escape from within the jeweled enclosure, seeking individuality, and therefore engaging in the struggle that illuminates compassion. Simultaneously, a human consciousness seeks stillness within the jewel, and therefore Union with the original Compassion itself.

"In all things, action is courageous, a right action, when human consciousness seeks to illuminate compassion through intuition, then act through individual responsibility and spiritual stillness. The future of human evolution lies in developing the human capacity for intuition.

"In simplest terms, intuition connects human emotion and intellect to Soul. Human consciousness has evolved, as it reaches the next millen-

nium, to the brain development and amount of brain use capable now of
fully discovering and, over the next decades, refining the use of this Intuition.

"You will recognize Intuition when you experience it. Intuition is the
deep well of human consciousness, yet when it occurs in the Self, it feels
like a lightening blast of insight. All paradoxes are paradoxes because they
require intuition to solve and thus free them. The mystic *knows* what is
known because intuition confirms it. The mystic *acts* as action is required
because intuition drives the being to do so. The web of human life is too
complicated to be navigated solely by intellect or emotion alone. The web
becomes simplified by the lightening blast of intuition, which does not destroy it but illuminates it.

"Intuition is the Oneness, the Union as a known act within consciousness. With its lightning a storm calls attention to itself, crying, 'I
have wisdom for you. Look. Listen. Beware.' It is the flash of intuition that
reveals the evolution of the Cosmos in human consciousness. It is the
light of intuition that reveals God in every atom of every mote of dust."

The Magician paused for me, as if to allow me to breathe deeply again.
I inhaled and exhaled, savoring the glow of the moment and standing still,
waiting, indicating I could put more into my consciousness. I intuited very
clearly that words between myself and this Traveler were not necessarily
important, so I simply thought within myself, remembering that I had
written on my paper of questions, "Should the Bible be taken literally?"
then crossed it out and written, "What is the function of sacred texts?" and
now felt the question come out more broadly. As I began to think the
question clearly, he spoke.

"You wonder what role religions play in spiritual life.

"Principle 9. Religions are the cup of spiritual life, not the water itself.

"All spiritual and religious visions, like the Bible, are divinely inspired, as your journaled story of your experiences in these last weeks is divinely inspired. It is essential to remember that the divine does not speak
in literal but in allegorical terms. Divine stories are fingers that point to
the full story of all seven realities, a story that cannot ever be fully told in

one text. Thus they are not fact, and thus they are not meant to be limitations. Your mystical narrative of your experiences with me is inspired by the evolutionary energy of the universe; it is not the energy itself trapped in a cage of words.

"Religion is a sacred tool to be taught by adults who have experienced the second birth and thus become capable in their communities of both mature attachment and mature detachment. These adults rise to Self, beyond their Ego needs, to manipulate and to institutionalize power; they become intuitive ethicians *before* accepting the ethical truths of the religious text. An adult person whose moral acumen is still based in the religious text of his or another's psychological and spiritual childhood is a danger to the world.

"The mystic approaches all religions as maps of questions to be asked, not as maps of answers to be enforced.

"Your species must revise its religions soon, for you have reached a point of evolutionary crisis, a crisis experienced in all tribes. Mechanical materiality, what you call 'materialism,' is the newest stage in religious development and has created the crisis of spirit that will make necessary the evolution of the new vision of *Homo infiniens*. This vision will be one about which its followers have the courage not to proselytize. If the vision is authentic, that authenticity will be found at its core, by intuition, without rhetoric, and found there to match the core principles of all other guiding visions and religions."

"Will the new vision be the one we live in for the rest of time?" I interrupted.

"The dominance of a religious vision should not be expected to last more than a few generations. For the most part, moral codes that derive from religion can last for many millennia, but the usefulness of the religious vision as the seat of spiritual life lasts only if followers enforce it. The idea of the literal infallibility of your Old Testament should have been dissolved a few generations after it was rhetorically codified; the New Testament similarly, and the Koran, and so with all the texts. Each has been given to you by Travelers who specifically called, at the time of its delivery, for the vision's adaptation when evolution required such adaptation. However, the call for adaptation is always stricken from the religious text by human organizers. Now, as the new millennium approaches, records are vast and computerized and my call for adaptation cannot be stricken. I have chosen you and your memory so that you will record these words and there can be no doubt in the minds of the people. When, after a number of generations, the seven messages are inadequate, they should be buried in a fertile earth where new spiritual codes will sprout.

"Your human brain was not able, when the sixth reality provided earlier religious maps, to see that religions must die and be reborn along with all else in the cycle of life. Now your brains are able to see: your society lives in danger. You have few spiritual rituals of the soul, too many of the religious ego. Too many religious leaders battle one another like dogs over a dead carcass. Your young do not respect you. The words of the wise are less revered among you than the fashions of the rich.

"You are not the first culture to be weakened. You are not the first people to mistake the spice for the meat. You will find your way. Let your intuitions guide you.

"Principle 10. The path to illumination and enlightenment can be walked by anyone.

"You, young Messenger, have lived a map. You have been led through the ten tasks of enlightenment so that the people of your era can have a contemporary vision of how to make the journey to God. The ten tasks of enlightenment you have fulfilled have been similar throughout the history of spiritual life, taught by all the Travelers. The individual human being's journey in the tasks is not limited to the chronology you have experienced, but the journey to enlightenment requires the accomplishment of all ten tasks, like the building of ten bridges to God:

"The call to Union
"Submission to the Master
"Immersion in the Senses
"Immersion in the Emotions
"Atonement
"Realization of Destiny
"Embrace of the Beloved

"Embrace of Nothingness and Death

"Ritual Initiation

"Illumination.

"While the mystic may emphasize in one phase of life one task more than the other, and sometimes more than one at once, ultimately it is your mission to master all ten. The mystic finds, of course, that after mastering all of them and celebrating, briefly, the experience of enlightenment, the urge to master each task again will occur. This is normal, as it is normal to realize oneself and, in so doing, realize that everyone is enlightened and everyone is a teacher.

"Messenger, you have been initiated into enlightenment in a clear and recorded way so that others can study your journey. In your many languages there are many words for enlightenment: Union, Hal, Samadhi, Satori, Nirvana, salvation. They are accessible to anyone directly, for God is accessible to anyone. The ocean is there. Anyone can dive in.

"Messenger, teach the people that every self is a door behind which the infinite ocean of love awaits. The ocean is always on the edge of breaking through. Each task opens the door by moving fear out of the way. Let everyone seek the initiations—the life events—that fulfill the tasks, and let the door open. Let everyone fulfill the tasks by which the soul becomes free to fully feel compassion in the body. Once this feeling is freed, it will flow constantly onto the shores of daily life.

"Our time is nearly finished, Messenger. Ask the questions you were born to ask."

I asked, "Now that I know you and know you as an emanation of God, should I say to people, 'I *believe* in the Magician'?"

"Belief is a child's path to truth. Knowledge and wisdom are an adult's paths to truth. Belief is more like prediction than prophecy. Knowledge and wisdom are prophecy.

"A believer will say, 'If I believe in God just right, I will go to Heaven.' This is a condition and a prediction. But God's love is not conditional.

"A mystic will say, 'I *know* God, so I am already *in* Heaven.' There is no condition, only the exercise of the prophetic mind.

"In your spiritual dealings, speak what you know, with intuitive knowing. Do not speak your beliefs except as humble questions. When you hear someone say he believes in something, help him learn that he is only asking a question; he has not yet found the intuition that provides the answer."

I asked, "How should we live our daily lives so that we become more intuitive and closer to knowing God in every moment?"

"You will know your daily lives in their essence when you walk their various changes as if walking delicately on a web that is the Union with God. Nothingness is ever present, a great teacher, challenging the self to courage and compassion. Nothingness, manifested as busyness, chaos, and control, creates the illusion that Union is a puzzle that the self, overwhelmed by life, cannot put together. Be it known that the mission of daily life is to recognize that there is not a puzzle but a flow, which you are when you live life as prayer to God."

"But how? What practical wisdom can you give me?"

"The wisdom and spiritual traditions of all mystical paths give you practical wisdom that your personal intuition will savor, weigh, then form into your personal path. This path will provide the daily tempo of spiritual practice by which you will guide your busy life. On this path, every day, you will pray in nature, you will pray in your nest, you will pray in recreation, you will pray in service. Should you choose not to pray, you will feel lost.

"Ask another question, Messenger."

"What do the seven layers of reality look like?"

"If you take the shell off the snail to view the snail, it looks no longer like a sacred spiral, but only a snail. So with Being. There are seven realities and seven horizons of mind. This is all your mind can perceive at this time in its evolution. Seek to perfect your knowledge of what you are capable of knowing. Seek not to falsely know what cannot be known at this time. Wait for messages from allies in your twenty-fifth century who will speak, with voices from the dead, of freedom."

"When you say the word 'freedom,' what do you really mean?"

"Freedom comes to those who, living lives of worry, deprivation, fear, and pain, rise above these lacks to feel love.

"Freedom is not a gift that can be given. It must be *taken* by a Self that chooses to leave the cage of transitory deprivations and discover Union with God.

"Beware false freedom. Your people work to be free by working to rid your lives of cares and worries. Money, your people believe, ensures freedom, for it seems to ensure the end of care and worry. But it rarely does. Seek money and acquired goods only for the survival and purchase of sacred time, time in which to take your freedom. Money and goods will limit your freedom and increase your alienation—unless they increase your time and space to know God."

There was a silence, then he continued.

"Tell the people to conquer the fear of inadequacy. It is the fear behind all other fears. When you have conquered it, you will find that as you meet your defects in your life, they will delight you, like eccentric elderly parents.

"Now, Messenger, let us speak of *Homo infiniens,* the multidimensional human.

"You will notice the evolution of a multidimensional human is already occurring in seven particular areas of human experience:

"Your patterns of intimate romantic relationship have evolved from single-dimensional animal reproduction to the multidimensional search for the integration of masculine and feminine in what you call 'true love.'

"Your religions have evolved from single-dimensional anthropomorphization of nature's elements into gods to multidimensional visions of illusion and reality. Simultaneously, your cultures have sought to incorporate the wisdom of other cultures' religions, and even the great faiths have moved toward more and more direct connection with God.

"Your art has emerged as a grand proliferation of dimensions of imagination, aided now by technologies of multidimensional art.

"Your ability to enter trances at will has increased manifold over the last few hundred years. You need only find the right substance, design, or practice. Whole cultures are now entering trances at given times of the day or year, aided by your technologies of trance.

"Your material world, especially its information technologies, bestowed upon you by certain Travelers who have spoken through messengers like Einstein, Edison, Bohr, and Bell, now work to break down dimensional limits of time and space, creating intermediary worlds of virtual time and space.

"Your experiments with institutionalized motivations for human action, for instance the institutionalized motivation for protection of nation-states, has led you to become as the creator God, creating in atoms the very agent of your own self-destruction. This in itself motivates the evolution of humanity to *Homo infiniens*, for there is no other path for protection of the species but to discover your Oneness.

"Your transcendental futurisms, emerging over the last few hundred years and culminating in your America of the late twentieth century, are the foundation for new thinking, and this America will be most remembered for its multidimensionality of society and creativity, a millennial scavenger country that seeks to synthesize all traditions, all dimensions, all visions.

"These are the signs of the next stage of your evolution. As you learn to use more and more of your brain, you will learn to exist in many dimensions at once. You, Messenger, in the last weeks, have used more of your brain than most people use in a lifetime. This has been your destiny, and you have been aided in this experiment."

"Have I truly been existing in many dimensions over the last weeks?"

"You have existed in the first reality of bodily action.

"You have existed in the second reality of imagination.

"You have existed in the third reality, the 'flying,' as it is called, where the membranes of the realities, the skins of consciousness, peel away to reveal the nonseparation between all places.

"You have existed in the fourth reality of unlimited time, apprehending messages and visions of the future that will become clearer in later years.

"You have existed in the fifth reality, in the intermediary world before birth and after death, the transitional world of energy transmutation.

"Now, messenger, let us speak of your duty. It is your duty to help others gain their abilities to exist as *Homo infiniens*, the multidimensional human."

"How shall I do this? What are the next steps in helping the brain expand to see and exist in the many dimensions?"

"In the next epoch of human consciousness, a particle field will be discovered, smaller than any particle imaginable and larger than any field, and capable of moving through solid form without obstacle because it re-forms solid form, as a ship moving through space re-forms space. This particle field will lead you to the next expanded reality of consciousness. Be patient. This will not happen in your present lifetime. But in your present lifetime you can inspire others to search, and you can teach others some of the aspects of the design they are searching for.

"Remember, however, that throughout the human search for all the realities, when you are in body you cannot know all seven realities at once. This is the limitation of body. The scientific paradigm that your mystical consciousness has created over the last few hundred years—culminating in the mystical sciences of unified field and quantum physics—is essential to envisioning the vibratory path of energy, but it must beware its arrogant assumption that one day scientific mechanism can know all realities.

"It is also essential to tell the people that trying to understand consciousness and reality without first becoming enlightened is a tremulous path, and not a path of full courage. The ten tasks of enlightenment await all searchers. Once accomplished, they begin the searcher on the ten tasks all over again; thus there is no 'end' to the journey of enlightenment simply because the tenth goal has been reached. But not to reach the tenth goal for the first time, and in this lack to attempt to understand or rule the world—this is a perilous path.

"Now it is time for our parting. Ask one last question, and I must then return to the world of light."

I had so many more questions. He remained silent. In his silence I saw again, as I had earlier, the need for my own. So I remained silent. I had no more questions.

He said, "I will leave you now, but I will never be far. Remember that the biggest mistake a Messenger can make is to seek an extraordinary life. Live your diurnal disciplines, entertainments, commitments, and activities with a prayerful and powerful heart—a mind searching always for meaning and a body open to love. With the help of others, as your intuition will show you, you must write for your people the initiatory journey you have made. It is your destiny to teach the world of Second Birth, for you have achieved the Second Birth, the Birth into Soul. Write your story soon, and make plans for its revelation after a time of patience more than ten years hence, as the millennium turns. It is not clear to me that I will return again to you and your people.

"Good-bye, Messenger, thank you for your love."

"Good-bye," I said, tears in my eyes. "Thank you for your love."

The light that he was folded up, like a Japanese folded-paper animal. It became a bird again, flying out over the ocean. Then it became a mere spot of light and disappeared into the glaring light of the ordinary day.

When the Magician had gone, I did not know what to say or do. The sun set red and gold on the horizon, mesmerizing me with a hypnotist's colors. I shook myself and moved to my paper and pen. Over the next few hours, relying on firelight, I recorded everything in the Message—the principles, the history, the Creation, the predictions, the wisdom, the story. As I wrote, I felt myself gradually returning to my body, like a boat returning to a dock. Now and then, I looked up from the page and gazed out over the sea, as if I were gazing back over my thirty years of life. I saw a string of memories, all falling into place; everything I had ever been through made sense, led me to this moment. Had my brain been scanned in those hours, I know the neurobiologist would have seen serotonin and natural amphetamines coursing through, washing me with the pure triumph of life.

It took me a few hours to write down everything I remembered. When I finished, I felt a wave of sadness that the Magician was gone. With the grief came a sudden welling up of fear as my new responsibilities matured in me. I had work to do. I had a purpose. I had to learn to teach and to serve. I had to learn to lead. I became as anyone who sees through fear and experiences vision; I realized that the greatest challenge lay in what to do with it. It suddenly seemed like an impossibly heavy load to carry.

Again I heard the Magician say that anyone who harnesses the power of intuition is enlightened and therefore becomes a teacher. Since anyone at all has the potential to harness that power, everyone can become a spiritual teacher. The method of this grace is obvious: Witness your first intuition clearly—that you are already enlightened. Intuit that, feel it in your deepest heart, and you have become who you truly are.

Over the millennia, hundreds of millions of people have been mystics. Today I was not becoming a singular exception but joining a historical community of enlightened individuals and prophets that spread across time and space. We were mystics. We shared a spiritual identity.

That thought dissolved me and simultaneously reconstructed me. I lay my writing tools down and walked into the water, floating in the cool insulation like a fish. Rising from the water, I raised my arms to the cliffs and called into the echoing rocks, "I. Am. Ben."

Then more quietly, like a prayer, I renamed my life, murmuring to the world, "I. Am. God."

That night I slept more deeply than I had slept in a very long time.

Joseph came the next morning. I was packed and ready, having awoken with a foreknowledge that he would come.

He said, "I heard you call me in my dreams, my friend. You have had your encounter."

I acknowledged him with a smile and an embrace. "I understand John now," I said. "John 3:7, 'Ye shall be born again.'"

I started to give a report but then asked for one last dose of silent island time. Speaking only as needed, we loaded up, then chugged around the island and back toward the mainland. Before we reached it, and as I saw the crowds far off in the town, I asked him to veer off toward the ruins of the judge's house. We sat on the beach below the ruins, and there, before we saw any of the others, gazing across the water at Lobos, I talked and he listened. When I could talk no more, he read my written record. This took him some time. I wandered up into the ruins and meditated there, feeling a beautiful calm.

When I returned, he had finished reading. His first words were "I don't know which will be more useful and more inspiring for people: the Message and its many teachings and principles or the story of your journey toward it. How good it is that you can give both to the world! How much ego terror and hatred and war we would have been saved if we had better records of the prophets of the past, accurate accounts of their *actual* journeys to mystical truth, not just the fragments or versions retold later by followers trying to create religions and dominate consciousness."

"It feels so egotistical to say, 'I'm a prophet. I'm enlightened. I. Am. God.' The words vibrate so big, and I'm so small."

"Yes," he said, "your life will be lived in a spiritual vigilance so that humility is always your guide."

"I'm afraid to report any of this to anyone. Look at me. I'm shivering in fear."

And I was. Even as the late-morning sun, already hot, beamed down on us, my skin had sprung goose bumps.

"The evolutionary energy requires that you have the compassion to give a message to the world. To fulfill your destiny of compassion, you must move through your fear, even your fear of what destruction you will cause. And you *will* cause destruction. It is inevitable. Every artist and every prophet has gone through this terrifying moment. Many have compromised, many have become paralyzed. You, I think, will see that compassion and courage are one in your destiny."

I thought: Yet again, I am not special, I am typical. Many people who have secrets want to keep them hidden.

"Everyone is waiting," I said at last. "Let's go."

"Are you ready for another wave of ecstasy, my friend? The crowd in the village will lavish you with praise."

"I'm ready as I'll ever be."

"Let me warn you of something. A true teacher is one who senses his own vibrations as he teaches. You must do this as you speak to the people. When you feel your own ego rising, intuit what person or cluster of energies has risen its ego in the audience to cause your own to rise. Right now, following your encounter, you are in a completely conscious, therefore vulnerable, altered state, a state you will from now on enter when you choose—in your prayer rituals, certain times in your writing, and certainly in your teaching trance. In those times you will learn the magic words that open and close the altered state not only for yourself but for others. You will find, often, safe community and solitude. But often you will be thrust into a throng, and some among the crowds will be damaged, groping, alienated, evil. You and they are one, for all is one. So their energy will cause the rising of similar energy in you. Watch this energy as it rises in *you*. Do you understand?"

"I think so. Will you help me?" I asked. "If I miss something—an evil or an ego rising or my own ego rising—will you help me? Tell me what you see? Even take me to safety?"

"I'll help you," he promised.

"As long as I live," I said in profound deference, "you will be the father of my soul. I know that now."

"Ah, my friend." Joseph sighed, tears forming in his eyes. "You have learned humility and gratitude." He stood up and embraced me. His embrace pulled my head down toward his. Accepting me into his heart, he clasped my head in viselike hands, in the way he had told me once Mwimbo had done to him. Pulling my face to his, he repeated Mwimbo's ultimate gesture of acceptance: he brought his lips to the portals of my soul; he gently kissed my eyes.

There were about a hundred people gathered on the beach in front of Aykut's house. As I told my story of what had happened, Joseph translated for the Turks and I heard murmured translations in other languages as well. As I spoke, my performance energy felt huge, stranger than I had ever felt before. It was a somewhat new kind of trance state. I had no defenses built up yet, so I felt buffeted by every soul in the group—by those I knew, such as Ragıp and Sela, Fusun and Mehmet, and by those I didn't know, including a few tourists who just happened to walk by and stopped to listen and must be thinking, "How bizarre, how crazy, how interesting." I looked crazy, I'm sure—disheveled, unshaven, eyes bloodshot, sunburned, T-shirt and swim trunks dirty, body welted and bitten, but my soul careening freely. I cried to them, "I am no different from you who have encountered the Magician, and we are no different from anyone else—just more capable of joy. That is the only difference, isn't it?"

"Yes," they agreed with smiles, murmurs, and nods.

I told the people what the Magician had told me, giving them the First Message. When I finished, a woman asked if the Magician would be back. I replied honestly that I didn't know; it was possible he would not. "But of course," I reminded them, "he is only one of the forms our companion spirits can take." Still, the thought that he was gone brought some people to tears. Questions were called out at me, sudden little conversations erupted, people shushed one another. I felt my ego rising, as a rock star must feel. I remembered Joseph's instructions and looked into the crowd carefully. There I saw a young man with an angry, jealous face. I smiled at him and bowed a little as I talked. His face melted, and I felt freed again. I had to do this a number of times, quieting many angers and even more fears in the audience and thus working to keep myself pure.

Then, gradually, I had no more to say, a child of exhaustion. Others could see it. They gathered to thank me, congratulate me, shake my hand, embrace me, and let me go. Seeing how overwhelmed I had become, Joseph escorted me through the crowd and into Aykut's house, where he helped me into Aykut's bed. Instead of feeling bizarre toward this place of death, I felt welcomed and slept deeply.

When I woke up, it was the middle of the night. The village slept, so I rose stealthily. The moon was out, and stars twinkled at me as I walked to the beach, avoiding sleeping bodies as I walked. I looked out at Lobos. Stripping myself naked of my T-shirt and shorts, I entered the water, swimming out toward the island.

Somewhere about a hundred yards out, I got tired of swimming and floated on my back, gazing upward. A shadow careened past me on the water. I looked up into the moonlight and found its source, a stork out, like me, to bathe in the moonlit darkness between land and island. It flapped a few more times and then turned and glided back to Lobos. It seemed to say to me: From now on, this is you, a tenant of this undefined oceanic world that bridges the realities together.

I swam back to shore, resolved as to where I'd go next—back to Istanbul. To the dock where I'd first seen the stork. And back to the carpet store. What had Sela said? "I hope you've left something here you'll want to come back and retrieve." How beautiful! At the carpet store, a moment of love had occurred between the salesman and me, a promise to hold the carpet for me. It had left a tracing of energy for me to retrieve. Ever since coming to Turkey, I had been in an altered state. I'd really seen little of Anatolia. I had accomplished the ten tasks, and I felt, as the Magician suggested I would, ready to start all over again. After a few more days here in Kadı Kalesi I would go back to the magical city that bridged Europe and Asia. I would retrieve the moments of the soul I had not fully lived. They would take me into new places of the soul. I would start my journey in Istanbul, and this time, having found my freedom, I would live it to the fullest, relaxing in the quiet, graceful, hardy spirit I truly was.

EDITOR'S ✳ AFTERWORD

I was dead, then alive.

— JALĀL AD-DĪN AR-RŪMĪ

*B*en Brickman is believed to have died in a car-bus collision on the road from Hyderabad to Madras, in south India, in the summer of 1990—yet he may only have disappeared. No one is absolutely sure if he is alive or dead, because there have been eyewitness reports that someone was seen walking away from the flames in the accident. A number of charred bodies were cremated, Ben's body assumed to be among them. Many people proceed with the assumption of his death. I prefer to believe he has only disappeared and will one day reappear to continue his work.

In the two years between his second birth and his "death," Ben visited Turkey numerous times, studied in India, did service work in both countries, and also taught to small, then ever-increasing groups. The healings and miraculous life readings he performed brought him a reputation, despite the fact that he asked followers to give him a great deal more "peace and learning time" before they pushed him toward a public life. Some followers called him the Second Coming, others the Godhead, others the Reincarnation of the Buddha.

Feza joined him in Madras. By the time I met her in early 1989, I had come to know Ben quite well. Ben, whom many of his friends call "an American mystic," never actually made it back to America. In his teaching in India and Turkey, Ben told the story of his two-month journey, presented his understanding of the ten tasks of enlightenment, and taught spiritual principles inspired by the Magician. He spoke candidly about the Magician's instruction that much of what was to be revealed not be revealed until just at the turn of the millennium. According to Joseph Kader, over the two-year period Ben recorded more than a thousand pages of automatic writing of the Magician's spiritual teaching. At this point, no

one knows where those thousand pages are. I have hired, at my own ex-
pense, a private investigator to search for them. There are rumors that
Feza is hiding those pages. She denies this.

Ben's ability to inspire and teach received notice in religious circles.
V. Muhktana, the founder of Ana Yoga, said in an interview for the Indian
paper *Hatha* that Ben's teachings were "refreshing, a voice of everlasting
love. I embrace his concept of a world mysticism, this 'millennial mysticism,' as he calls it. I too hope that it will be an accumulation of religious
and spiritual wisdom from around the world. It is time for this on this
earth. Though I am a religious man, I have nothing to fear from this young
man's metareligion. I have only new life to gain."

Sandra Lachey flew to Turkey and interviewed Joseph and Ben together, publishing her interview in the Spring 1991 *New World*, after
Ben's disappearance. In her opening remarks she wrote, "Ben carries
beauty in every nerve ending. Talking with him was like talking to shimmering water. In his eyes I saw concrete attention to the Now, and I saw
sorrow, beautiful sorrow turning, as we spoke, to joy, as if he took hurts in
me, in the air, in his environment, and fed them compassion." Ben's small
group of followers agreed he had a gift for altering, like a magician, the
moods around him.

Ben's detractors took another view. The Christian evangelist Harry
Schlesinger, who was asked to comment about the *New World* interview,
called Ben's ideas "New Age hooey." Iranian Imam Ayatollah Sabreyni
called them "an affront to real religion."

To the general public, Ben was barely known. He was no celebrity, just
a man who found himself, spoke up, and died or disappeared tragically
young, before he could tell all the secrets he knew, secrets that humankind
may desperately need. He was part of an unfolding story that has not yet
been fully told.

For more than a decade, since meeting Ben Brickman and Joseph
Kader, I have lived with the reality of millennial mysticism and an excit-
ing network of friends in this new spiritual tradition. For more than ten
years I have been a spectator of my own American culture, watching, listening, noting the validity of Ben and Joseph's claim that everywhere

these days mystical awakening is spreading in tiny, exploding slivers of human light. It seems that nearly everyone is seeking, in his or her own way, a direct path to God. The World Wide Web has crisscrossed the planet with a digital membrane of consciousness. In recalling the Magician's description of *Homo infiniens*, human beings now are indeed striving, through travel in outer space, through medical science, through television, cinema, virtual reality, and cyberspace, through prayer and practice, through spiritual search, to become the limitless, boundless human beings of the future.

And there is more truth than Feza knew to the energy-transfer technique of "temporal telepathy." A number of people are receiving visions of the future with the kind of texture, content, and prophecy that Ben experienced in his seven dreams. I will pursue these stories in future volumes. As an example, an incident happened to me in 1994. It "blew my mind."

During the winter of that year, I traveled to Los Gatos, California, invited by friends, the therapists Joel and Katherine Webb, to give workshops on one of my books, *Mothers, Sons, and Lovers*. The day after the workshop, Joel and Katherine's twelve-year-old daughter, Tara, an avid equestrian, took us all riding. We began shortly before dawn on trails in the Santa Cruz Mountains. Near the crest of an especially beautiful ridge, we stopped to rest, watching the morning sun light up the valley below. Two women in their fifties had stopped as well. I stood next to Tara, a gangly, talkative girl, who was, despite her usual vivaciousness, subdued in the face of the immense colors, the dreamy haze, and the delight of horses breathing beside us. We lived in the few minutes before the sun rose and the many purples dissipated into one yellow.

In our revery, we assumed that the two women—one tall, dressed in riding clothes, with flowing gray hair, the other medium height, dressed in a thick sweater, with black hair and sunglasses—would move away when they had finished with the scene. Our assumption proved incorrect; they made no attempt to hide their interest in us. They looked at Tara especially and whispered to each other. Moving toward us, reins in hand and horse in tow, the shorter woman took off her sunglasses. I saw that while her taller companion was Caucasian, this woman had the mottled brown skin, almost oriental features, and black eyes of a Native American woman.

Discomfited by the looks, whispers, and approach of the women, Joel and Katherine, who had stood away from Tara, came beside her now. As the women stopped before her daughter, Katherine asked firmly, "Can we help you?"

The older, taller woman spoke. "Don't be alarmed. We must talk to you."

Her companion spoke on her heels. "I am a Seven Rivers shaman. I received a vision in the sweat lodge, a vision of your daughter. In the vision, she sat with this man"—she pointed to me—"and four others, a very short dark man, a tall man, younger, with curly blond hair and a look of stars in his brown eyes, a large woman, young, a man of middle height and years, with straight blond-white hair and an energy like a whirlwind, and behind them stood another man, old, with thick glasses, dark skin, and a long look of suffering like the kiss of a weeping raven. This man had a name, Alfred. The others did not have names."

"How short was the other old man?" I asked.

The Indian woman held her hand up to about Tara's height—just under five feet.

"I know three of the men you speak of!" I exclaimed. "Ben Brickman, Joseph Kader, and Alfred Hecht. I don't know the other man, and I'm not sure of the woman. Please tell us more."

"Grandmother blesses my vision with purpose but not with clarity. The man, Alfred, stretched his hand through Grandfather Rock, and all of space opened. This girl and you men stood now in the heavens, looking down into space and onto our Turtle Island. You men liked only the looking but this girl liked the walking, so she walked down and you with her, following her wisdom, out of space, to Turtle Island, here to this hill. This is why I came here to this hill with Dolores. I knew this to be the hill in my vision. And now you are here." She paused, losing her train of thought.

"Tell them about the man in the prison," her companion prodded.

"Yes. Just there, where there are trees, there was a prison in my vision. A young man with gray hair, with a face like he was born from stone, sat in a cell. Sometimes his cell lit in fire and he sat through it, unburned. Other times it remained cold like ice and he sat through it."

"It lit in fire?" I asked.

"Yes. But it didn't really burn. It was a vision."

"Please go on."

"The man in the prison was of this earth but came from the stars. In his mind was written the sadness and aloneness of all two-legged creatures, for in space there were no other living sentient beings and he had discovered this."

"He had discovered that we are the only sentient life-form?" I asked, remembering that Ben had predicted this discovery in Joseph Kader's flat in Ankara. That had been 1988. He had said we would learn that we were, as *Homo infiniens*, alone in the universe, and thus our mission was all the more important.

"Yes. This girl and you men and the woman flew to his cell, speaking to him and bringing love to him. The woman touched his head with her hand, and he was grateful. The stone boy asked her, 'How could you come here to 2411?'"

"2411?" I exclaimed. "Are you sure?"

"Yes. Do you know of this?"

"Go on. Go on."

"The man named Alfred said, 'We have not come to you, but you have come to us.' The stone man said to the young blond man, 'Many are mystics now, because of you.' And so now I understood: this vision came from the future, the land of intentions. I do not know its meanings, but I know its source.

"The stone man said to you"—she pointed to me—"'I am Karver. We will speak often and soon.' You did not know how the speaking would occur, but the woman did. She pointed to this girl." The woman pointed to Tara, who stood stunned but mesmerized. "She will speak to her companion spirits in other times and bring them to our time."

"The stone man named Karver said, 'Look at the Speakers and the Listeners. All ideas in your present come from the future from Speakers, who speak to Listeners. These are the circles of energy. Travelers are everywhere on the circles, directing the energy. All stories and songs come in the circular path. There is no time. There is no present, past, or future. When you understand this, you will be free.'

"These were the words passed between these people. Then the teaching was done and the vision was done. Now I am here on this hill. Now you are here. So it is. *Ho-ma-tac-ma-hay*."

Katherine spoke. "Isn't your vision saying that all ideas in the present actually came from the future or past? We think they're *our* own ideas, but the creator, thinker, or artist is not a 'creator' per se but a listener to some energy or spirit speaking from the future or past?

"That's amazing," she exhaled, holding her daughter's shoulders. "And that you saw Michael, and Tara, and the others. That's quite something."

"Your daughter," the shaman said, "will become a woman of magic and psychic power. The large woman in my vision will become an important teacher to her later in her life."

We talked longer on that hill, each of us full of theories and explanations. The shaman's name was Sandy Two Rivers. Her "real job," as she herself put it, was, like her companion's, Dolores Hampton's, computer analysis at the nearby Livermore Labs.

Sandy Two Rivers and I have kept in touch. She has never had the vision again, but now, in her midteens, Tara has begun to experience a very rich dream life. And we have found "the large woman" from Sandy's vision, and the man with straight blond hair. Her name is Beth Carey, his Nathan Wondreski. He is the Nathan from Ben's first two dreams. She is the Beth from the Seventh Dream. Her story appears to be an amazing one that I hope I will have a chance to tell.

Joseph's death came in late 1991, in Paris. My wife, Gail, and I went there during his last days, as cancer took him. "I go to join God," he said one morning with a smile, and was gone. The night before, we had talked for a few minutes; each word, as happens with those near death, felt like a story. He blessed me with memories of his family, his own journey, his time with Ben. He passed on to me a letter from someone who wanted to remain anonymous, a young man who had heard of Joseph and wanted to tell him about a strange experience he'd had, of visions of the future.

As I write this epilogue, I am on a plane heading to northern California, to Nathan's research institute. Experiments are going on there that will, I believe, change the human condition. These were predicted by the Magician. Ben Brickman's dreams, of course, predicted an assassination attempt on Nathan that has yet to be fulfilled. After hearing about the premonitional dreams, Nathan has chosen to have bodyguards.

On this particular trip to Nathan's institute I am to meet with Beth Carey. I sent her a transcript of Ben's seventh dream. She was stunned by its accuracy. "It's as if he were watching me from back in 1988 do something that I did, by complete surprise, in 1994. How could this be?" Her own life experience is itself discovering an answer to that question.

The sleeper on the airplane beside me awakens from his snoring. The human species is awakening all around us. I am a searcher who has much to learn. I fly now like an astronaut, or like a tiny seed, toward the next story, the next truth, the next opportunity.

—Michael Gurian

A U T H O R ✻ B I O

Michael Gurian is the author of three books of poetry and eight books in the fields of parenting and psychology. This is his first novel.